BONFIRE NIGHT

Ricki Thomas

A Wild Wolf Publication

Published by Wild Wolf Publishing in 2013
This second edition published by Wild Wolf Publishing in 2016
Copyright © 2013 Ricki Thomas

Second print

ISBN: 978-1-907954-28-3
Also available as an e-book

www.wildwolfpublishing.com

Also by Ricki Thomas

Hope's Vengeance
Unlikely Killer
Bloody Mary
Holiday of the Dead (contributor)
Black Park
Wild Wolf's Twisted Tails (contributor)
Rings of Death
Deadly Angels

I dedicate Bonfire Night to my children, Ems, Alice, Joe and Tom, and to my wonderful Mum – I love you all.

Chapter 1
Monday 29th October

"Frank, it's Sue, I wonder if you would do something for me?" I was surprised to hear my colleague's wife on the phone as she normally called Ellen if she wanted or needed anything from me. I agreed, curious. "Jeff's father has had a heart attack. His brother just called and asked me to tell him to get to Scunthorpe Hospital as soon as possible."

"Well, I guess," I hesitated briefly, "why don't you tell him though?"

"You know he's not on good terms with his father. I didn't want to tell him on the phone in case his stubborn streak came out and he refused to go. Paul sounds really upset."

I knew all about the rift in Jeff's family, which infuriated and upset him in equal measure, so I understood Sue's reasoning. "I'll tell him, don't worry." I was about to ask how the baby was, but with Jeff in earshot I thought the mention of Jacob's name with the news I had would be callous, so I said my goodbyes and ended the call.

I motioned Jeff over, indicating a seat, and leant forward, my voice hushed. "I've just had your Sue on the phone. She wanted me to tell you that your father's in Scunthorpe Hospital.He's had a heart attack and Paul has asked you to come as soon as you can."

His expression transformed from instant distaste at the mention of his father to worry. "I hardly know him."

It was true – from the age of four Jeff had only seen Roland Mason twice – but I knew I had to do the right thing. "If you don't go and something happens you may regret it for the rest of your life."

Jeff raised a brief, confused smile. "Yeah, I suppose you're right, boss." I nodded and gestured towards the door as he glumly lifted his jacket from the back of his chair. He shrugged it on and paced towards the door, tugging his car keys from a pocket. A gentle, cool breeze blew into the room as he opened the door, and he was gone.

I couldn't help having a soft spot for Jeff Mason; we had become personal friends over the years and so had our wives, and I had a huge amount of respect for his calmness and the firm, yet polite manner he always used. We had been working in the same department – the regional Serious Crime squad – for just gone four years now, since he had eagerly trained as a detective, and our working relationship was great, regardless of the difference in age. From day one I had taken the younger man under my wing, which wasn't my usual way, but Jeff wasn't an ordinary detective. I had seen his enthusiasm for the job, the keenness and intelligence that glittered in his almost black eyes and, having reached my mid-forties when Jeff joined the team, I saw the man as, well, a protégé, I suppose. Someone to train ready to take my place when I took early retirement. And that day was approaching rapidly.

I returned to the latest case details spread across my desk, another child murdered in what was believed to be a domestic argument, and my brow furrowed. I loved my job; even though the majority of our investigations involved death, the benefits of putting the perpetrators behind bars were worth the pitfalls. But with child victims there was a questioning, an absence of understanding that made it hard to deal with.

With most child killings there would be something happen, something you saw, that would remind you of your own children, and this would instantly remind us fathers on the case how precious they were. And how disgusting and severe the murder was.

In the current case we were investigating, the scene of the crime had been the trigger to liken the victim to my teenage daughter, as Kaylee Robinson's broken body had been clothed in the same pyjamas my daughter had been wearing when I'd left the house that morning. We suspected that fourteen-year-old Kaylee had been strangled by her father, as is often the case – either the father or a close blood relative. With my daughter being the same age, in the same outfit, and having the same colour and style of hair, my stomach had lurched sickeningly when I first arrived at the scene. In my thirty years on the police force, I had never understood how anybody could kill his or her own child, but I'd sadly come to realise that such murders were not uncommon.

I sipped my thick, cold coffee with a sigh and returned to reading Kaylee's father's statement. A statement full of inaccuracies. A statement of blatant lies.

Jeff was jittery as he drove his silver Vectra towards the Humber River. He was typically a composed man, both at home and work, and would tolerate situations to an impossible level, but today he was impatient, eager to dodge the heavy traffic and drive at speed to get past the bridge, knowing the roads would be quieter on the other side. But the slow journey through rush hour traffic in Hull was frustrating. It took three quarters of an hour to reach North Lincolnshire, and thankfully only a further fifteen minutes to get to the hospital after the bridge. Worried he was rushing too late towards bad news, he wished he had cheated, taken a pool car and used the sirens to divide the traffic.

Jeff wasted possibly vital time searching for a parking space, which depressed him further, and by the time he had locked the car, his stomach heaved with stress. He raced through the main doors to the desk and breathlessly asked for assistance. "I'm a relative of Roland Mason. He was brought in a couple of hours ago."

No words were returned as the woman calmly typed the name into her computer, and Jeff felt like spinning the screen round to get the information himself to hurry the process up. He shifted from one foot to the other as less than a minute felt like an hour. "He's still in A and E, love. That's over the other side of the hosp..." She stopped abruptly when she realised he was already running along the corridor.

Jeff was grateful to know the layout of the hospital, having visited many times prior to the death of his mother six years previously of breast cancer. The mother who had taken him, but not his older brother, with her when she had left their father thirty-two years before. The painful memories of her passing flooded back as he scurried towards the emergency department, and panic raced through his veins, fearful he was about to lose his father too and become an orphan aged just thirty-six.

The department was familiarly heaving, with overworked staff humming in all directions, but a kindly nurse gently led him to a cubicle and pulled the curtain aside for him to enter. As he saw the aging man he barely knew, covered in wires and tubes, the information she was giving him about his father's condition paled into the background clatter and he steadied himself on the trolley. "I'll get you a seat, sir." He was grateful; his legs had turned to jelly.

Seated, and finally breathing steadily, Jeff turned to the brother he'd not seen since their mother's funeral. "Paul. What's been happening?"

Paul lifted his heavy head and returned his brother's gaze, with spent tears clinging to his ruddy cheeks, and Jeff was, as he had always been on the few times he had met Paul, taken aback by their family resemblance. By how much they both took after their handsome mother. Except for the reddened skin, which Paul had inherited from their father, whereas Jeff had Joan's creamlike tone. "He's had three heart attacks, but he's stable at the moment. They're going to operate as soon as possible. They want to put a tube inside, a stent, or something like that. They said it's to keep his blood thingies open." His head lowered again, returning to his private pain.

Jeff's eyes lingered on the frail, desperately ill man and his stomach twisted with angst.

The sun was long gone leaving a bitter, windy night in its place and Jeff drove slowly along the dirt track that led to the muddy parking space behind his father's garden. At Paul's direction he stopped the car, having not seen the house since the age of four, and he and Paul solemnly climbed out. They traipsed across the soggy lawn towards the back door of the run-down, neglected house – the house they had both been born in over thirty years before.

It had been a long, arduous day. They had waited, each of them mentally agonising with little interaction, while Roland was in the operating theatre, and eventually the welcome news that their father was alive, but asleep, came. The doctor stated they would be better off going home and resting, ready to visit with fresh eyes the next morning.

Paul went straight to the fridge as if on autopilot, eager to sink an ale or ten, but remembering his well-to-do brother's presence he turned and grasped the kettle instead, filling it from the tap. Jeff eyed the outdated heat-on-the-hob kettle, which was probably older than he was, and sighed. He knew his father and brother were frugal with money and it was a trait he wasn't comfortable with. Paul interrupted his thoughts. "Do you want a mug of tea?"

However, Jeff had noticed the shelf loaded with beer in the fridge. "I don't suppose you've got something a bit stronger? Tea feels a bit lame after the past few hours."

Without a word Paul turned the cooker off and grabbed two bottles from the fridge, handing one to Jeff. They shifted to the front room, sagging into two worn armchairs that Jeff swore he could vaguely remember. Paul took an opener from the coffee table and clicked the lids from both beers easily. He gulped his down and placed the empty bottle on the floor beside his seat, before reaching for some fingerless gloves and tugging them over his weather-beaten hands. Jeff was bemused. "Gloves inside? Why don't you just put the heating on?"

Paul turned his head, his raven eyes filled with bitterness. Or was it jealousy? "Me and my dad don't have much money, not like you. We can only afford to light the fire when it's really cold."

Jeff was truly surprised and he scanned the murky room for a radiator. "Haven't you got central heating?"

"It costs loads of money to install and we haven't got enough. So we can't have it. Anyway, the cold won't kill you." The image of their ailing father instantly sprung to the minds of both men and they avoided each other's eyes. Ashamed, Paul reached to a bottle of whisky beside his chair, no longer caring about drinking in front of his brother. He pointed to the side of the armchair Jeff was seated in. "Dad's bottle is down there. We don't bother with glasses; it saves washing them up. Go on, my dad won't know."

Jeff wasn't comfortable drinking from the bottle, it seemed uncouth, but a dash of liquor was tempting and today he needed it. "I'll get a glass and wash it up afterwards, okay?" Jeff rose, heading for the kitchen.

"There are no glasses. We just use mugs if it's a special day." Paul's monotonous voice was grating on Jeff, as was his laziness and antipathy. The two brothers couldn't have been more dissimilar.

"Then I'll use a mug." He pulled the thick, olive-velvet curtain to one side and left the room. Free of Paul's scrutiny, Jeff glanced around the room. The kitchen was filthy, a greyish tinge to the walls, the gloom enhanced by the dull yellow glow from the energy saving bulb, which had no light-shade, on the ceiling. Dirty crockery littered the sides, and greasy, dusty tins and jars cluttered the table. A dingy carpet covered the floor, spongy with years of fat spillages. Jeff poked inside the sparse cupboards, searching for anything clean that would hold a drink, and realised how grateful he was that his wonderful, cheerful mother had taken him to live with her when she had broken her marriage to Roland. Had she left him behind, he could be just like Paul now.

Or perhaps, had the tables been turned, Paul could have been as go-getting as him. Swings and roundabouts.

Their mother had never spoken about why she had split the family. She had admitted to Jeff that she'd been unhappy, and that Paul had always idolised his father. But he now understood why his mother had left the marriage: she had wanted a life.

Jeff found a chipped mug, rinsed it under a hot tap that supplied cold water, and resolved that if his father was in a stable condition in the morning, he would leave any aftercare to Paul and return to his comfortable, modern semi in Hessle. Return to his happy family and affluent life.

Hours passed with few words as they supped their nightcaps, and when Paul stated he was heading upstairs, he suggested their father's bed to Jeff, who declined politely, withholding a grimace, balking at the thought of what could be living in the mattress. He would stay on the armchair.

He waited for Paul, grunting a lame goodnight, to leave, and dragged the multi-coloured, crocheted blanket from the chair he was seated on, surmising his mother had probably made it by hand years before. He shrugged it around his body and snuggled into the stale-smelling wool, trying to find a comfortable position. But it was difficult to settle.

Jeff heaved for a while, the chair too small to stretch out on, and finally gave up, pouring another whisky. He shoved the blanket aside and leaned to the bookcase beside the armchair, considering reading until sleep came. Years of dust lay on the edges of the shelves, but the sliding glass doors had protected the row of hardbacks inside. Jeff's skin crawled – he detested mess and filth – but he persevered and was amazed to find a collection on a subject that interested him deeply: true crime.

Intrigued to have found a shared hobby with his father, he slid the murky glass aside and scanned the titles. "Never," the roar made Jeff jump, spilling drops of whisky onto the grotesque carpet, "ever touch those books. They're my dad's, and he always told me he'd kill me if I touched them."

Jeff held his hands up apologetically. "Sorry, mate, I had no idea."

Paul loomed over him and for the first time Jeff, a hefty, strong man himself, noticed how broad his brother was, how monstrously tall. How powerful. How much blacker the anger made his eyes.

Fearful, he instinctively tried to back away but the chair was behind him. "Get this clear, I am not your mate. I'm your brother. Don't poke around my dad's house any more or I'll get angry. I don't trust you." Bristling, Paul waited for Jeff to settle back on the chair. He switched the light off, folded the curtain back into place, and closed the hall door. "If I hear you poking around again there'll be trouble." Scolded like a naughty dog, the four-year old child within Jeff was scared to move an inch.

The night was long and on many occasions Jeff considered going home to Hessle and returning in the morning, but two large tots of whisky on an unaccustomed stomach made that impossible. He tossed and turned under the stale blanket, the coldness easily seeping through the holes, and the mixture of his father's and brother's unwashed, manly smells were sickening, but eventually the alcohol helped him to drift into a deep sleep. He woke the next morning, warm, and pleased to see the low late-autumn sun pooling through holes in the tatty curtains. The ordeal was nearly over.

Paul's droning voice floated from the kitchen. "Hurry up. It's time to go and see my dad."

Jeff had worn his clothes overnight and when he recalled the freezing water in the hot tap from the early hours of the morning, he chose not to wash. He went to the kitchen, the intense odour of male bodies now replaced by rancid grime, and sat beside the small, cluttered melamine table. Paul had prepared a steaming mug of sweet tea for him, regardless that he didn't take sugar, and forced it into his hands. "Get that down you quick. I want to see my dad as soon as possible."

Paul drained his own mug and refilled it from a large china pot, adding some milk and spooning in several heaped sugars, and Jeff sipped his scalding, thickly sweet and colourless brew. Although it tasted revolting, Jeff was grateful for the drink. Paul's behaviour the previous night troubled him and he assessed his brother's mood, before asking, "Those books I was looking at last night, why doesn't Roland want anyone to read them? They look interesting."

"My dad told me never to touch them. He said they were important and weren't to be touched." The stern statement teamed with a warning glare heightened Jeff's curiosity. His detective training screamed that the behaviour was unusual. However, with his father being ill, it was probable that Paul was simply being overprotective. Jeff decided to let it go for now. Maybe when the old man was better and back at home, he would come and visit, ask about the intriguing collection in person.

When they arrived on the ward Roland had been placed on, both sons were pleased to see him awake and propped up in bed. He smiled weakly when he noticed their approach. They sat at the bedside for what seemed an eternity, the trio barely speaking, until, eventually, a doctor beckoned the brothers to one side.

14

"He's had a good night, he slept very soundly, and we're not immediately worried about him."

"When can he come home?" Paul was grinning, a strange, lopsided smirk that replaced the usually grumpy expression, and Jeff realised he had never seen his brother smile before.

"A couple of days, I should think. But you must realise that his heart has significant damage from the arrests. He's not going to spring back to normal, even with the stents in place. You need to keep a close eye on him from now on."

"As long as he's alive, I'm happy." Jeff couldn't imagine Paul happy; it didn't fit his gruff persona.

They said goodbye to their father and Jeff dropped Paul outside his home in Colefield before gratefully returning to his life in Hull.

Chapter 2
Daytime, Tuesday 30th October

I wasn't expecting to see Jeff at work for a few days, so when he walked sluggishly into the room, eyes dull and face drawn, I indicated the door to an empty room where we could talk in private. The room was supposed to be my office, allocated when I had been promoted to Detective Chief Inspector, but I preferred the hustle and bustle of working in the incident room with 'the boys', I felt more involved. "Can I get you a drink, Jeff? You don't look so good." He shook his head and perched on one side of the massive desk, the centrepiece of the room. I sat on a nearby chair and leant forward, elbows on knees. "How's it going?"

Jeff shook his head slowly, focusing on the carpet before him. "He's okay. He'll be home in a couple of days."

I wasn't expecting that. Everything about him had the demeanour of somebody grieving. I didn't believe he would be up to working on the Kaylee Robinson case, so I couldn't understand why he had returned to work so swiftly and I relayed my fears to him.

This time Jeff was more open in his reply, for which I was grateful. "It was awful, boss, truly awful. I know they're my father and brother, but I don't know them. The last time I saw Paul was when we buried our mother six years ago, and the last time I saw my father was at my wedding, two years before that. I know they live in poverty but – my god, Frank – you should see the state of the house they live in. It's utterly disgusting."

It seemed a strange concern considering recent events. "Come on, Jeff, we see filthy houses all the time."

His charcoal eyes hooked me, intense. "No. It was different there. It has a weird atmosphere, it's sort of sinister." When he stopped, I hoped he had realised how stupid he'd sounded, but I was wrong. "In fact the whole village just seems odd." He paused and I sat back, lounging against the backrest. "The thing is… oh, this is so difficult to explain. Yes, the house is cluttered, and yes, they don't like housework, but as soon as I entered the village it was as if I couldn't breathe freely, like there was a secret hiding in the walls."

I'd never heard him say anything remotely spiritual before and these were definitely not the usual sentiments of the man I had grown to respect over the years. It sounded barmy, but I put it down to having a rough night in distressing circumstances. "I don't think you should come back to work yet, I…"

"I've got to, Frank, for my sanity."

I raised an eyebrow sardonically. "For your," I paused with the irony, "sanity?"

He was completely serious. "I reckon that if I don't have something to take my mind off yesterday – well, last night – I'll go crazy."

I sighed deeply. There was no comeback to that and I had to agree to keep him on the case. "Okay. But two things: firstly, if you want to talk about anything, anything at all, say the word and we can go for a drink or something; and secondly, if you need to go and see your father or brother, your absence will be covered with no questions asked."

He shook my hand, a gentle, sincere smile fleeting across his face. "Thanks, boss."

We returned to our desks in the incident room and Jeff busied himself by catching up with the developments of Kaylee Robinson's case. We now had her father in custody, with damning evidence to back our suspicion that he was the brute who had squeezed her innocent young life short.

Paul sat in silence, a cheese sandwich made with doorstop bread and a mug of tea on the kitchen table in front of him, both untouched. Dorothy, just three years older than his father, brought her own sandwich and tea across and sat on the empty chair opposite. "Come on, eat up, lad. You need to keep your strength up, what with your dad being ill."

He sagged further into the chair, reluctantly picking up one half of the sandwich and taking a large bite. He chewed slowly, the lack of appetite turning the food to cardboard. "I've got some washing upstairs. Are you taking it today?"

She reached over and patted his hand. "Of course I am, love. You need all the help you can get at the moment, and I need the pennies too, remember." It was her usual, unveiled hint and he replied with a grunt. Dorothy was used to his unsociable manner, having known him all his life. Paul had always been quiet and she had often said to herself that if she were thirty years younger, he would be exactly the type of man she'd have gone for, with his mop of hair so black it had a blueish tinge when the sunlight touched it, his equally black eyes, and the manly, ruddy complexion. He was also a bear of a man, just like her Ernie had been back in the day.

She took a dainty bite of her own sandwich, the slices of bread much thinner than the ones she had cut for Paul, and chewed it like a tiny squirrel nibbling on a hazelnut. "Are you going to see your dad again today?" She took another bite.

He raised his eyes with a sorrowful expression. "The trouble I've got is not having a car. It's a long trek by bus." It was his turn to hint and she was familiar with it.

Keeping a practiced, motherly smile on her face, Dorothy finished her mouthful and sighed. "I have to go to the supermarket today anyway." She didn't, but he didn't need to know that. There was no point upsetting him. "I can take you to the hospital, go shopping and pick you up on the way home if you like."

Again Paul raised his empty eyes, deadened by concern for his ailing father. "Thanks, Dot. Can you get some more bread and cheese while you're out? I'll give you the money back when I get paid."

Her smile waned. This advantage taking was becoming all too regular, but how could she stand up to him when Roland was in hospital? Through gritted teeth she agreed, mentally totting up how much money Roland and Paul owed her. Must be just shy of a hundred pounds by now, what with cooking for them most nights, doing their washing and ironing, cleaning the pots, shopping. They were supposed to pay each week for the services she provided, but that had tailed off a long time ago.

She also found it odd how they referred to being paid, because she knew Roland had been registered disabled for as long as she could remember and she had never seen Paul go out to work. Mind you, she'd not been further inside the house than the kitchen since Jeannie had gone, so maybe they ran a business from home. Everybody nowadays seemed to be using this Internet thing to make money. Quite aside from anything, although she was the village gossip, she conceded it was none of her business, and she loved their company anyway. She loved nurturing people. Without them, she would be alone day in, day out. Having chastised herself for being inconsiderate, her smile returned and she patted Paul's hand. "Let me get my purse and shopping bag, I'll be back in half an hour or so. And make sure you finish that sandwich or there'll be no bacon butties tomorrow morning."

As he walked towards his father, Paul was stunned by the contrast from earlier in the day. Roland's skin was pallid, his eyes and cheeks sunken, and his breath was laboured. A nurse was hanging a new drip by his bedside and when she saw Paul approaching, she pulled him to one side. "You're his son, aren't you, love?" He nodded. "I'll just find the doctor for you. I won't be long. Don't expect your dad to say much, he's very poorly."

Concerned, Paul dragged a chair closer to the bed and sat, taking Roland's limp hand in his. "I'm here, dad."

Roland's eyes opened a crack and he laboriously turned to face his eldest son. Paul was shocked at how grey his normally brown eyes appeared. The voice that came wasn't his father's. It was raspy and faint, not the usual thundering bark. "Is the other one with you?"

"What?"

Agitated with frustration. "Jeffery." His head sank to the pillow, quickly exhausted.

"No, dad, he's gone back to his posh life with his posh house and car."

"Good."

Paul smiled. He liked to please his beloved father.

Roland strained to lift his head again but it was too tiring. He beckoned Paul closer with a bony finger. "I need to tell you something without him here." He took a few shallow breaths. "It's important."

"Is it Mr Mason?" The chirpy, young voice behind Paul made him jump and he sprung away from his father. The doctor continued, an equal mixture of concern and friendliness on his face. "You are Mr Mason?"

Paul stood and shook the proffered hand strongly. "Yes, sir."

The doctor continued in hushed tones and Paul leaned closer. "I'm afraid your father's condition has deteriorated since this morning. We're all quite surprised to be truthful. We've increased his medication," he took Roland's chart from the end of the bed, scanning the page, "but things should have been improving with the stents in place. We're waiting to see if his condition improves overnight before reassessing the situation, but it may be an idea to make sure his affairs are in order."

Paul fell heavily into the still-warm seat, shock engulfing him. "Affairs? You mean he might..." The sentence petered to silence. Eventually Paul blinked and grasped the doctor's sleeve. "He can't die."

"Don't worry too much, Mr Mason, I'm just suggesting you make sure everything's in order as a precaution. Do you have anyone who could be with you? A wife, girlfriend, good friend."

"No." Jeff flickered into Paul's mind. Would his brother's presence make this blow any easier? He buried the thought. His dad had seemed keen for Jeff not to be there and he resolved he would handle this on his own.

Once the doctor had left, Paul leant closer to his father and clasped his hand firmly. "Dad, you wanted to say something to me."

"When you get home," each word was a struggle, "go into my room." He rested his head on the pillow with a pained grimace.

"Do you want me to get the doctor?"

Now Roland's eyes were wide. An inner strength arrived from somewhere and he unwittingly drooled with every struggled word. "Listen. The key to my safe is in my underwear drawer. In the safe is a notebook. I want you to read it through. All of it. In order." He was panting with the effort of speech, but if he was going to die – and he knew he was – he couldn't leave anything unsaid. "In the front is a letter to you. Read it and get rid of it. At the back is another, the notebook will tell you when to read that one. You must follow these instructions. Whatever you do, don't tell anybody – especially not Jeffery. Not until you've read the last letter."

"Okay, dad." Paul counted on his thick fingers as he burned the instructions to his memory. "Key in underwear drawer. Safe, notebook, letters."

"And the necklaces. Sell them. They're in…" Roland's voice tailed to a pained growl. His head fell onto the pillow and his grip on Paul's hand loosened. Before Paul could register what the odd whining noise was, the crash team shoved him aside as they rushed from the doorway. He viewed his father's transition from life to death from the side-lines, as if he were watching a dream unfold. A nightmare. People ran to and fro, strange words were shouted by an array of voices, until finally they left, one by one, and the doctor who had been so cheery just minutes before turned to Paul. "I'm sorry, Mr Mason, there's nothing more we can do."

I watched Jeff go through the motions at work over the course of the day, and was surprised by how normal he was considering his personal circumstances. But knowing him so well, I guessed he was tormented inside and just covering it well. It was nearly time to call it a night. Most of the team had already left and the Kaylee Robinson investigation was all but finished. With the approval of our superintendent, we would be charging her father with murder the next day.

Without thinking it through I picked up the phone and dialled. Jeff's wife answered and I could hear their baby gurgling in the background. "Hey Sue, it's Frank. I just wondered if I could borrow Jeff for an hour after work. He's been a bit stressed today so I want to drag him for a beer and make sure he's okay."

"No problem, it'll mean I can watch Corrie in peace." She chuckled and I was warmed that Jeff had such a wonderful family to support him at times like this.

"Thanks, Sue. See you soon."

"Before you go, I've been meaning to tell Jeff to ask, but how do you and Ellen fancy coming over soon for dinner and drinks?"

"Sounds good to me. Give Ellen a call, she does all the social arrangements." I bid her farewell and ended the call. Grasping my trench coat from the rack and briefcase from under the desk, I sauntered to Jeff's desk, fishing in my pockets for the car keys. "Come on, you. Sue's just told me I'm allowed to take you for a drink. If you leave your car here I'll drive and pick you up tomorrow morning so you can have a few tonight."

Jeff gave no resistance.

We always went to the Horse and Hounds in Hessle if we had a drink in the evenings. It was a fair distance from the office on the other side of Hull, but it was closer to home for both of us and beautifully quiet, which meant we could chat over our beers without having to shout. Not to mention the sumptuous food they served on the days we felt like indulging.

Usually, we would prop up the bar and make banter with the staff and regulars alike, but I wanted to speak to Jeff in private, so I directed him to a table and fetched the first two pints of smooth, along with a couple of bags of peanuts.

"Any news of your father since this morning?"

Jeff took a long, obviously much required, drink from his ice-cold glass. He held a finger up as he gulped to acknowledge the question and finally, satiated, shook his head. "No, Paul said he'd call if there were any problems, so no news is good news on this occasion."

We made small talk for a while. From past experience, I knew he wouldn't loosen up until he'd had a couple of beers. After we'd had two pints, I got him a third and a coffee for myself, as I was driving.

Knowing I was about to step out of line, I focused on the fussy coffee cup, fiddling with the handle, stirring a little too much. I steeled myself. "Jeff, are you going to tell me what's going on in that head of yours?"

He replaced his glass on the table. I could see he was weighing whether to say anything or not. "Nothing, just what's happened to my father and all that."

Fidgeting, I threw another sugar into the cup, not that it needed more sweetness. "You and I both know there's something else, I know you too well." At this point he broke and told me what had happened at his father's home. He told me, incredulous, about the collection of crime books, the angry brother. The oddness of it all. When he finished speaking we sat in silence for a while, considering his outpouring. "I don't think there's too much to be concerned about, really. Paul's obviously protective of your dad and maybe he's taken the rap before for touching the books. I'd let it drop if I were you."

Jeff sighed, distant and troubled. "I'm not sure I can. You'd have to see the house to understand. It's not just that it's dirty. Like you said this morning, I see that all the time. I don't know how to explain it, you'd have to see the house, the village. Feel it."

He was withdrawing and despite my concern for him, I thought he was being absurd. "Try and explain it, the more you try the more I can understand."

"Oh god, this is so hard to explain. Okay, here goes. There's a kind of doom and gloom about Colefield. It's so pretty, so picturesque, so well kept. But there's a filth. Not a physical filth, but a mental filth. It's almost as if it's evil, eyes everywhere, secrets. Like the walls are screaming for someone to listen."

And now I knew why Jeff had been reluctant to mention his fears. They were totally ridiculous. However, the name of the village rang a bell from somewhere and it always bugged me when my memory failed me. Colefield. How did I know Colefield?

Chapter 3
Evening, Tuesday 30th October

It was almost nine miles from the hospital to his rural home, but Paul had chosen to walk anyway. He couldn't face saying the words 'my dad has died' to Dorothy, and he didn't want to sit on a stuffy bus when his head needed clearing. He had pondered over Roland's mysterious final words, but wasn't sure he was ready to start rummaging about in his room to retrieve the curious items. It pained him that his father had passed in the middle of a sentence. Or was it an instruction? Neither wore jewellery, so what had his father been trying to tell him about necklaces?

Relieved to finally be home, Paul closed the back door behind him, gratefully shutting the icy, evening wind behind him. He stood in the kitchen, a little lost boy, and it hit him properly for the first time that he would never see his father again. There, by the kitchen table, were two chairs – he would only need one now. Roland's favourite mug, still with dregs of tea inside, sat on the hob beside the kettle. His coat hung from the peg. Tears began to fall. Copious tears spouting anger, denial, hate, love and, most of all, an overwhelming loneliness. Frustrated, Paul picked up the mug and threw it against the wall, smashing the 'Mr Grumpy' slogan on the side to smithereens.

Once the unwelcome sobbing subsided, Paul, with drooping shoulders, sloped to the front room and sagged onto his chair, half-heartedly lifting the cheap whisky bottle from the floor. He sank a few gulps, the bitterness making his teeth grind, contorting his unusual features to a grimace.

Whether through shock or simply the time of year, he began to shiver and reluctantly heaved himself forward to build up a fire in the grate. It didn't take long – he had grown up with the open fire so it was second nature – and within minutes he had thrown on a couple of scuttles of coal, enough to keep it roaring for the rest of the evening.

Paul yawned. It had been an arduous day and he felt empty inside. Sleep crept up swiftly and for a few hours he sat, head lolled to one side, snoring from the alcohol. In his deep slumber, the three drunken phone calls from Jeff went unanswered.

I dropped Jeff off and returned home to Ellen and our children, who sat in the living room watching some rubbish or other on the television. Ellen stood immediately when she heard my key in the door, sliding her slippers on. "I'll reheat your tea."

"No. No, you sit back down. I'll do it." I wasn't ready for company yet, still shocked by Jeff's ludicrous outburst.

I went to the kitchen and switched the sidelights on, the central spotlights too bright for my mood. I checked my meal was in the microwave, where Ellen usually placed it when I arrived home late, and pulled a can of beer from the fridge. Sitting at the table, I supped the cool drink as I mulled over Jeff's odd words.

He never behaved like that. He was one of the calmest, most rational detectives on our team, which was one of the reasons I had taken to him in the first place. Soon enough the microwave pinged and I ate my dinner at the table, whilst recapping the conversation without my three wayward teenagers either gabbling at me about irrelevant things or throwing tantrums. By the time I had finished, I'd become strangely curious about the village of Colefield – about Paul's house – and suspecting I wouldn't sleep easily, I decided to drive over and take a look.

The journey was pleasant, and with little traffic on the roads and the Humber Bridge clear, it gave me ample time to think. From the moment Jeff had mentioned Colefield the name had rung a bell, and I racked my brains as to why. I repeated the name in my head, over and over, trying to place it from my memory, but nothing had come to me by the time I passed the florally decorated signpost that heralded Colefield.

I hadn't reached any houses yet, so I pulled the car to the side of the road to decide what the next step should be. The clock on the dashboard told me it was approaching midnight and, with the village so peaceful, I didn't want to disturb the residents. Eventually I killed the engine, resolving to walk a bit at first, get the feel of the area that's impossible to experience from

25

being inside a car. With no idea of Paul's address, I decided to stroll around and see if any of the outrageous things Jeff had said made sense.

As I had suspected, the houses were actually cottages – some detached, some semis, some bungalows – and all of the gardens were spectacular, even without the arrays of blooming, colourful flowers I could imagine flourished in summer. Although the sky was dark, the dim lampposts glistened on the red, yellow, amber and brown leaves that danced furiously on the road in the gusting wind. On first impression it seemed to be a desirable area. Further up the road I could see a building that was possibly a barn, and a few steps further into the heart of Colefield showed me I was right. When I spotted a dirt track that lead to a farm gate, I decided to return to the car and park it by the fence; the wind was howling and my thin trench coat wasn't keeping the wintry iciness out.

The village wasn't much larger than a hamlet and I could see many of the houses from the new vantage point, warm in the car. Maybe forty or fifty homes, a small, dilapidated pub that couldn't have done much trade, and no shop. And, oddly, there were no signs of life. No wonder Jeff had been spooked, staying in a place like this overnight. I couldn't see a single glowing window anywhere and the only sound was the twirling leaves and whispering wind. I mused that if the streetlights were to go out, this place would become invisible at night. Maybe Jeff wasn't being so ridiculous after all.

I sat in the car for a while, watching, waiting for a sign of life, and suddenly a flash drew my eyes to a house I had driven past further down the road. There was life in Colefield after all. An upstairs light shone through net curtains, and with the farm being on an incline I could see a good deal into the room. I fumbled in the glove compartment for my binoculars.

Inside the room was a man, silhouetted by the light behind him. He appeared to be a giant against the low ceiling and he was opening and closing drawers, obviously searching for something. I wondered why he didn't close the curtains and then I remembered: what was the point if nobody was awake to watch? Except me.

Paul had woken from his much-needed slumber and glanced at the clock, amazed that five hours had passed since he had arrived home; it was one in the morning. A blissful second had passed before the tragic recollection that his wonderful dad was dead resurfaced. He'd thought of the death, of the moments leading up to the death, and his father's final instructions.

Resigned, he had taken another slug of whisky and resolved that the time had come to find out what his father's strange ramblings were all about.

Paul rarely went into his father's room. It had been shrouded in mystery since he was a child and being there felt uncomfortable. With the bright light contrasting the blackness outside, he opened several drawers before finding the one that contained his father's underwear. The key was at the back, underneath socks that Dorothy had neatly rolled. He took it and searched the room again, this time for the safe he hadn't known existed.

The room was as cluttered as the rest of the house – boxes on boxes, things stacked on other things – and after a while he wondered if the safe had been part of a dying man's imagination. After all, his father had never mentioned it before. Paul was about to give in to tiredness and try again in the morning when he opened the door of a forties-style wardrobe- solid oak littered with woodworm holes – for the second time and noticed the safe on the top shelf, almost completely hidden by pullovers.

He brought it down and placed it on the bed, unlocking it. As promised, inside was a leather-bound notebook, nice quality but very old. He opened the front cover and took the envelope that lay on the first page. On the front his name was scrawled in Roland's uneducated handwriting, above the words *'PRIVATE AND CONFIDENTIAL'.*

Still uneasy in the forbidden room, Paul replaced the safe on the shelf and took the letter and journal downstairs. The raw heat of the raging fire hit him, his face reddening further, and he slumped onto the armchair, swigging from the bottle before tentatively opening the envelope with his huge fingers. It had been written using capital letters only, a thoughtful gesture from

Roland, who knew his underachieving son struggled to read lowercase.

'PAUL, SON. READING THIS, IT MEANS I'LL HAVE

GONE. WE HAVE ALWAYS BEEN CLOSE, YOU AND

ME, AND THAT'S WHY I'M LETTING YOU KNOW MY

BIGGEST SECRET. DO NOT TELL ANYONE OR YOU'LL

BE IN DANGER. NOBODY ELSE MUST SEE THIS

NOTEBOOK.

MY FINAL WILL AND TESTAMENT IS IN THE SAFE. YOU INHERIT EVERYTHING. TRY TO READ THE NOTEBOOK, BUT IF YOU DON'T UNDERSTAND IT, DON'T SHOW ANYONE ELSE, JUST READ WHAT YOU CAN. WOULDN'T NORMALLY SAY THIS, BUT I LOVE YOU, SON.'

A surge of tears streamed down Paul's face, the impact of having lost his father heightened by the letter. He had never heard his father say he loved him, and although seeing it on paper wasn't the same as hearing the words, it had still been expressed.

Too distraught to examine the journal right now, he made himself comfortable in the armchair and shamelessly cried himself to sleep.

The light in the window had gone out, leaving the darkened village eerily silent once more, and I restarted the car, unaware that the man I had been watching was Jeff's brother. I headed away from the village. For the life of me, even though I had now been there, I still couldn't recall why I recognised the village's name.

I arrived home shortly after two and my house was also in silence. I crept to the study and clicked the computer on, fixing myself a brandy to see me through until bedtime while waiting for it to come to life. Eventually I typed 'Colefield' into the search engine and selected the first site. It was a tourism website that detailed villages in North Lincolnshire, and gave me nothing of interest, so I continued searching, sipping the warming drink. I checked the hallway to ensure Ellen was in bed and surreptitiously lit a cigar, deeply inhaling the musty smoke.

After a tedious few minutes, the information I was seeking was on my screen, and the memories instantly returned, taking me back to my teenaged days in nineteen-eighty, when a woman was shot dead at a bonfire display. The killer had never been found, and when a second woman had been shot the following year, the investigation had escalated. A third victim was shot in nineteen eighty-two. These displays had been held in a field on the outskirts of Colefield.

Now I recalled why the name was familiar, my mind took me back to the tender age of seventeen. When the first killing had happened I had been studying three A-levels with an ambition to join the police force, and over the next couple of years, I read about the Bonfire Night Killer in the national newspapers. At the time I was a southerner, living in Oxford, and the north was of little interest to me until I met my Hessle born and bred wife at university. After we graduated, I moved to Hull to be with her.

When the murderer wasn't found, the years passed and the investigation tailed off with no further leads. Satisfied now that Colefield wouldn't keep me awake, I flicked the butt of the cigar through the window, switched the computer off, finished my drink and went upstairs to sleep it off.

Chapter 4
Wednesday 31st October

By the time Paul awoke with a sore head and thirsty mouth, curiosity had arisen and he was eager to have breakfast and take a look at the journal. Still unusually cold, he stoked the barely glowing ashes, tipping some more coal on the top, and went to prepare a bacon butty and mug of tea. As the meat sizzled in the pan and the kettle boiled, he scooped up the fragments of his father's mug and placed them in the bin, not wanting Dorothy to see, knowing she would call round at some stage to have words with him about deserting her the previous day.

Finally, he settled at the table to eat and opened the first page of the notebook to begin the mysterious journey to his father's memories, intending to hide the book when he heard Dorothy's familiar 'yoo-hoo' as she approached the back door.

However, unlike the letter, the words were written in lowercase and joined-up, and he struggled to make sense of what they said. He was still labouring over the text when, without singing her customary warning of arrival, the door flew open and Dorothy bustled into the room, dropping her bag, rushing to Paul and holding his head close to her ample chest. "I heard about your dad, love. I'm so sorry."

With his left hand, Paul discreetly fed the book under a stack of paperwork to conceal it. He had managed to make out a few words by that time and could see why his father had instructed him not to tell anybody about the journal. What it contained was scandalous. He suffocated against the heaving breasts for minutes as Dorothy sobbed uncontrollably, her spent tears dripping onto his scruffy hair, salt and pepper at the temples. Eventually she pulled away, dried her eyes on her sleeve, and took Paul's used plate and mug to the sink, busying herself by clearing up.

In the aftermath of her sobs, her voice was stilted. "What were you reading that had you so engrossed?"

Startled and lost for words, Paul stuttered as he regained his composure. "Oh, nothing. Just a thing I found on the table. Junk mail stuff."

"Funny, the post hasn't been yet. All the same." She tutted at the obvious lie, her curiosity aroused.

Paul guessed Dorothy had seen more than he had wanted her to and he needed to change the subject to take her mind off it. Moments later it dawned on him. "How did you know about dad? I didn't tell anyone at all."

Her hand went to her hip as her mind transformed to gossip mode. "Oh, there's a nurse lives down the road, she told Eddie, who told Peter Graves, who told his wife Monica. I'm on the other side of her next door neighbour, Anne, so Monica told Anne and she told me."

Paul wished he hadn't asked, but at least she had forgotten the journal. However, he still needed to hide it securely, so would need her out of the room. "I think my brother left a mug in the front room, can you get it if you're planning on washing the pots?"

Dorothy, the book still at the forefront of her mind, guessed what he was doing. She pottered out of the room, leaving the door slightly ajar. She stopped to listen, shifting her hand about occasionally to make it sound as if she were working. She knew the kitchen from top to bottom; if she heard where Paul moved the book to, she could take a look later -nobody could hide anything from her. Seconds later she heard a cupboard open, a pan lid clang and a thud as Paul's hefty frame flopped back onto the chair.

Dorothy collected the single mug she had spotted from the doorway, had a nosy glance around the room she had not seen since Paul's mother had left, and was about to return to the kitchen when she noticed the letter Roland had left for Paul on a chair. She checked she wasn't being watched and picked it up. Skimming the words, she returned it to the chair, a satisfied smirk on her face.

Back in the kitchen, Dorothy filled the kettle, her mind whirring, devising a way to get Paul out of the kitchen without taking the book with him. Eventually the water started to bubble and the answer came. "I was about to make a brew, but in the circumstances, would you like me to make you a coffee with a little something in it to take the edge off your grief?"

Paul had always thought Dorothy, a strict teetotaller, was against drinking and his eyes lit up at the welcome suggestion. "Sounds like a good idea, Dot."

She waited a few seconds, studying him. "Well? Have you got anything to put in it?"

He stuttered an apology and nipped to the front room to grab his father's whisky bottle, his own being empty, and passed it to Dorothy, who had prepared a strong, overly sweet coffee substitute using a grubby bottle of *Camp,* which was years past the sell-by date. She tipped a hefty dash of the liquor into the drink and stirred it. The plan worked. Within minutes of drinking a second heavily-dosed coffee, Paul was asleep with his head resting on the table, the alcohol having topped up the excess from his overindulgence the night before.

Silently she opened the pan cupboard, peering with myopic eyes through the glass lids to see which one to open, and she pulled out the tatty book, glancing at Paul before turning her back to him to read it by the sink.

It was agonising for her to withhold the shocked gasps as she scanned the unbelievable words in front of her eyes and, checking every now and then that Paul was still asleep, she became engrossed in the unfolding admission from beyond the grave.

By the time Paul awoke, his neck stiff and harbouring a thundering headache, the book had been returned to its hiding place and Dorothy had long gone.

Jeff had received a call just after lunch from his brother with the sad, but not entirely unexpected, news about their father, and despite Paul insisting he wanted to be alone, Jeff was making his way through the drizzling rain to Colefield. Lost in driving he recalled the conversation that morning with me. I had been asking questions about the Colefield shootings back in the eighties, and whereas Jeff had heard about them, he had only been four when the first happened, so all he knew was hearsay. I had been astounded that Jeff wasn't particularly interested – a keen policeman and detective, not intrigued by killings on his back door – but Jeff reminded me that his mother had taken him to live in Scunthorpe around that time. I, however, had a life-long interest in unsolved crimes and wouldn't let the subject drop, leading tetchy Jeff to suggest I was obsessed.

Jeff slowly drove along the dirt track that led to the parking space at the back of the house, musing that maybe he would research the murders too. After all, he had the advantage of having been born in Colefield, and his brother living there made it slightly more appealing. If nothing else, it would take his mind off the emotional turmoil he was caught in.

Tugging his jacket hood over his gelled and tufted brunette hair, he trudged through the rain, over the lawn – muddy from the wet spell – to the back door and rapped. There was no answer. He tried again, harder. This time Paul answered, weary and pallid, and Jeff pushed past him, away from the cold wetness outside. "I know you asked me not to come, bro, but I really need to spend a bit of time with you. I've so many questions about Roland, it's driving me crazy."

Paul sighed. He closed the door and strode to the kettle, filling it and returning it to the cooker. "Call him dad. He was your dad too, not just mine. You'd better sit down, I suppose. Now you're here." Paul's eyes fixed on Jeff's. "We need to talk, I guess."

Jeff was unnerved, unsure whether the statement was ominous or not; surely hearing about his father's untimely death was enough bad news for one day? But as the minutes silently ticked by he realised the abruptness was just Paul's way. The light whistle from the kettle as the water boiled broke the peace and Jeff watched his brother prepare a large pot of tea using a single teabag. Now he understood why his brother took so much sugar: to give it some flavour.

Jeff studied the filthy room, the cloying stench of overused lard hanging in the air, and wondered how anybody survived in such conditions. He had seen worse – there was always worse – but he loved that he and his wife kept their house freshly cleaned and hygienic.

Paul brought the teapot to the table, covering it with a stained tea cosy, and sat opposite Jeff, who struggled to find some appropriate words. "So, how was the, er, death?"

Paul poured the pale tea into dubiously cleaned mugs. "He had a heart attack. He died."

"Okay, okay, stupid question. No, I mean, well, did he say anything before he died?"

Paul shifted on his seat, wondering worriedly if Jeff knew anything about his father's final instructions. No, that was silly, of course he couldn't know. "He said I get all his things. And that he loved me."

Jeff was unperturbed about inheriting nothing, he had been estranged from that side of the family for so long that it came as no surprise, and their mother hadn't left anything to Paul in her will. "That's nice, he didn't seem like the kind of guy who would say that often."

"First time that I know of. Then the machines started bleeping and he was gone. It was as quick as that." A calm drifted through the room as they digested the words, each confused and lost now both their parents were gone.

Again Jeff began, not really sure what to say. "So how have you been since?"

"I had a few too many beers, a bit too much whisky, and I've been reading dad's, er, I mean... reading dad's post. Yes, the post." Paul tapped a pile of paperwork beside him. "These. Bills and stuff." Paul focused on his mug as he spooned sugar after sugar into the tea, but this was Jeff's forte, he was trained to spot lies. He sipped his drink, burning his tongue slightly, and replaced the mug on the table. Something strange was going on. "How long are you stopping?"

Jeff sensed the eagerness for him to leave, which irritated him. As far as he knew, Roland had been the final member of their immediate family to die. They had no aunts or uncles, no cousins. It was just the two of them now and he had no understanding of his brother's reluctance to bond in any way. "Not too long today. I think I need a bit of a drink myself to get my head around Rol... er, dad being gone. Look, I can take the day off tomorrow. Do you want me to bring my wife and son over to see you, let you meet your nephew? He's only two months old. He's amazing."

Paul forcefully shook his head. "No. No."

Jeff's heckles rose further, along with his voice. "Damn you, Paul, why won't you let me in? As you yourself said, he was my father too. I didn't ask mum to take me away from you both, I was only four. And you're my brother, for god's sake."

Paul was taken aback, his own solitary, self-absorbed grief suddenly shaming him. "You're right, I'm sorry. No, no babies, no women. You can come though, perhaps stop over again. Bring plenty of booze with you and we can have a drink."

Jeff sighed with relief. "I'd like that. I really want to catch up with all the missing years. Find out who you are… who I am and where I come from."

As soon as Dorothy arrived home she had written down everything she could remember from reading Roland's journal. She'd not been able to digest the words fully in the short time she'd had, but had skimmed through the most important details, forcing them into her memory.

She recalled the Bonfire Night killings as if they had happened yesterday, having lived in the village all her life. The first was the biggest shock, she remembered. She and Ernie had been married just over ten years in November nineteen-eighty, and they were busy raising their three children, with the two boys in junior school and the youngest, daughter Freda, still in primary. As always, they had made sure the children were excited about the fifth of November, and this particular year was extra special as it was the first time a major display would take place in the adjacent fields, meaning they didn't have to take the car.

They had dressed the children snugly, two pairs of trousers each, gloves, hats, scarves, and they had looked so sweet with their big, brown eyes and pink button noses peeping out from the patterned home-made knitwear. Dorothy smiled at the memory. They were grown up now and had flown the nest many years before, providing – she had heard on the grapevine – a pleasing six grandchildren between them. Not that she had seen them; she'd been estranged from all three of her babies for years after some petty squabble she couldn't recall.

Dorothy and her family had seen Kath James with her children shortly before it happened. She had lived three doors from Dorothy and they liked to pass the time of day every now and then, talk about their children, gossip about the comings and goings of the villagers. Kath had been slightly younger than Dorothy on the fateful day and she also had three kids. They had walked together briefly before the firework display started, only separating when Ernie decided to buy his family a hamburger each from a mobile cafe.

The display had been announced and an expectant hush grew over the crowd, eagerly awaiting the light display, the first bangs and crashes. Soon the sky had become littered with colour. Golds, yellows, whites, reds – multi-coloured stars flashing and popping everywhere – and the entire crowd gazed into the night, whooping and delighting. Except for Katherine, it seemed. For it was during the display that she was raped and shot in a nearby copse of weeping willows.

Nobody had realised at the time. The gunshot had blended undistinguished from the cacophony of rockets, and it wasn't until Katherine's children arrived home without her that her husband had become uneasy and raised the alarm.

The same thing happened the next year, this time to a thirty-year old woman named Vanessa Walton, who originated from Lincoln and had recently moved to the village with her husband. Panic ran rife through the villagers. The police were sure her attacker was the same man to have killed Katherine James.

In nineteen eighty-two, when Bernie Smith, a local disabled woman with severe learning difficulties, was brutally raped and shot, the police investigation escalated and the council took the wise decision not to hold any more firework displays in the area surrounding Colefield.

Yes, Dorothy remembered it well, and now she knew who the killer was, she was about to have some fun. After all, she was owed a few pennies and could do with the money. And a little excitement.

Jeff got back to the office just before five and I beckoned him over. "How are you?"

He slumped onto the seat opposite me and leant his arm on the desk, sighing deeply and fiddling with some pens subconsciously. "Okay, I suppose. I'd sort of geared myself up for Roland dying so that's not really hit me as hard as I expected, at least not yet, anyway. But Paul's behaviour has, it seems as if he wants nothing to do with me. It's frustrating."

"How do you mean?" Now that Kaylee Robinson's father had been charged, we weren't working on a case at the moment, so a chat with Jeff would be a welcome interlude from catching up with the tedious paperwork.

He was clearly struggling to find the right words. "Well, it's two things, really. First, I've sort of gathered that Paul is a man of few words, he's very abrupt, but it seems like he's blocking me out. I really feel like I'm imposing when I visit, you know, getting in his way. But he doesn't appear to work, he has no car, and rarely goes out from what I can tell, so you'd think he would appreciate some company."

"Some people are natural loners."

"Yeah, but I'm not just anyone, I'm his brother."

How could I comment? It was an irrational, childish statement. "Uhuh. So what's the other thing?"

He hesitated, cheeks pinking with discomfort. "Well, this is weird, but I think Paul's hiding something. I don't know if it's to do with the will, but he's being secretive about something. He says he's been left everything in the will and that doesn't bother me, but I wonder if it's true. Something's not right, I just have no idea what."

I sank further into my seat and made a pyramid with my fingers as I digested his concerns. With knowledge, having lost my own father three years before, I explained that once probate had been granted the will would become a public document, so he would be able to see it for himself if he doubted what Paul was telling him.

It seemed to pacify him as he was quieted, lost in his private thoughts. I pushed the book I had started reading that morning aside and opened the file before me. Jeff grasped the book and flicked through. "You're still obsessed with the Bonfire Night Killer, then," he chuckled.

Needlessly, I felt embarrassed and hoped it didn't show on my face. "It's just a book I picked up earlier. Thought I might get my facts right about a killer I'm unfamiliar with."

"With a silly murder book that's probably written by someone who's conspiracy crazy?" He chuckled again and I snatched the book back.

"Sometimes it helps to have another perspective when I'm opening an old case."

Jeff smiled widely. "Well, I thought while I was driving to Colefield that I might join you with your obsession. After all, I was born there, I should know what nasty deeds have happened there over the years."

I was more than happy to do the research alongside my colleague and friend and there was no better time to start than right now, while we had no current cases to investigate. "I'll tell you what, I'll try and get permission from the Super to dig out the case notes, see if we can cast a fresh eye over the case." I wondered if I was asking too much of the man who was struggling to come to terms with the death of the father he had barely known, but I reasoned that the distraction would probably be beneficial. I was pleased when he nodded warmly.

Chapter 5
Thursday 1st November

Jeff had called me in the morning and I'd agreed he could have a day or two off work on compassionate grounds. He knew he was a lucky man to have such an understanding wife in Sue. They spent a leisurely day with their baby son, strolling lazily around the shopping centre in the morning, before having a healthy lunch at Mitzi's Salad Bar. Once they returned home, Sue spent the afternoon languidly preparing dinner and playing with Jacob, while Jeff tackled some minor jobs around the house.

Sue knew her husband well enough to know that keeping out of his way to let him come to terms with the bereavement was the best thing to do, and she had resolved to only mention the subject if he instigated the conversation. Jeff, not a do-it-yourself fiend, had laid out a few basic tools and the cheap drill he had bought when it was on special offer, and was marking the drill holes for the shelves he was about to hang on the wall of the spare bedroom. A wave of guilt, familiar throughout the day, washed through him and he laid the pencil and tape measure on the bed, sitting heavily. He placed his head in his hands.

He struggled to push himself back to his childhood, to try and recall something – anything – about his fourth year of age, the year his family had collapsed. He could vaguely remember the house in Colefield through a child's eyes, the greens of the fields and hedgerows, the azure sky and sparkling sun. He could remember happiness. Lightness, dancing, playing a superhero in the garden while his mum hung the washing on the line. Oddly, neither his father nor brother featured in these early memories, and they were basic, random snapshots, rather than specific times and situations.

His mum had never badmouthed his father, not to him anyway. All she'd said was that the marriage hadn't worked and they had left – no explanation, no reasons. And Jeff had been content with that. He remembered sitting on his bed in the house his mother had taken him to live in after the break-up, a boy of maybe ten or eleven, and wondering for the first time who his father was, what he was like, both in looks and personality. After one of the rare arguments with his mother when he was a gruff teenager, he had packed a rucksack and was ready to 'leave home', to find his father and live with him. But Joan had called him for his dinner, a sumptuous boeuf bourguignon with delightful creamed potatoes – his mother's speciality – and lightly steamed vegetables, and flying the nest was forgotten.

Joan had been a talented cook with a flair for knowing which herbs and spices to add to her dishes to deliver optimum flavour, and she hadn't been scared to experiment either. They had always eaten at the dining table, properly laid, with a jug of water, or a bottle of well-chosen wine on special occasions. The television and radio were always switched off, and often she would have classical music playing quietly in the background. A single parent, Joan didn't have excess money, her meagre wages from working at the school Jeff attended only just covered the bills, but she had always ensured they ate well. In reflection it was easy to see why Jeff had become a true gentleman.

Sue's voice calling up the stairs to announce that dinner was served startled him from his musing and he was shocked that the light shining through the window had dulled as the sun hastened towards the horizon. More shocking, though, was that even when trying to recall memories of his father, his mother and their life together took precedence. He genuinely had no idea who Roland Mason had been.

He trotted down the stairs to the dining kitchen. Just as his mother had insisted, Sue always served dinner at the table, but she drew the line at the classical music, thinking it ostentatious, which made Jeff chuckle. He sat as she switched on the wall lights and closed the blinds, and spooned the food onto their plates. "I didn't get the shelf up."

"Don't worry, there's no hurry."

Jeff finished his mouthful and reloaded his fork. "I sat on the bed for a while, trying to think about Roland."

"I suspected you would." Sue took a sip of water.

"How can I grieve for someone I didn't know? I barely feel anything, not for him, anyway. I still feel pain about mum dying, but there's nothing for Roland. It's weird."

She leant across the table and rested her hand on his. "There's no set process, Jeff. You have to deal with it in your own way, in your own time. Perhaps spending time with Paul will help to fill in the gaps?"

Jeff dropped his cutlery on the table with a start. "You've just reminded me, I told Paul I'd spend the evening with him. I'm sorry, love, I'd totally forgotten." He grasped the fork and hurriedly scooped some mash into his mouth.

She laughed lightly. "Slow down, there's no problem. I think it's the best thing to do."

The rest of the meal was spent in silence as Jeff shovelled, as politely as possible, his food up. He stood, kissed his wife with a hurried *thanks* and grabbed his jacket and car keys, checking his trouser pocket for his wallet. "We're drinking tonight so I'll stop over again, but I'll be back as soon as possible tomorrow morning."

Sue stopped clearing the plates and smiled. "Jacob and I will be fine. Try and have a good time, make it work for you."

Jeff's mind wandered again as he drove towards the bridge, this time to his beloved wife. Sue and Jeff had met at the police station as colleagues a decade before and, initially, they had hated each other. He'd thought she was an arrogant upstart, and she had thought him a 'waster'. Neither could have been more wrong. Once they'd realised their immediate judgements had been way off the mark, the relationship had quickly blossomed, and they'd married a couple of years later with a lavish wedding, courtesy of the bride's affluent parents, Jack and Brenda.

They had the kind of relationship everybody dreamt of. He was level-headed, quietly passionate, a gentle man, and over the years had become a wonderful husband and father. Sue, currently a stay-at-home mother while she rethought her future during her maternity leave, was understanding about his long hours. She was sweet, funny and hard-working. They loved each other implicitly and the visible tenderness when they gazed at each other was beautiful.

The glowing, yellow sign above the off-licence snapped Jeff back to reality, and without checking his mirrors properly he screeched to the kerb, causing the angry driver behind him to swerve. Embarrassed, Jeff determined to keep his mind on the road when he returned to the car. He picked up a bottle of whisky for Paul, a nice brandy for himself, and a six-pack of beer before restarting the car, this time ensuring his concentration was fully on driving.

Parking on the familiar spot behind the back garden, he took the carrier bag and traipsed across the wet grass, dismayed to feel the damp soaking into his thick socks; the house was cold enough already without the torture of soggy feet. He tapped at the door and when Paul opened it, Jeff brandished the bag with a grin. Paul's strange, lopsided leer that Jeff now realised was a smile beamed at him and Jeff was relieved that his brother seemed pleased to see him for once. There was no hello or handshake, but the antagonistic atmosphere had disappeared.

Once Paul had tugged the ragged curtains across the doors to keep the heat in,they sat on the armchairs in the front room and, delighted the fire was raging, Jeff took his trainers and socks off and placed them on the hearth to dry. In the soft glow from the un-shaded economy bulb on the ceiling, the room oozed comfort and homeliness, regardless of the dust and grime that covered every surface. Within an hour they had sunk the beers and the mood was relaxed and friendly.

Although it felt uncomfortable, his lifestyle the opposite of his brother's, Jeff opened the brandy and supped from the bottle this time. The gesture was less to do with politeness and more to do with having seen the mugs in daylight; the lip of the bottle was cleaner. Paul didn't seem to enjoy conversation, the silent gaps were long, and Jeff hoped his tongue would loosen with the alcohol so they could get to know each other better.

Five minutes passed without a word and Jeff scanned the room, taking in the small details to try and make sense of his dead father and dull brother. Once again, he focussed on the collection of murder books and leant over, head tipped to read the titles. Spotting the one he'd seen on his boss's desk the day before, he reached towards the glass sliding door.

Paul stood instantly, his hefty frame towering over his brother. "I told you to leave those alone."

42

Jeff frowned, quizzical, as he stood. He was a tall man himself, but not in comparison to his older brother. He shrugged his shoulders. "Come on, Paul, dad has gone. What harm can it do to flick through them now?"

Paul sat again, his head hanging, and it crossed Jeff's mind for the first time that his brother may be educationally subnormal. Shocked at first, it soon made sense. Paul glanced at him from the corner of his eye, head down and childlike. "I suppose it can't hurt now."

Jeff bent and slid the door across, pulling the book from the shelf. "*Murders in Lincolnshire.* My boss was reading this book yesterday. He's interested in the chapter on the Bonfire Night Killer. I guess you know all about it, living here?"

Paul's eyes widened, a rabbit caught in headlights. How did Jeff know about this? He couldn't have seen the journal; it was hidden away. He was confused and wanted to change the subject. "I don't know anything. Okay, I know a bit. Only what I heard, though, I don't read too well. I was only six when it started. Too young to remember properly."

"We're thinking about re-opening the investigation."

Paul took a large swig without a grimace and stuttered, "Why do you want to do that? What good can it do?"

Was Paul pleading? Jeff was confused. The answer seemed obvious. "To bring justice for the women who were murdered and their families, of course."

Paul frowned, shaking his head. "That was a bad time for us villagers, everyone in all the other villages hated us. They reckoned we was harbouring the murderer." He thought back to his father's notes and shuddered involuntarily. "Don't do anything. Please. It'll be dangerous."

"I don't understand you, Paul. How can running a few DNA tests be dangerous? The killer stopped years ago, and most serial killers only stop when they're stopped or they die, so he's probably long dead and buried by now."

Paul visibly relaxed for the first time since the conversation had begun, safe in the realisation that his brother definitely had no idea about the journal his father had left for him. "Yes, you're probably right." He would have hated to incriminate his father, but with him dead, and access to his DNA impossible after the cremation the next week, his father's secret would be kept with him.

Over the course of the evening they discussed many topics, from their separate experiences growing up, schools, their adult lives, family. Their father. And mother. The unbalanced conversation, with Jeff's eloquent ramblings and Paul's stilted half-sentences, was pleasant and informative on both sides. Jeff, his eyes watering with love at the memories of his mother, shared her funny habits, the cheerful way she skipped through life and her warm, comforting cuddles. In return Paul described their father's habits, his strength, mildness and logical ways. Soon, tears reached his own raven eyes, the loss of his beloved father raw and cutting. They comforted each other in silence, bathing their individual sorrows in alcohol.

Midnight came and went, and eventually Paul, staggering, climbed the stairs towards his tempting bed. Jeff snuggled as comfortably as he could under the blanket on the armchair. He had enjoyed the evening very much. There had been pain released on both sides, but he felt as if a bond had finally begun to grow with his brother.

Dorothy had stayed up later than her usual nine o'clock, busily preparing a surprise for someone who had once been a friend. In fact, he had once been more than a friend. She rarely threw newspapers away, sure she would be able to find a use for them one day, and now she had. They gave her plenty of letters to cut out and glue onto her blackmail note. Not a daft woman, she wore rubber gloves, awkward but necessary.

She surveyed the finished article, checking that the words made sense:

"I KNOW EVERYTHING AND I WILL TELL ALL IF YOU DON'T PAY UP. I WANT TWO THOUSAND POUNDS. GET THE MONEY AND I'LL GIVE YOU MORE INSTRUCTIONS LATER."

She placed it on the table, satisfied it was acceptable, and prepared a mug of hot chocolate before settling on the sofa, resting her aching feet on a footstool. She draped a blanket over her legs and clicked the television on with the remote control. Snug and warm, the trashy late night film mixed with the warm, milky nightcap lulled her to sleep in minutes.

Dorothy would never stay on the sofa all night as she had reached the annoying stage of maturity that required several trips to the bathroom overnight. But this was convenient now, as she planned to drop the note through his letterbox in the dead of night, and changing from and to her clothes and back seemed pointless. This way she could stay dressed until the shenanigans were over.

The sky was icy and cloudless, a threatening blue-black, when Dorothy, at two in the morning, took the folded note in her gloved hands and hastened through the rarely used side door of her pleasant family home. She snuck along the driveway to the front of the garden and glanced around, checking the lights in the surrounding houses were off. Quietly, she crept the short distance and posted the threat through the door, pleased there was no barking dog to alert him. Minutes later she was back in her own home, the freezing night locked outside, and now she was ready to change into her nightclothes and get some proper rest.

Chapter 6
Friday 2nd November

Bert had heard about Roland's death, as had virtually every other villager. A lifelong acquaintance of the man, he had intended to visit Roland's son with his regards anyway, but now he had some additional business to discuss. The two men weren't close, but knew a scant amount about each other through the village gossips. Mainly Dorothy. After knocking loudly, Bert was surprised when the back door was opened by an unfamiliar, dishevelled stranger, with heavy, bloodshot eyes, stifling a yawn. He stammered briefly, before, "I was looking for Paul Mason."

"He's still in bed. I'm his brother, can I help you?" Jeff glanced at the clock, irritated at being woken before nine in the morning on a rare day off, especially after all the alcohol that had flowed the previous night.

"I vaguely remember you as a small lad." Bert held out his hand and the two men shook in greeting. "Before your mam left with you. My name's Bert Rock, I live down the road. I just came to offer my condolences. Roly was a good man."

Jeff stood aside to let the older man through and gestured to a seat at the kitchen table. "Thank you for saying so. Can I get you a tea or coffee?"

"Get yourself one, I'm fine. Yes, I do remember you now I think of it. Jeannie took you with her when she left and Paul stayed with his dad. It had the locals nattering for ages." Jeff knew to keep quiet when being offered information; it was a common tendency for people to fill silences with more chatter. "She was a handsome lass, your mother. Tall, broad, but she had good features, did Jeannie. You look like her. Roly adored Jeannie, it broke his heart when she went. He never did forgive her, that I know of. I shouldn't say this, but," he winked and nudged Jeff on the arm, "she could be a vixen sometimes, a right temptress. She loved a good time. Tell me, how's she doing?"

"She died six years ago of cancer." Jeff withheld the instinct to deck the vile creature before him. How dare he speak about his mum that way. "Aye, lad, sorry to hear that."

Jeff finished preparing his mug of strong tea, an essential brew to eradicate the hangover that thudded painfully, and he brought it to the table, settling opposite Bert. "So you were a friend of my father's then?"

Bert chuckled. "We went to school together, well, one year apart. We were friends most of our lives. I tell you, lad, we were hell-raising teenagers together, the laughs we used to have. We had some good times. He quietened down after he got married, and then you boys came along and he got all sensible. He stopped coming to the local every night, spent more time at home, so I barely saw him. When Jeannie left, he needed his friends more than ever, especially me, but that petered out after a couple of years. He became a miserable old bugger, moping about the house all day, never going out."

Jeff was incredulous. This unpleasant old man had the audacity to slate both his late parents in virtually the same sentence. "He was disabled, of course he couldn't get about!" He was stunned at how quickly he was defending the man he didn't know.

Bert waved his hand, dismissive. "Pah, everyone can play that game if they want it bad enough. There was nothing wrong with the old sod. Disability mumbo jumbo, that all was."

Paul had seen Bert approaching the back door from his bedroom window. He had silently, avoiding the creaky steps on the staircase, crept through the front room and was standing behind the curtain in the kitchen doorway. Jeff had left the door open in his hurry to answer the knock at the door, which meant Paul could clearly hear the conversation, and he wanted to punch the unwelcome visitor, especially now he was reading the dark secrets that were detailed in the journal. He had never liked Bert Rock anyway, didn't trust him, and he certainly didn't want him in his house. But he also didn't want to face him and there was no way he'd popped over purely to offer condolences – Bert only did things that benefited himself, he had no compassion for other people.

Until Jeff had arrived the previous evening, Paul had been trying his absolute best, strongly hindered by his reading difficulties, to plough through the journal. Bert had been mentioned several times and it made terrifying reading. Also, Roland had always told him that it was a physical fight with Bert that had disabled him. Bert had punched him during the tussle and he had fallen onto a low garden wall. He'd never been able to walk without an unflattering stoop again.

He waited for what seemed like ages for Bert to leave and sighed with relief as the back door closed. Taking a deep breath, he strolled into the kitchen and headed for the kettle, pleased to find it still hot. He grunted an incomprehensible greeting, which was met by his brother's similar, hung-over, snort. Jeff took a loaf of uncut, crusty white from the breadbin and instinctively checked the sell-by date. "Do you want some toast?"

"Toast?" Paul stared at him as if he were crazy. "You've got to have meat for breakfast, toast won't fill you up. Anyway, don't eat anything yet. Dot will be round in a while to cook us a fry up. She always does."

Jeff and Sue had recently been on a health-drive. Sue had some excess weight to lose from her pregnancy and Jeff had a few extra pounds that bothered him. He shook his head, wishing he hadn't as the ache flooded from one side of his brain to the other, and sliced into the bread on the chopping board. "Thanks, but I'll just have toast. My wife and I are trying to get fit and lose a few pounds."

An odd snorting filled the room and Jeff realised it was Paul laughing. Not for long, just a short outburst of bizarre grunting, which Jeff suspiciously took as sardonic amusement. Since being a small child, he'd had a calm and quiet manner, without tendency to anger or passionate displays, and the boisterous male bonding that his contemporaries had displayed during his youth and early adulthood had never appealed to him. He was more refined in his ways. And he hated sport unless he was playing it. He ignored his brother's rudeness and dropped the two slices into the grease-splattered toaster.

Paul, calmed and silent again, poured steaming water into the oversized teapot on the table and sat heavily. "What did that Bert Rock want?"

48

"Nothing really, just offering his condolences." He paused for a moment, groping behind for the chair. "He's not a very nice person, is he?"

"You can say that again. He's dangerous. You'd be best to keep away from him. He's a bad sort. I've heard very bad things about him." Despite the outstanding accusations he was spouting, Paul's voice remained monotonous.

Jeff didn't have time to respond as a shrilling 'yoo-hoo' rang from outside and the back door flew open, filling the kitchen with icy wind. Dorothy bustled in, the bag in her hand filled with supplies taken from her own fridge, as usual. "Just thought I'd come and cook you breakfast, Paul, love." She noticed Jeff and stopped abruptly. "Oh, I'm sorry. Who are you?"

Paul introduced his brother and a grin spread across her face, her beady, blue eyes twinkling behind the thick glasses. She dropped the bag and rushed over to hug the bemused Jeff, planting a motherly kiss on his forehead. "Goodness me, I haven't seen you for, goodness, how many years would it be now since Jeannie left? Twenty-eight, twenty-nine?"

"Thereabouts." Paul was curt again. He didn't mind speaking to his brother about their mother, but he hated the local gossips mentioning her name. His tummy growled hungrily. "Come on, Dot, get on with cooking my food."

Without hesitation, and to Jeff's surprise, Dorothy busied herself at the cooker, collecting pans from the cupboard, noticing, as she had expected, that Paul had moved the journal. She was pleased she'd written so many notes the previous day as her memory wasn't quite what it once had been. "I saw that Bert Rock coming out of your front gate. Has he been round to see you, love?"

Paul jumped in before Jeff had a chance. "Yes. He was here."

Dorothy laid several rashers of thick bacon into the large, fat-laden frying pan. "Did he have much to say for himself?" She had never been able to conceal her prying ways and her quest for gossip was evident.

"Not really. He just paid his condolences, told us that him and dad used to be close. That sort of thing." Jeff was baffled that Paul was relaying the visit as if he'd been there himself, and again his suspicions that something odd was going on were aroused. He kept quiet and listened.

Dorothy sliced some of the loaf, buttering each piece thickly. "Oh, they were close alright. Thick as thieves, they used to be. Bert got your dad into a lot of trouble when they were young, I can say. That Bert Rock is a bad man, mark my words, but I always believe that what goes around comes around. He'll get his comeuppance for all the grief he's caused people over the years. Of that, I'm certain."

Jeff, finishing the final crumbs of his toast, was puzzled by the aging lady's sentiments and he watched her expressions as she toiled beside the hot stove. He wondered if maybe she and Bert had been lovers before they had married their own partners. Not that he knew if Bert had ever had a wife. He asked the question and Dorothy, always keen to demonstrate her vast knowledge of the lives of the villagers, informed him that Bert had never been, and probably never would be, married, and he had no children that she knew of. "He's too selfish to think of anybody but himself, that man. He's a nasty piece of work."

Paul settled onto his armchair, having stoked the fire until it was raging again. He wasn't sure if he was harbouring a cold, or whether it was a side effect of grief over his father, but since the previous Tuesday, after his father had passed away, he had found it impossible to warm up without the fire crackling red hot. Since his return from the hospital he had kept it alight constantly, which was far from his usual penny-pinching ways, but he couldn't shrug the chill from deep inside his body.

Glancing at the clock on the wall, he wasn't surprised to see that it had only just gone eleven in the morning. It had been an early start with Bert's inconsiderate morning visit and he wished he'd been able to have a decent lie-in to avoid the thundering hangover. He peeped through the net curtains to ensure no other visitors were heading his way, relieved that he was alone now that his brother and Dorothy had gone. He had never been keen on people in the house, apart from his dad. He enjoyed his own company and thoughts far more than having to make small talk. Not only that, he still needed to find somewhere foolproof to hide his father's journal for when he wasn't attempting to read it, now Jeff was becoming a frequent visitor.

He retrieved the journal from its current hiding place in the cupboard that filled the alcove beside the fireplace, hidden safely enough for now behind a stack of VHS videotapes that had been redundant since their television had broken down and not been replaced. He began the struggle to read from where he had finished the day before. He wasn't comfortable with the horrors that were emerging, but he didn't doubt for a second that his father's words were the truth. Regardless of the distressing content, the journal did answer a lot of mysteries about the man his father had been. Opening the can of beer he had brought from the fridge, the early hour irrelevant, he pondered over the confusing text for a while, soaking in as much detail as he could muster through the odd word he could understand. Momentarily disturbing his concentration, he heard a skittering noise in the hallway. Paul debated getting up to see what it was, but comfortable and warm for once, he reasoned it was probably just another neighbour dropping a sympathy card through the letterbox.

It wasn't until hours later, when he had struggled through most of the journal and was struggling to stay awake after four cans of beer and a third of a bottle of whisky, that Paul stumbled out of the room, ready to sleep off the excess. As he entered the tiny hallway he noticed a pale green envelope on the hall carpet and recalled the noise he'd heard earlier in the afternoon. He brought it up the stairs and threw it on the bed, intending to read it after brushing his teeth and donning his pyjamas.

Jeff and Sue had lulled Jacob to sleep after his late feed and were snuggling in bed, the gentle gleam of the bedside lights glistening from the wine glasses in their hands. Sue picked up the bottle from her bedside cabinet to divide the remains of the delightful Cabernet Sauvignon between them. It had been a hectic day, littered with appointments and chores, and this was the first real chance they'd had to talk to each other properly. Sue asked how Jeff's evening with Paul had been and he told her the details that seemed worth mentioning.

"That's reminded me…" Jeff jumped from the bed quietly to avoid waking the baby in his cot across the room. "My dad had this collection of books about true murders that he cherished but, now he's gone, Paul said I could borrow them." He fished *Murders in Lincolnshire* from his jacket pocket and returned to the warmth of the duvet. "Funny enough, Frank was also reading this book because it has a chapter on one of the old cases we're considering re-opening."

Though she was a policewoman, albeit on maternity leave at this point, murder didn't interest Sue. She was more enthusiastic about the community side of the job, dealing with the public, keeping the relationship with them running smoothly. She replied with an indifferent 'mmmm' as she grasped a glossy magazine from her bedside drawer and flicked through, browsing the colourful celebrities posing seductively in their borrowed dresses and lavish jewellery.

Jeff heeded her hint with a reluctant smile and leafed through to the chapter on the Bonfire Night Killer. He was immediately taken aback by the copious notes scribbled in ballpoint pen along the margins of the chapter. Intrigued, he turned to the next chapter to see if it had similar scribbled memos, but it became apparent that it was purely the Bonfire Night Killer that had held Roland's interest enough for him to deface his book. Jeff was curious, but he couldn't read the tiny scrawl. He resolved to check the other books the next time he visited Paul. In the meantime, he would get to work early the next day to photocopy the pages of the book, complete with his father's notes. Once he had returned the book to Paul, he could take some time to try and decipher what they could possibly mean.

As he snuggled under the covers, Jeff felt an unexpected urge to shed tears for his father, which he resisted defiantly. He was angry at not having had the chance to get to know him, of knowing little or nothing about the man. He felt as if he had been robbed and it appalled him that, for that moment anyway, he resented his mother for having broken the family and taken him away. His sleep wasn't peaceful, the frustration crossing from consciousness into his dreams.

In Colefield, Paul was also having a fitful night as he slept his way into his thirty-eighth birthday. It hadn't seemed appropriate to announce it, let alone celebrate it, after such tragic recent events. The note that had been posted through his door had been forgotten in his inebriated haste to climb into bed, but after nearly drifting off to sleep for the umpteenth time only to jump awake again, he remembered it. He was desperate to sleep, but curiosity eventually got the better of him and he cursed, switching the bedside light on in temper.

He grabbed the letter from the top of the duvet and tore open the envelope, withdrawing a mint piece of paper that matched its sleeve. In capital letters and written in black marker pen were the words 'THREATS MEAN DEATH'. Puzzled, he tucked the letter back into the envelope and threw it back on the bed, resolving that he was too drunk and it was too late at night to worry about the menacing message. He sat on the edge of the bed and surveyed his tired face in the mirror opposite.

He had never been a blessed child in any way. His father had always said he'd inherited his mother's features, and Paul surmised she must have been an ugly woman to look like him. He remembered her being strong and hefty, and he certainly had her height. But he'd gained his father's insipidity; maybe the manner was learned rather than genetic, but he was verging on being a sociophobe and he liked it that way.

Apart from the misfortune with his looks, Paul had also struggled at school. None of the words or numbers had made sense to him and he had given up at fourteen, preferring to take odd jobs at the farm across the road that needed little education. He would help at harvest time, feed the animals, any menial tasks that didn't require too much brainpower or thought.

He would have loved to have a wife one day but, awkward and embarrassed amongst the fairer sex, he had accepted it was unlikely to happen. He didn't have much confidence and the idea of approaching a woman filled him with dread. He thought back to what his father had admitted throughout his journal and wondered whether it was right or wrong. He knew the law saw it as wrong, which was probably why his father had been adamant Jeff shouldn't know about the journal. But who was to say the law was right? He knew his father well, and knew he wouldn't have hurt those women without them asking for it.

Paul switched the light off and settled back down, and as he willed himself to sleep, he wondered if the tendency to rape and murder could run in families, alongside eye and hair colour.

Confident that Bert Rock had no idea who had sent the previous note, Dorothy decided enough time had passed for her to instigate stage two of her cunning, and hopefully lucrative, plan. It had taken her a ridiculous amount of time to work out where she should request the blackmail money be dropped, and as much time again to ponder over how to not be discovered picking the cash up. It had been a quandary, but eventually she was satisfied she had solved the problem.

She took her scissors and searched for the right letters in the remaining newspapers to spell out her latest message. She'd decided follow the same plan as last time: she would doze on the sofa for a while after a mug of hot chocolate and deliver the note in the early hours when no prying eyes would see her. Bert was a creature of habit and, by all accounts, loved his sleep, so she was certain there would be no disturbances. As she drifted into a relaxed slumber, she felt a tingle of excitement from her cloak and dagger plotting and a soft smile settled on her lips.

Dorothy awoke from a pleasant dream at two-thirty in the morning and, stifling a yawn, she dragged on her coat, scarf, hat and gloves and took the note a few doors away, dropping it through Bert's letterbox. As expected, no lights went on as she scuttled away, and she gratefully returned to the comfort of her home, her night-time activities over.

Chapter 7
Monday 5th November

The first weekend of November had been a busy one for my investigation team. Another domestic violence related death had needed our time, this time a drunken man stabbing his teenaged nephew during a heated argument, and it had taken a while to find the suspect after he had cowered into hiding. By Sunday evening things had settled down and after we had formally charged the uncle with manslaughter, Jeff and I hoped we would have a chance to revisit the case notes we had started reviewing the previous week.

We were at our desks, concentrating on various parts of the original investigation into the Bonfire Night murders, when Jeff sat upright and faced me. "Oh, I forgot to tell you." He fished into his tan leather briefcase and brought out a replica of the book I had purchased the previous week, albeit a tatty and yellowed version. "This was in my father's collection."

I was dismissive. "Been there, done that, it didn't tell us anything of note." I tapped my copy of *Murders in Lincolnshire,* which was still on the desk.

"No, you need to see it. Really, wait for this." Jeff flicked through the pages as he strolled towards me. "Chapter eleven. Ah, here we are." He showed me the abundant notes in the margins and I was stunned.

"What is all that?" I frowned, squinting in a failed attempt to read the tiny writing.

"This must be why Roland wouldn't let anyone touch his collection. These notes show he held a keen interest in the Bonfire Night killings and I'm sure that, if we can work out what all the rambling is about, it could lead to the killer."

I took the book from him and studied the writing, bringing a magnifying glass from my top drawer when my reading glasses didn't make the script any clearer. "I can just about see. *Wrong. Was third tree from right, not left. There was no frost, it was pretty warm for that time of year.*" I paused, trying to make sense of the words, and as the horrible possibility of what the scrawl could mean dawned on me, I could see it also had to Jeff.

He sagged into the chair beside my desk, visibly paling. "Oh my god. My father was there. Either he saw it," he swallowed hard and his voice quavered, "or he did it." And now he remembered his brother's desperate pleas for them not to re-open the case. Exactly what did Paul know that he wasn't telling? Was this why Paul became aggravated when he had visitors? Because he was hiding something dreadful? Jeff gasped and placed his head in his hands. "What if it was my father who committed those murders?"

His pain was palpable and I felt torn between duty and friendship. On the one hand we could continue searching and request the investigation become official if or when we found something solid to present to the Super, and at the same time tar my good friend and his family with a vicious heritage. Alternatively, we could put the archive box back in the storeroom and never mention it again, pretend we had never seen it.

Could that work? Would two senior police detectives really be able to brush something so potentially colossal under the carpet and live with the lies? At that point I had no answers and chose what I could see as the only option presently available. I glanced around the incident room at my team, all busy at their desks on the phone or immersed in paperwork. There had been no witnesses to our conversation. "Let's take time out on this case for now, have some time to think. Both of us."

I returned the notes on the old murders to the box neatly, closing the lid, and shoved it under my desk rather than returning it to the archive room straight away. I needed to consider the options carefully, maybe talk to some people off the record. My thoughts drifted to an old friend and colleague, Peter Barrymore, a retired Detective Superintendent who had once been my mentor. I remembered him mentioning once that he had worked on the case and resolved to call him when Jeff wasn't nearby.

I didn't have to wait long, because moments later Jeff snatched his jacket from the chair, shrugging it over his suit, and took his car keys from the pocket. He took his father's book from my desk. "I'm going to see Paul." I waited until the door had closed behind him and picked up the phone, flicking through my address book to find the number I wanted, and dialled. "Peter, it's Frank."

The journey through Hull was frustrating, the heaving Monday morning traffic slowing Jeff to a snail's pace, or so it seemed. He was unsure whether he was doing the right thing, confronting the issue, but he guessed that if they at least discussed the book – the notes – maybe Paul would volunteer what he knew about the situation. Perhaps there was a rational explanation, an innocent outcome that he hadn't considered.

He arrived just after ten and Dorothy was already at the cooker, brandishing a frying pan and utensils as she prepared a delicious-smelling feast for Paul. As always he sat by the table with a mug of tea, the pot warmed by the grubby tea cosy. The three exchanged greetings, and Dorothy offered to put some more bacon in the pan for Jeff, but he declined once more, still dieting, and still dubious about the cleanliness of the cooking equipment. "Paul, we need to talk."

Paul's charcoal eyes moved from the middle distance to focus on his brother. "What about?"

Jeff mouthed 'in private' and imitated himself eating hungrily, before pointing at the door to the front room. Paul's brow furrowed for a moment, then he nodded.

"What do you need to talk about, love?" Dorothy was always searching for the latest news to tattle to her neighbours and fellow villagers, especially as Roland's sudden demise was now old news.

Jeff's mind raced as he inwardly berated himself for mentioning anything in front of the nosy woman. "Oh, um, just, well, we need to discuss sorting dad's old room out, that's all."

"I see." She flipped three rashers of bacon over in the frying pan and paused. "Oh, I'd better mention this, Paul. You see, my son's dropping a small parcel off for me at your back door. It'll be overnight sometime, so don't wait up. Can you take it in safe for me tomorrow morning?"

Paul grunted a yes without thinking, but Jeff was intrigued and the interrogator in him surfaced. "Why doesn't he just drop it at your house? And why overnight?"

Turning to face them, Dorothy rolled her eyes dramatically and her hands dropped loosely onto her hips. She sighed. "Bleeding coppers! My son is travelling overnight from Scotland to London, he says the roads are clearer at night. He'll visit me on his way back up. And both my side and front door are visible from the road, so if he left the package there it might get stolen. Paul's back door is concealed, so it's safer." With a fatigued 'tut', she turned back to the sizzling breakfast, leaving Jeff childishly chastised.

Dorothy was pleased with her off-the-cuff imagination. She dished the greasy breakfast onto a large plate and handed it to Paul, along with some cutlery, and he tucked in voraciously while she cleaned the pans. Jeff waited in silence, eager for Dorothy to leave so he could have the discussion that was burning him from inside with Paul.

Finally, she breezed from the house, leaving the kitchen barely tidier than when she had arrived, and Jeff took Paul's empty plate to the sink, leaving it to soak in some water. "I wanted to talk to you about that book I borrowed from dad's collection, and I think I already know what you're going to say."

From the look of puzzlement on his face it was clear that either Paul was a brilliant actor or he had no idea what Jeff was talking about. "I don't know anything about them, except that my dad won't let me touch them."

"You must have seen inside them at some stage, it's not like they're new."

"No, I've never looked inside those books, I swear." Paul's face had paled and he was defensive. "Anyway, I find books difficult to read when they've only got little letters."

Jeff found the comment surprising, he learned something new about his brother every time they met. He fished the book from his pocket and set it on the table. "*Murders in Lincolnshire.* Do you have any idea why, when it comes to chapter eleven, which is all about the Bonfire Night Killer, there are loads of notes in the margins, written in what I assume to be dad's handwriting?"

He flicked through to the chapter and showed Paul, whose heart had started to race at the mention of the notorious murderer. "No. No idea. No. I don't know anything." He leant forward to try and work out what the words said, but gave up swiftly. "No idea what that is." Paul needed to devise a plausible explanation or Jeff would keep needling him about his father, and knowing the contents of Roland's journal, he couldn't take that risk. "He was probably interested because it happened nearby."

"No, it's more than that. My boss scrutinised the words under a magnifying glass and they seem to be correcting the author's account about the exact location of the murders and other small details that someone would only know if they had been present when the murders happened."

Paul couldn't cope with the unwanted words, he was frightened and concerned. "My dad was not a killer. Alright? So just leave it. Just leave it." He clasped his huge, fleshy hands to his ears and squeezed his eyes shut, rocking gently. Long sentences and so many questions. His head was pounding and he didn't want to say another word in case he said the wrong thing and dropped his dead father in trouble.

Jeff realised he would have to stop examining Paul, figuring his surprising outburst was remarkably similar to how somebody who suffered with mild autism, or even bipolar disorder, would behave, and it showed he was stressed. He laid a hand on his brother's shoulder. "It's okay, Paul, I won't ask any more, but can I take a look through the other books while I'm here? Just out of interest. I'm a copper after all, it's my thing." He paused, thinking hard of the best way to calm his brother. "Anyway, we've decided not to re-open the case, if that's what you're worried about." The decision hadn't been taken, but Jeff knew that if they chose to go ahead with an investigation, he would have to be the mentally strong one of the two brothers.

Paul stopped swaying and grunted his approval, before downing his fourth mug of sickly sweet, anaemic tea. Jeff slipped through the curtain to the front room and took the books from the shelf, one by one. Most were about true crimes from around the world, but five contained sections about the Bonfire Night case. As suspected, they were covered in notes, the writing size dependant on the size of the book – the bigger the letters, the larger the hardback.

He took the five books to the kitchen. "Can I borrow these? Just for a few days so I can photocopy the notes in the margins?"

Paul's face contorted, he slammed his fists on the table and stood abruptly. "For god's sake, just bloody leave it, will you? We don't need you bloody nosy buggers poking around in my village. People will be turning in their graves. Just let it go, damn you."

Jeff was fed up with the odd behaviour and he, too, was angry. "What are you scared of, Paul? What is it that you know and I don't? Who are you covering for? Is it dad? Did he kill those women and you know about it? Did…"

All Jeff heard was a crisp thud and the next thing he realised was that he had fallen to the floor, his brother's formidable fist looming over him. He clutched his smarting jaw, clambering back to the table. "Point taken, bro. I'd better get home now. Ouch! That really hurt." Jeff could see that if the truth was ever going to come out about the murders from the past, it wasn't going to be through Paul's lips.

Bert had been furious when he'd found another vulgar blackmail note at the bottom of the stairs that morning. He thought he had dealt with the problem effectively, but clearly Paul was more stupid than he looked. Well, he was going to get his payment, that was for sure, just not in the way he expected it.

Bert had a history of crime, not that many people in the village or the surrounding areas knew, most too young to remember him before he had taken a respectable job at the steelworks and ceased breaking the law. He and Roly had been born in January, one year apart, with him being the older of the two. A year had seemed a lifetime as young teenagers, but once they both left school, neither with an exam result to speak of, they had started hanging out together. They committed petty crimes at first, for fun, but when they realised how lucrative it could be, they had planned their lawbreaking more seriously. Shoplifting was a favourite and there were a few attempts at minor burglary, plus sales of rabbits and poached fowl on the local black-market kept the pennies rolling in.

They had been a good team, as neither achieved a criminal record until their early twenties, from which time they both had a series of short convictions, interspersed with honing their crimes to the point where they were no longer being detected. But Roly had become involved with Jeannie. They had already known her from the dance circuit in Scunthorpe where they went for the occasional night away from the village, but at first it seemed Bert was the one who was going to get the girl.

Jeannie hadn't been pretty, far from it, but she'd had a curious, strong face. For an unfeminine woman her eyes were beautiful. Big and black, doe-like, framed by copious long eyelashes. She was tall with a large frame and kept her shiny, raven hair in a neat ponytail. Being a spinster in her twenties, still at home with her parents and desperate to get married to gratefully tend a husband, made her appealing. And easy.

One night, without explanation, she transferred her affections to Roly, and Bert had no idea why. She wasn't the first to spurn his affections, though. He'd been in love with Dorothy, seriously considering marriage, until she had fallen head over heels for handsome Ernie. And now the unusual, compelling, sex-crazed Jeannie had chosen Roly.

He hadn't been able to forgive any of them and his friendship with Roly had been replaced with a burning envy. He watched from the lonely side-lines while Roly and Jeannie, blissfully and sickeningly in love, held a modest wedding and proceeded to have two sons in relatively quick succession. Coupled with Dorothy's early leap into marriage and motherhood, Bert had despaired at losing the two women so easily, and his ability to trust, or even like, females had been destroyed.

Bert, without his partner in crime, had continued to poach every now and then, but eventually he had taken a sensible job at the steelworks to pay the bills the honest way; the fun had gone from breaking the law now his partner in crime had become a responsible family man.

Scanning the crude attempt at extortion in his hands, he was certain it was stupid Paul Mason who was pathetically attempting to scare him. He had always suspected his past would come back to haunt him one day, and maybe Roly had given him some titbits before he died. But Bert was far cleverer than Paul and he began to devise a shocking finale that would stop the irritating problem for good. An hour later, he was satisfied and he shrugged his jacket on.

Dorothy was the only person in the village to insist her side access wasn't used by visitors, demanding they use the front door, and Bert ambled awkwardly, his back kinked through age, and knocked. She answered, failing to raise a smile when she saw the visitor, crossing her arms defensively. "What do you want, Bert?"

"With it being Bonfire Night, I'll be out in the fields tonight, so I could do with a pair of wellies, but mine have split. The sole's come away. I just wondered if you've still got a pair of Ernie's lying around anywhere that I could borrow."

Dorothy was taken aback, it was the last thing she had expected to hear, knowing what she thought they both knew, and she bustled awkwardly behind the door for a few moments. She produced a large pair, still mud-encrusted even though her husband had been in his grave for years, and held them up.

"There's these, but they'll be way too big for you, my Ernie was a big man."

Bert snatched them willingly, tucking them under his arm. "No matter, that'll mean I can wear a few pairs of socks underneath to keep my feet warm."

The fireworks started cracking and fizzing as darkness fell over the village. Because the fifth of November was on a Monday this year, the celebrations had started the Friday before and tediously, for those who disliked the environmental ramifications and financial waste, continued throughout the weekend. Domestic pets and farm animals were traumatized, cowering and yelping with every exploding rocket, and the poachers had given up the hunt until the crashes stopped startling their prey. For the lighter hearted, though, the colourful arrays twinkling in the sky, the smell of barbecuing meat, the neighbourhood camaraderie was delightful, raising smiles and laughter from house to house, street to street.

Everything was prepared for the second stage of Bert's plan to frighten Paul Mason, and his silly blackmailing attempt, away. He'd had a lengthy nap in the afternoon to avoid falling asleep early, as he was frequently prone to do as his years progressed. He squeezed the equipment he would need into an old, yet immaculate, workbag and donned his jacket and gloves, covering the bald patch on his head with a tweed flat cap. He slipped his woollen-socked feet into the borrowed boots, an easy task as they were several sizes too large, and left the bungalow via the back door. Heart thudding with excitement, he was stealthy, fast, and soundless; attributes gained from years of poaching and thieving.

Merriment and whooping drifted from the neighbourhood gardens. Families and friends together, celebrating Bonfire Night with an abundance of food and alcohol, fireworks and sparklers. Silvery ashes from bonfires flitted through the air, gliding like feathers, and flickering, coloured stars exploded into glistening flowers before disappearing into the night sky.

Once inside Paul's back garden, Bert crept to the door, dropped a well-stuffed envelope onto the step, and hastened to the nearby shed, letting himself through the door quietly. He made himself comfortable on a foldable tripod seat he had brought and took a gun from the bag, placing it on his lap. After pouring a plastic mug of tea from the flask, he cracked the door open to watch for movement in Paul's house.

Finally, the kitchen light flickered on, Paul's elongated silhouette shadowed on the cement path between Bert and the back door. He grasped the gun and pushed his gloved finger through the metal gap onto the trigger. The figure moved, rounding a corner, and Paul's massive frame was clearly visible through the frosted glass panel of the back door.

Bert raised the gun as Paul stepped into the garden, but instead of bending down to pick up the package as Bert had expected, he strode outside, kicking it with the trailing foot. Stumbling across the cement he regained his balance and glanced back, confusion on his face. He dropped the carrier bag of rubbish he had been taking to the wheelie bin and returned to the step, collecting the parcel, and his brow furrowed.

Bert lowered the gun to his side, stood, and strolled from his hiding place towards Paul. "You weren't expecting that, were you?" His voice was bland now he realised Paul wasn't the blackmailer, and that whoever it was must be cleverer than he had thought.

Paul straightened, startled by the visitor. "I don't think so." He noticed the gun in Bert's hand and a tremor shook his cumbersome body.

"Inside." Bert, annoyed now, waved the gun at Paul, who followed his instructions. Bert entered and closed the door behind him, trapping out the cold, and motioned for Paul to sit. Bert would never have admitted it aloud, but Paul's broad beefiness intimidated him, a huge guy, whereas he was just a little, old guy with a dodgy gait. With Paul seated, he didn't feel so pathetic in comparison. He angled the gun at Paul, as if prepared to shoot if necessary, though he had no intention of doing so. "With them fireworks crashing and booming nobody will notice a single gunshot, so behave."

Paul was terrified. He had no idea what was going on. What was a strange parcel doing on his doorstep? Why was Bert

Rock standing in his kitchen with a gun? He glanced to the floor and gasped. Why did Bert suddenly have unbelievably huge feet? "I don't remember your feet being so big."

Bert fidgeted, irritated and oddly embarrassed. "Who's the package for?"

Paul threw it on the table. "I don't know, I… wait." Bert saying *package* had triggered a vague recollection and he grinned excitedly as it dawned on him. "I know what it is. It's for Dot. She was over this morning. She said her son was dropping a package off overnight. She asked me to take it in for her, said her doors could be seen from the road."

With a sigh, Bert withdrew the gun and tucked it into his jacket pocket. He rolled his eyes. "You have no idea what's in the package?" It was more a statement than a question.

Paul shook his head, eyes widened from having a revolver trained on him, and Bert sagged. "What could she possibly know? Maybe she's talking about something completely different. What bad things have I done lately? Bloody meddling woman, always sticking her bloody nose in." Paul instinctively kept quiet while the rambling continued, and finally Bert's self-questioning slowed and stopped.

Feeling braver now the firearm was packed away, Paul was ready to talk again and he was becoming tetchier by the second. "Are you going to tell me what's going on?" Bert remained quiet and Paul's anger rose. "You've come into my house and held me at gunpoint. I think I deserve to know why." He stood, towering over his father's one-time friend.

Bert chose his words carefully. He didn't want to give too much away, but was concerned about the size and strength of the man before him. "Somebody's been blackmailing me, lad. They told me to leave some money in a large envelope at your back door tonight. I didn't put money in. I put in two pairs of folded, unwashed socks instead."

"Blackmailing you? Who would do that?"

"Jesus Christ, Paul, top marks for bloody stupidity. Dot, obviously. Come on lad, even you can't be that thick." Bert hadn't prepared for any possibility other than Paul being the blackmailer, and discovering it was Dorothy Webber had come as a colossal shock. He figured he would have been tempted to shoot a man in such circumstances, but a female was a different matter. Plus, the woman was the love of his life, and hurting Dorothy was out of the question. His plans now awry, he needed to think the latest revelations through. "Just give me the package back. Don't tell her about me coming here, just tell her no package arrived."

Dorothy hadn't seen any of her offspring for many years. She had been a strict parent, having had her first son at the tender age of twenty, and all three of her children had rebelled against her. She had not been lying when she'd mentioned her son's impending visit, he had called her out of the blue a few days before, asking to drop by on his arduous overnight journey between Scotland and London, but she hadn't foolishly raised her hopes. She missed her children every day of her life, but they had chosen to cease contact with her and there had been nothing she could do to change their minds. She had never met any of her grandchildren. Not a birth announcement, a photograph. Nothing. She had only heard she was a grandparent through the rumour mill.

David, her first borne, had always been her favourite, in contrast to Ernie's ill-disguised antagonism towards the boy. He took after his mother in looks, petite and spindly rather than tall and broad like his father. Ernie had always teased her that he wasn't the boy's biological father. Dorothy had no idea that it was a real suspicion that had grated on him throughout his unfortunately short life, passing away from colon cancer twelve years before.

"Ma."

She stood, unmoving, as she drank in his fine features, with greying hair and deep-set laughter lines. She was unsure if an attempt to hug him would be rebuked and chose not to after a moment's deliberation. "David." Dorothy moved aside to let her son into the house, glancing furtively around before closing the door. She followed him to the lounge and they both sat. "It's good to see you, son. You've grown old." Although uttered jokily, his expression remained blank. "You haven't been here for over twenty years, David. Why now?"

"I had to pass through the area on business anyway, but I decided to visit you because I want to know who my real father was."

Dorothy's heart leapt to her mouth, the thudding in her chest almost painful, it was so pronounced. "What are you saying, David? You know who your father is. Was."

"Ma, don't waste my time, dad told me everything. If you insist on continuing to bleat your innocence, then try this one: I've been speaking to a good friend, he's a doctor of genetics. Dad, Ernie, he had blue eyes. You have blue eyes. It's virtually impossible genetically for him to have fathered me because mine are brown. Blue is a recessive gene. I know there are exceptions to this rule, but let's be realistic, I have never looked like Ernie in any way. Who is my biological father?"

Dorothy drew her hands to her head, distraught. Yes, she had been a rebellious youngster, the sixties had been her teenage heyday and she had dabbled in drugs, excessive alcohol, and more than a little free love, but when she had committed herself to Ernie it had been for life. What an impudent question. "David, I don't know why you're doing this, why you have this bee in your bonnet, but I can tell you, hand on heart, that Ernie was your father. We got together when I was eighteen and we loved each other until he died."

David sighed. "Has it ever occurred to you why all three of your children stopped having anything to do with you twenty years ago?"

"Of course it has, it's been one of the most painful things I've ever had to cope with in my life."

"I was twenty-five years old when Ernie told me, Dan, and Freda that he was infertile. He told me you'd had affairs with two other men, and either of those men must have fathered us. He told me he stayed with you because it was the easiest thing to do." Dorothy was aghast, eyes wide, and for once she was totally speechless. Her jaw moved swiftly but no words came, although the brimming tears were about to. Her obvious pain was of no concern to him; he continued, his words abrupt and uncaring. "I heard that one of them, Roland Mason, recently died. Was it him? Was he my real father? Or is it Albert Rock?"

Dorothy stood abruptly and slapped her son sharply across the cheek, and he recoiled, stunned. "You need to wash your mouth out, young man. That's a dreadful accusation to make. Your father was most certainly not infertile."

David sighed again, irritated by the tedious lies. "I got married for the second time a couple of years ago and we decided to have a baby; my wife's much younger than me. Our son was born in January, and we learnt soon after that he has Down's Syndrome. I had some blood tests and apparently I'm a translocation carrier. I must have inherited the gene from either you or my real father. So, are you a carrier?"

"Of course I'm not. That's ridiculous. Down's isn't genetic, it's caused by the mother being old. You just had babies too late." She waved her hand with disgust.

"No. My wife has only just turned twenty-six. We've done plenty of research and I inherited the gene from somewhere, and if you had even an ounce of goodness in your heart you would tell me exactly who my father is. I need to know for the sake of my child and his well-being."

"I'll tell you nothing, David Webber, and how dare you accuse me of being unfaithful to your father. Bert Rock! Roly Mason! As if." Unable to control herself Dorothy lurched toward her eldest son for the second time, her hand swiping his face, leaving a painful, reddening welt on his already glowing skin. He grabbed her wrist and twisted, defensive, furious. Out of control. Within seconds the old lady was lying on the carpet, her surprisingly strong son's knees over her arms, hand across her mouth, blocking her airways. Her frightened eyes pleaded hopelessly as years of pent-up anger forced him to keep his firm grip, squeezing away her life. She tried to scream, the gurgling of her trapped breath barely there. "I'll tell you, just get off me."

Shocked by his unprecedented violence, David released his grip, and Dorothy puffed for over a minute, her breathing easing eventually while she rubbed her sore neck. "Tell me, then." It came as a low growl. David, having backed away, was scared of the rage and brutality he'd never realised he was capable of.

Dorothy was indignant, arms crossing her bosom with hostility. "What your father probably omitted to inform you when he told you he was infertile was that he was also impotent, and I was desperate to have children. I was young, full of hormones, and I knew that Bert and Roly were both keen on me, so I started seeing them while Ernie was at the pub. They meant nothing, but I soon got what I wanted from them and fell pregnant and it seemed the best thing to do – tell everyone you were Ernie's kids. I suppose, realistically, that I suspected he knew, but he never said a word to me. Not once. Apart from the lack of sex, we had a happy marriage. There never was any emotion in it for me. I knew Bert had strong feelings for me but they were never returned, and Roly was in love with Jeannie, he made no secret of that. Quite simply I was in love with Ernie. I just wanted a family."

Breaking the moment, the doorbell chimed, and both mother and son glanced at each other with the same confused expression. David nodded and Dorothy clambered up, smoothing her skirt as she walked through the hallway, tending to her dishevelled hair.

Controlling her breathing, she steadied herself against the doorframe before calmly opening the door. She was stunned when Bert pushed her aside, wielding a gun, and slammed the door behind him. "I'm so bloody disappointed with you, Dot. I know that it's you who's been blackmailing me. What the hell are you playing at? I want to know what you have on me that makes you think I can just pay up two grand every time you want a bit of extra cash."

Dorothy backed away in the direction of the lounge, and David slipped silently behind the door, listening to the unfolding drama intently. "Calm down, Bert, there's no need to be brandishing guns and suchlike, it's all a silly misunderstanding."

He strode towards her, trapping her against the wall before she reached the living room, and her eyes were wide with fright. "I asked you what you've got on me."

He pushed the gun towards her face and her hands blocked him defensively. "Okay, okay! I found a diary that Roly wrote before he died. He said you were the Bonfire Night Killer from the eighties. He said he did the rapes, but you shot the girls."

Bert drew a sharp breath. "The bloody lying bastard. I knew that filthy arsehole would do something like this, I just knew it. He swore he would get his revenge one day."

She could never hold her nosiness back, whatever the situation. "Revenge? I thought you two were pals."

"He bloody found me with Jeannie one night, didn't he. Swore he'd make me pay one day." He realised he had digressed and snapped back to the present, angrily thrusting the gun at her face again. "Where's the diary now?"

She stuttered as she desperately tried to ignore the weapon. "I don't know, I honestly don't. Paul hid it somewhere."

"So Paul Mason has also read this pack of lies, then?"

"Paul doesn't read that well, so I don't know how much he managed. He's not said a word to me. In fact, he doesn't know I've seen it. I only found out about it because I came across a note from Roly telling Paul about the diary."

"So he's left instructions for Paul to frame me for something I didn't do."

Dorothy was desperate for Bert to leave. She stared at him, her eyes imploring. "No, he said in the note not to tell anyone, not even the police."

"Then what was he playing at, what's the point of all this?" Bert's arm fell and he took a step back, no longer threatening.

"Maybe he knew his days were coming to an end and he wanted to get things off his chest." She hoped the words would pacify him.

They didn't. He re-aimed the revolver at Dorothy's head. "By writing a bloody pack of bloody lies about me? I wonder how many years he was planning this bloody revengeful farce." He was silenced but his mind was whirring, figuring what the next step should be. He waved the gun towards the door. "Well, he started it, so now I'm going to finish it. Move. Get your coat, you're coming with me." Dorothy followed the barked order. She was terrified, but she knew her son had heard every word, and she trusted he would come to the rescue.

David waited until he heard the front door click shut and moved from behind the door, shaking faintly with nerves. "Just the nice bloke I remember. I hope Roland Mason is my natural father and not that tosser." He zipped up his overcoat and let himself out of his mother's house. London was almost two hundred miles away; it would be a while before he could sink into the comfortable hotel bed that was already booked.

Chapter 8
Tuesday 6th November

It wasn't planned, but Jeff and his small family had ended up having an early night. They had been to see Sue's sister and her husband in the evening, and while Andy had slaved over a barbecue in the chilly breeze, Amy had flitted about the kitchen arranging paper plates, salad and rolls. Meantime, their two young children had run amok, unsupervised, in the garden. After they had eaten, Andy lit the first firework, a simple Catherine Wheel, but the fizzing had made baby Jacob cry, and every time a rocket was launched by a neighbour he would scream, terrified. The decision to take him home early had been easy and after they'd settled the baby in his cot, they had shared a bottle of Claret before going to bed.

As a result of falling asleep before ten, Jeff was awake at five in the morning, and unable to turn his whirring mind off, he tiptoed to the kitchen to prepare some breakfast. Just before six his mobile phone chimed and he answered my flustered, sleepy call. I explained to him that the body of a young woman had been found in a copse of weeping willows in a field close to Colefield. I could imagine him shuddering in the way I had when the location of the body had been reported to me minutes before. I told him I was coming to pick him up so we could attend the scene immediately.

Twenty minutes later, Jeff was dressed and running towards my car. He jumped in and we made our way towards the familiar village. Guided by our uniformed friends, we drove along the dirt track behind a row of house and parked. A huge, scruffy man, who I soon discovered was Jeff's brother, was standing beside his back fence, watching the police scour the field behind his house – the field where three other women had been killed over thirty years before. Paul spotted his brother and tried a brief smile that looked more like a grimace. "What's going on?"

Jeff dismissed the question with a shake of his head, he didn't really know himself yet, and we traipsed across the long, dewy winter grass towards the copse. We glanced at each other as we neared the crime scene and I was certain Jeff was thinking the same as me – how eerily familiar the willow copse seemed now we had both studied the photos in the books about the Bonfire Night Killer. I was pleased for the brown-green grass, the pale-blue sky scattered with lacy clouds, as the colour separated the scene from the grim, dated, black-and-white photos we had been researching.

From the lividity on the victim's hands and face, the only exposed skin, it seemed she was lying as she had fallen, probably from a seated position. There appeared to be a single bullet wound to her head. Her eyes were open, dull and opaque in death, and her lips pouted wide, as if she had been speaking as she died. A trickle of blood had dribbled from her mouth and was now black and scabbed. Jeff shoved his hands in his pockets and stretched his shoulders with a barely hidden yawn. "It was Bonfire Night last night."

I nodded, not knowing how to follow the ominous statement.

"You don't think…" He didn't finish. He didn't need to. I knew exactly what he meant.

"No. It must be a copycat murder. No serial killer would stop for thirty years and then start randomly murdering again, it just doesn't happen. The details of the Bonfire Night killings are out there for anybody to see, in books, on the Internet, it would be easy for somebody else to replicate the crimes." Wouldn't it? I wasn't sure what to think and realised my internal musing had tumbled out aloud. But one thing I did know, now, was that the decision whether to re-investigate the original murders or not was out of my hands. I hoped desperately that we were wrong about Jeff's father being involved.

Paul had returned to the house after his brother had snubbed him; there wasn't anything to see of the unknown crime the night before as the police had cordoned off the area. He set the kettle on the hob and chucked a teabag into the oversized china pot, dragging the tea cosy nearby. He realised he was hungry and it dawned on him that he hadn't seen nosy Dorothy poking around for gossip. That wasn't like her. Rather than cook bacon for himself, he cut two doorsteps of bread and buttered them thickly, stuffing them down in less time than it had taken to prepare them.

Occasionally he glanced through the window to see if there had been any developments, but apart from different faces strolling about each time, nothing changed.

Still hungry, he again thought of Dorothy, this time with a little concern as the conversation the night before floated into his mind. Dorothy may have been blackmailing Bert. He had been prepared to shoot Paul until he realised he wasn't the blackmailer. Had Bert done something to Dorothy? Was it her frail, old body lying out in those trees? Pouring the boiling water into the pot, Paul shook his head to dismiss the ridiculous thoughts and decided the best way to set his mind at peace would be to visit his friend, to make sure in person that she was safe and well.

Unwilling to use the back door due to all the police activity, he collected his wellies from the inner porch behind the kitchen and took them to the front room. He sat on his armchair beside the gently crackling fire to drag them over his socked feet, and slipped a lumberjack shirt over his sweater. Stepping into the small hallway, his eyes were drawn to a pastel green envelope that lay on the carpet beneath the letterbox. It looked just like the one he had received previously, which had stated the enigmatic words *'threats mean death'*. Curious, he scooped it up and dragged the paper from inside, but the joined up letters meant nothing to him. He tried for a while to work out what it said, but the words had been hastily scribbled and he couldn't understand any of it. Eventually he decided to take the letter to Dorothy when he went to check on her; maybe she would read it for him, perhaps even recognise the handwriting.

He slipped the paper back into the envelope and folded it into his pocket, before going outside to the chilly, yet sunny day. His first knock wasn't answered, nor the second, louder this time. When the third went unheeded, he gave up and trudged home, skirting along the alley to the back garden so he could see if there had been any changes with the police and medical activity.

Nothing had changed so he let himself through the back door, tugging his boots off and discarding them on the porch floor beside the coir doormat. By the time he had locked the door behind him, tugged off his jacket and gone reluctantly to the kitchen to prepare a more substantial breakfast, the green letter was forgotten.

The grass had been parted nearby in several places, evidence that people had been walking through it, but the area was heaving with constables and technicians, so which path the perpetrator and his victim had taken wasn't clear without further analysis.

Jeff and I had seen all we needed to and staying longer was pointless. All we could do was head back to the station to await the results of the post mortem and see if the forensic team had managed to collect anything useful from the crime scene.

We reached the car and Jeff stood beside it while I climbed in, grateful to be out of the cold. "Can we take ten minutes to go and see if my brother saw or heard anything, boss?"

I didn't want to, but reasoned there wouldn't be a huge amount we could do at the station at this early stage, so I got out again, closing the door behind me. He led me a short way along the dirt track and through a gate at the back of the garden where the odd-looking monster had been standing before. As I followed Jeff across the grass I considered the house may be the one I had been watching several nights before from the main road. A pair of muddied wellies standing upright beside the back door caught my eye and I thought back to the footprint at the crime scene. They seemed a similar size.

Jeff rapped on the door and presently the large man I now knew to be Paul opened the door, moving aside to let us in. With the benefit of knowledge, I could now see the resemblance between the brothers, although Paul was much harder around the

75

edges. He had the same black eyes, but his hair was raven, his features twisted and battered, skin tougher. With Jeff's refined, well-groomed appearance and manner, the two brothers were chalk and cheese.

Jeff didn't wait for Paul to offer a drink; he filled the antiquated kettle and set it on the hob. I leant against the sink, leaving the spare chair for Jeff, but he indicated that I sit. "Have you any idea what happened last night, Paul?"

The bear of a man shook his head, his unkempt hair, black interspersed with grey, flopped from one side to the other with the exaggerated movement. "I don't know anything. The police cars and everything were all there when I got up this morning."

Jeff placed a teabag in each of three mugs, and I watched as Paul removed them. He placed one in the teapot and put the other two back in the box, furnishing Jeff with a disgruntled glare. I almost laughed at the pettiness. "What time did you go to bed? Do you remember?"

Paul became nervous, fidgeting and squirming, and I couldn't fathom why until he spoke finally. "I haven't done anything. Why are you asking me?" He began to rock gently and I glanced at Jeff, questioning. Jeff nodded. He had never mentioned his brother was autistic before. In retrospect, I wondered, why would he?

Jeff laid a hand on Paul's arm. "You're not in any trouble, we just wondered if you saw or heard anything unusual last night, that's all. The more we go back to the office with, the quicker we find the culprit."

Paul's rocking continued, slightly faster. "I don't even know what you're here for, I don't know what happened. Dot's not told me and she knows everything."

"Dot," Jeff brought the mugs to the table and set them down, "isn't she the woman who cooked your breakfast the other day?"

"Yes, she helps us – me – a lot. She was supposed to come round this morning to pick up a package, but she's not been and she's not answering her door. She'll know everything though, she always does."

My eyes met Jeff's and he shook his head, letting me know that the broken victim we had seen wasn't Dorothy. "The vic was too young. We can pop round there after our drink and ask if she saw anything. If she's the village nosy parker, she's bound to know something."

Paul was still agitated and it interested me. "No, I told you, she's not in. I tried. I wanted her to read a letter that came this morning because I don't understand it."

Something felt very wrong to me. As we had been walking towards the back door I had seen a postman wheeling his bicycle, a bunch of letters in his hand, on the main road at the front of the house. He wouldn't have reached Paul yet. "What time did you get the letter?"

"I don't know what time. It was after you got here this morning, but a long time before you came round."

I strode into the front room without asking and Paul swiftly rose behind me. I guessed he was irked at my familiarity, but I wanted to see what was happening on the main road. Scanning through the glass, I could see the same postman further along the road, delivering to a bungalow. I turned to find Paul behind me, his chest puffed out in readiness to defend his home from intruders like me.

I felt uneasy and caught Jeff's eye as he surveyed the scene from the kitchen, holding the dividing curtain aside. "What were you looking for?"

"Have you got the letter, Paul? I don't think it came through the post, so it must have been hand delivered. It might be important."

He glared at me with sinister eyes for a moment. "It's in my coat. Go back in the kitchen and I'll get it." He followed me out and as I sat back down, he grabbed the checked shirt from a rack in the back porch and dug around in the pockets, finally pulling out the crumpled mint envelope. I read it and, on noticing two quizzical faces watching me, read it again, aloudthis time. "Paul, my son picked me up and I've gone to stay with him in London. Dorothy."

"Oh," Paul muttered as he returned to the porch to hang the jacket back up, before sitting on his favourite wooden chair. "Now who's going to make my dinner?"

I tucked the letter and envelope into my pocket with the intention of having them forensically analysed, because my gut feeling told me something was untoward about both the letter and Dorothy's disappearance. I asked a few questions about the woman, but all the answers were negative. Paul didn't know much more than her address, surname, and roughly how old she was. He told me he hadn't even remembered she had a son until she had mentioned him the previous day. I nodded to Jeff when he again suggested we check Dorothy's house before heading back to Hull.

For a village that didn't see much action, plenty seemed to have happened the night before, and my team was going to find out exactly what, who – and why. And quickly.

Now there had been a murder, it was expected that both Jeff and I would work non-stop until the case was solved, unless, of course, something drastic happened and we had no choice but to leave the office for other business. Neither Jeff nor I minded, however times like these did take their toll on our families and relationships, and this was the third murder we'd had to deal with in the past two weeks. But we were professionals, we were good, and we wanted the answers as much as anybody. Maybe more so.

After leaving Paul we had tried Dorothy's door but, as Paul had told us, there was no answer and my suspicions were aroused further. We had a quick stroll around her house to see if there were any open windows or signs of forced entry. Seeing inside was impossible as all the curtains were drawn, which seemed unusual for the time of day. Eventually, we radioed through for some uniforms to try and find a relative or friend who had a key and we headed back over the bridge and into Hull.

The traffic was dreadful, as it always seemed to be in the centre of the city, and I was impatient. Jeff was a much calmer person than I could ever be and he retained his composure while I rapped on the steering wheel, huffing and puffing, swearing copiously. If I hadn't been so stressed at the time, the chasm of contrast between our personalities would have been laughable.

We barely spoke during the journey, but when I finally crawled out of the city centre traffic and could actually use the accelerator, Jeff revealed what was on his mind. "I know we have to re-open the Bonfire Night Killer case now, but boss, can you do me a favour? Can we keep the old part of the investigation as much between ourselves as possible? I've got some awful suspicions and I don't want to end up the laughing stock if I'm on the right track."

I glanced at him. "You do realise I should be taking you off this case because of the possibility of your father being a suspect?"

I could feel his dark-chocolate eyes boring into the side of my face and I kept mine on the road. He sighed and the viper stare was gone as his head dropped. "I know, you're right. I just wish I could investigate, I don't want other people knowing my business and taking the piss behind my back."

I indicated left for the station's car park, weaving beside an exiting squad car. "I'll tell you what. You can research the original case, for now, and I'll get Reeves and Townsend to take charge of the latest murder. I'll oversee you all. But I don't want you compromising this, Jeff. Even if the finger starts pointing at your father I want you to be unbiased."

I felt his body relax as he acknowledged my concerns and told me how grateful he was. I couldn't begin to think how difficult it was for him, having never been in that position, but I could empathise.

Paul opened the door, surprised the knock had come from the front; only the postman used that entrance on the rare occasion a package was delivered. A delightfully attractive police constable stepped forward and Paul blushed, the presence of a pretty female making him nervous. "We were just wondering if you have a key for Mrs Dorothy Webber's house. We're a little worried about her and want to make sure she's alright."

"No, I haven't. But, wait a sec, my dad might have one. I'll look in his room." Paul had a vague memory of his father doing 'his bit' while Dorothy wasn't well after her Ernie died. Normally he wouldn't have taken the trouble to help the cops, but this was about Dot and he missed her cooking already. He opened the door to his father's room, remembering from the previous week, when he had been searching for the safe, roughly where the skeleton ring of keys he had seen was. He took them to the officer. "There's a few on there, but one of them might fit." She glanced at him curiously before strolling away, calling to a colleague who was also doing house calls.

The two constables struggled with the keys for a while, before coming up with the idea of removing all the keys from the ring, selecting the ones that would possibly fit the door, and trying just those. The fifth one they tried was the lucky one. They hammered and called out before entering and, adrenalin pumping, they burst in and proceeded to check each room. There was no Dorothy. There were no signs of a struggle and nothing seemed out of place. Just no Dorothy. They knew the next step would be to find the son she had written about visiting, and for someone to check it was her handwriting on the note. The constable grasped a shopping list from the kitchen side and tucked it in her pocket, and searched through a few drawers in the kitchen for an address book, which she retained in the hope that the son's details would be inside.

Back at the office, as Jeff slipped behind his desk, I bent to bring the case box for the Bonfire Night killings out from under mine once more. I placed it on his desk without a word and called for my team to gather round so I could allocate tasks to them, as was the norm. "Do we have anything on the identity of the victim yet?"

A detective nodded, hand raised. "We have a possible. A woman of a similar description was staying with her sister and didn't come home after a walk. The husband is on his way from Birmingham to see if he can identify the body.

"Good, good. What about a post mortem report?"

Another colleague took over. "It's being done right now. I'll get the results to you as soon as I hear anything."

"Right. Do we know if she was raped?"

There were a few glances around the room, and finally Debbie spoke. "Nothing was apparent at the scene, there appeared to be no injuries other than the bullet wound and her clothes were intact, but it's better to wait for the post mortem results to be sure."

I carried on for a while, mentally taking notes, and after asking everyone to report any new findings to me, I sent them off to work. I sat behind my desk, deep in thought. One case was probably going to lead to the perpetrator of the other, and there were two probable solutions: either the original killer had resurfaced for some reason, which was highly unlikely; or somebody had read about the original killings and decided to re-create them, which wasn't an uncommon scenario. That theory was more likely if the victim had been raped, but still feasible if not.

I glanced over to Jeff, who was engrossed in the original case reports, and from what I could see of the file he was studying, he was learning everything he could about the first victim and her untimely demise. Her name was Katherine James:

'Victim 1 – Katherine James, 14, Oakleigh Close, Colefield, North Lincs (death 7/11/80)

D.O.B. and Age – 2/2/50   age 30
Family – Husband, Richard James, age 34 (pipe-fitter, Scunthorpe steelworks)
Son, Russell, age 7
Son, Christopher, age 6
Daughter, Sally, age 4

Employment – Part-time shelf stacker at Mini Mart supermarket, Westerton'

It was basic detail that wouldn't help much, but every file needed a title page. Behind was a bundle of statements from family, friends and people who had seen her on the evening she died. Jeff pulled out her husband, Richard's, and read:

'I'm just like every other man around here, I can't stand fireworks, none of us can, so I didn't go to the display with my wife. I was more than happy watching television and reading, ignoring the noise. She left the house with our children. Sally was in the buggy because she might fall asleep. It was about six in the evening. The display was due to start at six-thirty, so I knew she was going early to have a natter with her mates. I gave her five pounds so they could all have a hot dog. She was in good spirits, as were the children.

I had no reason to worry until the children turned up at ten without her. I asked where she was and the eldest, Russell, said that she had bought them hot dogs during the interlude, and then asked if he could take the buggy while she went to talk to her friend. She told him to stay by the burger van. He said they waited for ages, watching the second half of the display, but after it finished he got bored and began pushing the buggy around the site, along with his brother Christopher, looking for her. When they couldn't find her, they came home.

I waited until midnight, when all the revellers had returned home and the pub had closed, and then rang the police. They refused to send anyone round until the next day. The next morning her body was found.

I have never hit or hurt my wife. We had a good relationship, and when we argued it was always settled amicably.

I have a firearms licence, most men in the village do as hunting is one of the villagers' major pastimes, but I am confident and responsible with my rifle, it is locked away as it should be, and the lock hasn't been tampered with.'

Jeff was interested in the suggestion that most of Colefield's men had a firearms licence, and he raised it with me as a possible detail to check with the latest case, then sat back down and continued to read. In turn I called a couple of officers over and instructed them to look into the firearms certificates and weapons of the village members.

Jeff found that the children's statements correlated with their father's, and the majority of the others were as simple as having seen Katherine at the event and passing the time of day. Nobody had seen her go into the copse of willows where she had been murdered. Nobody had knowingly heard the gun amongst the cacophony of fireworks. And nobody had noticed anyone suspicious hanging around, although there were plenty of unrecognised faces due to the influx of people from the surrounding area.

The gun that had killed Katherine used .44 calibre bullets, and the ballistics experts had focused on the gun being a Ruger, possibly a Blackhawk. The weapon had not been located.

Swabs had been taken from Katherine's body and stored in the anticipation of scientific advances, and Jeff immediately arranged for them to be tested and compared against the archives in HOLMES2, the police national computer database.

There didn't seem to be a motive for her rape or death. There were no reported disputes with neighbours, no signs of adultery within the marriage on either side, and no vendettas with relations. It appeared it was a random attack; she had simply been in the wrong place at the wrong time.

Dusk had come and gone hours before and been replaced by a cloudy, black sky, illuminated gently by the lights from busy streets. Many of my staff had packed their things away and left the office, with families to return home to, when I received the call from the morgue to tell me that our victim had been positively identified. Her name was Fiona Bethany Malik and she was twenty-five years old. She was married to Neel and they had two daughters, both pre-school. She had not been raped. Death had been caused by a single bullet from a .44 calibre gun and the bullet had been sent to ballistics for examination.

I sat in silence, aware the original murders had also been committed using a .44 calibre weapon. Was that merely a coincidence, or was it more sinister? I trotted to Jeff's desk and told him the latest news. "Can you look in the evidence boxes to see if the bullets were retrieved from the other victims? Might be worth getting them to the lab to see if there are any comparisons."

A wave of concern flickered across Jeff's face. "When do you want it done?"

"Well, now. Why, is there a problem?"

Jeff shuffled, sheepish. "It's just it's Sue's birthday today, I was going to take her out for a meal. We've booked a babysitter."

I looked at my watch, surprised to see it was nine already; the hectic day had flown by. I raised my voice so all personnel left in the room could hear me. "Come on everyone, let's all go home, it's been a long day and there's nothing we can do today that can't wait until tomorrow. "

Chapter 9
Wednesday 7th November

I arrived at my desk early in the morning, so eager to solve the case as soon as possible that my attempts to sleep had been worthless. My mind was buzzing with the drama in Colefield and I wanted my team to be the one that would find the killer – or killers. Jeff wasn't far behind me, trundling to his desk with a wide yawn, and I was glad I was past those hectic and wearing new-baby days; I could remember the tortuous sleep deprivation well.

As always, I booted my computer up, preparing the coffee machine while the programs loaded, and once I'd had a hot drink to wake me up, I checked my emails. One had an attachment of a statement given by Fiona Malik's sister to my colleague, Alan Reeves, and I printed it out to read:

'Fi had come over for the night. She'd had an argument with Neel, which was becoming more common lately. Normally they would just sleep apart, but this was a bad one. She wouldn't tell me what had happened, and as we got more and more drunk, I got heavy on her, telling her she had to let me know what he'd done. Suddenly she grabbed a bottle of vodka and her fags, and stormed off out the back.

I thought she'd just have a couple of swigs with a couple of fags while she calmed down, but an hour later she was still gone. I hate saying it but I was mad at her; I suspected Neel was getting heavy handed on her and I couldn't help her if she wouldn't let me in. I left the back door unlocked for her and went to bed.

The next thing I knew it was morning and the street was filled with police cars. I checked on the sofa where Fi usually slept when she stayed over, but there were no signs that she'd been there; the blankets were still folded. I checked the conservatory, then the back garden. I figured she'd just gone home, still mad at me, so didn't report her missing until I phoned Neel and he told me she hadn't turned up.'

I glanced over the personal details of the sister. At forty-one she was much older than Fiona, with two older teenagers living at home. She was separated from her husband. I wondered if age had made her wiser. Certainly ignoring a tantrum in the way she did — by not giving the thrower the attention they were seeking — was an excellent way to reduce toddler troubles, but was it appropriate with an obviously troubled and upset adult?

That was irrelevant, I told myself. In all likelihood Fiona had chosen to leave the property boundaries, thus becoming an unwitting target to the hunter, and that was a foolish act. The increase in crime over the years must surely have taught the woman that walking about alone at night was not safe in today's violent climate. The unlikelier option was that Fiona had been snatched from the garden physically but, so far, nobody had mentioned any unidentifiable fibres on her clothing, which would indicate there was no physical contact between her and her killer.

Returning to my inbox, a new email had popped up from Jeff and I gave him a wry glance, which made him chuckle. He was letting me know that he had found all three bullets from the older murders and they were on their way to ballistics for examination. Now the wait began. If they had been fired from the same gun, then either the murderer had suffered a psychological trigger that had made him want to kill again or, more chillingly, he had a son or close relative who had decided to take up where the killer had left off.

I felt the blood drain from my face when I thought of Roland and Paul Mason. Paul could have done it, he was troubled. Maybe he knew Roland had committed the crimes. Maybe he was finishing the job for his father out of grief. I wanted to know all the details about Jeff's father and brother. However, I definitely didn't want Jeff to know what I was doing, because if he found out, I would have to take him off the case completely due to personal conflict. I already should have.

I had asked the Scunthorpe branch to keep me informed about the search for Dorothy Webber and late in the morning, just before Jeff and I were planning to head for lunch and a pint at the local we went to whilst working, an email told me that her three adult children had been found. None of them had seen her for years, the entire family being estranged, apart from when Ernie Webber had been buried twelve years earlier following his early death. They knew of nobody whom she might refer to as a son and they

86

had no idea of her whereabouts. I replied, instructing them to get the family to report her as a missing person, and to begin an investigation immediately. Disappearing was one thing, but on the same night and place as a murder was worrying.

While I was considering Fiona and Dorothy's cases, Jeff appeared to be reading the file about the second shooting, back in nineteen eighty-one.

'Victim 2 – Vanessa Walton (Known as Nessa), 32, Broadside Close, Colefield, North Lincs. (death 6/11/81)

D.O.B. and Age – 28/4/52   age 29
Family – Husband, Ralph Walton, age 34 (Solicitor)

Employment – Trainee Solicitor at Morgan Bryant and Sons, Scunthorpe

The husband had provided a comprehensive statement that had given far more detail of the circumstances than had been available for the first murder. He and Nessa had been together since their schooldays, but waited to move in together until they married, two years before her death. Both high earners, they were able to follow Ralph's job and move from their home city of Lincoln to the affluent village of Colefield, where they had purchased a two-bedroom semi-detached stone cottage a few months before.

He stated they were both placid in temperament and rarely argued. They were also considering the possibility of having a child once Nessa had finished her training, and this forward planning virtually ruled out the husband as a suspect.

The villagers had been excited about the major fireworks display taking place the evening after Bonfire Night on the main field for a second year running, and most of the women and children had planned to see it, regardless that most could see the airborne display from the comfort of their homes. Ralph and Nessa had arrived late due to their high-pressured jobs, but by eight they were eating burgers and enjoying the sparkling decorations whizzing through the sky.

Nessa had needed the loo and Ralph suggested they went home, but she was reluctant to miss anything and, being a practical girl who relied on common sense, she told him she would nip into the bushes and discreetly do her business. He ordered another burger after she'd gone, eating it while waiting for her, but by the time he had finished the snack he was becoming concerned that she hadn't returned. He followed her steps to the bushes, yet couldn't find her, and he began to worry. He searched further into the trees and undergrowth, eventually tripping over her body in a nearby copse of weeping willow trees. Neither he, nor Nessa, as far as he knew, had known about the shooting the previous year.

There were barely any more witness statements; during the few months that Nessa and Ralph had lived in Colefield, they had not become involved in village life, partly because of their desire for privacy, and also because they worked such long hours, they were barely home. Hardly anybody knew even their names.

Again, the only real piece of evidence had been the bullet. With the field crowded and the area so noisy, shoe-prints had been all but worthless. A sample of her rapist's semen had been taken from her during the post mortem and stored. The bullet was found to match the one removed from Katherine James's body and the investigation had been stepped up, but nobody had any information. The gun hadn't been found, and nor had the gunman.

Immediately Jeff arranged for the second semen sample to be tested and compared to the records on the database.

Paul was comfortably dozing on his armchair, a swift shot or three of whisky having warmed him after his walk earlier, when a sharp rapping on the front door stirred him. He sighed sleepily and hoisted himself up, not totally surprised to see two constables when he opened the door. "Mr Paul Mason?" He nodded. "We'd like to have a few words about a Mrs Dorothy Webber, who has been reported missing by her family."

Paul widened the door and moved aside for the officers to enter, and they gratefully stood close to the crackling fire to warm their frozen legs. "So what's going on with Dot?"

Constable Myers opened her notepad. "She hasn't been seen since Monday and we understand that it was a key in your possession that allowed us to gain access to her house yesterday."

"It was my dad's. I got it from his room." Paul slumped onto his seat, hand hovering over the whisky beside his chair briefly, before deciding that drinking liquor from a bottle in front of police officers wasn't the best of ideas.

"Have you ever used the key to let yourself into Mrs Webber's house?"

Paul shook his head over-exaggeratedly, worried. "I didn't even know he had it until you lot used it."

The two officers glanced at each other. "Is your father here?"

Taken aback, Paul explained about the heart attacks, that he had been in his dad's room to begin clearing out and had noticed the keys on the side. He insisted he had not seen them before. The constables realised they weren't going to get much more information, regardless of their suspicions of the massive, unkempt man before them.

Once they had left, Paul panicked and dialled his brother's home number. Sue informed him Jeff was at work and gave him the number. He was distressed by the time he reached Jeff and his voice shuddered. "Why are the police asking me lots of questions about Dot? I don't know anything about her not being at home, except she went to her son's to stay like that note said."

Jeff was surprised, having not been told any further details of her disappearance since the day before. He was truthful. "I don't know. Give me five minutes, I'll call the Scunthorpe station and see what's going on."

I could see that Jeff was struggling with the phone call, not that I knew who was on the other end of the line. Rolling his eyes dramatically he slammed the receiver down and marched over, flapping his arms about as he tended to on the rare occasion he was disgruntled. I pulled a chair round for him. "Go on then, what's made you so tetchy?"

He sat heavily. "It's about the old lady, Dorothy Webber. The bloody Scunny force reckon Paul's a suspect in her disappearance." I was equally shocked, more down to the fact they hadn't informed me than to Jeff's unusual brother being a suspect. I asked him what reasons they had given. "They wouldn't tell me anything because I stupidly mentioned I was his brother. Why did I do that? I should have known better."

I shaped my fingers into a pyramid as I thought about the ethicality of my next sentence, but I didn't see what harm it could do. "Leave it with me, I'll see what I can find out."

He mumbled his thanks through tightened lips and wandered back to his desk. I was about to follow him, knowing he wouldn't be able to concentrate on his work whilst so tense, but the desk sergeant brought a pile of papers over and shoved them into my hand. "It's the results on the bullets from ballistics."

Jeff was forgotten in an instant as I hastily scanned through the findings, eager to see a link. When I found what I was searching for I called Jeff, Alan Reeves, and Dom Townsend to my desk. I waved the papers in the air. "These are the results from ballistics. The bullet recovered from Fiona Malik's body is a match to the three bullets from the shootings in the early eighties. I can confirm that we're probably looking at either the same gunman, or a close relative who may have inherited the gun."

I noticed the pained frown that briefly formed on Jeff's face, and he implored me with quizzical eyes. I nodded at him. "I'll speak to you alone in a minute, Jeff. In either case it explains – somewhat – why there was no rape this time. If it was the original killer he may be too old to restrain his victim, or it could be that he's impotent through age. If it is a new killer using the same gun, he would have a different MO, and maybe rape isn't his thing."

"So what do we do next?" Dom Townsend's deep voice commanded attention every time he spoke, always oozing with confidence and authority.

"I think house calls are the next step, collecting DNA…"

"DNA to compare with what, exactly?" Dom was asking a fair question, but his tone aggravated me. I glared at him, but his eyes didn't waver in the slightest, which irrationally made me want to punch the smug git.

I continued, glowering. "I want you to collect voluntary DNA samples from all males from the age of sixteen upwards."

Alan waved his hand meekly, his presence always timid in contrast to his partner. "No, you need it from the women too. If rape wasn't involved, it's possible it was a woman who fired the gun. You can't rule it out." He blushed, shrinking back to the camouflage of the wall.

I conceded to his well-made point, stating we would follow that route if our initial searches drew a blank, and presently Reeves and Townsend donned their jackets and left for their journey to Colefield.

I nodded and Jeff followed me to the spare office, where I perched on the desk. He was furious and remained standing. "What are you doing, Frank?"

I sighed, knowing that the next few weeks were going to jeopardise my friendship with Jeff, and there was nothing I could do about it. "I'm sorry, but as you know, there's strong reason to suspect your father in the original killings, and you have to admit that the recent loss of your father may have triggered Paul to complete his father's work."

He was normally so calm and composed, regardless of whatever horrors he was working on. This one had clearly wormed its way under his skin, and quite understandably with the family link. I'd never seen Jeff so aggressive as he shouted, "So I'm off the case? Is that it? Off the case while you lot poke about in my business when I haven't done anything wrong."

I noticed heads turning to watch through the glass and I kept my voice low. "Come on, Jeff, you know I have to follow protocol. The choice isn't in my hands."

He punched the desk, more with frustration than anger. "Frank, this is important to me, this is my heritage. At least let me keep on researching the shootings from the eighties. I won't be on the case officially, but that way I'll be able to keep up with things. Imagine if it was your family. Nothing would stop you investigating, nobody."

I swore I could see tears of vexation brewing, his passion was obvious, and I had to admit he was right; if anybody hurt any member of my precious family I'd personally leave no stone unturned to find the perpetrator. I sighed, knowing I was about to break the rules. "Keep your nose down. Keep in mind that any work you do is unofficial, and if anything else comes in while we're working on this case, you'll be leading that investigation instead without any further debate."

He instantly calmed, his shoulders relaxed and his jaw unclenched, and he nodded, his eyes and slight smile radiating his appreciation. He sloped back to his desk, instantly opening a file as if time were running out.

'Victim 3 – Bernadette Elaine Smith (known as 'Bernie'), 4 Hanging Gardens, Colefield, North Lincolnshire (death 5/11/82)

D.O.B. and Age – 14/2/1952   age 30
Family – lived with parents, Hugh and Margie Smith

Employment – none (disabled)

Jeff read the statement on the top of the file, which had been taken from Bernie's mother:

'Bernie had always loved Bonfire Night. Although she was thirty she had the mentality of a child. Her body was disfigured in the womb – she was born with stumps for hands and a cleft lip – which made life difficult for her right from the start, but she also wasn't good mentally. We always knew she was different to other babies. She didn't reach her goalposts anywhere near as soon as other children – if at all – but we still loved her. She struggled at school, and eventually we took the decision to educate her at home. It worked, she picked things up slowly, but it was tough on me and Hugh. We always celebrated special days, it was any excuse to see the joy on her face.

The major display for the third year in a row was due on Friday 5th, and we got her so excited, she was really looking forward to it. Of course we knew about the two previous shootings, but didn't think it would happen again. Nobody did. We brought her out just before the display was about to start and told her to stay with us.

Halfway through the display the organisers had a break, so I got her a hot dog from one of the stands. Hugh and I got chatting to some neighbours and we didn't notice Bernie wandering off. By the time Hugh realised she was gone we couldn't see her anywhere. Because of the other two shootings we were really concerned, and we started searching for her, through the crowds – everywhere – but then they started the fireworks again and it became really difficult after that.

We tried asking people to help, but they were all enjoying the display too much to be bothered. We aren't the most popular people in the village, not because we've done anything wrong, but our decision to keep a disabled and autistic child back in nineteen fifty-two was scorned on by everybody, and that distaste had stuck through the years.

Once the display had finished we searched high and low. I went home in case she returned there, but shortly after, Hugh came back and he told me he'd found her body. I wanted to break down there and then, but he told me to run to the phone box and get the police and an ambulance. Of course, when they arrived she was already dead.'

The father's account was similar, there was no doubt they were telling the truth. Again, as in the two previous killings, the lack of statements that said anything of worth was incredible considering all three murders had been committed in public at a major event. There appeared to be no evidence apart from the bullet and semen, and unless the gun was found or the DNA matched a sample in the police database, it was difficult to see how those investigations could progress without a confession. The only hope was the latest death. If they could find Fiona Malik's assailant it would possibly – probably – lead to the original gunman.

Jeff was aware I was taking a huge risk in letting him stay on the case, even unofficially, but I could tell how important this was to him. He had grown up not knowing his father and brother, and had told me that in his teens, to his mother's disgust, he had searched for and found them, but the relationships had never got off the ground due to their vastly contrasting lifestyles. Both men had been present at his wedding, and Paul had come to their mother's funeral, but that was the last time he had seen either. Until now.

Maybe it was part of the grieving process now that his father was gone, but he felt the need to know everything about his forgotten family, and he was also spending more time than normal thinking about his mother. But the possibility of a dark and murky past wasn't something he had envisaged, and he felt even more lost than he had whilst painfully accepting he was an orphan. If his suspicions were true he would need a lot of strength to deal with the situation.

Over an hour passed as we both burrowed our heads in the copious paperwork, and finally Jeff finished reading the file and dropped it onto his desk. He sauntered over to mine. "Did you find out anything about Paul being implicated in Dorothy's disappearance?" I hadn't even thought about it since I had been interrupted with the ballistics reports and shook my head in shame. "I'm going to see Paul. He's getting stressed with the investigation happening around him, and that's on top of the funeral coming up. If you find anything out can you call me on my mobile?" I nodded, reprimanding myself for being so forgetful.

Paul had worked himself into a state after the police had visited, so when they knocked on the door for the second time that day he was terrified, unable to cope with the questions. Jeff was driving past the small, ordinary semi, heading for the dirt track that led to his usual parking spot, when he noticed Reeves and Townsend interviewing Paul on the doorstep. He turned his head slightly, not wanting his colleagues to know he was related to Paul. Obviously they would find out eventually if the investigation continued along this line, but he wasn't ready to deal with that yet. He wanted to find some answers for himself first.

Shivering by the door in the back garden during the short wait for the questioning to end, Jeff was thankful I called to update him with the details I had learned from the Scunthorpe team. This whiled away the time a little. Once he heard his fellow detectives leave the property, Jeff knocked on the back door.

Paul answered, his face a mask of worry, and gratefully let his brother in. "I need a whisky. Those police people are scaring me."

Jeff followed him through to the front room and they both sunk onto the armchairs. Paul lifted the whisky bottle to his mouth, the cheap drink relaxing him, and Jeff grimaced. "What's going on then, Paul?"

The words were right on the edge, ready to tumble. "They think I know where Dot is, and they think I killed that girl." His shoulders began to heave as he gasped for breath, upset and scared.

Jeff chuckled lightly, an attempt to brighten the situation, but it was unconvincing. "No they don't, honest. Look, those two men are my colleagues, I know them. They're just routinely asking at all the houses in the village to see if anybody saw anything that might lead to Fiona Malik's killer. It's not just you. What did they ask?"

His breaths were shallow, hands wringing together, and he sobbed without tears, frightened. "They said did I have a gun, so I said yes, because I have." His face was reddening more than usual with the recalled conversation. "All of us men go shooting. We only shoot rabbits and birds, but they said they wanted to see my fire licence."

"Did you show it to them?" Jeff kept his voice calm.

Paul became more vexed; he didn't like all the questions, they confused his mind. His dad would have known what to say, but he didn't. "I don't even know what a fire licence is. I don't think I've got one."

"I think you mean a firearms licence. Is that what they asked for?"

Paul clutched his tummy tightly and rocked gently, back and forth. "Yes." The word was greatly extended, a whining child.

Jeff thought laterally about how to probe more softly to calm his brother. "Now, the gun you're talking about when you say you shoot birds and rabbits, was it dad's?"

"No, it's mine, he got it for me. It was a present."

"It would be helpful if I could see it. Can you show me?"

With fear in his eyes Paul rose, nodding exaggeratedly. He trotted up the stairs and was back in an instant. He passed the air rifle to Jeff, who laughed with welcome relief. "That's okay, the police will know it wasn't you who killed Fiona, it's the wrong type of gun. Do you know if dad had any guns?" Paul shook his head, which surprised Jeff. From what he had been reading, with shooting being a popular sport for the male villagers, he couldn't imagine his gruff, unlikeable, alpha-male father not being part of the hunt. "You've never seen him with a gun? Didn't he go on the shooting trips with the other men?"

"No, he couldn't be bothered since he got his bad back. He gave me my gun so I could go, but he didn't go."

Jeff was uncomfortable. His father not owning a gun didn't make sense, but he decided to let the subject drop for a while. "My boss has spoken to the Scunthorpe police about Dorothy going missing, and why they came to see you. They say you have a key to Dorothy's house."

Paul began rocking, violently this time, the questions overwhelming him. "I haven't. I just told those men. Why won't people listen to me?"

"Hey, it's okay, Paul. Tell me about the key."

"My dad had it. I saw a bunch of keys in his room the other day when I was getting the, um, getting something, so I gave it to them and said that her key might be on it. I never let myself into her house. I never once went in there. I would never be rude to Dot."

"Okay, but you must be able to see why the police find it suspicious?"

"I didn't do nothing wrong. I like Dot, she gives me lots of food. I wouldn't hurt her."

Jeff balked; he'd not mentioned anything about Dorothy being hurt. Did Paul know more than he was letting on? He dismissed the untoward thought, hoping – praying – that the evidence mounting up against his family was circumstantial, that the real killer would be found soon.

Jeff's mobile rang and, excusing himself, he answered. "Jeff, it's Frank. I thought I'd let you know that I've had a memo from our forensics team. Apparently there was a small amount of blood found a few feet from Fiona Malik's body. They've tested it and it's not her blood."

He gasped. "The murderer?"

It was the first conclusion I had jumped to as well. "It came from a different female."

"Are you saying that the killer was a woman?"

"Either that, or another woman was present and she was also hurt."

He whispered to avoid upsetting Paul. "Dorothy?"

"We can't tell until we get some of her DNA to the lab, so while you're in Colefield, can you go to her place and get something we can take a sample from for testing."

"I will do, boss."

"One more thing, I didn't know at the time, and it's a long story that I won't bore you with, but I saw Paul take what looked like a safe out of a wardrobe in the front bedroom the other night…"

There was undisguised venom in his voice. "You did what? You've been watching him? That's bloody out of order, mate."

"No, Jeff, it wasn't anything official. I just couldn't sleep and I wanted to see the village after you'd told me about it, I recognised the name and I thought the drive would tire me out. I didn't know it was Paul I was watching – not then, anyway -but his was the only light on in the village as it was the early hours, so my eyes were drawn to it." Jeff grunted, clearly still annoyed with me. "Anyway, just check the safe out, okay. Rather now than later, eh?"

Jeff was rattled, even after the explanation, but he didn't mention anything to his distressed brother. He asked if he could use the key to Dorothy's house to check on things. Paul explained that the officers hadn't returned the key after using it, and Jeff's heart sunk at the thought of the inevitable long wait for a constable to bring the key to him. Reluctantly he phoned Scunthorpe Police Station and PC Myers promised she would be there, with the key, within the next hour. He asked her to text him before she left, which meant he could be at the house ready for her to avoid the fact he was Paul's brother becoming public knowledge just yet.

Jeff watched Paul rocking gently and felt a strange bond with his older sibling. He felt protective of the scared man, but he also wanted to find answers that would exonerate any family member of involvement in the filthy, cowardly crimes. "Paul, have you ever wondered who shot those three women in the early eighties?"

"I was only a lad." Paul lifted the bottle to his mouth and took a large gulp, and Jeff was surprised that he looked shifty.

"Yes, but it must have been gossiped about for years, a small place like this."

"I don't know nothing. Why won't you all stop asking me about it? It wasn't me and it wasn't my dad."

"I can see it upsets you, but wouldn't you rather it was me asking than the other policemen? He was my dad too, I don't want anything linked to either of you, but the fact is, because of the shooting two days ago, the old case has been re-opened and they *will* find the answers. All I want to do is prove that you and dad are innocent, not the other way around. But you need to be honest with me."

Paul made no attempt to answer, a trait Jeff had noticed was apparent when he was confused. He locked himself away, with mental barriers protecting him from any subject he disliked. Eventually, fed up with the silence, Jeff stood. "I'm going to take a look around dad's room, okay?"

Instantly Paul was standing, his full height intimidating. "No. My dad's room is private."

"Look, if you're hiding something, or covering something up, they're going to find out. Tell me the truth, damn it, and I can work out what to do for the best. As soon as people find out I'm related to you they're going to take me off the case, and then I won't be able to help you anymore. It won't be me questioning you, it'll be officers who don't know you. Officers who want to find the killer and lock him away. You've got to trust me, Paul." Not uttering a word, but clearly disgruntled, Paul unwillingly followed Jeff up the stairs. He opened the door to his father's bedroom and let Jeff through. "I heard that dad had a safe. Do you know where the key is?"

How Jeff knew about the safe didn't cross Paul's mind. He reached into the underwear drawer and presented the key to his brother, then brought the safe from the shelf in the wardrobe and set it on the bed. Inside there were documents, title deeds, nothing unusual except for an envelope addressed to his brother. He waved it at Paul. "Did you know that there's a letter here with your name on it?"

"I can't open that until I've finished the b…" He hadn't remembered in time that Jeff wasn't to know about the damning journal, his second slip of the day. "Um, Dad told me to read some of his books before I'm allowed to open it."

Jeff had come to realise the difficulties Paul had reading anything but capital letters, so spotted the outright lie, but there was nothing he could do about it at this point, not with Paul watching. He would have to come back later, maybe on the pretence of visiting the toilet. Searching through the boxes and drawers, he wasn't sure what he was looking for and, as Paul had already stated, he couldn't find any firearms. In fact, apart from a dated black-and-white photograph of happier times – he assumed the subjects were his young mother and father, together and smiling with both their sons – there seemed to be nothing untoward. He didn't find anything that pinpointed his father as the Bonfire Night Killer, and the relief was overwhelming. The only thing that concerned him was the envelope addressed to Paul.

Ellen had been calling me repeatedly and I was becoming annoyed. I loved her very much, but sometimes she had no inkling of what working on my team involved, and that the get-together with friends we were due to attend that night paled in comparison – to me, anyway – to finding the person who had brutally killed a young mother two nights before. On the final call I regrettably snapped at her, which I knew would leave the air bad between us for god knows how long.

On entering, Jeff informed me he had taken a toothbrush and comb from Dorothy Webber's house and forwarded them to the forensics department. Now we had another waiting game to see if the second sample of blood matched her DNA. I suggested we go to the pub around the corner and have a couple of pints, which pleased Jeff, weary from the emotional roller coaster he was riding.

The glasses of cold ale were welcome and we both drank the first quickly at the bar, before sitting at a table with a second pint each. Jeff told me about the chat he'd had with Paul, and of searching his father's room. I could tell he was trying to sway me from suspecting his father, but the scrawled notes on the crime books were firmly lodged in my mind. I commented in the right places, keeping my side of the conversation non-committal. If Roland Mason had anything to do with the murders I knew Reeves and Townsend – both excellent detectives – would find out, even if the results were regrettable.

We were about to order a third pint when my mobile beeped. I took the call, stopped Jeff from asking the barmaid, and dragged him back to the office with a brief explanation: "The other blood sample was from Dorothy. We need to find her, or her body, and quick."

Dorothy's house was soon cordoned off, and for the second time in as many days, forensic investigators swarmed the small village of Colefield. There seemed to be no signs of affray within her house, and apart from the blood underneath the weeping willows, there was nothing else to link her to the murder scene. Either she had been wielding the gun, or she was a victim, and if that were the case, we had no idea how badly she had been hurt.

I thought of Paul. He was strong enough to restrain two women, especially with one being elderly. He didn't see the world in quite the way we did. Maybe his autism made good and bad behaviour indistinguishable, and I didn't know enough about the condition to make any judgement. However, if perhaps he had known Roland was the original killer, maybe he was now trying to implicate somebody else to get the police off his father's trail. After all, Roland Mason couldn't have killed from the grave. But it was just as possible that he was a crazy psychopath who wanted to finish his father's work.

The officers checked the house from top to bottom and couldn't find the slightest clue indicating where she may be.

There were no notes on the calendar that hung on the kitchen wall, apart from what appeared to be an appointment of some kind – the destination had been written in initials, and it was for a week later anyway. Her suitcases were in the cupboard and there were no gaps for a further one to have been removed. There were no signs of packing, no lists or discarded clothes, and the daily basics for personal hygiene were in place in her bathroom. No traces of blood were found. I felt for the pale green envelope, supposedly from Dorothy, in my pocket and dragged it out, wishing I had run tests on it before now. My memory was atrocious sometimes.

I found a diary in the top drawer of Dorothy's bedside cabinet and compared the writing inside against the letter. They weren't a match by any means. Dorothy's writing was rounded and large and the scrawl on the letter was forward slanting and elegant. I sighed deeply. Her disappearance was becoming more mysterious by the minute and I sat on the bed, nonchalantly flicking through the pages in the hope that her private words would give me a lead. Most entries were dreary drivel, a quick summary of the spent day, a bit of moaning and complaining, nothing of note, but the ramblings during the week leading up to her disappearance were far more hopeful and happy, with some surprising revelations. It seemed that Dorothy had been expecting a sizeable sum of money to arrive soon, although the diary didn't reveal from what, or whom. I looked at the green letter again, stating that she had gone to stay with her son, and it occurred to me that I hadn't seen any similar correspondence sets during my search of her home. If I could find who possessed the unusual writing set, it was probable the owner was the person who had abducted and hurt her.

I returned to Dorothy's diary. She had clearly expected whoever owed her money to pay up as she frequently mentioned her finances improving, where she would be able to go, and what she'd be able to do once she received the money. From an eleven-month snapshot into an old woman's life, the only excitement appeared to have been in the past week. She had obviously been enjoying this interlude of adventure in her monotonous existence. Tucking the book into the large hip

101

pocket of my well-worn trench coat, I decided to go home and face the sulky silence that was bound to be greeting me from my wife.

Chapter 10
Thursday 8th November

On the way home the previous night I purchased some close to wilting flowers at the garage when I stopped for petrol and presented them to Ellen with a flourish when I got home. She rolled her eyes without smiling, but the mediocre apology had been enough to repress the argument she'd had planned. After I had eaten a simple cheese and onion sandwich for my main meal of the day, I slipped upstairs to bed and was shocked to see Ellen already there. I guessed the quarrel that hadn't yet happened was still bubbling away – our total conversation that evening had consisted of a sombre three words – and I resolved to be on best behaviour.

I had bought Ellen one of those Kindle things for her birthday and, being an avid reader, she had barely put it down in the evenings since. True to form, her nose was deep in an electronic book, oblivious to me in her concentration. I hadn't been sure what to do with myself. I changed into my pyjamas, languidly to waste time, and climbed into bed, messing with some meaningless junk mail that lay on my bedside cabinet. Bored, I padded about the room, folding my clothes, neatening my chest of drawers, still wasting time. I brushed my teeth for a second time, flossing too. Eventually, I nipped downstairs to pour a large measure of brandy and returned to bed, this time with a notepad and pen.

I sat in bed with the covers over my knees and wrote anything I could think of about the old shootings – and the latest. I tried to be completely impartial about Jeff's family, but it still felt as if I was betraying him. The oversized measure of alcohol had lulled me closer to sleep, but depressed me at the same time. I increasingly wished I had never heard of the Bonfire Night Killer and his revolting activities. Maybe it *would* be better if the past stayed in the past. Realising I was thinking rubbish, I had turned my lamp off and buried myself under the covers. Thankfully sleep had come easily.

I turned up refreshed for work in the morning, pleased to have somehow avoided the row with Ellen, but as soon as I entered the office and saw Jeff's unhappy face, everything came hurtling back to me. I had no choice, now he wasn't officially working on the Bonfire Night killings, but to exclude Jeff from the daily morning meeting, and I also knew he would have to be excluded from the case completely. There was no other way. I was unsure whether to tell him before or after the latest briefing I was painstakingly preparing. But as a new bundle of paperwork from the forensics lab hit my desk, and with the meeting due in half an hour, the decision was made for me. I would take him for a beer at lunchtime and explain the dilemma with my fingers crossed behind my back in the hope that our friendship didn't deteriorate any further than it already had.

Instead of calling the team together as I normally would and holding the briefing at my desk, I strolled around the office, telling them to go to the office, the one that should have been mine. I was being a chicken, I suppose, but with Jeff's desk close to mine the idea of asking him to leave for half an hour so we could hold the meeting seemed callous, and I thought it the most diplomatic solution. Nevertheless, I could feel Jeff's eyes boring into my back as I followed the officers and detectives through.

The meeting was full of positives, which led to everybody feeling more hopeful about solving the case. The scientifically estimated distance between the killer and Fiona, based on the impact, injuries and gunshot residue, was just over six feet, which meant that the only clear, full footprint in the mud, which had been found at this distance, had probably been made by the killer. A cast had been taken of the print and we now had a shoe size, and the lab reported it probable that the print had been made by a Peter Storm Wellington boot, due to the distinguishable pattern on the sole. It was size fourteen, made by a man's boot, which made sense in Colefield as most of the male villagers marched around in wellies and sensible body warmers. If we could find the boot it would virtually solve the latest killing. I again thought of the muddied boots beside Paul's back door.

I asked Townsend and Reeves to the front to summarise the house visits they had completed the previous day. They had been asking simple questions at this stage, and requesting a voluntary DNA sample from the male adults, which most of the men had been happy to supply. There were just over ten households that hadn't answered the door and they intended to keep returning to these houses in case the occupants had been out.

Once the meeting had concluded I kept Reeves and Townsend behind as the room emptied and asked for a more in-depth report of the interview with Paul Mason. They glanced at each other, before Townsend related their thoughts. "Are you considering him as a suspect?"

I hung my head, drowning in betrayal. "Yes. Tell me what he said to you."

Reeves, a quiet, timid man, complimented Townsend's self-assuredness; they made an excellent team. He leafed through the notepad in his hand, knowing exactly which page he was looking for, and tapped the pen on the paper. "Paul Gareth Mason. Date of Birth: second of November, nineteen seventy-four, aged thirty-eight. Lives alone."

Dom Townsend stopped him, eyeing me curiously. "Jeff wasn't at the meeting and his surname is Mason. Is there something going on here we should know about?"

My shoulders sagged and I cursed under my breath, wondering if a white lie would be in order. Instead I returned Dom's stare directly. "This information is to be kept strictly confidential, and I mean that. If word gets out about this, you boys won't know what's hit you. Is that clear?" They nodded like puppies and I felt strangely powerful. "Paul is Jeff's estranged brother, and for that reason Jeff cannot be involved with the investigation. Because of the nature of the crime Jeff has asked me to keep his name out of the records as much as we can, which I've agreed to. Paul's father has recently died which could be a trigger, especially if he is aware of the atrocities we suspect Roland Mason may have been involved in."

Townsend took a deep breath, digesting the shocking news. "Whoa. Poor Jeff, that's shit stuff to deal with."

Reeve's agreement with the comment was like a gentle breeze after Townsend's tornado, and he swiftly returned to his notes when he noticed me staring at him. "Um, Paul Mason didn't object to a swab being taken. He said he didn't go out on Bonfire Night, said he doesn't like fireworks."

"Most of the men in the village said that." I didn't give credit to Dom's quip. The situation was too dire for me to have any humour.

"He said the noises made his head angry, which I thought was a strange thing to say."

I held my finger up, pausing the conversation while I found the next words and placed them in an acceptable order. "Of course, yes. I should point out there's a possibility Paul has some form of autism. I met him a couple of days ago and he was displaying some common signs. When you get the chance can you find out what surgery he's registered with, see if they'll answer that question without the kafuffle of getting a warrant? Also, he keeps his wellies outside by the back door, I want you to get them and send them to forensics to compare them to our footprint cast."

Reeves nodded and returned to the notes after scribbling his latest tasks a few pages ahead. "He said that normally Dot, who is apparently a neighbour…"

"Dot is Dorothy Webber, the old lady who's gone missing."

"Right. Well, he said that normally Dot would spend time with him – cooking, cleaning the dishes, clearing up – but she didn't come over that afternoon so he prepared his own tea and washed up afterwards. Then he went to bed after a few slugs of whisky."

I drummed my fingers on my chin as I thought the statement through. The story was suitable to the lonely man, but something felt missing. Between teatime and bedtime is a good few hours, and washing dishes for one doesn't take long. Supping a few whiskies? Yes, but not without something else to do, be it reading, watching television or a DVD. Even wasting time on the Internet or doing a hobby, but not drinking without any external stimulation. I had not seen a television in the front room, nor a computer. I told them as much and Townsend reminded me that they'd had no idea he was a suspect, so why would they have thought to take supplementary details? I asked them to return today and question him in more detail when they went to pick up the Wellington boots.

I followed the detectives from the office and noticed Jeff sitting at his desk, which was unusually tidy. His face was like thunder and I felt my guilty conscience rise again, a grey, disloyal bile. I swallowed hard, steadying myself for the inevitable confrontation that was brewing, and used my thumb to indicate the office I had just departed. I retraced my steps, this time with sagging shoulders.

This 'angry' Jeff was taking some getting used to, it was totally unfamiliar. He stomped through, slamming the door behind him, and his tirade lasted too long. It was impossible to get a word in edgeways to pacify him. I waited for him to finish and simply stated that I had no choice. Things were too close to home for him to remain on the case. "That's the bloody thing, Frank, I understand that. What I don't get is you having secret meetings. I'm unofficial on this case, but I can still help."

I knew I should calm him down, but something inside me snapped. I was fed up with tiptoeing around the case trying not to offend him. "Not any more, Jeff. I'm afraid you're officially – and unofficially – off the case as of now." I tapped my watch needlessly. "You have some holiday you can take; it's probably best you have a few days off."

I could see Jeff was struggling to find words for his defence; the shocked expression on his face was pitiful. Not only had I seen a new facet to his personality, but he had found one with mine. "I know my family is in the clear," he boomed, "and I will prove it with, or without, your help. I won't forget this, Frank, this isn't how friends treat each other."

I stood motionless as Jeff marched from office. He stopped by his desk to collect his briefcase and stormed away. His stunned colleagues, including myself, watched, dumbstruck.

One of the things Sue enjoyed most about being at home all day was having more time to experiment with cooking. She'd rarely had the chance to prepare a meal from scratch when she had worked full-time, so the fridge had always been stacked with convenience food. In contrast to preparing exotic dishes, experimenting with spices and herbs and experiencing unfamiliar tastes and textures, there was something peaceful and homely about having a baking day. The customary batch of sugar-free cakes, some low-fat scones for Jeff to take to work, granary bread and crispy wholemeal rolls. The simple preparation and hands-on involvement never failed to leave her tranquil and contented. And her mood reflected on the baby, who happily sat in his recliner and gurgled. When Jeff let himself through the back door, tired and downtrodden, Sue wiped her floury hands on her apron and hugged him. "I wasn't expecting you so early. What's up, you look dreadful?"

Jeff, still reeling from the argument at the office, realised that the time had come to explain what was going on to his wife. Until now there had been nothing to tell her, but he needed to explain his suspension somehow and he favoured the truth every time. He filled the kettle and dropped a couple of teabags into waiting mugs. "I've got something to tell you and you're not going to like it. Finish up what you're doing and come and have a tea with me."

Worry clouded Sue's face as she fed the final baking tray into the oven and set the timer, before scraping the used flour from the worktop and dropping it into the bin. She sat at the table just as Jeff brought the two hot mugs over and set them down. He dragged out a chair and sagged onto it, chin in hands, despondent. "My brother and late-father are being investigated for possible murder. I acted out and got myself suspended." Her mouth hung open in disbelief. "Frank asked me to use up my holiday."

Sue gasped. "Our Frank? Frank Butler? Frank Butler suspended *you*?"

He raised an eyebrow, with a mirthless, sardonic smile. "I know. He's supposed to be a fucking friend."

"Jeff," she tapped his hand, indignant. "Not in front of the baby. Now, what's this about murder?"

He related the old and new killings, the proximity to Paul's house, the notes in the margins of his father's books. The suggestion that Roland's death had triggered a murderous streak in Paul. An hour later, after two strong teas and nearly all the hot cheese scones, each spread with low-fat margarine and sprinkled with ground black pepper, Jeff was sure he had covered everything. He dusted his hands over the plate, swallowing the last delicious mouthful, and dropped the bomb he thought would be met with absolute objection. "I want to go and stay with Paul for a couple of days."

He let the sentence hang without elaboration and she didn't fill the lengthy gap, instead busying herself by clearing the table and rinsing the plates ready to wash. She kept her head down, avoiding eye contact, as if she'd not heard him. But she had, and he knew it. Eventually he continued. "I think he needs me there while the police are visiting, that's one reason." He hesitated. What he was about to tell his wife had to be kept a total secret, because if word got out it was possible he would be kicked off the force. He was certain she was trustworthy. Perhaps? He grasped the moment, no longer having anything to lose. "While the team were in a meeting I photocopied everything I think is necessarily relevant to the original murders, and what I could find on the latest killing." Sue gasped again and he spoke quickly to avoid her interrupting. "I want to keep working on the case without Frank knowing. Please, Sue, don't ruin this for me."

Slowly she stopped the mindless housework and shuddered with the weight of the admission. Bouncing each word against the next, thinking about the potential consequences, she tried to make sense of the serious situation that threatened to send her perfect life into turmoil. The moments ticked by and when Jacob, now snoozing in his bouncer, began snuffling, she had never been more grateful to hear him wake up. She spoke succinctly. "Go and stay with Paul if you have to. I'll be fine with Jacob."

"Really? What about the... the, er..."

"I'm going to have to imagine you never said a word. This is all too much to take in. I don't want to know anything else, just keep me out of it."

Knowing there was nothing he could say to appease her, Jeff quickly gathered some clothes and essential items together. He kissed his wife and son and set off towards the ominous Colefield again. Clearing the family name wasn't the only priority;

he hoped helping with the disastrous mess would bring him closer to his brother. And father.

Jeff arrived in the village with shoulders tense and stressed. He'd spent the past mile following an achingly slow refuse lorry and was impatiently eager to reach his destination. As he drove past Paul's house towards the dirt track that led to the back of the house, he noticed Townsend's car parked on the roadside, and realising they were still completing house calls irked him irrationally. However, he knew they had visited Paul the previous day, so had no qualms about letting himself through the back door when his knock went unanswered. Paul wasn't in the kitchen, but when Jeff entered the front room and heard his brother in the hall talking, he realised they were questioning him again. His uncommon anger resurged and it took all his strength not to go and give his colleagues a piece of his mind. He reached over the armchair for Paul's bottle and took a calming swig, replacing it swiftly with a mental note to buy some more alcohol for the evening.

From the snippets of conversation Jeff was able to hear, it was obvious that Dom and Alan had no intention of leaving any time soon, and that Paul had no intention of either letting them into the warm house, or answering their questions coherently. He paused, he complained, he whined, all in equal measure. Jeff's thoughts inadvertently turned to me and he contemplated our four years of friendship. Ex-friendship. He believed I was treating him unfairly, that he was completely able to cast an impartial eye over the case, regardless of the truth awaiting discovery. He reasoned that he was unlikely to forgive this turn of face and questioned any form of trust on a higher level than before. He was thirty-six; how many more times did he have to waste his belief in someone, only to have it thrown back in his face? By the time he heard the unwelcome visitors end the questioning, he had wound himself into a foul mood, and he smiled listlessly at the thought of Paul's expression when he entered the room and found him sitting there. But Paul barely noticed, his mind absorbed by the thousands of questions that had just been barked at him. Jeff needlessly helped his brother to his armchair. Grasping the frightened man's arm, he explained,

"It's okay, Paul, I've come to stay with you. A few days, maybe. We can get all this nasty business out of the way without you being hurt. What did they ask you?"

Relaxing slightly, Paul sagged onto the armchair after busily stoking the fire and throwing on another scuttle of coal. "They think I killed that girl, and they think that I hurt Dot. Where is Dot? I don't like cooking my tea. It doesn't taste so good as when Dot does it."

"I'll make sure you eat, Paul. In fact, why don't I show you how to cook while I'm here? I could show you curry and chilli, spaghetti Bolognese, all sorts. What do you reckon?" It was the second time in one day that his words had gone unheeded, so he gave up and changed the subject. "Do you have the letter from Doro – Dot? The one that told you she was staying with her son."

Paul felt his pockets and shook his head, worried. "I think your friend took it. I couldn't find it in my pocket when they asked me at the door."

"Damn." Jeff paused, preparing to phrase his interrogation in a way that wouldn't panic his brother. He reached between the armchairs and laid a gentle hand on Paul's forearm. "Paul, I need you to understand that I'm here to help you. I have been asked to take a break from my job because I'm related to you, and I'm going to spend that time with you. I know that you haven't told me everything, but you are a suspect, and so is dad. I don't believe that's the truth, but unless you tell me everything you know, I can't help you."

Without hesitation, Paul hoisted the bottle of whisky to his lips and sank a good few gulps before grimacing his reply through gritted teeth, his mouth twisted with the sharp bitterness. "I would never hurt Dot. And I would never hurt that girl. I only ever shoot rabbits and birds."

Jeff reasoned that Paul had been given enough to deal with for the moment. Eager to leave the house, secure himself some alcohol for the evening, he suggested they drove to the nearby town of Westerton to buy the ingredients for cottage pie, to which Paul readily agreed. They hastily shrugged on their winter coats – Jeff's a nearly-new thermal-layered jacket, and Paul's a beaten anorak that reeked of stale sweat – and made their way across the garden to Jeff's car.

At the shop, along with the mince, vegetables and onions, Jeff bought an exercise book and pen for Paul to write down the recipe and instructions for preparing basic meals, aware it was necessary that he learn to cook confidently on his own now. It was highly unlikely that Dorothy would be coming back.

I watched the two detectives stroll up to my heavily stacked desk. "Go on, anything?"

"Well, we've just interviewed Paul Mason again like you asked us to. He said that Dorothy Webber was due to visit him on Tuesday morning to pick up a package from her son. He told us that she didn't turn up, and that he received a note from her stating that she had gone to stay with her son, but he couldn't produce the letter." Reeves was reading from the notes he had taken.

I felt a stab of guilt when I remembered the note that remained screwed up in my jacket pocket, I should have sent it to the forensics lab immediately, yet I'd forgotten once again. I wavered over the embarrassment before meekly producing it for my colleagues. "He did receive it, it's here, but I don't believe it's Dorothy's handwriting. I think whoever wrote it was the person who is responsible for her disappearance that night, and I strongly believe this is linked to Fiona Malik's murder in some way, so…" I passed the note to Reeves who, furnishing me with a withering stare at my lack of adherence to protocol when storing a possibly vital piece of evidence, immediately dropped it into a plastic bag. Sheepish, my orders became less forceful. "Can you send that for testing. Please. I'd also like you to instruct the Scunthorpe boys that we will now be in charge of the investigation into Dorothy's whereabouts, alongside our search for Fiona's killer."

The phone rang on my desk. I answered, listened briefly, and replaced the receiver with a heavy sigh. "Paul's wellies were a match to the footprint found at the crime scene, and specks of Dorothy's blood were found on the right boot." The news was good, but I still felt like a traitor, and that reflected in my tone. "I think we have our man. Get a report ready as quickly as you can, we should be able to arrest him soon." Okay, I was a turncoat. I was betraying my friend. But this was my job and I was a professional. It had to be done.

"Soon? Why not now?" I could imagine Dom stamping his feet in temper, but thankfully he didn't. "His boots place him at the scene of the murder and he had a key for Dorothy's house in his possession. There's no alibi, nobody to vouch for…"

I held my hand in the air, halting him. "I have a friendship to protect." I winced; had I really just considered myself a professional? "Look, I have to be one hundred percent certain.

"How much more…"

"Just do as I bloody well say."

Dorothy was in agony, it felt as if every bone in her body was in smithereens and that her organs had been liquidised. As she slowly opened her weary eyes she could see a thin stream of daylight, but had no idea where she was, and she had little memory as to how she'd arrived at wherever she was, either. She sensed she had been unconscious, and for a while. Unable to move she lay stilled, her head pounding. Nearby she could hear movement, but every attempt to speak, to raise the alarm, was futile; her dry throat wouldn't emit a single sound. Her fingers moved tentatively, trying to work out where she lay, but on one side all she could feel was solid lumps, on the other everything was slimy, a sickening texture. The vile odour that engulfed her, trickling through her nostrils, through the pores of her skin, was gut-wrenching. Distant voices – men's voices – sounded every now and then, but she had no way of gaining attention in her putrid grave. Instinctively she knew it was imperative to stay awake.

Dorothy watched as the shaft of daylight that hazily reached her face receded until it turned grey, then black, and the voices could no longer be heard. The unceasing agony told her she was badly injured, and she had a vague recollection of a man, a silhouette, creeping up in the darkness, immediately followed by a sudden, extreme pain in her head. The brief memory disappeared as quickly as it had come, leaving her frustrated. She wanted to get out of whatever hole she was in, but every time she moved it seemed to upset whatever she was lying on, a domino effect that had rancid matter falling beside her, over her, everywhere around her. Forcing herself to stay conscious – sleep would be so easy – she listened to the scurrying noises around her as the night settled to a deep, freezing blackness. Dorothy reasoned that if she could have some water she may be able to find enough strength to move, but the nights had been clear recently and there were no signs of impending rain. She lay, stilled, her hazy mind trying to find recollections and concentrate on them, rather than fall into the tempting slumber that beckoned so welcomingly.

Paul and Jeff had spent a surprisingly pleasant day together, with Jeff showing his brother the basics of how to cook a rudimentary meal. With the kitchen cleaned and their tummies fit to burst with the delicious dinner, they finally sat, Paul in his armchair supping his preferred budget whisky, and Jeff in their father's with a bottle of Three Barrels. It was a cheaper brandy than he would normally buy, but he'd conceded that the point of drinking on this particular evening was to get drunk, not to savour the taste. Picking up threads from their previous conversations they continued to relate memories to each other, trying, step by step, to rid over thirty years of separation in an attempt to establish a sound relationship. Both parties wanted this desperately, each at the helm of an empire, albeit an unimpressive one.

Despite the emotional aspect of being in Colefield, Jeff was also still, as far as he was concerned, working on the Bonfire Night Killer's case. He hadn't told Paul his plans, reluctant to distress him by mentioning the killings. Having not been hands-on with the public side of the investigation, the only familiar names, apart from his father and Paul, were Dot and Bert. He had read a little about Fiona Malik, but didn't think for a second that Paul was capable of murder, and he was certain the police would realise that before the investigation went too far. He knew his brother disliked Bert Rock, but he asked after him anyway.

"I haven't seen him for a few days. Last time was when the fireworks were banging and he scared me with a gun."

Jeff sat up straight, alert now. The statement was totally unexpected. "What? A gun?" He breathed deeply, calming himself. "Paul, can you tell me exactly what happened."

Paul shrugged, sipping from the bottle before answering. "I don't know. He said he thought I was blackmailing him, but then said it was Dot. Not me. I thought he was going to shoot me, but he didn't."

Jeff had sobered up immediately. "Do you know anything about Dot blackmailing him?" Jeff shifted forward to the edge of the seat, leaning towards his brother, eager.

"No." Paul was tired, both from the whisky and the excessive questioning of the day, and his answer was a childlike whine. He raised the bottle to his lips and Jeff was surprised that over half the contents had gone. He had only bought it for his brother that afternoon, and that was on top of the six-pack of beers they had shared. He realised he needed to keep an eye on how much Paul was drinking, along with everything else.

"Okay. Look, we can go to bed in a minute, sleep off the booze, but before you go, just let me know a few more details. It'll give me something to think about overnight."

Paul sighed deeply, irritated, and answered huffily. "I'd cleared up the kitchen and I was putting a bag of rubbish out. I tripped though because there was something on the step. I picked it up, then suddenly Bert was there. He had a gun in his hand and he asked me something. I don't know what it was. Then he came inside and he was angry because of Dot. He didn't want to shoot me anymore because he was angry at her instead."

"Why did he think you were blackmailing him?"

Paul shook his head in an attempt to shake away the unwanted questions, and his voice was an irritated moan. "I don't know. He said something about two pairs of dirty socks in an envelope."

Jeff choked on his drink, stopping himself from laughing at the mental image that popped into his head. If there hadn't been a gun involved, this would be a ridiculous farce. "You what?"

He sighed, bored. "That thing I tripped over outside. It was the package Dot was expecting that her son was dropping off. I'd forgotten about it. I picked it up and brought it in. Bert said it was full of socks. I didn't know why Dot would want used socks, but I guess she knew what she was doing."

"Do you still have it? The package."

"No, I think Bert took it with him. He was angry with Dot. I don't know why."

Jeff was concerned that the unofficial grilling was getting too much for his brother. He suggested they say goodnight and Paul heartily agreed, yawning to confirm the point. Jeff was finally about to get the chance to see what was inside the envelope his father had left for Paul, but he would have to wait until he heard his brother snoring before he sneaked to the safe in his father's room. Paul lumbered up the stairs and soon Jeff heard the chain flush, the bathroom door unlock, and the bedroom door close. He waited ten minutes before creeping stealthily to the kitchen and placing the kettle on the hob. As silently as possible, he collected the letter and reached the ground floor just in time to stop the boiling water triggering the whistle. He unhooked it and returned the kettle to the heat, steaming the glue on the envelope over the spout until the flap loosened. Carefully he took the letter out and read the message, which was written in capital letters:

'PAUL, NOW YOU KNOW THE TRUTH. GET BERT BEHIND BARS WHERE HE BELONGS. FORGIVE ME FOR WHAT HAPPENED TO YOUR MOTHER. LOVE, DAD.'

It sounded ominously like Roland had left some kind of confession to Paul. Jeff thought back to when they had seen the envelope in the safe. Paul had told him that he wasn't to read the letter until he'd read something else. He had said at the time it was Roland's books, but that hadn't sounded true at the time and definitely didn't now, and Jeff reasoned he must have left a letter, or document of explanation about something, in a bid to free his conscience before dying. It would be in the house somewhere, but how would he find it with Paul constantly there?

Jeff copied the words into a notebook taken from his overnight bag. He resealed the envelope and tucked it into his jacket, intending to return it to the safe the next day. Tonight he was too tired.

Chapter 11
Friday 9th November

One of the civilians who works for our team, Kaye, had been searching the national firearms register and found that forty-four of the seventy-six adult males in the village of Colefield had Section 1 firearms certificates, of which one also had Section 2, which enabled him to use his modified Beretta long-barrelled shotgun. No women in the area held a licence. She printed the names and addresses of the men, and further reduced it by removing the twelve men who had solid alibis for the previous Monday from the list: three had been away on business, two on holiday and the other seven had been verified as working the night shift at their places of work.

Kaye brought the findings to me and I called Townsend and Reeves across. I briefed them, handing the list over. "I'm surprised to see there are no firearms licences for Paul or Roland Mason, so if they have any weapons, they're owned illegally. If you take this list back to Colefield, ask to see each man's firearms certificate. And the guy with the Section 2 certificate, get his membership number for whichever target or gun club he uses. I also want you to see where they keep their weapons, and that bit is important." I paused for questions but none came, so I continued. "First, you can see that their guns are securely locked away as the law states, and secondly you'll be able to see all of their weapons, not just the ones they want to show you."

They agreed and prepared to leave, gathering their necessary items together, and I kept Kaye back with me. "As I just said, Paul Mason wasn't on the list, can you check again? And also check Roland Mason. His might have been cancelled after his death, so look back a couple of months." I put the back of my hand to my forehead as I dredged my memory for the questions I knew were in there, somewhere. "In fact, I want you to find out everything you can about both of them. Both Roland and Paul Mason, and I mean everything, public records, you name it. I'm so close to arresting Paul, just one small detail may be enough."

Kaye went back to her desk and I debated phoning Jeff. Our falling-out had left me deeply uncomfortable, I felt dreadful after the events of yesterday and was desperately hoping there wasn't going to be any permanent damage to our friendship. But as I hesitated, my hand hovering over the phone, another email labelled 'URGENT' from the forensics lab popped into my inbox and distracted me. I skimmed through to the end, and then read it more thoroughly. The results were as I had expected, but not wanted. All three of the semen swabs had degenerated completely, so there was nothing forensically to link the old killer to the new. We would need a confession and I knew how unlikely that was.

The phone rang on my desk. I scooped it up nonchalantly, still studying the report on the screen, but soon I was sitting erect. I soaked in the details the caller was giving, and once she had finished, I dropped the phone and shrugged on my trench coat as I ran to the door. I charged down the stairs, into the car park, and climbed swiftly into my car, easing it into the less congested late morning traffic. The drive took just under an hour and I hastily made my way to the bed in the intensive care ward at Scunthorpe Hospital.

I caught my breath when I saw the severely bruised lady in the bed, her face contorted and swollen. She was barely alive. Her breathing was assisted by a ventilator, eyes closed in her unconsciousness, and every exposed part of her body was battered, with black-blue-green-yellow bruises covering her pallid skin. Her feet and hands were swathed in bandages. There was nothing she could help me with in the state she was in. I left the room and found a nurse, showing my badge and introducing myself. "Can I speak to a doctor about the circumstances that led to Dorothy Webber being here?"

She shrugged. "You can ask me. I know a fair bit."

I thanked her and she sat, indicating a seat across the nurses' station for me. I remained standing. "When was she brought in?"

"She came up to the ward at about ten this morning. Even though A and E have worked hard on her, her condition remains critical. She was found by some bloke who works at the landfill site near Colefield, do you know it? Anyway, rumour has it she was put in a bin and the dustcart took her away."

"You're kidding, right?" I felt nauseous just thinking about it.

"No, apparently that's what the bloke told the ambulance men. He said the area she was found in is where the lorries dump household waste."

I could feel bile threatening from my lurching stomach and I swallowed hard. "Don't they compress the waste in those things? You know, like squash it all together." I couldn't remove the horrified mask from my face however hard I tried.

She shrugged again, apparently unconcerned. "We're guessing that's why she's so black and blue. We suspect she has multiple bone breakages, at least one collapsed lung, and her interior organs are threatening to shut down. She's had one cardiac arrest since she's been here and we believe she has internal bleeding. We're waiting for an operating theatre to become free before we take her to have a look inside."

I stroked the grey stubble on my face, wishing I had been less lazy that morning and had a shave, while I thought the scenario through in my head. If somebody had put her in a bin, she wouldn't just have waited for the refuse lorry to collect it without making a fuss. She must have been incapacitated in some way when she was put inside, whether by physical restraint or unconsciousness. "Were her legs or arms tied when she was found?"

"Not that I know of."

"Has she been awake at all, you know, said anything, maybe?"

"No, she's not woken since she's been here. Oh, it's irrelevant but there seems to be a nasty ulcer on her hip. It's nothing to worry about, they're common in the elderly, and to be honest, it's the last thing we're concerned about at the moment. She's in a critical condition. Oh, and also, unfortunately, after spending a night on the landfill site, four of her toes and seven fingers have been gnawed to the stubs by wild animals. You know, foxes, rats, that kind of thing. Apart from that, the only other injuries appear to be from her ride in the dustcart."

"Which is most of them." I didn't like the nurse. She didn't care about that poor woman in the slightest. Was I being a hypocrite though? Did I *care* about Dorothy?

I hung my head, forcing my thoughts to the apparently harmless old woman who loved to take care of people. I couldn't help it: my mind drifted once more to Jeff's possibly murderous brother and late father. "Will she pull through?"

She shook her head, frowning. "Highly unlikely, I'd say, but don't quote me on it."

I arranged for a local officer to sit with Dorothy once she'd had her operation, giving strict orders to contact me immediately if and when she regained consciousness, and headed back towards Hull. I passed a sign for Colefield and, without reason, took the turn, soon finding myself near to Paul Mason's house. I hadn't planned the detour, and as I pulled into the dirt track that led to his back garden, I had no idea what I was going to say. I was stunned to see Jeff's silver Vectra parked up; I'd not even considered him being there.

I strode through the dew-damp brown grass and knocked abruptly on the back door, but there was no answer. Again, I rapped, but there was still no reply. I wandered along the alley to the front of the house, this time tapping on the main door. After trying several times, I had to accept that either they weren't in, or were ignoring visitors. I returned to my car. Luckily I had some crisps, a pre-packaged chicken salad sandwich, and a bottle of water that I had picked up that morning from the garage, so I satisfied my hunger and thirst while I watched the house.

Jeff and Paul had been standing outside Bert's house for a while, freezing in the crisp November air, and finally Bert answered, his hair mussed and a dressing gown draped over his vest and pyjama trousers. Slippers warmed his feet. "You bloody woke me up. What do you want?"

Jeff barged in, rudely shoving Bert aside, and Paul shrank away, scared by the hostility. "I want to know what you were doing, turning up at my brother's house late at night with a gun." He beckoned Paul who tentatively stepped inside, and Jeff closed the door behind him before pushing Bert through to his lounge and onto the sofa. Jeff was dominating the room, and worry was etched on the other men's faces. "Well?"

Jeff was a detective, trained to spot a lie, especially an elaborate one, which is what Bert would need to cover up this story. He tried to get up, but Jeff shoved him into the seat again. "I was just going to show you the notes I got, then you'll understand properly."

Huffing, Jeff stepped aside and Bert hobbled to an ornate walnut bureau, pulling the flap down and rooting through some papers. Jeff had already been surprised at the clean, dust-free tidiness of the room, and the neat organisation of the inside of the bureau was equally intriguing. Jeff decided he would closely study the man's body language as there was a remote possibility he had an obsessive-compulsive disorder, which didn't fit with his outward scruffiness. It would tell him a lot about the man.

Bert brought the notes he had received to Jeff and presented them to him with a flourish. "I got the first one after Roly died, and because Roly and I haven't always been good boys, I thought Paul had found something Roly might not have wanted him to see. Then, when I got the next one a few days later asking for the payment to be dropped off, I wanted to scare him, so I took my rifle. It wasn't loaded."

"Rifle? Paul, you said it was a shotgun."

Paul, relaxed now, nodded his head with vigour. "It wasn't a big gun. It was a little one."

Jeff stared at Bert, who avoided the intensity. "Do you care to elaborate?"

"He must have been scared so he got mistaken. I only have a rifle. I can show you my licence if you want. All us old-timers hunt in Colefield, it's tradition."

Jeff strolled to the window for more light and scanned the glued letters that formed the words on the notes closely, his experienced eye looking for clues in both the content and layout. "This is definitely prepared by a novice. Anybody could make one of these. We've all got skeletons in our closets and there's nothing specific at all. It could even be from excitable children. Have you any idea who it was from?"

Bert glanced at Paul and shook his head. "No, I don't. No idea at all."

Jeff knew from what Paul had told him about the late-night altercation in the kitchen that Bert was fibbing, he had implicated Dorothy and now she was missing. "What have you done to Dorothy Webber?"

He was angry and frustrated. "Nothing, that's what. I've explained why I turned up at Paul's the other night, just as you asked, so now you can bugger off and leave me alone."

Paul found the denial too uncomfortable to accept and he interrupted the spat. "But you were angry at Dot. You said it was her, not me. You were going to give her those dirty socks you told me about."

"Yes, I was angry with Dorothy, but I didn't shoot her. If she's disappeared, it's nothing to do with me."

Jeff had never considered that Dorothy may have been shot, and as far as he was aware, the newspapers hadn't implicated such a weapon. Why would Bert assume something like that? In fact, why would he even assume she was hurt? He knew more than he was letting on, but Jeff had no jurisdiction to press any further due to his enforced 'holiday'. He could let his boss know, but he and Frank weren't seeing eye-to-eye and his stubborn streak had kicked in. "I never said she'd been shot."

Bert fidgeted, mouth opening and closing silently, and he shifted from one foot to the other. It was obvious he was involved somehow, and now the enigmatic note his father had written for Paul, the comment that Bert should be behind bars, made more sense. In all probability Roland had left something for Paul that incriminated the man before him, and he wanted to see it. Jeff had no idea if Bert's DNA had been taken when the police were doing house-to-house calls, and to ask the question would raise a warning flag with the short, chubby man. He knew he should call his boss. Not doing so would be irresponsible, but if he did, Frank would know he was interfering with their investigation.

Jeff caught Bert's furious stare and smiled lightly. "I'm watching you." He dragged Paul away, slamming the door behind them.

I watched through the windscreen as Paul and Jeff came along the side alley that led to the garden from the front of the house. Jeff spotted my car immediately and stomped towards me, eyes flashing, and snarling. Paul let himself into the house, disinterested. I wound the window down as Jeff approached and he leant through. "What are you doing here?"

"To be honest with you, I don't know. I was on my way back from the hospital when I decided to come and see Paul."

"Why do you want to see Paul?"

Jeff's temper was fraying too easily recently, and a surge of irritation ran along my spine. "Official police business," I spat childishly.

Jeff's hands rested on his hips, cocky. "I didn't think you'd be wanting to sell him bloody fairy cakes, for god's sake. Let's get this straight, shall we. You have no official business. You suspect him and you're fishing for clues, and that's taking advantage of his mental incapacity. If you have something solid, you can take him to the station, but if not, sod off and leave us alone."

Jeff marched away, slamming the picket gate behind him, and then the back door. I sat, flummoxed. Never in a million years did I believe I'd be on the receiving end of Jeff Mason's rare temper. My blood simmered with embarrassment, leaving me as furious as he had been. I wasn't going to tolerate that. Not from him. I left my car and strode purposefully to the door and, without knocking, let myself in. They both gawped at me. "I want to search your father's room."

"You can't just burst in like that. You're either invited in or you get a warrant."

I'd had enough. Of his anger, of his ridiculous family loyalty to a man he barely knew. Of his rudeness. At this moment I hated him. I could feel the air supping deeply into my lungs and, shocking me as much as Jeff and Paul, it flew out in a bellowed gust. "Let me search the fucking room."

Jeff was as irate as me and he yelled back. "Get a fucking warrant. You know as well as I do that you won't be granted one because you have nothing to go on."

"I have the notes in the books on your father…"

"You have a dead woman, killed after my father died, shot using the same gun that killed three other women over thirty years ago."

"And I think that woman was murdered by Paul." Silence rang around the kitchen, the dreaded words having been spoken at last. Paul was shivering in the corner, trying to render himself invisible, and Jeff was wordlessly seething. I knew I had overstepped the mark, taken advantage of our friendship and allowed emotions to flood the argument. It wasn't a police role I'd just played, but a child's game of 'I want, and won't accept no for an answer'. I was ashamed of my behaviour. However, if I backed down now, I would lose my credibility as a detective and superior. But if I didn't, my friendship with Jeff – and the respect he had for me – would be gone. How many times had I told myself to go with my gut feeling? On the flipside, how many times had I had to caution myself for being too hot headed and impatient?

I felt like a bleating sheep as I tried to justify myself. "The soles of Paul's Wellington boots match a footprint found at the crime scene, and he has no evidence, or witnesses, to prove he was at home on Monday evening." I wasn't shouting any more, I wasn't proud of this. Neither Paul, nor Jeff, spoke. I crossed the small kitchen slowly, my decision made. "I'm arresting you, Paul Mason, on suspicion of withholding knowledge from a murder investigation. You do not have to say anything, but it may harm…" Jeff grabbed my arm, tugging at me for attention as I handcuffed Paul's wrist to mine, and I ignored him, proceeding with the caution.

"What are you doing, Frank? This is crazy. You've got nothing on him and you know it. For god's sake, he couldn't kill anybody."

I knew that I would never be more to Jeff than pond life from this moment on, and that was a cross I had to bear. For the sake of the victims. For Dorothy and her poor battered body. For justice. After I'd finished stating his rights, I radioed for assistance to bring Paul in for questioning. While we waited for another police car to arrive, Jeff stayed in the front room, shutting the door for privacy, and I could hear him speaking on the phone. I guessed he would be finding a lawyer, and knew he'd have me rapped for wrongful arrest if I didn't pin something watertight on the massive brute handcuffed to my arm.

I felt like a lemon standing around, waiting for the patrol car to arrive. To relieve both the boredom and discomfort, I slowly scanned Paul's tatty attire. His clothes, all old and faded, were long overdue for a wash. They were un-ironed, frayed at the seams and hems, and I choked on the stench of stale body odour when I got too close. His hefty, strong-jawed face was anything but handsome and his eyes were dull pools of black with an evil nothingness about them. I was grateful that Paul didn't put up a struggle as we waited for what seemed like eternity because, although I was expertly trained in self-defence, his sheer size was a worry.

Jeff was calmer when he returned to the room. "I assume he's going to Scunthorpe for questioning, so I've arranged for a solicitor to meet us there."

I debated taking him to Hull just to be spiteful and, again, berated myself for the ridiculous childishness. I had been worried that Jeff was taking this case to heart too much, yet here I was, behaving like a toddler. I deeply wished I had never gone to work that morning. And that I'd had a shave.

Bert was washing the few dishes he had used at the breakfast table that morning, and had watched a police car pull up a few minutes earlier in front of Paul's house. He had remained by the sink purely to see what was about to happen, if anything. Half of him expected them to hammer at his bungalow to follow up Jeff's line of inquiry, yet the other half knew that Paul was a suspect. He took a tea towel and slowly dried a cup, polishing the rim as he kept an eye on Paul's front garden. Presently a uniformed officer, handcuffed to Paul, led the way along the path to the car. Bert was astonished, relieved, and full of mirth. From the earlier altercation, he'd been concerned that Jeff had found something on him, but now it appeared he had been setting his brother up for arrest. Nasty thing to do, Bert chuckled to himself, as he compared the man to his mother, Jeannie. She had been sly and conniving herself when she had shown her true colours. Silly bitch.

As the patrol car drove past his bungalow he moved the net curtain in the kitchen aside enough for Paul, sadly gazing through the back window, to see he was being watched, and he grinned crudely, the black hole where a tooth had once been amplifying the foul, amused grimace on his face.

He returned to the housework and had almost finished drying and putting the crockery away, when there was a knock at the door. Dom Townsend and Alan Reeves explained that they were routinely checking the gun licences held by residents of Colefield, following the murder of a young woman the previous Monday. Without hesitation, Bert showed them to his immaculate living room and opened the bureau for the second time that day, producing his Section 1 licence easily from the organised paperwork.

Dom scanned the details and asked to see where his weapons were kept. Bert, smiling gently, led them to his bedroom. In one corner of the impeccably clean room was a single bed, and a few small items of dated, yet handsome bedroom furniture fronted the walls. Bert opened the sliding door of a built-in wardrobe and indicated a steel gun cabinet, tightly fixed to the wall and locked securely. "What weapons are in there?"

"I've only got the one, sir. A Remington SF 22-250 rifle. I use it on the hunts."

"Could you unlock the cabinet and show us, please." Reeves spoke for the first time.

Bert nodded agreeably. He pulled a key from the bedside drawer and opened the cabinet to display the gleaming, beautifully kept rifle. "Lovely, isn't she?"

"What do you use it for?"

"I told you, the hunts, and occasionally I'll use it on a rat in the back garden; we get a lot of them from the farm and the landfill site in the summer and autumn, sometimes even as early as springtime. You don't want them, they're thieving, destroying little bastards and a bullet's quicker than poison." Alan thanked him politely and was about to follow Dom from the bedroom when Bert stopped him, his hand on his jacket. "Why are you still doing the rounds, anyway? You lot have just arrested Paul Mason."

Reeves glanced over his shoulder, questioning, and Dom shrugged, irked that he had not been notified. Alan thanked Bert again and followed his colleague from the house.

I sat at the desk that had been hastily allocated to me at the Scunthorpe station, while waiting for Paul to be booked-in, his personal details and those of the charge documented. He would be taken to an interview room and an officer would let me know he was ready. I used the time to call Reeves, asking him to arrange forensic processing of Dorothy's dustbin – and Paul's – to see if there was any evidence to show that her body had been squeezed inside. I also asked them to arrange a warrant to search Paul's house.

I put the receiver down and a nanosecond later it rang again, this time with an irate Dom on the line. "Reeves was too shy to say anything, but I'm bloody not. Do you want us to keep up our house-to-house or are we wasting our time? Did it ever occur to you to tell us what was going on? We've just been totally humiliated because we weren't kept in the loop."

I felt like pining for Jeff, pitifully begging him to come back. He would never talk to me so abruptly; it wasn't his way. I choked slightly as 'the angry Jeff' resurfaced and suddenly I couldn't be bothered with office politics any more. Sod Domineering Dom and his bloody arrogance. "Sorry." I left it at that and replaced the phone.

I reached for my machine-made coffee, tepid dishwater in a plastic cup, but before I could take a sip my mobile announced an incoming call. I was tempted to ignore it, but noticed it was from a landline and picked up. It was the hospital and they were letting me know that Dorothy had died on the operating table. It was a shame, but having seen her injuries, I truly believed she was in a better place than had she survived, with the disabilities and daily agony they would have caused. And I had an opening line for the interview now.

I rose from the desk when the thumbs-up came from the desk sergeant and made my way to the allotted interview room. Jeff stood outside. "You know we'll be throwing the book at you, don't you?"

I stopped, pained at the good friendship gone bad. "How many times over the past four years have you agreed when I've suggested trusting your gut instinct? You're too close to this to be impartial." My words were quietly spoken, my demeanour withdrawn.

I was surprised by his equally reticent reply. "The one you want is Bert. That's not just my gut, it's informed. Search his place and you'll find the gun that he used to threaten my brother with on Monday night. And I have no doubt that it'll be the same one that killed all four women."

Jeff had instructed a well-known – locally, anyway – criminal lawyer, Benjamin Roberts, to act on Paul's behalf, and with his greater knowledge of the case than a regular relative, Jeff had imparted everything he knew, including the show-down at Bert Rock's house that morning. He stated that he had no reason professionally, or personally, to suspect his brother of any misdemeanour.

I was sitting opposite Paul and his brief, a graffiti covered, well-etched wooden desk between us, and we were ten minutes into the interview. I directed my next question to Benjamin Roberts. "You do know that Paul's Wellington boots match a footprint found at the crime scene?"

"Yes. My client's brother informed me."

Paul became agitated, his eyes imploring his solicitor. "But I don't get that. My boots are on my feet and nobody's looked at them, so how can they match anything?"

Instinctively we all glanced under the table. It would have been a funny sketch on the television, but today, here in the dingy room, there was nothing comedic at all. "Paul, we'll have taken your other pair. The ones you keep outside by the back door."

"These are my only pair of wellies. And I don't keep them outside. The spiders get inside and I don't like that."

I coughed slightly, biding my time, and returned my queries to Benjamin. "You also realise that the key to another woman's house – a woman who died of her terrible injuries today, having gone missing on the same night as Fiona Malik – was found in Paul's possession?"

Benjamin nodded and was about to speak when a small, pained voice interrupted. "Dot? Is Dot dead?" I nodded and Paul's shoulders began to heave as he tried to catch his breath.

Benjamin leant forward, the stench of stale tobacco swirling into my mouth and nose as I breathed his exhaled breath. "I think you'll agree that Paul's distraught reaction is an excellent indication of his innocence, don't you?"

I discreetly leant back to avoid inhaling any more rancid air and crossed my arms. "Or an indication of his impressive acting skills." It was bravado on my part; he had a valid point.

Jeff waited outside the room for a while, before being informed by Mr Roberts that the police would be holding Paul in a cell overnight while they searched his house. Jeff wasted no time in returning to his car and driving the few miles back to Colefield. Luckily Paul had given him his father's key when he had informed him of his intention to stay a few days, and he let himself in, locking the door securely behind him. It wouldn't take long in a case like this for a search warrant to be issued and he wanted to scour the place first. He was past caring if it would get him into trouble.

He went to his father's room first, his stomach churning again at the mounds of junk covering the majority of the worn carpet, and he searched as quickly and thoroughly as possible. Remembering the safe in the wardrobe, he was pleased he had forgotten to return the letter addressed to Paul; that would really stir things up, even if it did point the finger of suspicion at Bert Rock. Failing to find anything suspicious, he moved on to the second bedroom.

Paul's room was equally messy; it couldn't have been cleaned for years. Piles of unwashed clothing contributed to the body odour that hung in the stuffy room like a cloud, and the thick dust stifled Jeff's breathing. For a few frenzied minutes he opened drawers and cupboards, finding nothing, until, upon lifting the mattress, he saw an opened envelope with his father's handwriting on the front. A determined hammering sounded from the front door and he hastily tucked it into the back of his trousers, pulling his shirt and jacket over the top. Closing both bedroom doors silently, he crept to the bathroom and flushed the chain, before darting down the stairs and tugging the door open. "Sorry, I was on the loo. Can I help you?"

Four uniformed officers stood on the step, one of them brandishing a search warrant. Townsend and Reeves were by their car on the main road. They noticed him and Townsend shouted, "What are you doing here, Jeff?"

"Don't treat me like I'm stupid, Dom, you know it's my brother's house. Why do you think I'm here?"

"You need to come out while we search the house." Dom had stood to his full height and Jeff pictured him as the school bully, picking on others to make himself appear stronger. He felt tetchy and uncooperative.

"And you know that's not necessary. I'll be right inside the house watching you, and if you do anything wrong I'll have your arses, believe me." Returning inside, he sat on his father's old armchair and watched resolutely as the officers and detectives ransacked the house. Presently, one constable came down with Paul's air rifle. "You have got to be joking." Jeff stood, incredulous. "An airgun is legal, what are you taking that for?"

"We're under orders, sir."

To Jeff's surprise, another officer followed with a shotgun and two rifles and he had no comment this time. How on earth had he missed those? When the officer returned to the house Jeff meekly asked which room they had been found in, and upon hearing it was his father's, he was slightly relieved; he had believed and trusted his brother and would hate to be proven wrong about his innocence. The safe came next. Dirty clothes from Paul's floor had been thrown into a black plastic bag, and the crime books containing his father's notes were dragged from their home in the bookcase. As Jeff watched the officers, some colleagues and some he'd never met, take parts of his father's life away before he'd had a chance to find out who the man that spawned him was, he realised with a sinking heart that I, his so-called friend, was intent on finding his family guilty. It seemed to Jeff that he was the only person in a position to prove me wrong.

It was several hours later, after the officers had finished their painstaking search of the house, that Jeff had the opportunity to read the letter he had found underneath Paul's mattress. He peeled the envelope from where it had stuck to the skin of his lower back and pulled out the message, scanning the words formed in capital letters. He gasped, reading the astounding words aloud: "And that's why I'm letting you know my biggest secret. Do not tell anyone or you'll be in danger. Nobody else must see the journal."

He dropped the letter onto the arm of the chair and reached for the poker to stoke the dwindling fire back to life. "So Paul does know something he's not told me. Whatever this journal is about, I hope the police didn't find it." And now he realised his early suspicions about his father's youthful activities might be true. He took his mobile from his chest pocket and dialled his wife. "Sue, I just need someone to talk to. How are you? How's our baby?"

Chapter 12
Saturday 10th November

I hadn't managed to get anything of worth from interrogating Paul the previous day, especially as his brief was one of the best in the area and kept Paul's answers in check. The business about the boots had irritated me. I was sure Paul was acting more of an idiot than he really was – obviously he had two pairs of wellies and was just hindering the investigation. Worrying about the next step had kept me awake for most of the night, tossing and turning, annoying Ellen to the point that she eventually sent me downstairs with a sleeping bag and pillow. I arrived at work, tired and hungry, and fetched a ridiculously strong coffee from the percolator. I stirred in a portion of cream and a few sugars and took it to my desk, hoping the caffeine would perk me up and place me back in the real world.

When my computer had finally booted up, I scanned the list of emails for anything important, clicking open a couple of files and printing the details. Dorothy and Paul's bins had been processed and nothing untoward had been found on, or in, either, which surprised me. It was only guesswork that led us to conclude that Dorothy had been placed in a bin, and I debated the other possibilities, surmising there were three options. One: that she was placed in a bin, just not her own or Paul's. Two: she was taken to the landfill site in person. Or three: she was placed in a skip that was subsequently taken to the dump. I tapped out a hasty email to the morgue, asking for the results of Dorothy's post mortem as soon as they were finished.

Townsend and Reeves approached my desk, both sprightly and business-like, and I felt like a haggard, old man in comparison. "Rough night, boss?"

I chuckled mirthlessly. "What did you get from the search yesterday? Anything worth me knowing about?"

They dragged two chairs up to my desk and sat, Reeves opening the file he had brought, reading. "There was a small safe, you know, the cheap, fireproof ones you can pick up anywhere.

We opened it and most of the contents were everyday things, documents, certificates, guarantees, normal stuff."

"I'm sensing a 'but'." I leant forward and sipped the creamy, overly sweet coffee, savouring the soft smoothness with an added caffeine kick.

Townsend grinned. "Not for the safe, but we did find – and I think you'll like this – three small envelopes hidden inside an old metal tobacco tin at the back of one of his drawers." I leant forward with interest. "Get this, boss. They were each labelled." He brought out three photos, dropping them on my desk in front of me and pointing as he elaborated. "KJ80, VW81, BS82. What do you make of that?"

I studied the photos, one by one, slipping my reading glasses on with embarrassment; I hated wearing them, they made me feel ancient. "Katherine James, nineteen eighty; Vanessa Walton, nineteen eighty-one; and Bernie Smith, nineteen eighty-two. What was inside?" I could feel the adrenaline pumping through my veins with the gravity of the new evidence.

"There was a necklace in each one. We're going to show them to the friends and relatives of Katherine, Nessa, and Bernie to see if anybody recognises them."

I took a deep breath, the air suddenly fresher, waking me properly. "So he kept trophies. Good work, boys, that's pretty incriminating stuff. Check the post mortem reports to see if any of them showed an injury around the neck where a necklace could have been ripped off."

"Already done, boss. All three do, but my research shows it wasn't a lead that was taken particularly seriously during the original investigations."

"I see. Was there anything else?"

Reeves scanned his notes. "Two rifles and a shotgun, some bullets, forty-fives and twenty-twos; ballistics are taking sample shots for testing after analysing the guns. I made a list of the items we took and emailed it to you this morning."

He'd emailed me? And I'd skimmed past it? "Good, good. I'll take a look in a minute."

Townsend stood, eager to get on with his day. "I think the necklaces are the best lead we have in implicating Roland so far.

If a relative of the victims recognises one, I think that's the original Bonfire Night Killer pretty much found, don't you?"

I finished my coffee and replaced the cup, aching for another, while Reeves studied the carpet with no intention of moving. Townsend urged, "Well, what should I do about it, boss?"

His enthusiasm was impressive, but I was uneasy; something still felt out of place, yet I couldn't put my finger on what. "I can see where you're coming from, but having the jewellery is circumstantial, really. It'll take something more solid to positively attribute the shootings to Roland."

He grunted, aware that I was right if we wanted to find the naked truth of the case. "Yes, but it's still good evidence." Townsend slipped back onto his chair with a face like soured milk.

"Did you find anything that may link Paul to Fiona Malik's murder?"

With Townsend sulking, Reeves took over. "Paul doesn't seem to do much but drink, eat, or play Atari games on a broken telly in his bedroom."

"Atari? That's a blast from the past. I remember my brother having one in the eighties."

Townsend gave me a moody glance. "Showing your age, boss."

Reeves searched in the file and found a transparent evidence bag. "The only thing that was suspicious was this." It contained a note – 'threats mean death' – written in capital letters by a black marker pen on pale-green paper, with a matching envelope in a bag behind.

"Pale green." I studied it closely. "The note, apparently from Dorothy Webber, stating that she was going to stay with her son in London, was written on a sheet of pale-green paper just like this, and it also had a matching envelope."

Townsend hit the desk with the palms of his hands, triumphant. "There you go. Obviously he was blackmailing Dorothy, but disposed of her before he gave her the note. All we need to do is work out the series of events that will place Paul at both Dorothy and Fiona's deaths, and his father in the older

shootings – at the scene – and we can go ahead and charge him."
He rubbed his hands together, subliminally dusting the awkward
case into the past.

I shared a worried glance with Reeves. "I'm sorry, Dom,
but I don't think these things are enough. In all honesty I haven't
seen anything that has convinced me, one hundred percent, that
Paul is a killer. I mean, yes, I agree that the evidence mounting
up against Roland Mason is strong, but that doesn't mean his son
took up where he left off."

"I agree with the boss, Dom. Paul is definitely an odd
character, but a psychopathic tendency to kill doesn't just spring
up like that, even with his father's death acting as a trigger, and I
haven't seen anything in the details we have on him that suggests
he's been leading up to this."

Dom growled, irritated at being contradicted. "You know
what, Alan? You need to get a life. You read too bloody much."

Reeves rolled his eyes, and I was keen to cool the
atmosphere. "As I said, the note that Dorothy was supposed to
have sent to Paul – do you remember me showing it to you?"
They nodded. "And this one," I tapped the bag, "we need to see
if they're from the same set. Take this to forensics, they'll be able
to prove that."

"When they find that the handwriting matches, it will prove
that it wasn't Dorothy blackmailing Bert, like Paul suggested
when he mentioned the package, but that Paul actually wrote
them himself." Townsend stared at me, confident once more.

Reeves didn't share the conviction. "But the letter
supposedly from Dorothy was in lowercase and joined up. I
thought Paul couldn't…"

"He's not as dumb as he makes out, I'm sure about that."
An excellent actor, though, I conceded.

"Exactly." Townsend was smug. "Look, it's simple. I'm
right on this, I know I am. The sooner that hunchback is behind
bars for good, the safer Colefield will be." The conversation had
ended resolutely and I returned to my computer as Townsend
and Reeves, glaring silently at each other, strutted away.

Jeff had woken early and, having slept in his clothes for two nights, was desperate for a shower and a clean outfit. Although he was becoming more relaxed with Paul's tardy housekeeping in general, he struggled to cope with the bathroom. It was disgusting, it couldn't have been cleaned for years, and he decided to head back to Hessle. He would tidy himself up a bit, then spend an hour or so with his wife and son.

Sue was pleased to see him, as was Jacob, a cute open-mouthed grin spreading across his face when he saw his daddy, and she prepared a healthy continental breakfast while her husband showered. They sat at the small, antiqued-pine table in the kitchen while Jacob was having a nap and shared the rye bread, meats and cheeses, both satisfied by the filling meal. She asked after Paul and Jeff explained, in more detail than he had during their phone conversation the night before, about the arrest, the house search – Dorothy's disappearance – just as the sound of the newspaper being delivered echoed from the hall.

Sue collected it, dropping it on the table. The cover of the local daily grabbed Jeff's attention and he looked closer. *"'Woman Dumped in Landfill Site Dies'."* While he read the front page, Sue took her whimpering son from his pram and made herself comfortable enough to breastfeed him. "That's Dorothy Webber, the old lady I just mentioned, Paul's neighbour and friend. It says she was crushed by the dustcart's hydraulic compressor and died later from her injuries. Now I know why they were messing with the bins yesterday, they were looking for her DNA. They checked Paul's bin. I reckon they're trying to hang that on him as well as Fiona's death. I don't believe this."

Sue laid her hand on his arm calmly. "If he's innocent like you believe, the truth will come out in the end."

Jeff jumped up, angry, his face reddened. "You just don't get it, do you?" Sue had never seen her gentle husband in a temper before, it was completely out of character. "Paul isn't capable of murder. He's autistic, of that I'm sure."

Sue instinctively knew not to react to his burst of rage, but it was necessary to state the truth and she kept her words soft, ensuring her tone wasn't confrontational. "I recently read a study that showed a link between high-functioning autism and murderers, especially those with Asperger's Syndrome."

Jeff glared at her. He had seen papers on the research and knew it was true to a small extent, but he didn't think for a second that Paul had committed any crime, let alone one so dire as murder. He had seen Paul with Dot, there had been no malice, and he had been watching Paul through the interview room window when he'd been told Dot was dead. Nothing in his manner had been suspicious. The only way Paul could have acted that way after murdering a person would be by disassociating himself from the crime, basically blocking the memory out. "It wasn't Paul. The original killings may have been dad, I can't deny that, although I'm trying to, but Paul didn't kill Fiona Malik. Or Dorothy."

"I think it may help to get him to a doctor, have his head checked out."

After dealing with my emails, I took my coat and slurped the dregs of my third coffee before announcing that I was off to Scunthorpe to see the suspect. I arrived more than an hour later, having been caught in the tail end of the morning's heavy traffic – cars full of people determined to waste their money in the shopping centres buying things they didn't need. Paul seemed pleased to see me in a childlike way, as if he wanted a playmate and was relieved to see a familiar face. It irritated me and I stupidly let it show. "Guessing you're after an OSCAR." Mildly relieved by my sarcasm, I leafed importantly through the paperwork on my lap. "Why Dorothy, Paul? She was good to you. Why did you kill her? Why were you blackmailing her? Is that what this," I produced a photocopy of the 'threats mean death' note that Reeves had taken to the lab the previous day and laid it on the desk between us, "note is about?" I tapped the page. "What were you threatening her for?"

Paul's head whirled with the multitude of questions, he could feel his brain bouncing from one side of his skull to the other. "I didn't kill Dot. She was like a mum to me, all the years."

I was thankful Paul hadn't requested the presence of his brief, which Jeff would have insisted on had he been there. "Maybe it was an accident. Was it an accident?"

He had his hands to his head and was nodding gently to relax himself from the stressful questions. "I saw her on Monday morning. She didn't cook me dinner. She cooked me breakfast. She said she'd pick up a package tomorrow."

"A package?"

"Her son was bringing a package and leaving it at my back door." I would have to check, but I was certain the relations we'd traced had all said they'd not had contact with Dorothy for years after a family dispute. "I never saw her again after that, and she doesn't cook dinner or breakfast anymore."

I leant forward and spoke quietly. "You know what, Paul? I think you're playing games with me. Drop the dumb act, you're not stupid and nor am I. You know exactly what happened, and if it takes me getting a medical examination to prove that all your faculties are all there, I will." Paul seemed to cower, his eyes scared and distrustful. He was a damned fine actor. "What did you know about Dorothy that made you blackmail her?"

His face scrunched in puzzlement. "I wasn't blackmailing her."

I sighed with irritation and waved the copied page again. "It's right here in your handwriting, Paul. Stop messing with me, I'm not a patient man."

Paul became excitable, pointing at the note. "That's the green letter, isn't it? I didn't write that. Someone else did. Someone posted it through my door a few days ago."

"The note has got your fingerprints on it." I spoke with a bored huff.

"Of course it's got his bloody fingerprints on it. He was being blackmailed and he read the letter, using his hands to open the envelope and hold it." I'd not realised that Jeff was listening and I swore under my breath at his intervention. "Frank, you're well out of line on this. I bet you never asked if Paul wanted legal consult present this morning. You can see he doesn't understand half of what you're saying to him. Don't frame my brother,

Frank, I'm warning you. I'll be fighting you all the way on this one."

I tidied my paperwork away neatly and stood to leave, but stopped as I passed Jeff at the doorway. "We almost have enough evidence to proceed on all four murders, Jeff. You won't be fighting for long." I wasn't sure any more what I had liked about Jeff Mason four years ago, and he had turned aggressively arrogant recently. Finally showing his true colours, I surmised. I turned away from Jeff, my head raised proudly, and left the interview room.

Glancing at my watch, I realised we only had five hours left to hold Paul before either charging him or letting him go. We had the Wellington boots as good evidence, placing him at the scene of Fiona's murder, but he was denying they were his. I called the lab and asked them to check the inside of the boots for fibres, hair, anything to prove he had been wearing them. If we had that, we could formally charge him with Fiona's murder at least, while still working on Dorothy's. I was also pretty certain that the post mortem case against Roland Mason was in the bag.

Jeff sat with his confused brother for a while, before asking Paul what was going on. "I don't know. How do they know my boots were near the body? They haven't looked at them."

Jeff thought about the odd comment. "They took them from outside the back door. You know that."

"But I don't keep my boots outside." The childish whine had returned. "If they were outside, they weren't mine. Nobody's taken my boots."

Jeff remembered seeing a pair of Wellington boots by the back door of Paul's house the morning after Fiona's murder and had assumed they were his, but looking at him now, he realised he had seldom seen Paul without his olive green wellies on. And the ones by the back door had been a darker shade of green. Somebody – the murderer – must have placed them there to frame him. And it was working.

Jeff debated asking about the notebook that had been mentioned in the letter he had found under Paul's mattress, but the instructions had been clear – nobody else was to know about it – and he knew his brother's loyalty to their dead father was fierce. He tried a different direction. "You know the police have searched the house, don't you?" Paul nodded; he was tiring of all the questions and was eager to return to his cell. "Was there anything in there you wouldn't want them to find?"

Paul's intense eyes met Jeff's – black meeting black – and Jeff felt a shiver run along his spine. "I hide things well. If I don't want somebody to find something, they won't." Finally, Jeff knew there was a ray, albeit a small one, of hope.

After leaving Paul, Jeff headed for the medical practice in Westerton, hoping it would still be open. He hadn't made a prior appointment as time was short, but when he showed his police badge at the reception desk and told them it was urgent, an impromptu appointment was scheduled for as soon as one of the two doctors working this Saturday, Doctor Aggarwal, finished with the patient he was currently seeing.

Jeff was directed through to the bland, hygienically clean room and he sat beside the doctor's table as directed. He explained what had been happening the over the past few days, and when the time came to relate the morning's events, he became agitated and exasperated at how his brother was being treated. "Do you have access to Paul's medical history to see if he has ever been diagnosed with any form of autism?"

Dr Aggarwal was taken aback; he hadn't been expecting that to follow Jeff's lengthy explanation. "I would need a warrant to disclose personal information without the patient being present."

"I understand that's the case, but I think he's about to be charged with a murder he didn't commit. I need everything possible to buy him time while I find enough evidence to prove he's innocent."

"I'll see what I can do." He clicked through the notes, not sure he wanted to give any personal details, but it turned out there wasn't anything confidential to tell. He could see from the notes the patient's name, age and basic information, but since the records had been computerised several years before, Paul Mason hadn't made a single visit or call to the practice, from what he could see.

Jeff became concerned by the oppressive gap in the conversation. "Is there a problem? The screens look pretty blank."

Dr Aggarwal swivelled in his chair to face Jeff and he crossed his arms. "We began storing data on our computer system nearly fifteen years ago. In that time, we have no entries for Paul. There is nothing on his records to suggest autism or a condition of any kind. Why do you think he's autistic?"

Jeff explained the head nodding, bobbing and shaking, the vagueness. He mentioned the stilted conversations, Paul's lack of hobbies. His lack of ambition. The doctor drummed his fingers on his desk, the softly ticking clock on the wall hammering out the seconds that were swiftly passing in silence. "I haven't heard anything specifically that makes me suspect autism. Of course we can arrange for tests, if you wish to go down that route, but the world is made up of all sorts of people, some bright, some not so..."

"When can the tests be done?" Jeff wasn't prepared to waste time with a meaningless, irrelevant lecture.

"Um, I think maybe," he opened a file on his computer and scanned through, glasses balanced on the end of his tiny nose, "if I refer him today, the waiting list is about two to three months at the moment, but keep your eye out for a cancellation." He turned away from the screen to notice the impatient man storming through the door without even a thank you.

Sue swore she knew her husband of eight years better than he knew himself, and she guessed he would heed her advice to take Paul to a doctor. She could also see, and understand, that this case was weighing heavily on his shoulders. After feeding Jacob and settling him into his baby bouncer, she searched for details of autism on the computer that was set up in the lounge. Shocked to see that a proper, full diagnosis of autism, even if paying privately, would take a while, she dialled a friend whom she knew from the psychiatric department of the Royal Infirmary in Hull. Within a few minutes of ending the call an email pinged into her inbox and Sue printed the attachment. She stapled the pages together, checked Paul's house number in her address book, and carefully squeezed Jacob into his all-in-one, waterproof baby-suit. "Come on, son. I think it's time we went and helped your daddy. The sooner this case is solved the sooner you get your real daddy back."

She drove her aging car to the quaint village of Colefield. She had not been before and was intrigued to see that such a beautiful place still existed, being so used to the hustle and bustle of city life in her native Hull. From what Jeff had mentioned recently about the village, she knew that the house her husband had been born in was on the main through street and she slowed the car, searching for number thirteen. She pulled the car close to the stone boundary wall and parked, hoping she had left enough room for the tractor that had been following her to pass. It chugged through safely and she went to the passenger side of the car to collect Jacob, cosy in his car seat, and his changing bag.

Not used to the unusual ways south of the Humber River, Sue knocked at the front door, unaware that most locals would automatically use the back. Jeff answered and was stunned to see his wife and child. He moved aside to let them through, kissing them both as they passed. He took Jacob, in the car seat, from his wife and set it on the floor, before helping Sue to remove her coat. "What are you doing here?"

"I didn't trust you so I thought I'd check up on you."

Jeff laughed. "No, really, why did you come all this way?"

"It's only ten miles." Sue brought some folded pages from her handbag and passed them to Jeff. "I thought this might help. I did a bit of research into autism this morning."

Jeff looked at the printed pages. There was a list of questions entitled *'Autism: Pre-Diagnosis Test'*, and he hugged her close, grinning. "You're a star, Sue. How did you know it would be hopeless at the surgery?"

Sue tapped her nose. "I visit ours once a week with the baby, I know these things. No, I saw on the net how long it takes to get an official diagnosis, so I called my friend for advice. She sent this. It won't give a medical diagnosis, but it'll give us an idea of what we're working with." Sue pointed to the questionnaire. "Do you want me to fill it out, or shall I observe as a neutral bystander?"

"Maybe a bit of both. How long are you stopping?"

"Well, obviously I'll have to get Jacob to bed at his usual time, but apart from that I have no plans, so as long as you want." She lifted Jacob from his seat and started to undress him from his outer clothing; the glowering coal fire emitted more warmth than she would have thought possible.

Jeff leaned forward and kissed her cheek. "Sue, I don't know why, but Frank's determined to frame Paul for this. They've still got him in custody. It's going to take a miracle for me to prove his innocence against the might of the police force, especially when they're ignoring important information to make the case fit the solution they want. Please, I know you're busy and all that, but please can you help me. I'm not sure any more that I can do this on my own."

She stroked his cheek gently with her soft fingers, physically feeling the love she had held for him for so many years. "You know I will. You name it, I'll do it. Within reason, of course."

I spent the afternoon preparing a report of all the details we had that linked Roland Mason to the Bonfire Night Killer. We had a series of crime books with intensive notes scrawled only on the chapters regarding the killings. The necklaces, two of which had been positively identified as belonging to the victims by bereaved relatives, that had been found in a drawer in his bedroom. Kaye found that he had held a Section 2 firearms licence, which had expired several years before, and in his original application in nineteen seventy, he had been unspecific as to which type of gun – within the legal boundaries – he intended to use. His house backed onto the field where the shootings took place. His wife had left shortly before the first murder, which could have triggered a spate of violence. On top of those facts, we almost had enough evidence to formally charge his son, Paul Mason, with the latest two murders.

I summoned Townsend and Reeves over. "Did you pick anything up that contained Roland's DNA when you were at the house yesterday?"

Townsend glanced at Reeves and mouthed 'did we'. Reeves smiled expressively. "If you look at line twenty-seven on the email I sent you, it says that we took his toothbrush and comb. I instructed the lab to re-test everything linked to the original murders to see if there was a match to Roland's DNA. We already have Paul Mason's DNA from the swab we took during the initial questioning. I must point out that Roland's cremation is due to take place on Monday; may I suggest we request the body is taken into our possession for an extended period?"

As I nodded my agreement the phone rang on my desk. I held my finger up to indicate I hadn't finished with the two detectives yet and answered. I listened, bidding my thanks to the caller after asking him to fax me his report, and replaced the receiver. "That was the coroner. Bring some chairs up, then you can get us a mug of coffee, Dom, and you, Alan, can pick up the fax that's about to come through for me. It's the post mortem report for Dorothy Webber."

Five minutes later the document was in my hand, my cup was refilled, and I made the first unexpected discovery. "Dorothy had been shot! A forty-four-calibre bullet entered the top of her right hip, hit the ball joint and lodged. The coroner has removed it and sent it for testing." I pondered briefly, thinking back to when I had seen the nurse at the hospital. "The nurse told me she had a nasty ulcer on her hip. I bet that was actually the gunshot wound.

"It says that she had signs of restraint on her wrists and ankles, and a ligature imprint on her neck. From the bruising, these are believed to have been done a number of days before she died." I turned to face Townsend and Reeves. "My guess is that she was bound and gagged when she was dumped, be it in a bin, skip, or at the landfill site."

"That wouldn't make sense, how would she have undone them?"

I was embarrassed to miss something so obvious, but didn't show it. "She could always have taken them off while she was trapped." I sighed, safe in the knowledge that I was talking rubbish. "Okay, you're right. But if she was dumped unrestrained, then she had to have been unconscious or she would have struggled to get out, tried to raise the alarm in some way by hammering and shouting. Maybe her attacker presumed she was already dead. He must have."

"What was the actual cause of death?"

I scanned through the document. "She had suffered from compressive asphyxia – I assume by being squashed in the dustcart – severe hypothermia, and massive internal bleeding. In conjunction, these led to progressive heart and organ failure." Sipping at my scalding, yet welcome, coffee, I checked my watch. We only had another hour to keep Paul and, even with prompting, I couldn't see the bullet being tested that quickly. I typed a quick email to the Chief Superintendent, requesting permission to keep him an additional twelve hours. "I'm trying to buy a bit more time, but can you try and speed ballistics up with the analysis of the bullet they removed from Dorothy's hip. I know it's the weekend, but explain we can't hold the suspect much longer. If it's from the same gun that was used on the other four women, it's almost certain that Paul killed Dorothy."

"I've got to get going, I have to get the baby to bed." Jacob was asleep in his car seat, Jeff and Sue on the armchairs. "Why don't you come back with me and have a comfortable night for once? With Paul's custody extended until tomorrow, we can't do much more here."

The suggestion was tempting, but two problems cropped up instantly. "The thing is, they wouldn't have been granted extra custody without having good evidence that he killed Fiona, and possibly Dorothy too. I know nothing about that part of the investigation because I was only involved with the eighties murders. And anyway, if he's released at six in the morning, I want to be there for him."

Sue laid her hand on his arm, concerned. "Jeff, you must understand, accept even, that he probably won't be released."

"I know that." The words were severe and Jeff was

suddenly lonely. The thought of Sue leaving, alone again in the

dank, murky house. It was unbearable and he caught her eye, his expression desperate. "Look, there's something I haven't told you yet and I think it may be vital to helping Paul. You see, I checked in dad's safe the other day and there was a letter for Paul. I wanted to open it but he said he wasn't allowed to until he'd finished reading dad's books, but I think he was lying, because I know for a fact he can't read lowercase very well. I think Dad left him some kind of document explaining something, but I've not been able to find anything."

Sue sighed. To have received a stay of custody meant the police had plausible evidence. Jeff seemed to be the only person who believed Paul was innocent, and that was understandable, but maybe he was wearing rose-tinted glasses. "If there had been anything here, they would have found it in the search, and the solicitor has mentioned nothing about a diary or letter."

"Yes, I know all that, and I know Paul is slow, but he's not stupid. Not at all. After I'd found the letter yesterday I asked him in a roundabout way if he was hiding something. He said that if he doesn't want something to be found, it won't be found. But maybe if I think about who he is, what he does, how he would react in a situation. Maybe I can find this document and try and clear both his and dad's names, because that's the next one that'll be thrown at us." She was bound to rebuke the suggestion, but it was worth a try. "Why don't you put Jacob to bed here, maybe in dad's bed? I changed the sheets. You could sleep with him."

Sue couldn't stand the mess, the grimy dust collected from years of little or no housework, but her husband needed her. "I suppose so, I've got just about enough nappies for overnight. But you've got to try and be more impartial in all of this, you have nothing to suggest the police are wrong."

"You're the best. Go and settle Jacob down, I'll search Paul's room again. With your help we might just find something."

Chapter 13
Sunday 11th November
The Nightmare Begins

Jeff woke in the early hours, stiff and aching from another night in the armchair. Sue had been happy to sleep in Roland's bed with Jacob, having tucked a sturdy pillow behind his back to prevent him from falling, but Jeff preferred the familiar chair. He fortified himself with mug after mug of strong, steaming tea, mindful of his mobile in case the police rang. Six o'clock came and went with no call, and he tetchily waited until seven to phone his brother's lawyer. It was an unearthly hour on a Sunday morning and Benjamin was furious. "I sent you an email explaining what was going on."

Jeff was surprised at his long-time acquaintance's hostility. "I haven't checked them, it never occurred to me." He felt the smartphone in his pocket, embarrassed.

Benjamin sighed, reluctantly hoisting himself up the pillow. "He was charged with Fiona's murder last night and his custody was extended. He'll be in until he appears in court on Monday. I'm not sure if they're charging him with Dorothy's death yet, but they're convinced he's their man." He felt guilty for being so rude to the man whose head must be in turmoil.

Jeff ended the call in shock and hammered the arm of the chair, frustrated, angry and scared. He reached deep into his memory, trying to remember every little detail of the latest murder, but it was futile; he'd had scant involvement, only familiar with the eighties murders. What did they have on his brother that warranted the charge?

He thought of the mysterious notes he was sure his father had left for Paul to read. He and Sue had searched the house for hours the night before, finally giving up after midnight, bored, tired and disheartened. Jeff was hounded by his brother's words: *'if I don't want somebody to find something, they won't'*. He knew there was something and he had to find it, because Paul was in serious trouble.

Weary, and despondent after the short conversation, Jeff whiled away the time by re-searching the front room, dredging through pile after pile of irrelevant paperwork, things that could have been thrown away years ago, but there was nothing. At eight, he was grateful to hear Jacob's plaintive, hungry cry and trotted up the stairs to his late father's room. "I'm so glad you're awake. I've been going stir crazy downstairs. They've kept him in, Sue. They're doing him for murder. I've been up since about five this morning, searching for dad's notes again, but I still haven't found anything. It's really bugging me now."

Exhausted and un-refreshed from the few hours of restless sleep, Sue was irritable. She stretched sleepily, stifling a yawn, and pulled Jacob to her chest for a feed, while her head screamed 'just let me sleep for one more hour'. Why couldn't her husband accept there was nothing to find? "Look, we must have missed loads of places last night, we can keep trying. But for god's sake, can I at least have a cup of tea before we start?"

Jeff returned ten minutes later with two steaming mugs, and he clicked the light on with his knuckle as he walked through the door. He set the drinks on a box beside the bed and sat on the edge of the mattress, snuggling up to Sue. The past couple of months tending to a new-born had exhausted her, but she had to pull herself together because Jeff needed her, whatever the outcome of the sorry mess they were in. "What exactly are we looking for?"

"But…"

"No, I mean, think logically. Think what it's liable to look like and try to follow Paul's thought processes." Her tone wasn't as enthusiastic as the words.

Jeff sighed. "I don't know. The letter said, *'now you know the truth, get Bert behind bars where he belongs'*, so it was a diary of some kind."

Jacob had settled into his feed, leaving Sue relaxed. "So it's a confession, well, more an accusation by the sound of it. Something personal and dangerous. It has to be in Paul's bedroom. If you have something intensely private, you keep it where you're at your most vulnerable: where you sleep."

"But we looked."

"Not hard enough, though, was it? Anyway, we'll deal with that after breakfast. For now, there are other important matters. Your dad's being cremated tomorrow, and as they're keeping Paul in, what are you going to do about it?"

Jeff sagged. "Shit." He reached for his tea, cupping his hands around the mug to soak in the warmth. He had forgotten and the question added a further worry. "I don't know. I can't deal with that at the moment. Look, get ready as quickly as possible, we've got to get moving on this. I'm going to see Paul and get him to be honest with me somehow. Tell him we know dad's notes exist."

Sue rolled her eyes. "So much for a Sunday lie-in." She adjusted her top and held Jacob out to her husband. "You take the baby. I'll have a quick wash and then I'll keep looking for the notes while you go and visit Paul."

A quarter of an hour later, clean and refreshed, Sue returned to Paul's bedroom. She could hear Jacob downstairs, gurgling merrily, and decided to leave him with Jeff while she started the logical search she had planned while washing. Thinking laterally, she had figured that in, or around, the bed would be the most obvious place to hide something confidential. She carefully stripped the bed, aware the police would have already found anything suspicious. The odour of rancid sweat belched from the dislodged covers and Sue leaned across to open the ill-fitting metal window, desperate for fresh air. She checked the mattress – sides, top, bottom -for any loose or open stitching, but it was intact. The next step was to move the bed out and, hands on hips, she scoured the floor, disheartened by how much junk needed to be shifted before the bed was going anywhere.

She moved boxes, stacks of magazines, clutter, balking at the disgusting, used tissues, and was about to start tugging at the single divan when Jeff strolled in with Jacob cuddled to one shoulder, and a mug of tea in his other hand. "You sounded busy so I brought you this."

"Just in time. Give me Jacob, then you can pull the bed out so I can see underneath it."

"Okay, but don't be too long up here. The sooner I get Paul to tell us where it is, the sooner we can see what it's all about." The bed was much heavier than he had expected, and although the scuffed material that covered the frame was tatty, it was apparent the bed was solidly made and probably as old as he was. The carpet underneath was disgraceful and Sue inadvertently groaned. Jeff grimaced at the thick dust, littered with dried tissues, scraps of paper, rotting food and mouse droppings, and he glanced at her. "Not nice, eh?"

She clutched her mouth with her spare hand and pulled Jacob's face into her shoulder to shield him from the putrid air, dense with floating dust. Her words were muffled. "No. Bloody revolting. How can someone live in this filth?"

"I know, but…" Jeff leaned over the mattress towards the wall,"well, what do you know," he pointed to where the head of the bed had been. "See the disturbance in the dust over there? The carpet's been pulled back recently."

"I had to shift ten tons of junk to move that bed. If he's put it down there he definitely didn't want it found." Sue had backed to the doorway for the slightly fresher air of the landing.

The carpet wasn't fixed, so Jeff flipped it over to expose a broken floorboard. He smiled at Sue before lifting it, and underneath was a leather bound notebook with his father's writing on the label. "Bingo," he flicked through the pages, "I knew it. Now we've just got to hope and pray that there's something that can help in it."

"Amen to that. I take it you won't be going to see Paul now." Jeff was already reading the first page and shook his head, engrossed.

"Don't get your hopes up too much, love. Remember that your father wrote this journal before he died, so it won't have any effect on Paul going down for the murders of two women after his death. I know it's important for you to believe that Paul is innocent, and I know he's your brother and everything, but if I was still at work, I know he'd be a major suspect in my eyes. I mean, he's borderline autistic, he has anger issues, he…" Sue realised her words were falling on deaf ears and gave up.

"Oh my god." The words were quiet, under his breath. Sue craned her head over Jeff's shoulder. "Oh my god, I didn't expect this. This is worse than I ever imagined."

Sue was as horrified as her husband by the time she had read the first few pages. She looked at Jeff, concerned. "Do you want to put it back?"

He grimaced. The temptation to pretend the book didn't exist was strong, but he had a duty to his profession. "No. I'm going to read it through. Once I know the whole story, I'll decide what the next step should be."

"Do you want me and Jacob to stay?" If Jeff intended to read all day, she would end up tidying the squalid house, and that was unappealing. She would rather be at home.

Jeff waved, still absorbing the enormity of the confession. "I guess not, now we've found this. I'll try and get the fire going properly again and read some more. Anyway, Jacob probably needs a bath by now."

"You know, I think you should let the solicitor know about the journal, he might have some idea of what to do." Jeff shook his head, overwhelmed and confused, but Sue was insistent. "Please, love, I know it's Sunday, but he needs as much time as possible to prepare the defence, and this is essential reading."

"I suppose you're right. But this isn't going to do Paul any favours at all."

"Sweetheart, you've got to start considering the possibility that Paul might be guilty." He stared past her, a thousand-yard stare.

Grateful to be leaving, she trotted down the stairs with Jacob. "I'm off home to get Jacob cleaned and fed properly."

Following her, Jeff pecked her cheek tenderly when they reached the front room, and threw himself onto the familiar armchair with the journal. "I'll keep reading until it's a decent enough time to phone Benjamin again."

"Do you want me to come back later?"

He hesitated. "I don't know. Give me a call this afternoon and we can see what's going on then."

Benjamin Roberts hadn't slept after Jeff's call, and eventually he had prepared a delicious full English breakfast for his family, before donning his suit and heading to the police station. After the routine humdrum of filling out a couple of forms and signing a few boxes for the police records, Benjamin was allowed to see Paul. They sat opposite each other, Paul on the bed, Benjamin on a chair. "You do understand what's happening, don't you, Paul?" Paul said nothing, but gave the lawyer a wry glare. "You will be attending court tomorrow and…"

"Tomorrow is dad's funeral. I've got to go to that."

Benjamin had forgotten that particular gem. He eyed his client tentatively and the consternation he felt over the man's size wasn't irrational. "It doesn't work like that, I'm afraid, Paul. The crime you're accused of is serious. They're not going to let you out of here." He stood and, subconsciously concerned about the reaction the next bombshell might trigger, backed towards the metal door. "That's even if your father's funeral goes ahead, which is looking unlikely at the moment." He paused, waiting for the inevitable rage, but Paul remained calm and Benjamin relaxed slightly. "The police have applied to keep his body in their possession due to the investigation into the original Bonfire Night murders."

Paul's face contorted, deep wrinkles on his leathery forehead under the dishevelled mop of raven and grey hair. "They can't do that. He's dead, I don't want him going off."

Benjamin sighed, fanning the paperwork in his hands. "They can, I'm afraid, and permission will most likely be granted. Paul, we need to talk about your appearance in court tomorrow. Are you going to plead guilty?"

Paul banged his fist on the worn mattress. "I didn't kill anyone."

"The police have a good case against you, Paul, this isn't going to go away just because you want it to."

"I didn't kill anyone."

Benjamin's mobile rang. He answered and turned towards the door for privacy. "I'm with him now. You what?"

Jeff briefly mentioned the diary, without giving any details away, explaining he needed see Benjamin as soon as possible. He was out of his depth, despite having only read half the journal, and had reluctantly accepted that content wasn't only going to change Paul's life, but the lives of every member of the family. The revolting tale unfolding made horrific reading and it was too much for him to deal with alone. Benjamin ended the call, completely lost for words at the meagre information Jeff had given him. He gave his excuses to Paul and made his way to Colefield to visit his client's brother.

It had been a while since I'd had a day off and I was tempted to laze in bed, but we needed to get our paperwork in order for the court appearance the next day. I sat at my desk, poring over the case notes, yet something kept bugging me and I couldn't put my finger on it. I was convinced that Paul had murdered Fiona Malik and Dorothy Webber, and I firmly believed that his father was the original killer. However, something was out of place, something didn't fit, and I wouldn't be satisfied unless I worked out what it was. I told Reeves I was popping to Colefield and drove to the strange village that was steeped in mystery. I let myself into Dorothy's house with the key I had taken from her file. I wasn't looking for anything in particular, only to familiarise myself with the woman, her daily life and how her mind worked. How she ended up in a wheelie bin, before being crushed and dumped.

Her house was tidy, well-organised and somewhat dated. The kitchen – so small it was as if the architect who had designed the property had added it as an afterthought – was orderly, the space utilised to the last inch. I poked my head into the lounge, and walked up the stairs to look in her bedroom. The bed was neat, patiently waiting for the woman who would never return home. Poor Dorothy. I glanced in her drawers, over the shelves, searching for the missing link.

Opening the wardrobe, I dragged a heavy, battered cardboard box from the bottom. I took it to the bed and removed the lid. It was full of memories: paperwork, diaries, photos. I pulled out a battered black and white photograph with four smiling adults and guessed from the clothing that it was from the late sixties, maybe early seventies. Dorothy had been an attractive lady in her twenties, and I guessed the towering, solid man with his arm around her shoulder was her late husband, Ernie. I didn't recognise the other two, but surprisingly the man had his hand on Dorothy's hip, much too personal an area to be a simple friendly gesture. Whoever the man was, he had undoubtedly been intimate with Dorothy. The other woman bore a strong resemblance to both Jeff and Paul Mason, and I was certain she was their mother. I sagged to the bed as I realised that their father and Dorothy must have had an affair.

"Who are you?" I hadn't noticed the unfamiliar man enter the room and I was surprised. Standing, I told him my name and the reason for my visit, and returned the question. "I'm David Webber, her eldest son." He grinned and shook my hand, shocking me with his carefree composure; hardly the behaviour of a man whose mother had just been tortured and killed. "Obviously we've heard the news, and I guess I just came to make sure she was dead." My jaw dropped as my mind raced to find words to follow the callous comment. He noticed and his expression became serious. "We weren't close. Her death isn't a great loss, not to me, nor to society. She was a selfish, self-absorbed cow."

I dropped the photo on the bed, stunned. "I see. I was just trying to find out more about your mother." I should have questioned him further, but instead, "We have a man in custody, but there's not enough evidence yet to convict him of your mother's murder. I'm trying to find the missing link. Have you anything you could tell me?"

"I haven't seen my mother for over twenty years, apart from at my father's funeral, and even then I didn't speak to her. My brother and sister don't have anything to do with her either, as far as I know. Mother had no redeeming features. She was a bossy, controlling busybody who had no inkling of what the word private meant. Growing up was horrendous; the only thing that made it bearable was the presence of my father. He was a weak man. Psychologically, not physically; he was built like a gorilla. He was like a little lapdog for mother, jumping to her every whim, at her beck and call. But at least he was good-hearted and loving. That photo," he leant down and tapped on the telling picture that lay on the bed, "is an excellent example of her selfishness. That's her with my dad, and Roland and Jeannie Mason."

"Thanks. I thought that was who they were. I obviously never met either."

"You've missed the point." He tapped the photo again and I realised he had reached the same sordid conclusion as me, be it now or years ago. "She wasn't faithful. My father did everything in his power to give her whatever she wanted and she thanked him by being the village tart. You know they killed her, don't you?" He tapped the photo for the third time and I was confused. "Jeannie Mason. They killed her. My mother and Roland killed her. That bullshit-tale they spouted about her moving to Scunthorpe, that's rubbish. The younger kid went to live with Jeannie's sister, who was also having a fling with that philandering arsehole."

I hadn't been prepared for that and I was flummoxed. "You do realise that what you've just said is a serious accusation?"

He sat on the bed and I followed suit, disbelieving, yet intrigued. "My mother was what you would call a slag nowadays, Mr Butler. Not only was she shagging Roland, but she was also knocking off another neighbour for many years, on and off. A dreadful man named Bert Rock. My father told me when I was in my mid-twenties that it was impossible for him to have fathered any of us three children. He'd found out from some test or other that he was sterile, and would have been from birth due to a congenital defect that had only just been diagnosed. I don't know what it was, I'd been too shocked to listen much following the bombshell he'd just dropped. He told us about her affairs, and that either of the two men could be our biological father. Apparently the rumours had circulated for years about my mother and her lovers, not that I'd ever heard anything. Finding out he'd brought up three children who weren't biologically his broke my dad's heart, not that he made us feel unwanted – he was still our dad. But he insisted he would stand by her. He wasn't going to tell her what he knew because he doted on her and didn't want to rock the boat, so he swore us to secrecy. All three of us had already left home, but one by one we decided that building a relationship with mother was futile, because we couldn't handle the lies and hypocrisy, the way she acted so little-

157

miss-perfect when in fact she was an adulterous whore. Of course, there was also the dreadful fact that none of us had a clue who we were any longer, now the heritage we knew had been stripped. My mother didn't deserve his loyalty. We kept in touch with dad until he died, but I haven't spoken to her since that day. None of us have."

"Was she seeing Roland throughout the marriage?" I was fascinated with the revelations. The Dorothy I had prepared the prosecution on bore no resemblance to the woman her son described.

"I don't think so." He wrung his hands, delving into his memory. "I think it was all going on when I was a young boy. I suppose that if my father was sterile and she wasn't falling pregnant, well, I guess having kids meant more to her than her marriage vows."

I strongly felt that David was judging his mother harshly. After all, she had given him life, but it wasn't my place to intrude. "What about Jeannie Mason?"

"I remember her clearly, I was older then, maybe eleven or twelve. She went missing. It was completely out of the blue. Everyone was saying she'd taken the younger lad and moved to Scunthorpe, but let's be realistic, if she'd moved away she would still have visited and called her friends. It's only a few miles away, that's how it works. I thought I had an overactive imagination at the time, but now I'm older it fits, that my mother and Roland had conveniently disposed of her."

I sat up straight, jaw clenched with irritation. "So as an impressionable boy you guessed she was killed, but you have no evidence or anything. Nothing to back up your suspicions." The silly man was a timewaster, and as big a gossip as his mother had apparently been.

His chestnut eyes flashed and he took a deep, calming breath. Having his credibility questioned clearly irked him, and while he took his ten steadying breaths I studied him. He had a ruddy complexion and what was left of his hair was grey. He wasn't a large man, about average height. His features were from his mother's side, but I couldn't see a resemblance to either man in the photo. "Look, all I know is that one night Jeannie and the

158

little lad just disappeared. Roland told everybody who would listen the story that she'd left him. He played the wounded husband, but I'm sure he and my mother had killed her and sent the youngest kid to live with Jeannie's sister. That was my final conclusion."

I shook my head, dismissive. "No, maybe a hundred years ago somebody could have covered that up, but not in the late seventies, early eighties. I think you were right about having an overactive imagination. You've got the wrong end of the stick."

He stared at me, lips twisted to a smirk. "Really? Come on, Mr Butler, it's big news that Paul Mason has been arrested. A murderous son, a murderous father..." He left the sentence hanging and I wasn't interested enough to prompt him. Eventually he continued. "I occasionally kicked a ball around with Paul Mason, I was a fair bit older than him – five, maybe six years – and I didn't like him. He was thick as pig shit, totally stupid. But Jeannie and my mother were close friends and they urged us to get on. When dad told me my mother had cheated with her best friend's husband, well, I'd had it with her. How can you respect a mother who can't keep her legs together?"

I shifted uncomfortably. I wasn't a psychologist, but even a layman could see that David's utter distaste of his mother was less about her extra-marital excitement and more about a deep-rooted trauma. Obviously I had no idea what, but a good counsellor would probably guess from the first sentence. "Before she met my dad, Ernie, she was with Bert Rock, and dad said that he never got over her, always made any excuse to see her. I think my dad had more going for him and that's why mother left Bert for him. He was a well to do man and gave her a more affluent lifestyle than Bert would ever have been able to afford. Dad told me that Bert settled down, stopped being a crook and got himself a regular job, but it was too late for mother. She was already married to my dad. But I don't think she ever truly loved dad, and as soon as the opportunity to screw Roland and Bert came up she didn't waste any time.

"My dad told me that Jeannie knew about it. I remember her as a nice lady, and I guess in those days, affairs were brushed over, ignored in the hope the problem would go away. People

159

didn't get divorced at the drop of a hat like they do nowadays. One day Jeannie was gone, and I knew she hadn't left Roland like he said; it was all too convenient."

I was reluctant, but still had to do my job. "David, you know I'm going to have to look into this, don't you?"

"Yes, and I'm glad." His forceful resolution stunned me. "I don't want everyone thinking she was just a helpless little old lady that ended up beaten and dumped on a landfill site. I want people to know what a traitorous cow she really was."

I swallowed hard, still unable to reconcile the Dorothy that had just been painted to the one I thought I had known. "Will you be prepared to give me a statement?"

"Why would you need a statement? You've already got Paul Mason in custody for her murder."

This new information, if true, would pretty much confirm Roland was the Bonfire Night Killer – once a murderer, always a murderer, right? But how much *was* true? Or was I being sidelined by a young boy's fanciful imagination. I wondered if Jeff or Paul knew of the rumours about their father's sex life, or that he'd killed their mother. I cleared my throat. "No, I said we had a man in custody, you suggested it was Paul Mason. A man has been arrested on suspicion of the murder of a completely unrelated woman, but we are investigating the possibility that he may also have been involved with your mother's death."

"How did the other woman die, just out of interest?"

The story had been all over the papers, so was no secret. "She was shot."

David Webber laughed and I squirmed. "As I said before, I never liked Paul, but I'll tell you what: I owe him nothing, but if you ask me, I don't reckon he's your guy. He was always dumb, but not violent. While I was busy frying ants with a magnifying glass or pouring salt on slugs to watch them die, he was busy re-homing caterpillars or tending injured birds. And who knows what else, he'd look after any old lame duck. Shooting is a violent crime, and the Paul I remember didn't have a cruel streak at all."

My eyes dropped to the yellow candlewick bedspread and I nodded. I was unconvinced that anything David had told me was worth the time of day. "Right. Noted." The sarcasm was thinly veiled and it rattled him.

"I think you should understand what living in here is like before you make judgements. It's like the village that time forgot, Colefield. When you walk through this place you feel like each step you take is treading on some dirty little secret or other. Curtains twitch, eyes watch you everywhere you go, it's intimidating. It's a revolting place and I couldn't wait to get away when I was growing up. It wouldn't surprise me if you named any of my parents' male friends as a killer, and probably their sons too. But the one that would shock me is Paul, because I don't believe he's capable. If you convict Paul Mason, you're just sweeping a bigger problem under the carpet."

A prickle ran along my spine, deeply aware of my own discomfort in the quaint, silent cluster of flower-fronted houses. I don't know why, but suddenly I needed, *really* needed, to speak to Jeff. He would understand. "I've got to make a call. Will you be here for couple of hours so myself and a colleague can take a statement?"

"I have a few days off work. The conniving cow named me as the executor of her will, so I'll be staying here. The truth should have come out years ago, especially when the Bonfire Night Killer struck and the place was swarming with police."

For the first time since the murders had happened, I was doubting my conviction that Paul was wholly responsible for the latest two killings, and I left the room to call Jeff, who was as surprised to hear from me as I was to be contacting him. I gave him a concise overview of the revelations, ensuring he knew I was unconvinced, but his reply was urgent, which surprised me. "Her son's on the right track, Frank, although I know for a fact that Dot wasn't involved in my real mother's death. I have a document in my possession that places her sister, Joan, in the room with Roland on the night she supposedly left. I was always told she was my mother, but apparently I've been lied to for a long time. Are you letting Paul go?"

I hesitated, knowing he wanted to hear yes, but not sure I could justify it yet. "Paul may still be involved with Fiona's murder, Jeff, you know that. Look, I know there's bad blood between us at the moment, and I hate that, but I just want to find out what really happened, even if it means admitting I'm in the wrong. Why don't you let me come over and we can go through things?"

"Frank." He sounded pained so I paused while he prepared himself. "Paul and I know more than either of us want to about the original Bonfire Night killings, but I'm not sure how much I want you to know until I've got it clear in my head. Things are very personal and I'm finding this difficult."

I shuffled, pulling the bedroom door closed to shield the conversation from David. "Jeff, what are you trying to tell me?"

Now he had the upper hand. "Let Paul out and I'll tell you. You know he's not strong enough to cope with what's happening and you know as well as I do that he's not involved."

"Come on, Jeff, you of all people know it doesn't work like that. His boots were placed at the scene by a clear footprint..."

"They weren't his boots and you've found no evidence to suggest he was wearing them."

He was right, no fibres matching any of Paul's clothing had been found, no fingerprints, DNA, and Paul had denied they were his from the start. "Everything you have on him is circumstantial, you're framing him. I know who committed the murders in the eighties, and he probably killed Fiona Malik. Dorothy too. I just need to prove it and that would be easier with your help."

I hesitated. What Jeff was saying made sense. The evidence we had was enough to hold Paul, but nothing solid enough to convict him, despite my efforts to find something. It pained me to admit this having been so adamant. "Frank? Are you still there?"

I had to make a decision. I thought of my colleague, how I had trusted his gut instincts and consistent excellence for the past four yours. How he was firmly stating he knew the Bonfire Night Killer's identity, so must have found something our search had missed. "Jeff, my neck's going to be on the line for this." I sighed, resolute, yet unconvinced of Paul's innocence. "I'll phone through an order to let him out and arrange for someone to bring him home, but in two hours, okay, because I want to speak to you without his hostility before he arrives home."

"Stop covering your arse, Frank. Make the call now, tell them to release him in two hours."

"You're a hard bastard, Jeff. I'll call now."

He sighed, relieved. "Thanks, Frank. Look, I'm at Paul's. Call me when you've arranged his free ride home, then you can come over and we'll discuss things."

"Right. I'll be bringing David with me, by the way, Dorothy Webber's son. I think you need to hear what he's told me. "

"Alright, but nobody else. Until we've got to the bottom of this mess, I want my family history kept strictly private."

I returned to the bedroom and explained to David that we would be taking his statement at the Mason family home. He was naturally surprised, having assumed it would be taken at his mother's home or the police station, but I bluffed that it was easier as the other officer was already there. He accepted my excuse and I was relieved; I didn't want him to know any of the details about the eighties murders that Jeff had mysteriously hinted at, or that Jeff was Paul's brother.

As agreed, I called Scunthorpe Station and ordered Paul's release at lunchtime, stating I had new information that didn't warrant holding him any longer. They seemed confused but, due to my rank in the investigation, didn't question my decision. I told them I'd send an email from my smartphone.

Quarter of an hour later, as David and I strolled the short distance from Dorothy's house to Paul's in silence, I thought about how the village had made me edgy from the first night, when I had driven there through curiosity. About the dense atmosphere, the inexplicable sensation of whispering and dark secrets.

Jeff and I greeted each other coldly, the friendship wavering on both sides. "Why is Benjamin Roberts here?" Jeff hadn't mentioned that Paul's solicitor would be present.

Jeff led us to the front room, his shoulders heavy, and I was briefly ashamed at how I had recently treated him. "As long as Paul's in custody, Ben will be a witness. Can I get anybody a drink?"

We declined and Jeff dragged the two wooden chairs from the kitchen for us to sit. After introductions, nobody spoke for a while, the room strangely silent, until Jeff mustered some bravado. "I have a journal written by Roland Mason. I'm not sure how Paul found it; he doesn't know I have it. The journal was clearly written for him, and it details events until the early eighties. It clearly states who the Bonfire Night Killer was."

"There, I knew it was Roland." David was momentarily self-satisfied.

"It wasn't. Roland and Dorothy," Jeff swallowed, "had an affair." He glanced at the woman's son, unaware he already knew.

David crossed his arms, content that his theory was proven. "That's what I was telling you, Mr Butler."

I was pissed off with the condescending bastard and corrected him. "Detective. Chief. Inspector."

"Do you remember me, Jeff?" I was gob smacked that David recognised him; he had only been four when he'd left. Jeff was also shocked, and David continued, "I thought I recognised you as soon as I walked in, and obviously the name confirmed my suspicions." I mentally chastised myself for stupidly introducing Jeff by his rank and surname. "I'm Dorothy's son, David Webber."

"I know."

"I knew you and Paul when you were youngsters, and I remember when you moved away from the village. I left home as soon as I turned eighteen, I was desperate to get away from this shit-hole and all the lies and deceit. Did you know that the woman who brought you up was not your mother?"

Jeff stood, eyes flashing. "It's detailed in the journal."

I set a hand on Jeff's shoulder and pushed him down gently. "Come on, mate, it's time the past was buried. Do you remember anything about leaving?"

"It makes sense to me now. I remember Roland putting me in the back seat of a car, I'd been in bed and was half-asleep. The next morning, I woke up in a new house. In retrospect I think I must have realised she wasn't my real mum, but she looked just like her and she was happy and loving. She turned out to be a

164

wonderful mum, birth mother or not. I guess at that age it didn't matter.

"I vaguely recall – now, anyway – an aunt they called Joan. I suppose it was easy to mess with my memory at that age, and after a while I must have just accepted that this aunt, Joan, was actually my mother." His eyes fell sadly to the floor, voice lowered. "I trusted them."

I'd had the benefit of David's suspicions, but Benjamin Roberts was clueless. "Am I supposed to know what we're talking about?"

Jeff's gaze was hollow. "My father was not an honourable man. He was having an affair with his wife's sister – the woman I, until now, believed was my mother – and also with Dorothy Webber. It seems that one night Roland, my birth mother, Jean, and her sister got involved in a heated argument and Roland struck Jean. She fell backwards and hit her head on the mantelpiece. When they realised she was dead, the two of them decided to cover up the truth. They put my mother into a dustbin bag and sealed the top." He paused to regain his composure. "Joan, her sister, took me to live with her. I vaguely remember asking about my mother, but she always replied that she was my mum. I guess I heard it so many times that it became the truth for me."

"What did they do with Jean's body?" It was a callous question, but necessary, and I knew Jeff understood my position as a police officer.

"Roland took her in the boot of his car and dumped her near Manchester. That's all I know. If her body was ever found, it wasn't linked back to here."

I could understand Jeff's despair, why he had reverted to calling his father Roland, rather than the affectionate 'dad' he had been using recently. It was a terrible discovery, one we would have to investigate, but I couldn't see the relevance to the Bonfire Night killings and said as much.

Jeff was pale and resigned. "Roland didn't kill those women, but he did rape them. That's all I'm going to say until Paul is here."

I smiled encouragingly. "I've arranged for his release. He should be home shortly after one. We don't need him here to carry on. You know how annoyed he'll be when he sees me here, he'll make things difficult."

I had assumed Jeff's anger a few days before was as bad as it got, but I was wrong. He leaned forward, furious, his spittle splashing my face as he shouted, "Let's get this straight, shall we? I have in my possession a diary which details all three rapes and murders in the eighties. It shows that my father raped the victims, but his accomplice was the killer. It also states, with plenty of detail, who the killer was. The man who probably also killed Fiona and Dorothy. I know what happened, but I want assurance that my brother has been exonerated from this before I fill you in with any further details."

I squirmed, uncomfortable with his rage, but I still had a job to do and he knew that. I was about to lay the law down when I became aware of another presence in the room. The four of us turned to the doorway where a stocky, older man stood, aiming a gun in our direction. If it was loaded, we were buggered without back up. "He told me he'd do this. Roland Mason was a bastard through and through. Obviously none of you can leave now. You see, I don't fancy spending the rest of my days in prison."

Nobody moved, but I sensed Jeff wasn't as surprised as me, David and Benjamin. He wore a grim expression, as if he had expected this would happen. "I knew something was going on as soon as I saw dear old David Webber – yes, I recognise you, you haven't changed a bit – walking in here with a copper. Where's the diary?" Jeff, the only person I was aware had the answer, didn't reply, keeping his eyes to the floor and face expressionless. "I said, where's the diary?" Jeff didn't respond and Bert lunged forward, whipping his head with the gun, knocking him to the floor, a mass of thick crimson oozing from his temple. He swayed as he pulled himself to his feet, unstable, and fell onto the chair.

Between the four hostages, Jeff was probably the most capable in a situation such as this, but now he had been weakened, our freedom was down to me. I stood, hands in the air, submissive. "Sir, I can see that emotions are running high. If you just put the gun down, we can…"

A shot rang out and I roared in agony as I fell to the floor, intense pain radiating from my thigh. I was staggered. It was totally unexpected. Agony exploded in waves through my leg and hip and I realised that I, too, had no control of the situation. David, although average height, was skinny, as was the short, balding Benjamin, and I doubted either would have the strength, knowledge, or courage to disarm a man with a gun, even if he was elderly. The man I assumed to be Bert Rock was definitely in charge of the room.

"I want you all to move upstairs. And who are these men, anyway?" Bert's glare was cold, his yellow-brown eyes pools of hatred. I was grateful that the pain in my leg was subsiding, my body pumped with adrenaline.

Jeff, dazed from his injury, had found inner strength. "Benjamin Roberts is Paul's solicitor. David Webber, as it seems you already know, is Dorothy's son. DCI Frank Butler is the detective in charge of investigations into Fiona Malik and Dorothy's deaths. You know who I am."

"Get upstairs and don't be making any sudden movements. I've killed before and I'll do it again at the drop of a hat," his mouth twisted to a grim leer, a black hole where a tooth should have been, "because I enjoy it."

David helped me stand, supporting my wounded side, and we stumbled up the stairs, vulnerable. Benjamin assisted Jeff, who staggered, seriously concussed. As the stairs rounded at the top, Benjamin grabbed a heavy cardboard box in an unexpected, sweeping movement, hurling it down the stairs at Bert.

Bert retaliated, shooting him accurately through the centre of his forehead. His body collapsed and Bert moved aside as it tumbled down the stairs, unquestionably dead, brain matter spattering the wall where he had been. Now I had seen how serious Bert Rock was, the terrible danger we were in sank home. The chances of getting out of the situation without more fatalities was remote. It was going to be a long and frightening day.

Chapter 14
Sunday 11th November
Hostage Situation

Bert directed us to the bedroom at the front of the house, reminding me of when I'd watched Paul's silhouetted figure searching for something in the early hours of the morning on my first visit to the curious Colefield. The memory sent a chill along my spine. I could now confirm my assumption that this was the late Roland Mason's room. From the way Bert confidently held the gun, aimed at us with his right hand, while the left deftly unhooked a backpack and dropped it to the floor, I could see he was a skilled hunter. He ordered us to sit on the double bed in a triangle, facing outwards with our arms interlinked. We did so without hesitation. Jeff and I had been trained to appease such a situation verbally, but neither of us knew enough about him to predict how he would behave, so we remained silent.

He glanced through the window, checking the gunfire hadn't aroused suspicion, and drew the curtains. Without provocation he pistol-whipped David, whose head involuntarily jerked back into ours as he whelped in pain. Now all three of us were injured. Bert took a loop of thick, nylon rope from the bag. Having spent a fair amount of time in a gun club over the past decade, I recognised a number of weapons and guessed the one he firmly held was a Ruger Blackhawk; it appeared to be old style and, although I was no expert on firearms, I suspected it was an Old Model Flattop because of the distinguishing three screws visible on the side of the bloodied revolver.

Tying one end of the rope securely to the sturdy oak leg at the base of the bed, he wound it around the three of us, and I was surprised how agile he was, considering his age, as he clambered over the bed, again and again, coiling us constrictively until virtually any movement, apart from breathing, was impossible. He tied the end of the rope to the leg of the bed on the other side.

I supposed I was the only prisoner able to see him when he stood beside the ominous backpack that lay opened on the floor.

168

He brought out two Hessian sacks, placing one each over Jeff's head and mine. "I only brought two bags, didn't think I'd need a third." We were trapped and blinded. I could hear shuffling and some movement from the position where David was, and I suspected Bert had found something to blindfold him. None of us spoke. Finally, I heard him dragging furniture, guessing it was a chair. "Tell me where the diary is or I'll kill the three of you."

Although I was bleeding, the bullet in my leg hadn't punctured an artery, so I wasn't in immediate danger of collapsing. However, Jeff's reply was not only muffled, but also slurred, and I knew he needed urgent medical attention. "I've hidden it well. If you kill us, you'll never know where it is." I was unsure whether he was being brave or stupid. I heard a thud, then a blinding flash in my head, and realised Bert had struck Jeff again with such a force his head had cracked painfully into mine.

"Then I shall torture each and every one of you until you tell me." A bland, matter-of-fact statement and I realised with horror that he was devoid of emotion. I was terrified, yet sensible, thinking laterally for a way to escape. I wasn't sure if Jeff was capable of rational thought after the second blow and hoped I'd have a partner when I worked out a solution. We remained silent; our attacker was too unpredictable.

I felt my mobile in my trouser pocket, but we were bound so tightly it was impossible to move. I wondered whether Jeff or David were able to access their phones. Ironically, on cue, Jeff's mobile rang its familiar chime.

"Fucking bastard things." Bert's rage was palpable. "Where is it? Give the bastard thing to me."

"I can't reach it." He sounded as if his tongue was larger than his mouth and I was increasingly concerned about Jeff's condition, more so when his head cracked against mine again. He managed a gurgling noise before slumping forward, his body relaxed. With horror, I realised he was unconscious.

I had to rely on instinct and guessed being helpful was the way to go. "He keeps it in the chest pocket of his shirt."

I felt tugging beside me and the call ended abruptly. "Where do you two keep yours?"

"I left mine in my overcoat back at my mother's house." David sounded terrified, exactly how I felt.

"Mine is in my trouser pocket." If David was telling the truth, taking my mobile would lose our final lifeline, but I couldn't risk Jeff being hit again. Or any of us. Our tormentor ripped my pocket open and stole my last hope.

Sue had arrived home early, the Sunday traffic moderate, and bathed the baby before feeding him. After playing with Jacob for a while, he tired and she laid him in his pram for his midday nap. Her mind had been solely on her husband and the plight of his estranged family, and she phoned Jeff for an update. She was used to him ignoring her calls while he was working, but he wasn't, and the call ringing off before the answerphone played disturbed her.

She prepared a mug of chicken noodle soup, warming to fend off the chilly, wintry day, and sorted a basket of laundry while it cooled enough to drink. However, the mindless job didn't quell her concern. Maybe once Jacob awoke she should drive back across the bridge and see how he was. Or maybe she should stay in her cosy, tidy house and try calling him again later. Maybe he'd not taken the call because he was deep in conversation with Paul's solicitor and the timing was inconvenient. She busied herself in the kitchen, putting the dishes away, cleaning surfaces, trying to ignore the ominous sense that something was wrong.

Scooping the final noodles to her mouth with a teaspoon, Sue hesitated before dialling a familiar number; Jeff and his boss were on ill terms at the moment, but she was still friendly with his wife.

Ellen was pleased to hear from her as they hadn't had a natter for a while. But when Sue mentioned her concerns about Jeff not answering the phone, Ellen laughed. "You've got too much time on your hands now you've had that baby, young lady. Take advantage of not being at the beck and call of either man or baby. Get your feet up and watch some telly for a change."

When she ended the call, Sue realised how dramatic and paranoid she must have sounded and flumped onto the sofa, closing her eyes and trying to enjoy the peace.

A mile away, Ellen put the phone down. Her husband's mobile had transferred straight to the answerphone. Like Sue, she had an ominous feeling that all was not well.

The door to the cell clanged open and Paul, who lay forlorn on the uncomfortable bed, looked at the young constable. "We've had word from above that you're allowed to go home."

He didn't move, a flash of confused disbelief fleeting over his face, and she moved towards him, annoyed. Alicia's tone and manner were curt and cutting. "I don't know why, but I do know it's highly irregular." She grasped his shoulder, her face close to his and her words quiet. "Get up, you lazy fuck. Obviously some strings have been pulled by your bloody brother, so you might as well take advantage of it, mate."

He laid still, weary and indifferent. "I'm not your mate. I don't even know you."

"Whatever." She stood tall and sneered. "I've arranged your release forms. You need to come with me and get your stuff. Then I've been told to drive you home. Don't know why your precious brother or counsel couldn't do it, but obviously some people round here get special treatment. Get up and do as you're bloody told, arsehole."

Paul glared at her. He stood, stretched and followed her from the cell. Once he had signed the documents confirming the return of his belongings and his release, she led him, still unspeaking, to a pool car and he sat in the back. As she filtered onto the road, he leant towards her and whispered menacingly, "If you think I'm a killer, why are you alone in the car with me? I could murder you."

A shiver ran along her spine as she realised how vulnerable she was. "Shut the fuck up and sit back, arsehole."

The journey passed in silence, with Alicia frequently checking the rear-view mirror for movement, but he behaved, gazing through the window, soaking up the architecture in

Scunthorpe and relishing the few brief miles of countryside towards Colefield. After five miles – the longest Alicia had ever experienced – they drew up outside his home. "You can get out now."Her voice was as icy as the temperature.

He focussed through the window, still, and full of consternation. "Somebody's been in my house. My dad's curtains are drawn."

"Well you'll have to ask your bloody brother about that one. Get out." He climbed onto the freezing grass on the verge, tentative, and as soon as he had closed the car door, Alicia sped off, showering him with mud and leaves whisked up by the skidding tyres.

Bert had watched the patrol car drop its passenger off through a gap in the curtains and he flicked the drape across, furious. "What's your bastard brother doing here, I thought he was locked up."

I heard a crack and Jeff's limp head smacked against mine for the third time. He was clearly unconscious. I was relieved that Paul was back, hoping he would be flanked by a couple of officers when he discovered us. I didn't dare speak in case Bert pistol-whipped me, but David had no idea of the danger he was putting us in. "You mean help's here?"

A shot rang out and David's body jerked and sagged. In my blindfolded darkness, I couldn't tell whether either man was alive or dead. I could hear a distant, persistent rapping, a male voice shouting, but I couldn't make out the words. I heard Bert slide quietly, the hunter in him stealthy, from the room. I groped with my hands, trying to wriggle free of the trap. The rope was bound tightly, our arms interlinked, and as we were secured to the bed, I couldn't lever from my position. I squirmed as much as the constraints would allow, my injured leg pounding with pain, but the rope didn't budge. Silently, I shifted my feet back and forth, trying to locate something, anything, that would help me break free. There was nothing, but I didn't lose hope.

I concentrated on what I could hear to try and make out what was happening. I had guessed it was Paul hammering at the back door, imagining his fury at being locked from his own

172

home. I heard him try the front door and assumed he had checked if any windows were open. The banging re-started at the back of the house for a short while, then stopped. The silence was haunting.

Bert was in the kitchen, out of sight of both the door and window, and he could hear two men outside talking. Agitated, Paul told elderly Mr Carver that he was locked out, and the next-door neighbour helpfully offered to get the spare key Roland had given his wife years before for moments such as this. Paul explained he had a key, but the door was bolted on the inside.

"Don't get yourself upset, lad." He pointed to the dirt track. "Your brother's car is there so it must be him who's done it. Can't you just phone him and get him to let you in, instead of making all this bleeding racket?"

Paul relaxed on seeing Jeff's car, comforted that the intruder was family. "I don't have his number. It's in the address book inside."

"Surely you must have it on your mobile phone? That's how you youngsters do things nowadays, isn't it?"

Paul growled, "Never had one and I never will."

"Then come inside and wait for a while. Mrs Carver will make you a cup of tea and we can wait until you see some movement. There's no need for all this banging and shouting, you'll scare the devil."

Bert let his breath out when the voices dissipated, relieved. His plan was going too well to have it ruined by the lumbering idiot son of the man he detested now more than ever. Mr Carver's voice had been calm, meaning the gunshots hadn't been a cause for concern in the village. He tugged the curtain across the window in case they came back and opened the fridge, pulling out a beer, which he sank within seconds, his dry throat easing. Snatching a couple more, he took them to the front room so the open fire could warm him; the house was freezing. At the age of sixty-one, he was unaccustomed to the activity and needed a break. The prisoners were tied securely, there was no chance of them breaking free, and he figured he would have a breather before searching for the journal. There was plenty of time.

I was confident Bert hadn't returned to the room, despite making more noise than I had hoped to in my quest to break free of the restraint. I heard a low moaning and realised at least one of the men I was tied to was still alive. I whispered, "Who is that? Is that you, Jeff?"

The moaning continued and I was worried it would disturb Bert, wherever he was. "Don't make so much noise or he'll come back. Is that you, Jeff?"

"David. It's David."

"Did he shoot you?"

"I think so. In my stomach. It hurts."

"Okay. David, you're going to have to be really strong. If we don't get out of this trap I'm sure he's going to kill us all. Have you lost much blood?"

I felt his arms move slightly, gauging the wetness on his clothes as an indication of his blood loss. "A bit, yes, I can feel it on my shirt."

"You've got to be strong, okay. Are you blindfolded?"

"Yes." His wavering voice told me he was speaking through gritted teeth and I despaired at our helplessness, but David and I had to work together if we had any chance of escaping.

"Turn to me. Use your teeth and drag the sack from my head."

He followed my orders, whelping with pain, and I felt the Hessian scraping over my skin, inch-by-inch. "I can't do this. It hurts too much."

I had been trying to assist with my teeth and tongue but it wasn't easy. "Don't stop. You're doing really well, there can't be much further to go." I felt him bite the sack and it shifted a little further. "Keep going, you're doing really well. Not far to go now." The rough material scraped up and I gratefully felt the cold air on my chin. "Keep going, David." My eyes were clear again. I shook my head vigorously, leaning back, and the sack fell to my shoulders behind me.

"Well done, I can see. You did it, David." I leant as far to my left as I could. The blood spillage on David's shirt and trousers was shocking and my heart leapt. Leaning to see Jeff on my right side was more difficult as his limp body followed mine with every movement. I sighed, exhausted mentally and physically. "Okay, listen carefully. I'm going to give you instructions and I want you to do exactly as I say."

He was sobbing, his animalistic moans agonising to hear, and though I was in pain from the bullet in my thigh, our only chance of getting out of this hellhole was down to me. I hadn't heard a sound for a long time, so something must have happened to Paul. Maybe even to Bert. I focused on the moment. "I am facing the door, Jeff is facing the window and you are at the end of the bed. The rope is tied to the foot end legs of the bed. We need to try, between us, to get to the floor in front of you and somehow either untie, or unhook, at least one side of the rope. You have to be strong. It will hurt both of us, but I'm sure we can do this."

"What about Jeff?"

"Don't worry about Jeff, it's down to you and me. Focus, David, focus." I knew that with Jeff's limp weight, and mine and David's injuries – plus the limiting position of our arms – my suggestion was nigh on impossible, but if we didn't try we had no hope of surviving. We edged forward, maybe a millimetre or so at a time, but each movement was progress. Time was the essence, because Bert could reappear at any time, and if he found us attempting to escape I was sure we would be dead men.

Sue had followed Ellen's advice and relaxed on the sofa until Jacob woke, but she had been restless; the niggling feeling that something wasn't right wouldn't leave. She breastfed the baby and prepared a pan of Jeff's favourite chilli-con-carne for dinner, but the worry continued. She was a policewoman, trained to act on instinct. Ellen wasn't. She tried Jeff's number again, willing him to answer and tell her she was being a silly, paranoid new mother, full of hormones.

The ringing stopped and her heart jumped, fear and relief. "Jeff, I've been so worried about you."

"Who is this then?"

It wasn't Jeff. The voice was old and gruff. "Who are you? Why have you got my husband's mobile?"

"It's okay, love, Jeff's just popped out for a minute, he left me to hold the fort. He's nipped out to get a bite to eat as there was no food in the house." Bert took a gulp from his fourth can of beer, smiling, enjoying every moment of the atrocious game he was playing.

Sue sensed it was a lie. Jeff was a creature of habit and always kept his mobile in his chest pocket, no matter what. He would never have left it with anyone, even Frank. She should have trusted her instincts. Something untoward was happening and it was essential she choose the right words to appease the stranger on the phone. She forced a grin to make her voice sound bright. "Oh, that's okay. I'm his wife, and I was just wondering if he's going to be in for tea tonight. I thought he was with his brother Paul at the police station, but obviously I'm wrong. Did he go back to Colefield?"

"Yep, he's been at my house. We've been having a beer and a chat. He's just collecting a takeaway but I'm sure he'll be back soon. I'll tell him you called."

She needed him to stay on the phone and concentrated on keeping her voice cheery. "Okay, thanks. Hey, I don't recognise your voice. Have we met?"

"I don't think so, love."

"Well, go on then, tell me your name," she chuckled lightly.

"Just a friendly neighbour, love." He cut the call and threw the phone into the fire. The flames encompassed it, sizzling and popping, and as an afterthought, he shielded it with the metal fireguard in case the battery exploded.

Before the call, Bert had been half-heartedly searching the room for the journal, but had found nothing, and this irritated him.

A thud on the ceiling startled him and he realised his prisoners were on the move. He took the gun from the armrest and moved slowly, footsteps silent, through the doorway, past Benjamin's body and up the creaking stairs.

As soon as the call ended, Sue called the emergency services. She explained the situation and her position in the police force, hoping this would ensure they took her suspicions seriously, but they patronisingly reassured her that they would look into her allegations soon. She insisted they locate Jeff's car using the tracking system and send patrol cars to find him. The control room operator, sure the caller was simply hormonal and over-imaginative, repeated that the situation didn't warrant any urgency. Frustrated, Sue swiftly dressed Jacob in his winter suit and dropped him at her parent's house. They were fortunately at home and she practically threw the baby and his bag of essentials at them. "I can't tell you what's wrong because I don't know myself, but Jeff's in trouble and he needs my help."

She raced through Hull to the police headquarters, where she had worked before having Jacob, and explained to the desk sergeant, an old colleague, that she had to see Frank Butler, Alan Reeves or Dom Townsend immediately. "Look, Sue, you're on maternity leave and you have no jurisdiction here."

"Something is wrong, really, I'm not crazy. Jeff is missing, there's a strange man with his mobile, and you know how anal he is with that phone. Please, just get Dom or Alan."

The smirking man sighed dramatically. He picked up the phone with a flourish, keeping an amused eye on her as he dialled the offices slowly – painfully slowly – with the end of a pen.

The main doors opened and Dom strolled in, closely followed by Alan, and Sue ran over, thankful. "PC Mason, what a surprise. What are you doing here?"

"Stay here, Alan, Dom. Don't go anywhere." Sue rapped on the front desk window to get the sergeant's attention. "Have you traced the car yet, Jeff's car? I placed an emergency call about thirty minutes ago." He rolled his eyes, languidly calling another constable in a sardonic tone.

Dom was confused. He and Alan were returning from a late lunch and hadn't any idea about the fuss Sue had been creating. "What's going on?"

She rapped again on the window. "Well?"

"Yes, sweetheart, we have. It's in a place called Colefield, it's on the…"

Sue dismissed him, grabbing both Dom and Alan's wrists. "Come with me, it's urgent."

She dragged them both through the doors and the desk sergeant and his colleagues burst into laughter, shaking their heads. "Must be missing the job, the bloody woman's gone crazy."

Paul had become bored of Mr and Mrs Carver's company, of their vast collection of twee ornaments and the overly strong tea served in china cups, the cloying, musky, overly-hot house. He wanted to be in his own place with all its familiarities, especially the tempting whisky that sat beside his comfortable, well-worn armchair. Without explanation, he thanked them for their time and left.

Instead of wasting time knocking, he went to the shed and rummaged about for the crowbar amongst the disorderly stacks of tools, wood, gardening equipment, weed-killers and fertilisers. He strode the short distance to the back door, fed the metal lever into the thin gap beside the lock, between the door and frame, and used his strength to tug, the wood splintering and cracking. Within a minute, he was inside.

Immediately, Paul could see he'd had unwanted houseguests. He had expected his brother to be there, but Jeff knew he liked the place kept in his own unique untidiness. Instead there were a couple of empty beer cans on the table, unwashed plates he hadn't used scattered around, and the fridge door was open, which Jeff would never do. He grasped a carving knife from the kitchen side and tucked it into his belt, and held the crowbar tentatively over his shoulder. He crept through to the front room. The fire roared in the grate and two discarded beer cans lay on the table, alongside his emptied bottle of whisky. His anger surged to boiling point; he'd been looking forward to a drink.

He slunk through to the hallway and gasped. On the carpet, slumped by the front door, was his solicitor's body, the head lying in a deep-red pool of blood. His heart quickened. Immediately defensive, he heard muffled voices coming from upstairs. Adrenaline surged and he tiptoed up the stairs, avoiding the steps that had squeaky floorboards. He neared his father's room and the voices became clearer, one that he recognised from somewhere but couldn't put a face to. The other he knew well: Bert's. His fists tightened around the steel rod in preparation for a fight. Heart pounding, he listened through the door.

The voice he couldn't place was barely more than a husky whisper. "You've already killed at least one, maybe two men, where do you think this is going to end?"

"Shut it, fuckwit."

"I'm a senior police officer; do you really think they're not going to find you, Bert? I mean, what will you do with our bodies when you've finished with us? Your DNA will be all over us. Plus, the journal will tell everybody what you did thirty years ago."

His guttural voice was loud, fuming. "That journal is a pack of lies. Roland always said he'd do this, but he was the killer, not me. All you have is a bunch of meaningless words from a dead man who's about to be cremated."

Paul slowly pushed the door ajar and the first thing to hit him was the heady smell of iron, of blood. He struggled not to gasp at the scene before him. Bert, who hadn't noticed him, was crouching, facing away, a gun poised in his hand. He leant over three men, who were tightly tied together in a bloodied triangle. One was motionless and had a sack over his head that was soaked in crimson, reflecting the light from a crack in the curtains. Beside him, a man he didn't recognise was blindfolded, his clothes dripping with blood. The third was the man who had arrested him, mouth spitting droplets of ruby as he spoke. His eyes were blackened, his grey trousers scarlet with oozing fluid. Paul raised the crowbar above his head and crashed it onto Bert's back between his shoulder and neck.

The crack resounded through the filthy, blood-soaked room. For me, things seemed to happen in slow motion: the gun fell to the floor and Bert slumped forward, curling in agony, gasping and gurgling for breath. Paul kicked Bert, who clenched his chest and whimpered in pain, and grabbed the gun, throwing it angrily aside.

My fight disappeared the moment I saw Bert incapacitated. I could feel blood – taste it, smell it – and I wanted to succumb to the powerful urge to close my eyes and sleep. "Paul. You came. Thank you." I was so proud he hadn't killed our tormentor, yet guilty I'd labelled him a brute. Paul wasn't a brute; he was a hero.

"Where's my brother?" He withdrew the blade from his belt and deftly sliced through the rope that held me tightly against what I suspected were two dead men. I felt the restraints loosen, and exhausted, my battered body fell to the side, lying helplessly on the worn carpet. I couldn't reply, my strength had disappeared and I wasn't sure I cared if it never came back. I tried to fight against my closing eyelids, knowing that if they shut, my injuries were so severe they may not open again. In the duskiness, the sun behind the curtains, low as the wintry day headed towards evening, I saw Paul step over me, his huge, gallant body trying to help his brother -the brother he lost years ago but now clearly adored. I was in a dream-like state,my mind floating as I lay there, oddly bereft of pain. Dancing amongst the shadows, drifting from one moment to the next, knowing we had been rescued but no longer clear from what anymore.

I could hear noises that may have been in a different land, but I soon realised they were in the room with me. The words weren't clear. They came and went, coasting into my psyche and back out, flowing, ebbing. A light went on and it was too bright so I closed my eyes.

"Put your hands up and step away from the men. Paul Mason, I am arresting you on suspicion of…" The voice I thought I recognised drifted away and, exhausted with the struggle, I let go.

Chapter 15
Monday 12th November

I sensed I was lying on a bed, and I couldn't move. My breathing was laboured and my throat was dreadfully sore, raspy. I tried to swallow but it was impossible, and I couldn't move my arms or legs; they were dead weights. Voices came every now and then, but what they said was unintelligible, as if spoken in an unknown foreign language. A wonderfully pleasant warmth pulsed through my body, the sensation of being on the crest of a gentle wave, floating on my back, basking in the sun.

Someone took my hand and a woman's voice drifted in and out of my ears, sometimes urgent, sometimes soft. I didn't know where I was, what was happening, who was around, but I didn't care. I let the blackness take me again.

The doctor approached the bed, his face stern, and Ellen tensed with worry. "Mrs Butler, Frank's going to be here a while, his condition is very serious." She gulped, unable to find any words. "His injuries are severe and he has suffered massive blood loss. The surgery was a success, we've contained the bleed on his brain and sealed the vein in his thigh. He'll need further surgery to repair the damage to his leg in the future, but I must advise you that the trauma to his head is what worries us the most." He took Ellen's hand. "Do you understand what I'm telling you?"

"I think so. I'm not sure. When will he wake up?" Ellen ran another soggy tissue through her fingers, scared, tearful and guilty for the recent arguments. Had she known she may never see her husband awake again, she wouldn't have let the pettiness in.

The doctor lowered his head. "To be honest, Mrs Butler, he might not. And if he were to, we would need to put him into a medical coma to allow his brain time to heal. The damage is extensive."

The tears flowed again. She had shed enough already, but they wouldn't stop and her stomach muscles ached from sobbing. She scanned her husband's face, his head cocooned with a bandage, a thick white tube in his mouth from the ventilator that breathed for him, the mottled purple bruises and swelling around his eyes, cheekbones and jaw. Ellen pointed to a flexible tube fed into the head bandage and choked, "So what's this?"

"It's draining fluid from around his brain to take the pressure off."

"Is," she faltered, a sob catching her breath, "is he in pain?"

"We are giving him morphine intravenously. He's in no pain, and he's also having anticonvulsant medication to stop him having a seizure."

"Can he hear me?"

"We don't know, but keep talking to him just in case. Mrs Butler, or may I call you Ellen?" She nodded tearfully. "Thank you. Ellen, he's in the best place, and we're doing everything we can. Please try and stay positive. Do you have anyone who can be with you? This must be very traumatic."

"My children," she surveyed Frank's broken face and lifeless body, the only movement his breathing, "our children. They'll be taking turns to come and visit. I won't be leaving."

The doctor laid a hand on Ellen's shoulder gently. "You need to get rest too. You need to be strong. When they visit, take advantage and have a break; get yourself drinks, food, we have a canteen…"

She waved her hand, dismissive. "I'm not the important one here. Doctor, I have to ask, will he survive this?"

He paused, awkward. "In all honesty, we don't know."

In an adjacent room across the corridor, Sue sat beside her husband ina scene similar to mine and Ellen's. Jeff was also in a coma. He hadn't been shot, thankfully, but the trauma to his head was extreme, having been pistol-whipped a number of times. Several areas of his skull had been shattered and he'd had emergency surgery the previous evening to remove bone fragments from his brain. In addition, his heart had given up at the scene and the paramedics had successfully revived him three times on the way to the hospital. Of the two of us, his injuries were the most critical and it was unlikely he would survive. Poor

David Webber hadn't. He had been declared dead on arrival at Scunthorpe Hospital, taking his knowledge of Colefield's past to the grave.

A realistic person by nature, Sue wasn't handling the situation well, berating herself with guilt. If she had listened to her instincts, she could have been at Colefield several hours earlier. While she had been lounging on the sofa, supping hot soup and reading a pointless novel, her husband had been enduring violent torture. She could have nipped back to Hessle, collected more supplies for Jacob and returned to help Jeff. More sickeningly, she had known the murderer wasn't Roland, that he wasn't dead. None of this would have happened had she done things differently. Jeff's condition, my condition, David's death. Her fault.

Jeff's prognosis was dire, hanging to life by a thread. Would she soon be a single parent, little Jacob growing up and never knowing his father? Her baby was still with her parents. When she had called them from Paul's house, her words nonsensical through panic, they had pacified her, assuring the baby would be fine. They would keep him for as long as necessary, start him on bottled formula with the guidance of their medical centre. She wasn't to worry.

But whatever anybody said, this was her fault.

In her desperate state, her husband's recovery the only thing that mattered, it didn't occur to question Paul's arrest. That an innocent man had been charged with the abomination.

Townsend and Reeves had roughly handcuffed Paul as he had struggled, pleading his innocence, and after ensuring medical attention had arrived for their colleagues, Bert Rock and the stranger, they had taken him directly to the police station in Hull, rather than returning to Scunthorpe. His appearance in court was a priority, due to the severity of the victims' injuries, and was scheduled for the afternoon.

Paul had adamantly refused to talk in the interview room, only repeating his innocence. But Dom and Alan had seen him, leaning over four injured men with a carving knife in his hand, and nearby lay a bloodied gun and a crowbar. Not to mention the dead body of another man, now known to be a criminal lawyer based in Scunthorpe named Benjamin Roberts. There was no doubt he would be sent down for life.

In the cell, Paul lay motionless on the bed, as he had done in Scunthorpe after being arrested for the murders of Fiona Malik and Dorothy Webber. His father had told him on his deathbed not to mention the journal to anybody, and he hadn't, so why was he being punished?

He couldn't understand why he was in trouble for trying to help his brother and the two other injured men. What had he done wrong?

With Benjamin Roberts dead and his brother incapacitated, Paul had to accept a legal advisor arranged by the police, and presently a wiry, short man was allowed access to his cell. "My name is Simon West, I'm the solicitor allotted to your case."

Paul didn't move, his unseeing eyes focussed on the grimy grey wall. Simon sat beside Paul's legs and laid the paperwork he'd brought on his lap. He skimmed the notes. "Is there anything you want to tell me?" No answer came. "Paul, I'm here to help you, but I can't unless you start talking to me. You're due in court in," he checked his watch, "two hours exactly, and I need to know your plea. You have been accused of murdering four people and critically injuring two."

Paul slowly sat, his hefty legs swinging over the edge of the bed. "I haven't killed anybody."

Simon scribbled on his notepad. He scratched his ear – a nervous habit – and a sprinkling of skin from a patch of eczema fell onto the paper. He dusted it away, showering the floor with tiny, white flakes. "So you plan to plead not guilty. I must advise you that the evidence against you is strong, and it would be in your best interests to plead guilty; it will act in your favour and could well lessen the sentence you will receive."

Simon flinched at the intensity of Paul's glare. Deep, glistening black pools that warned and threatened danger. "I didn't kill nobody. I went into my dad's room and saw my brother. I tried to help him."

Simon coughed, flicking through the paperwork, unwilling to catch the evil stare again. "Paul, your fingerprints are on the gun, the crowbar and the knife. The gun was used to shoot three men, killing two, and two men are in a critical condition after being beaten severely. It is also believed that the head injuries of three of the men, including your brother, were caused by the gun. Which, may I point out, you have no firearms licence for, amongst other things."

Paul was tired, wishing the stupid situation would go away. He wanted to sit in his armchair with his bottle of whisky and exist. He wanted Dorothy back to cook him breakfast and dinner. He wanted his dad back, for that matter. He wanted his life the way it was before his father died. He had enjoyed it then. He stood, filling the room. "It isn't my gun. Bert dropped it. I killed no-one."

Simon sighed, expelling the air slowly, uncomfortable in the huge man's intimidating presence. "You are also being charged with the murder of Fiona Malik, who was killed with the same gun, and the court is also going to take into consideration the circumstances of Dorothy Webber's death."

Paul was agitated at having to repeat himself, especially regarding the two women's deaths. "Don't you hear straight, mister whatever? I said I killed no-one."

Simon returned the paperwork to the orderly file and snapped it closed. "You will be able to spend ten minutes with me before the court hearing. If you can think of anything that may help your defence, please let me know, because I'd like to help you if you'd let me. The charges against you are serious and the evidence strongly backs them up. Please, my legal advice to you is to change your plea to guilty." He rose and a guard unlocked the cell door.

Paul lay on the bed, once more staring sightlessly at the wall, and listened to the footsteps as they diminished along the corridor.

The police had released details of Paul Mason's arrest, and outside Hull Combined Court, local journalists struggled for position against the bullyboy national reporters, confident and brash with their fancy television cameras and microphones. It was mayhem for the driver of the secure van that carried the suspect, edging as closely to the doors of the building as was safely possible. In the back of the vehicle, a blanket was thrown over Paul's head and he was led outside by a team of officers, who guided him through the deafening, thronging, vulture-like crowd. Chanting and taunting, hurling obscenities, the crowd hounded the suspect angrily.

Paul was scared. He hadn't killed anyone, unless Bert was dead. He was taken to a tiny room where Simon West was waiting and they shook hands. "Have you decided to change your plea?"

"I won't tell people I'm guilty if I'm not. My dad always told me not to lie. He told me it was a bad thing to do."

"If you really believe you're innocent Paul, you need to tell me why. From what I can see it's impossible for you *not* to have committed these crimes." Simon scratched his ear with a pen, flakes of dead skin falling over his suited shoulders like a light snow shower. He had never represented somebody charged with multiple murders before and was completely out of his depth.

"I never killed that girl. I didn't even know her. And I would never kill Dot; she was my friend. Bert tied them all up, not me. I was next door at Mr Carver's house. I saved them all by hitting Bert and trying to set them free. Then the police hurt me and took me away."

Simon coughed nervously, scratching the unsightly eczema vigorously and thickening the layer on his jacket. "You know that Mr and Mrs Carver have each issued a damning statement against you, don't you?"

Simon noticed the genuine shock in Paul's eyes. "What?"

He huffed as he leafed through the paperwork in his file. "This is the statement from Mr Frederick Carver, taken yesterday: '*Paul was making a right racket outside his house, he tried the front and back doors, he was shouting and hammering. I went out to see what all the fuss was about. He said he was locked out of his house; that someone had barricaded himself in using the bolt on the back door. I suggested he come back to mine and had a cup of tea. I said his brother's car was there and it was probably him inside the house. I had no idea the poor man was trying to keep Paul out. He came back to mine, my Joyce made a pot of tea, but he was really agitated; he wanted to get back to his own house. He was swearing and shouting, completely out of control.'"*

Paul's eyes were wide, confused. "But I never swore. I wouldn't swear in front of a lady, especially Mrs Carver."

Simon tapped the pen on the page. "I'm just reading the statement that was taken by an officer of the law and signed by Mr Carver after having it read back to him. Shall I continue?" Paul sat on the chair beside the desk, head down, mouth hanging. "He says: *'He was like an animal in the end, desperate to get home, and we had no choice but to let him go – by that time Joyce and I were frightened for our lives. He went, and the next thing I saw he was jemmying the door open using a crowbar. I bolted the door, worried. Just a couple of minutes later, if that, I saw the police turn up, and then there were ambulances, crime scene tape, the lot.'* That's as far as it goes."

Paul's eyes pleaded, looking to his solicitor for a ray of hope. "What about Mrs Carver?"

Simon turned the page and glanced over Mrs Carver's statement. "It says pretty much the same thing."

"But they're lying. It wasn't like that at all."

Time had run out. An announcement crackled through the Tannoy, and Paul was escorted from the office and taken to the courtroom. Guided by officers, he made his way to a seat at the front.

The charges were read and it took just over a minute before the judge, pleased to have a cut and dried case, remanded Paul to HM Prison in Hull while the police gathered evidence against him for his trial. He was led away, handcuffs clinking.

Sue had fallen asleep a couple of hours before, seated on an uncomfortable chair beside the bed where Jeff lay, her head resting on the pale-blue blanket under his hand. The door opened quietly and her parents, Jack and Brenda Dawson, strolled through, her father carrying sleeping Jacob in his car seat.

Brenda drew a chair beside her daughter and took her hand. "Sue, love, it's your mam."

Sue stirred, confused initially as to her whereabouts. "Mam, what are you doing here?"

"We've brought Jacob to see you, we thought you might be missing him." Brenda sat, tucking Sue's curly mahogany hair neatly behind her ear and stroking her hand lovingly.

Sue glanced beside her feet to Jacob's car seat and gazed at her slumbering son. "I'm not sure the nurses…"

"Shhhh, don't worry. We phoned before we came. They said it might be a good idea for Jeff to hear him, it might help. How are you, love?"

Sue sat straight and stretched, yawning. She turned to Jeff and surveyed his peaceful, yet bruised and swollen, face, his closed eyes, the bandages that wrapped his head reminding her of the atrocious injuries her dreams had forgotten. "I'm the last of my concerns, mam. Do you know if there's been any change in his condition? I must have been out of it for a while. I'm exhausted." Sue noticed the curtains were drawn and realised that night had fallen during her much-needed rest.

"We had a word with the nurses, they say there's been no change, but that's not a bad thing. Sleeping is the best thing for him while his head recovers from the operation. We have some good news for you, though."

Sue eyed her parents sardonically. "It can't get much worse."

"The man who did this has been to court today and he's been sent to Hull Prison on remand. The case against him is straightforward, it's just a matter of formalities, and they expect him to get several life sentences. He shouldn't ever come out of prison."

Sue was quizzical. In the panic over her husband she hadn't realised they had a suspect already. "Really? That was quick."

Brenda glanced at Jack, worried. "Love, we told you yesterday, but maybe you were too distraught to understand what we were saying. Jeff's brother Paul, he did this to him."

Sue sat up straight, stunned. "No. No he didn't. Paul didn't do this. I know, I was there." The fragmented memories of the previous, tortuous day pieced themselves together in her muddled mind. "Paul was helping him. He'd cut the rope."

Jack reached out and pulled his daughter close for a fatherly hug, but she resisted, angry. "Come on, Sue, calm down. You've had a dreadful shock."

"You don't get it. Paul was being framed for Fiona Malik and Dorothy Webber's murders, and the police believed that Jeff and Paul's father, Roland Mason, was the Bonfire Night Killer from the nineteen eighties. Jeff has a notebook somewhere that says otherwise. I've seen it. It was written by Roland before he died. Either Frank or Jeff arranged for Paul to be let out of custody. Paul didn't do this, it was Bert Rock, the other guy who came to hospital with injuries."

Jack leaned over, whispering. "Perhaps we should take you for a break. I'm not sure it's a good idea to talk about this in front of Jeff; he may be able to hear. Come on Sue, Brenda, let's take Jacob down to the canteen. I'll get us all a bite to eat, something hot to drink, and we can discuss things there." They shuffled from the room, quiet now, bar the

beeping machines and ventilator. Jeff had heard every word. He lay, trapped in his useless body, floating high on morphine, anticonvulsants, and muscle relaxants, and knew that he had to get better somehow, or his brother would be spending the rest of his life locked in prison for crimes he hadn't committed. And Bert Rock would walk free, able to continue his violent web of lies for as many years as he had left.

Back home after having his injuries treated at the hospital, Bert sat in his impeccably tidy, organised house, lounging on the sofa in glorious freedom, able to relive the enjoyable moments of the past thirty-two years, safe in the knowledge that every scrap of potential evidence against him was now gone. He awkwardly levered himself up and limped to the drinks cabinet.

Pouring from the crystal decanter with his left hand wasn't easy, his right arm resting in a sling to protect it from movement to prevent further damage to his cracked collarbone, but he managed, and took the large measure of Remy Martin back to the sofa. Sipping to his victory, he thought of the months ahead. His injury was expected to take roughly six weeks to heal, which meant he would miss half the hunting season, but he should be

189

better in time to enjoy the final two months of shooting partridges, pheasants, ducks and geese. He smiled. Life was good.

Chapter 16
Wednesday 14th November

Sue hadn't left the hospital since Sunday evening, when she had travelled in the ambulance, lights flashing and sirens blaring, after Jeff had been attacked. On hearing the news by telephone, Ellen had also rushed to the hospital and stayed with her husband. Both women were shattered, physically and mentally, but neither man had shown much improvement. They had discussed the situation in detail during infrequent trips to the canteen to fuel themselves with little more than mugs of tea or cocoa; both had lost their appetites, unimportant compared to the very real possibility that they would lose their husbands. Sue had explained about Roland's journal, the intricate detailing of the historic crimes in Colefield that had shocked the nation over a period of three years. And she had convinced Ellen that Paul was not the man who had hurt their husbands. Ellen was impressed enough with Sue's conviction that she agreed to help investigate, if that became necessary.

The morning visiting period was due any minute and Ellen, satisfied that her husband's condition was stable, sat with Sue at Jeff's bedside to await Jack and Brenda, whom she had become acquainted with over the previous two days.

They arrived, as usual, with Jacob in his car seat, and for a few minutes the four adults cooed over the baby. Having missed him so much, Sue gave him extra cuddles. She was deeply grateful that her parents were caring for him, knowing she would be unable to cope while her future was potentially in tatters.

Having allowed Jacob to gurgle and chuckle beside Jeff for a while, Sue suggested they head for the canteen, explaining she had an idea she wanted to discuss, and that Ellen was willing to be part of the plan.

Brenda and Jack sent the two fretting wives to a table with Jacob while they collected a couple of trays laden with hot, nutritious meals and the beverages of choice. Ellen and Sue picked at their meals, while Brenda and Jack devoured theirs heartily. Soon, Brenda laid her fork down and Jack scooped her leftovers onto his plate. "You said you wanted to discuss something with us."

"Have you thought any more about what I said to you on Monday? About Paul not being guilty of this."

Brenda held her daughter's hand. "Love, we've spoken to the police. The case they have against Paul is watertight."

"No, it's not. It's convenient, but it's not the truth."

The Dawsons exchanged a concerned glance. "Sweetheart, you…"

"Look, if I hadn't seen the journal for myself I'm not sure I'd feel so strongly about this, but I saw the words and they were shocking. Jeff has that journal somewhere, but I don't know where. There's nothing more I can do for him here – he doesn't move, wake, nothing – but I know that if he was capable he'd be out there freeing his brother and putting the guilty man behind bars where he belongs. I can do that for him, rather than sit around here like a lemon hoping the truth will out in the end."

"Sue, you're on maternity leave and your husband is in a coma. This is the last thing you should be worrying about at the moment."

Sue snatched her hand back. "Yes, mam, it is. The police seem hell bent on locking an innocent man away, and I know for certain he's not committed the crime. How could I live with myself if I let such a travesty happen? And if, by some miracle, Jeff does wake up and see that I stood by and watched it happen without trying to stop it, how could he ever respect me again? I have to do something, not only for my husband, but for the only remaining member of his family. And for justice."

Brenda shook her head slowly, her disinterest unsurprising to Sue, who faced her father. "Dad, you've only recently retired from the force; you know what it's like. Surely you must understand me?"

He nodded, slipping some lukewarm mashed potato into his mouth. "I understand, but I don't know where you're going with this."

Sue implored, "Mam, if I were to come and stay the nights with you two, would you look after Jacob for the rest of the time?"

Brenda sighed, lips pursed. "I'm prepared to have him as long as you're in here with Jeff, but…"

Jack raised his hand to stop her. "Brenda, let Sue speak. Let's hear what she has to say."

"Dad, I still want to spend time with Jeff, but I can't stay day after day just watching him sleep. I need to be proactive. As far as I'm concerned there's a dangerous man in Colefield who has now murdered what, three girls – that we know of – in the nineteen eighties, and two more women at the beginning of this month."

Ellen jumped in, keen to support her friend in the difficult conversation. "Plus that solicitor and the other bloke, David Webber. Not to mention the vile attempts at taking both our husbands' lives."

"That's a fair amount of deaths." Jack took the last piece of gravy-soaked steak pie, emptying his plate.

"I want to find the journal and get a good solicitor on our side, because I can guarantee that Simon West isn't up to the job; I know him. That way we can free Paul and vindicate Roland at least for the murders, albeit not for the rapes, which he's admitted to."

"And to make damned sure we put the real guilty party in prison, where he belongs," Ellen emphasised, "because if he's killed this many people and been let off scot-free, I'm sure he won't stop there."

Clattering and noise, doctors, nurses, auxiliaries, visitors, patients, all eating and buzzing. Canteen staff serving, dishing up food, clearing discarded crockery and cutlery. But the table was silent. Eventually Brenda voiced the suggestion that Sue and Ellen were expecting. "Why don't you just tell the police what you know?"

Sue sighed. "I've tried and they won't listen. As far as Alan Reeves and Dom Townsend – they're the detectives who are now in charge of the case – are concerned, they caught Paul in the act. But I was there too, before them, and I'm certain Paul was rescuing Jeff and Frank, not attacking them."

"Please, we need your help." Ellen saw the sense in what Sue had told her and she wanted justice, not only for her husband, but for all the victims.

Jack pushed his plate to the centre of the table. "Sue, how certain are you that Paul is innocent?"

"One hundred percent."

"And that this Bert Rock is the attacker?"

Sue wanted to repeat the sentence but knew she couldn't, personally. "Jeff believed he was the real criminal and I trust his judgement."

"Then I'm on your side."

Brenda gasped. "For heaven's sake Jack, at least let's think about this. Haven't we all enough on our minds?"

Jack stared into his wife's eyes. "You can manage with Jacob; you're doing a fantastic job already. Whether you like it or not, we're standing by our Sue on this one."

Jack had driven reluctant Brenda home with Jacob and returned to the hospital to collect Sue and Ellen. Brenda had been following the sensationalised coverage of the case in the newspapers and fully trusted that the police had the right man, despite being troubled that he was related through her daughter's marriage. However, Sue and her father shared a stubborn streak that she'd had to live with for the past thirty plus years, so accepted it wasn't about to change.

Meanwhile Sue searched Jeff's belongings, unsuccessfully, for the journal, but she found Jeff's car keys, with what she believed was Paul's house key on the ring. She spent half an hour with her husband, explaining what she was doing and that she would return later. She wasn't sure if he could hear, but knew that if he could, he would be completely supportive.

Ellen knew Jack had been high in the police force – the subject had been discussed during a dinner party with Sue and Jeff at some stage – but wasn't sure how high. She asked him as they drove from the hospital to Colefield. "I was a Detective Chief Inspector, but I chose early retirement. I've been out of the game for a couple of years now."

"It wasn't really your choice to leave though, was it dad?" Sue glanced lovingly at the father she resembled. Sue turned towards Ellen in the back seat. "You see, dad had a mild heart attack when he was fifty-six. We all thought it was best if he left work."

Jack chuckled, peering over his shoulder at Ellen and winking. "I was coerced; I could have gone on for years."

The car was quiet for a few moments. "Dad, have you had any thoughts about which solicitor we can instruct to help Paul?"

Jack drove left onto the country lane leading to Colefield. "As far as I'm concerned there's only one choice: my old colleague Peter Barrymore's son, Kyle."

Sue was astounded and her eyes widened. "He's only about twelve years old!"

He chuckled at his daughter's amateur dramatics. "He's only four years younger than you, young lady, and by all accounts he's a brilliant lawyer. If anybody is going to clear Paul's name, it'll be him. If he agrees to come up from London, that is, but I'm working on that." Neither woman commented so, nearing the village, Jack continued. "I've talked to his father; he's going to get back to me today hopefully. Right, we're in Colefield. Where's the house?"

"Stick on this road," Sue was pointing ahead, "it's just down there, round the corner, on the left."

As they rounded the bend both Jack and Sue gasped, each cursing themselves for their stupidity. "I didn't even think of that," Sue whispered with frustration. Several constables guarded the house, which was surrounded by crime scene tape.

Jack parked on the grass verge in front of the house. "Leave this to me." He climbed out and approached the policeman who stood, clearly freezing, by the door. Jack chatted to the officer, who shook his head every time Jack spoke. He returned to the car, despondent. "They won't even consider letting us in. I told them I needed to get some clothes for Jeff, but they weren't having any of it." He slammed the door to keep some warmth in the car. "We'll have think of another way to get inside. Any ideas?"

195

"I do, but I'm not sure how it would work." All eyes turned to Sue. "I was there when Paul was arrested. Maybe if I go and see Bert he'll assume I'm one of the arresting officers and let me take a statement."

"I'm not sure I like that. If you're right and he is the killer, that's a lot of danger you're putting yourself in, love."

"Then you come with me. How is he to know you're not still on the force?"

"A small matter of a badge? I would say that's a good start, wouldn't you?"

"Then I'll go on my own." Before Jack could stop his strong-willed daughter she had let herself out of the car and was striding towards a short row of bungalows. Seconds later, her father had joined her, huffing and complaining about the danger she was putting herself in, not only with a possible killer, but with the police force for impeding an investigation.

Sue brushed him aside and hammered determinedly on the door. "Albert Rock?" Bert nodded, his expression wily. "I'm Detective Inspector, um," she racked her brain to find a suitable name, already guilty for lying about her rank, "Smith, and my colleague, Detective Chief Inspector Dawson. I'd like to take a further statement from you regarding the events of Sunday, the eleventh of November. Would you mind if we came in?"

"Yes, I would. You lot have already spoken with me three times now. I can't imagine there's anything more I can possibly say." He tried to shut the door, but Jack put his foot in the way, still uncomfortable with the situation.

"Mr Rock, we only have a couple of questions, we won't take up much of your time."

Bert stared at them, snake-like, yellowy eyes. "What?"

"May we come inside?"

He paused, but finally moved aside and led them to his neat living room. He sat on the sofa and rested his sling-protected elbow on the arm. Sue and Jack remained standing. "When Paul Mason attacked you, why hadn't he tied you with the other three men?"

"I've been through all of this. Can't you just read the last statements and stop wasting my time?"

"Mr Rock, we are trying to convict the man who assaulted you. Surely it isn't wasting your time to ensure we have the facts clear before the trial?"

Bert shot Sue a withering glance, and she fought the urge to step back, away from the evilness. His aggravated tone became bored. "I heard gunshots coming from the house. I let myself through the back door and went upstairs. When I saw the three men tied together I went to help, but Paul struck me on the shoulder with a heavy bar, which disabled me. The police arrived moments later. What more can I say? I was trying to help and got struck for the pleasure. End of story."

Sue remembered entering the house herself on the fateful day, recalling that the back door had been jemmied open. "How did you get through the door?"

He thought for a moment. "The key was in the lock so I let myself in."

"So you didn't use force in any way?"

"No, I didn't need to."

Jack had been glancing around the room, observing anything and everything. He had noticed Jeff's silver Vectra on the dirt track behind Bert's back garden and knew where they would be heading next. The bureau lay open and when Bert noticed Jack surveying the contents, he struggled up and hastily closed it. "What's in there that you don't want us to see?"

The question caught Bert off guard. He stared at Jack, mouth moving glibly as he concocted an answer. "Nothing, I just like my house to be clean and tidy. A place for everything and everything in its place, my mother used to say." Jack attempted to pull the flap down and Bert stopped him. "Have you any more questions?"

"Yes. Where were you when you heard the shots that made you want to investigate Paul's house?"

Bert faltered, eyes darting between the two bogus detectives. "I was walking outside, in front of the house."

"So why not knock on the front door? Why let yourself in through the back?"

Bert's face reddened as he fabricated a plausible excuse. "It's what we do around here, we always use the back door. Look, is this going to take long? I have an appointment to go to."

Sue crossed her arms. "You would have had to step over a dead man at the bottom of the stairs to get to the action. Surely at that stage you would have left and called the police?"

"I could hear," he swallowed, thinking, "I could hear noises upstairs, groaning noises. I was worried."

"Surely you would have taken a weapon? I mean, a man is lying there, either dead or seriously wounded, and there are clearly people in trouble up the stairs. Common sense would tell you to call the fuzz, but…"

"I'm a good person, what can I say." He gave a woeful, holier-than-thou smile. "My only thought was to stop the gunman taking any more lives. I didn't think. It was an instantaneous decision."

"You must have lived here a while, Mr Rock."

"All my life. Most people here have."

"Then you'll remember the Bonfire Night Killer in the eighties."

"I, I, err, yes," he was a rabbit caught in headlights, "yes. Dreadful business, that was."

"Did you know that the gun used for those murders was the same one that was used on Sunday?" Sue had no idea if it was or wasn't, she was fishing for information.

"Yes, Paul must have inherited it from Roly, and everyone round here knows that Roly did those murders. The vicious streak must run in the family."

"So how did you know? We haven't yet released that information publicly."

Bert marched to the hallway and held the front door aside, gesturing for them to leave. "I guessed. As I say, everyone knows Roland Mason was the killer."

Outside, the door slamming forcefully behind them, Jack and Sue strode back to the car. "Well, love, I wholeheartedly believe you now that I've met the man. I was unsure at first, but now I'm fully behind you on this and I'll enlist every bit of help I can from anybody who owes me a favour. Have you got Jeff's car keys?"

"Yes." Sue fumbled in her coat pocket. "Why?"

"I want you to go along the side alley of Paul's next door neighbour's house, go to the end and you'll find Jeff's car. Drive it back to my house and I'll meet you there with Ellen."

Jeff lay, unmoving, a ventilator breathing for him, but despite the heavy, intermittent doses of morphine being pumped directly into his body, his bruised mind was periodically active. He was determined to recover. He knew that his wife was putting herself in danger and he could do nothing to stop her. The only thing he had was his thoughts and it was essential he use them to his best advantage until his body was willing to let him return to clearing his family name. He thought back to the journal, trying desperately to remember the pages he had read of his father's demons from the past:

'I was never a good boy. My family were poor and I wanted things that my parents couldn't afford so, at the age of nine, I turned to petty crime. At first it was stealing things, small things that nobody would notice, but by the time I was a teenager and began hanging around with Bert Rock, I was more daring. We made a good team, me and him, and we stole way more than we earned from whatever pathetic wages we were getting from any random jobs we picked up. We got caught a couple of times, but only got our fingers rapped. The worst punishment was a few spells in jail.

'All through our teenage years he'd been in love with Dot, and eventually I got with Jeannie. We all used to hang around the village together, with nothing else to do, but then Dot began showing affection for Ernie Webber. I married Jeannie, Dot married Ernie, and Bert just stayed on his own, angry at the world.

'Dot married Ernie pretty quickly, and she must have become bored pretty quickly too, because she started coming on to me. I was about to marry Jeannie, but figured she'd never find out, so we went for it. The affair stayed pretty intense even after I got married, but then Dot started having babies, so seeing each other became sporadic – great when it happened, no bother when it didn't.

'Dot had just had her third kid by the time we had you, and she was busy being a wife and mother. Ernie paid all the bills without her having to work and they still had enough left for a caravan holiday at Cleethorpes every year. So she was happy with her lot and it seemed I'd just been a bit of excitement on the side in the early years of her marriage.

'I stopped stealing at night and got myself a decent job at the steelworks. With a son now I had to be more responsible for my family. Then Jeannie had Jeffery and things got hard. He was a difficult baby, always awake and wanting attention, and Jeannie got tired, so tired she stopped caring about her weight, her looks. Sex wasn't happening any more. Her sister was pretty broody and hung around all the time, cooing after Jeffery, and it took a matter of days before we were shagging. She was young, slim, pretty, and so bubbly – it made a nice change. Both Dot and Joan, they were just flings, a bit of excitement on the side. I didn't love either.

'Over the next few years you boys grew and Joan and I continued to see each other at any opportunity, but she began to change. She was needy, she wanted me to leave Jeannie and go and live with her. She even said she'd take you boys on if I wanted. And she often spoke about having a baby of our own after we'd done the business. I began to wish we'd never got together, and eventually I told her our affair was over.

'That night you boys were in bed, and Joan turned up uninvited. She was really upset, howling, crying her heart out. She told Jeannie about our affair, and Jeannie went crazy, shouting and screaming at me and Joan. I tried to calm her down, but she threw herself at me. I promise it was an accident, but I pushed her back, I was defending myself, and the next thing there was a loud crack and Jeannie was lying on the floor, completely still.

'I bent down to her, but blood was pouring from the side of her head, and her ear. We panicked, we didn't know what to do.'

Jeff's own thoughts returned, wondering what could possibly have been so wrong with calling an ambulance and getting medical attention for his real mother. He heard people around his bed and one of them mentioned he was agitated, that his body had been jerking and eyelids flickering excessively. "I've prescribed diazepam, haven't I?" He heard a doctor leafing through some paperwork. "Yes, he can have some now."

Realising he was about to be forced to sleep again, Jeff recalled as much as possible before his mind became inevitably blank.

'We put her body in a black garden sack, and then I got a tarpaulin from the back of my van and we wrapped her in it. I put her in my van while Joan scrubbed the blood from the hearth before you boys came down the next morning. Joan promised she wouldn't tell a soul if I let Jeffery go and live with her and raise him as her son. I'd never been close to him, he was too soft, too emotional, so without Jeannie there it didn't seem to matter. I never saw Joan again and I only ever saw Jeffery a couple of times after that, once he was an adult. I told you, well, everybody, that Jeannie had become bored of the marriage and left.

'I dumped her body in a factory skip I found on an industrial estate in Manchester. If she was ever found, I certainly never heard about it.'

Blackness fingered Jeff's mind, creeping through his thoughts and silencing the world as the sedative pulsed through him, ensuring several hours of restful sleep.

Bert wasted no time after Jack and Sue had visited; he phoned Reeves and explained he was dissatisfied with his treatment by the last two detectives who had been to question him. Reeves was only aware of his and Townsend's visit on the Sunday, after he had been released from hospital, and he said so. Bert detailed the two officers, and when he mentioned that the woman had dark red hair, Reeves realised they had a problem. He apologised for what seemed like the hundredth time and dropped the receiver on the desk. "I think Sue Mason has been poking around the crime scene. She's been to visit Bert Rock."

Townsend sat abruptly, his brow furrowed. "Sue Mason? As in Jeff's wife?" Reeves nodded, his face grim. "Why on earth would she be poking around?"

"I don't know. Hasn't she been going on about Paul being innocent?"

He raised an eyebrow sardonically. "Yes, she has." He wasn't sure why, but PC Mason had always grated on him. "Look, arrange for a car to go and pick her up," he waved his hand, dismissive, "she'll either be at the hospital or her house in Hessle. We need to find out what she's up to before she does something stupid and messes up our investigation."

Reeves called the hospital, but the nurses informed him that Mrs Mason had left a few hours before, and the officers who visited her house insisted there were no signs life indoors. Townsend was irritated, wanting to order her to back off, but Reeves was more analytical. He sat calmly at his desk and found the details of Sue's call to the emergency services three days before. It had been made at twelve forty-nine in the afternoon, requesting a trace on Jeff's car, meaning she had already suspected that something was amiss. She had bumped into the two detectives roughly an hour later and insisted they take her to Paul's house. He checked the record of Paul's release from the cells, which stated he wasn't released until one, and that PC Alicia Myers had signed the release forms and driven him home.

So why had Sue been panicking prior to his release? There were two possibilities: either she knew Paul was about to be released and feared for her husband's safety; or she knew her husband was already in danger, regardless of Paul. He vowed to keep an open mind once they found Sue Mason. He would listen to her theory and make his own mind up, despite Dom Townsend's unwavering conviction that Paul was guilty. He didn't know Sue that well, their paths had barely crossed before she'd had her child, but he respected Jeff Mason as a fine detective, sure he wouldn't have married a bimbo.

Townsend wasn't as impartial. "Right, Alan, that's your job. Go and find the interfering cow and tell her, in no uncertain terms, that she's to butt out of this and let us do the investigating. I know she's traumatised at the moment with Jeff and all that, but this is a multiple murder inquiry and I don't want her cocking it up." Reeves stared at him with distaste. "Well? Go on, get out of here."

Alan followed the orders from the man who was the same rank as he with gritted teeth, wondering why Townsend was pulling the punches now their boss was incapacitated. He would find Sue, be it today or the next, but he wasn't about to dismiss her story as he knew his colleague would.

It had taken a while, but Jack finally managed to get through to the big-shot London lawyer. "Kyle, I've been trying your number for ages. It's Jack Dawson. You might remember me; I worked alongside your father for many years."

"Yeah, I remember you, sir. My father told me you might phone. Are you calling in a favour then?" He laughed, a loud, proud, arrogant chortle that could only come from a man with no cares in the world.

"You could say that. Pete's told me a lot about you over the years, and how well you're doing down in London."

"It's going very well, indeed. I've got a triple figure salary, a generous expense account, top of the range company car, a subsidised company flat, and you know how the women like the money." Jack was sure he heard the brattish man wink. "What more can a man ask for?"

The last time Jack had seen Kyle, he had been a young boy, not quite in his teenage years, but even then it had been obvious he was incredibly intelligent and astute, and was going to make a name for himself. Peter Barrymore and his wife had only the one child, and he had worked desperately over the years to provide Kyle with the best education at a private, all-boys school in North London. Tiresomely, he had bragged from that moment on about how wonderfully his son was doing, his high achievements, the splendid exam results, which led to an early place at Cambridge University where he had studied criminal law. Before he'd finished his education, he had secured a position at a leading London-based law firm with a lucrative starting salary. It wasn't just a silver spoon in his mouth that had led to his ultimate success, because his aptitude within his career had shone immediately, and he was soon successfully defending hardened criminals, making a solid name for himself in the legal world. The fact that he was extremely young and devilishly good-looking hadn't hindered the rapid rise of his career at all.

"I want you to help me to prove an innocent man innocent, and a guilty man guilty. I can only pay expenses, and that's where the favour comes in. Whatever it takes, though, to stop this miscarriage of justice. Your dad says you're the best man for the job."

"Well," Jack heard a stiff drink splashing into a crystal glass, or so his cynical mind told him – it was possible he was just running water from the tap, "Dad's right there, but I'm very busy at the moment, I have a big case going on here in London."

Jack's teeth grated at the pomposity emanating from the man, knowing he needed some bait to lure him onto his side. "I understand, but realistically, what case could be bigger than the infamous Bonfire Night Killings from the eighties."

"Are you kidding? Dad never told me that."

"Kyle, I wouldn't ask if I wasn't desperate."

Again, the conceited chuckle tinkled along the phone line. "No, I meant *'are you kidding'* as in *'I would bite off my own arm to work on that case'*. What do you have?"

"I can't say on the phone; you never know who may be listening. How soon can you get here?"

"Ahah, very cloak and dagger, old man. I'm in court tomorrow and Friday, and the Friday night traffic is dreadful heading north. How about sometime Saturday?"

Jack knew he was pushing the boundaries, but he had nothing to lose. "Can't you get here quicker than that? A man is on remand and I have no idea how much the police have on him, but I'm not the only one who thinks he's innocent."

"Just a moment." Jack could hear Kyle leafing through some pages. "I can't avoid court tomorrow, it's impossible. Friday, I could probably be out by two. What if I was to take the train up, then the traffic wouldn't be an issue?"

"Done. We've got cars so transport won't be a problem. What can I get to you so you can prepare yourself for the case on the journey up?"

"Everything you have. Scan it and send it to my personal email account, old fella. Have you got a pen?"

Darkness had fallen by the time Sue returned to the hospital, driving Jeff's car rather than her tatty Micra, which had been abandoned at the police station in Hull when she had found Dom and Alan. As she anticipated crossing the Humber Bridge regularly, she purchased a weekly pass. The wind was bitter, the sky clear, and the temperature gauge on the dashboard registered a mere two Celsius. It was going to be a harsh winter.

After spending half an hour with Jeff, his condition still critical, she ventured to the adjacent room where Ellen calmly sat beside her husband, therapeutically knitting to while away the time. "No change?"

"No. He's no better and no worse." Ellen laid her knitting on the small suitcase her children had filled and brought for her. She stood and stretched, yawning widely.

"Right, same as Jeff. He's stable but not improving or worsening. Look, come to the canteen with me, we can talk about what dad and I have been up to today over some supper and a milky drink."

"I thought you were staying at your parent's house from now on. That's what you said when you asked them about this."

Sue took Ellen's hand as she led her from the room. "I know, but mam's so stressy with me and dad, I'm not sure I can face it until she's calmed down. I told them I'd spend one last night with Jeff. Anyway, I want to tell him what we've been up to."

Ellen stopped and stared at her friend. "Do you think he can hear you?"

"Yes," Sue patted Ellen's hand, clutching it softly, "yes, I do."

Chapter 17
Friday 16th November

A DCI had been transferred from another station to take over my work, pending my recovery, but due to Dom Townsend's vast knowledge of the Bonfire Night murders, the DCI had put him in charge of the investigation, much to Alan Reeve's consternation; he was always overlooked, and he supposed it was because Townsend was the more outspoken of the two. Alan hated being shy and nerdy, but he did the job as well as any man. Townsend barked in his direction, "What do you mean you haven't found her yet?"

Reeves and Townsend had been working together for two years, and although Townsend had always been dominant, he had really let his new responsibilities go to his head, and Alan was peeved. He glared at the man who was now effectively his superior. "I've been in touch with the hospital, both Wednesday and yesterday, and each time they told me she wasn't there. They said she's only visiting once a day now. I've tried her home a few times and she's not answering, and there have been no signs that she's in. Her car's still in the car park outside where she left it on Sunday before this ugly mess kicked off."

"Do you know what I'm hearing? Blah, blah, blah, blah, that's what. Bert Rock is threatening to make waves and I could do without that, especially as that bloody Sue Mason isn't even working at the moment. We need to handle this investigation by the book and I don't need some stupid, post-natal community officer, with nothing better to do than meddle where she's not wanted, messing with my case. For god's sake man, I would have found her within a shot if it had been me. Find her and shut her up."

Alan had so many words he wanted to say – *if you're so fucking good, you find her then* – but he didn't dare. He reminded himself he was an excellent detective. So what if he was timid. He was a thoughtful man, preferring to think before speaking, assess the facts before discussing them. He hated Dom. Frank was a far more palatable boss.

Tense and on edge, Alan left the room and headed for the personnel department. "Have you got any personal details for PC Susan Mason? I need to get in touch with her regarding the case we're currently working on. It's important."

The aging lady propped her glasses on the end of her nose and opened a large, grey filing cabinet, withdrawing a green folder. She set it on the desk and leafed through the papers inside. "What do you need to know?"

"A mobile number, if you have one, or a number for a next of kin other than her husband, maybe."

The woman's bony hand slid down page after page, she tutted and puffed breathlessly as she glanced through the notes. "No, my love. Nothing apart from her husband's details as next of kin, and no mobile number is recorded."

"Damn. Can I use your phone?"

The woman eyed him sardonically from above her reading glasses, a single eyebrow raised. "Please."

Weary, Alan conformed and was soon speaking to the intensive care ward at Scunthorpe Hospital, introducing himself for the hundredth time. "Has Mrs Mason come in today?" He swore under his breath at the negative answer. "Look, have you any idea what time she'll be there?" He waited. "After six, she's been coming in. Okay, if I can't catch up with her before then I'll meet her there. I don't suppose you know where she goes to during the day, do you? No, okay." He ended the call, no closer to finding Sue than he had been ten minutes before in the aftermath of the belittling from his colleague.

Brenda was in the kitchen, preparing a packet soup with a mound of bread and butter for lunch. She set the table for three and boiled the kettle to make a pot of tea for after they had eaten. She called Jack and Sue to the table. Sue came first, baby Jacob nuzzling sleepily in her arms, and Jack soon joined them.

"I've just been speaking to Kyle Barrymore. The case he was working on has been adjourned until Monday, he said he's at King's Cross Station and will be with us as soon as he can. He has to change at Doncaster, but says he should get into Hull at just gone two. I suggested I pick him up, but he said he'd get a taxi."

Brenda, her lips pursed indignantly, ladled soup into three bowls and brought them to the table. "Why are you two insisting on doing this? It's crazy." She slammed a bowl in front of her daughter, the chunky vegetables sloshing up the side dangerously. "You should be concentrating on your husband and child, not gallivanting all over looking for a criminal who's already been caught."

Jack received his own soup, dropped so harshly it spilled onto the placemat. "Brenda, I've met the man Roland claims is the killer and…"

"I don't care, Jack. Don't you get it? You retired, remember, you retired from the force because of your heart problems. Are you really so bored spending time at home that you have to start chasing killers who have already been caught, men who are already off the streets?"

"You're being totally unreasonable, Brenda…"

"Dad's right. Don't you care that an innocent man is in prison?"

"No." She dropped her own bowl heavily before seating herself and snatching a piece of bread. "No, I don't. They've arrested Paul because he's guilty and there's no more to it than that. You know, I think that you," she jabbed a finger at her daughter, "can't be bothered to look after your child properly, so it's easier to swan off on some redundant man hunt, and that you," it was Jack's turn for reprimand, "hate being retired so much that you can't let your police work go." She threw her spoon on the table. "Oh, stuff the soup, I've lost my appetite." Brenda pushed the bowl aside, dropping the bread into the steaming liquid, and stormed from the room.

Jack and Sue sat in silence, their food untouched, and avoided each other's eyes. The minutes passed with only the humming of the washing machine for background noise until, eventually, Sue broke the spell. "If it's easier for you not to help any more, I'll understand, dad."

He caught her gaze. "Hell, no, I'm right behind you. Look, there's something I've never told you before, but I want you to know now as it's become relevant." Sue was intrigued. "I'd been on the police force for five years when the first Bonfire Night murder happened. We'd heard about it, but in those days, cases like that were dealt with locally rather than regionally and we weren't involved. When the second happened we still had no involvement, but the third was different. By then the police had realised they had a serial killer on the loose and they drew in as many nearby forcesas possible, including us, to help with the investigation.

"I was thirty then. You were a toddler and your brother was on the way. I had a growing family and I was keen for promotion to give you kids a good life. I offered to help on the case, as did many other officers. I was one of the men who made house calls to the residents of Colefield, and one of the calls I made was to Bert Rock."

Sue gasped, her eyes wide. "Why on earth didn't you tell me this before?"

Jack shrugged. "It didn't seem relevant, it's history. In fact, it wasn't until after we'd been to his house the other day that I remembered. But what I can tell you is that I never liked him the first time round, and I certainly don't the second."

"What did he say back then?" Sue had the only spoonful of soup she would manage.

"He had an alibi, just like everybody else did. It seemed like Colefield had a zip on it, like the residents knew something dark but weren't saying a word. It was weird, mysterious and, to be honest, a little frightening. When the fuss died down we were all sent back to our own stations, and the case was soon forgotten. Well, not forgotten but, well, you know."

"Life moved on." Sue laid her spoon on the table, intrigued. "So what was he like back then?"

"Just as shifty. If I remember rightly, he said he hated fireworks and always stayed in on Bonfire Night. We would have backed his alibi up, but I can't remember how, it's been too long. Anyway, the point is I was disturbed that he wasn't questioned further, but it wasn't my place to make waves, and maybe it isn't now, but you're involved and my son-in-law's involved, and I want to make sure that Bert Rock doesn't escape the law this time."

Sue laid her hand over her father's. "Mum's overreaction, it was to do with that wasn't it?"

Jack looked at his untouched food, sheepish. "She had a dreadful time when she gave birth to Jason and I wasn't there for her. I was too busy in Colefield to return to Hull and be with her. She's never forgiven me."

Sue pushed her chair back and stood. "I'll go and have a word with her, maybe that'll help."

He gave her a wry smile. "Good luck!"

Jeff had no concept of time, unaware he had been incarcerated for five days. To him, the days and nights merged into one long blur, his mind at the mercy of the well-meaning doctors who saw any mental activity as a sign he was in discomfort, which usually led to being heavily sedated until his mind blackened.

In his brief lucid periods, he did his utmost to remember his father's journal, but he supposed this clarity made his body twitch and as soon as the movements were noticed, the medical staff would administer their powerful drugs and take the thoughts away. So every time he began to recollect, he had to make the most of the moment before it was physically stopped.

'When Jeannie died, or left as I told everybody, I fell to pieces. I still had you with me. I would never have been able to let you go. We were two peas in a pod, but I wasn't a great father, and being thirty years old at the time, I was interested in the ladies. Dot refused to see me anymore, she claimed that Ernie was suspicious, but I suspected she had guessed that Jeannie hadn't really left me. Mind you, she said nothing, for that I was grateful. Joan was out of the picture, as was Jeffery. I tried to find a replacement mother for you, but nobody was interested.

'I began to spend time with Bert again, we were the only young, single men in Colefield. Neither of us had any real interest in thieving or petty crime any more, we'd grown out of that, but he still had tendencies I wasn't sure about. One Saturday night we got drunk and I joked that I could really do with getting laid. He said he could arrange it, and I was up for anything.

We went to Scunthorpe on the bus. I left you sleeping in your bed, you were only six but I knew you'd be okay.

'We went to the Blakeney Bar. I'd heard before that it was a good place to pick up women and I had a few brews. We found a couple of girls who seemed up for it and we left with them. But as we walked through the town centre towards the bus stop they said they were going. I thought they were prick-teasers and before I knew it, I had the girl with me in my arms. I dragged her into a side alley and screwed her. She kept saying no, but I found that a turn-on. Her friend began screaming, but Bert put his hand over her mouth, making her watch.

'I hadn't been laid for a long time and, with the excitement of it all, I didn't last long. Soon we were back on the bus, laughing wildly as we remembered her face, her pathetic attempts to fight me off. I guess you could say that I got the bug then. It was better than straight sex. It was dangerous. Great fun.

'That was in the October. Bert and I never mentioned it again, but he didn't seem bothered by what I'd done, and I certainly wasn't.

'We kept hanging out together over the next few weeks, but didn't repeat the night out in Scunthorpe. Then we heard on the grapevine that they were going to hold a major firework display in Colefield. We both hated fireworks, but we also realised that there would be lots of women there, it would be dark, and there would be plenty of noise to cover any screams. I told Bert I wanted him to cover for me if I snatched a woman. He was more than happy to as long as he could watch.

'On the night, you went to stay with Dorothy. She was annoyed that I wasn't going to take you to the display, so I knew that Bert and I needed to keep ourselves well hidden in the trees so word didn't get back to her that I'd been out after all.

'I'd fancied Katherine James for a couple of years, she was a right looker – blonde, big bouncy tits, and she had a neat wiggle when she walked. Bert saw me watching her and asked if I was going to do her. I said I wanted to, but her kids were with her. We sat hidden beneath the branches of the weeping willows and waited, and as luck would have it, she left the kids and walked nearby, chatting to a friend. When the fireworks started banging I grabbed her from behind, my hand gripped over her mouth so she couldn't scream, and I dragged her into the copse with us.

'I had her pants down in no time. Women didn't wear trousers much in those days, so it was easy. I gave her a really good seeing to, and I couldn't

211

get the smile off my face after I'd finished. I put her panties back in place, lifting her skirt down, and I asked if she'd enjoyed it. I couldn't see her face, it was too dark and I couldn't really hear her with all the racket going on, but then she clearly said my name.

'Now everything seemed to go into slow motion. She was there, lying on the ground, making no moves to get away. But Bert pulled out this gun and he shot her in the head. I saw the blood trickle out. It was black against the pale skin of her face. I was fascinated, I watched it glisten in the tiny streaks of moonlight, mixed with the glare from the fireworks, and I was rooted to the spot, like time was hanging still.

'Then everything started happening really quick. Bert grabbed me and dragged me away from the body, further into the copse. It was dense in there, but he knew his way around because he was a keen night-time hunter. We seemed to run for miles, but really it was only to the outskirts of the village, and from there we made our way back from the other direction to my house to avoid being placed at the scene.

'I got the whisky out and me and Bert shared a whole bottle, just drinking it, not speaking. Eventually I asked him why he'd shot her and he simply said that she'd recognised me. If she'd gone to the police we would have been busted. It made sense, but I felt pretty bad about it.

'There were lots of police after that, poking their noses in, but Bert and I had concocted a solid story: that we were both at my place, drinking all evening. Because we hated fireworks. The police never looked further than that.

'After it had happened, after I'd gotten used to the fact Bert had killed her, I kind of forgot the bad things and just remembered the fantastic sense of power and control that I'd had when I was pumping her. She couldn't move away, her struggling had excited me more and more, and when I finished it was like someone had placed a firework inside my body. I just exploded. It was intense, it went on, and on, and on. So I wanted more. I knew that wouldn't be the last time I grabbed a girl and fucked her. Somewhere along the line Bert and I decided we'd do the same thing the next year.'

Jeff heard the medical staff buzzing around his bed and knew he was about to be sedated again. This time he wasn't too dismayed, because the recollection of his father's words disgusted him. How the man who gave him life could treat a woman so dreadfully, let alone enjoy it, was impossible for Jeff to fathom. He wondered how different life would be if his mother had never died; if Roland had never accidentally shoved her, cracking her skull on the mantelpiece. Would Roland have still ended up a rapist? A party to murder? Would he have been a good father who supported his children and wife?

The familiar tingling and flashes of light sprung behind Jeff's eyes and he was pleased that, until the sedation wore off, the visit to his father's history was halted. He succumbed gratefully to the blackness.

Kyle Barrymore was a handsome man and he knew it. The only child of a Detective Superintendent and an accountant, he had been sent to top boarding schools by his overindulgent parents, who believed they had made the appropriate sacrifices to enable him to achieve an affluent future. They had been right.

He had always been a top-class student, reaching A grades in most subjects, and a meagre B at least. It had come as no surprise when Cambridge offered him an early place to study law, specialising in criminology, and over the next few years he had continued to excel. Leading law firm, Gladstone and Peterson Partners, poached him before he left, arranging for him to start working two months after his graduation, which allowed him some time to travel to India and America, two dreams planted in childhood.

Not only was he acutely intelligent to match his refined features, but he was athletic too, playing a multitude of team sports to county level. Although he'd ceased competing once he had begun his adult life in London, he maintained his fitness levels with an exceptionally healthy, well-planned diet and frequent trips to the gym. The numerous activity-filled holidays were a bonus.

Now, in the twenty-ninth year of his charmed life, he was well in demand in his lucrative career. The cases he defended were often front-page national news and criminals would fight over who was going to benefit from his impeccable charm. His personal life also sparkled. Well known and loved on the capital's party circuit, he never dropped his playboy façade, and celebrity

213

magazines loved to photograph him adorning sofas and beds. Any picture of him with a female would spark dating, marriage, or even pregnancy rumours. He was one of the country's most desirable bachelors.

He made the most of the hour and a half train journey, reading the emails, full of details and attachments, about the case his father's ex-colleague, Jack Dawson, had sent. He knew of Paul Mason's predicament and the evidence the police had against him. He knew about the accusatory fingers pointing at the prisoner's late father. He knew about the journal full of damning recollections that appeared to be missing.

Kyle changed trains at Doncaster, grabbing a quick sandwich while he waited on the platform, and although the train to Hull wasn't as comfortable as the previous express, he managed to finish reading the emails. When he arrived in Hull, his back uncomfortable, desperate to walk around and ease his stiff joints, he took a taxi to the address Jack had given him.

He knocked on the door and waited. Presently a face he vaguely remembered from many years before, albeit now craggy and wrinkled, opened the door with a fixed smile. Kyle thrust his hand forward confidently. "Detective Jack Dawson. I haven't seen you since I was a nipper."

Jack's false smile waned. He wanted to like his friend's son, but the too-good-to-be-true youngster didn't do himself any favours by being so smarmy. He chastised himself for his disagreeableness – Kyle wasn't smarmy, he was polite and genial. All the same, everything about Kyle Barrymore and his fascinating lifestyle made him want to retch. "Come in and sit down, Kyle, I'll put the kettle on." Jack led his visitor to the kitchen and indicated a wooden seat. "Coffee? Tea?"

"Thank you, do you have any herbal tea? I'm on a bit of a health kick, I'm in training for a charitable bike ride, you know. I always do my bit for the charities, bless them."

Jack's teeth grated, restraining himself from punching the irritating, patronising weasel who sat smugly behind him. He opened a cupboard above the kettle. "I think my wife may have some up here. Ah, yes, there's some chamomile, um, and some green tea."

Kyle's voice trickled smoothly, "I'll have green tea with a drop of lemon." He chortled. "I don't dare have the chamomile, it relaxes me too much, and we don't want that, do we."

Wondering where his wife kept the lemon juice stopped Jack from hitting the annoying idiot. He brought the drinks to the table, just as Sue came from the hallway. She strolled to Kyle and shook his hand warmly, with an open smile. "I'm guessing you must be the notorious Kyle Barrymore."

He chuckled sweetly. "Notorious indeed, my fair lady. May I ask your name?"

"I'm Sue Mason, Jack's daughter. My husband is one of the detectives who was critically injured in last Sunday's attack."

"I'm so sorry about that." His tone was creamy, a velvet treacle. "I hope I'm going to be able to help you with this, well, I can't call it anything but bizarre, case."

"So do I. I take it dad's told you all about how Paul has been framed for this – oh, Paul is Jeff's brother. My husband, Jeff, that is – I, err…"

Laughing again, Kyle patted Sue's hand. Women often became tongue-tied in his presence. "Your dad has told me everything and I'm a hundred percent revised on the notes, so you have nothing to worry about." Jack cringed; he intensely disliked the man who was willing to freely give his time to help members of his family, and realised how hypocritically ungrateful that was. Kyle turned to Jack. "So, did you make an appointment for me to visit the prison like I asked to you to?"

"Yes, you have an official visit at four this afternoon. I also arranged for Paul to be seen by a doctor, as you asked, to see if we can get confirmation of autism."

"Yes, good. It will be beneficial if he's on the spectrum, guilty or innocent." He glanced at his watch, brow furrowed. "That's just over an hour away, when will we be leaving?"

"Any time now." Jack tapped on the table. "Drink up, we need to be there in good time to get you through the searches."

Paul was confused. He had been told that his latest solicitor was being replaced by another and he couldn't understand what he had done wrong for the second one to leave. Maybe it was because he didn't talk much, maybe Simon West had become bored of him. Paul hadn't liked the greasy man, and the way his skin scattered everywhere was perturbing, but Paul also didn't like change and he was concerned he may somehow make this new one hate him too.

At five to four a warden opened his cell, cuffed his hands behind his back and led him through the echoing, grey corridors, each footstep resonating on the multitude of metal bars surrounding him. Eventually they reached a secure room and he was led to a seat, fronted by a small glass pane. He waited and presently a young man, neatly, yet casually, dressed, sat behind the glass and gave him a Hollywood dreamboat smile. He stared, unwavering. He wasn't sure he liked the handsome man, or trusted him, for that matter.

"Paul, hi there. My name is Kyle Barrymore, I'm a criminal lawyer and I intend to represent you in your trial unless you have any objection to that." Paul neither spoke, nor moved, his black eyes boring through the glass to meet the sparkling baby-blue pair, framed by flopping blond curls. "Once you have signed the paperwork agreeing to my representation, I'll arrange to come back and talk to you in detail. I'll have the files from your previous solicitor and I'll request documentation from the police and court, but in the meantime – today – I simply want to hear your version of what happened last Sunday."

Paul didn't want to speak, the man before him seemed too young and inexperienced to instil his confidence in, but there was something compelling about him, a cheeky glint in his eye that made Paul want to volunteer everything he knew. Once he had started, he couldn't stop and was sure he'd never talked so much in his life. He told Kyle about being in the cells at Scunthorpe, about suddenly, unexpectedly, finding he was allowed to go home. How his house had been locked. The time he had spent with his neighbours, Mr and Mrs Carver. How he had become bored and broken in only to find his solicitor dead at the bottom of the stairs. How he had seen Bert torturing three men, who were bound together, and had struck him with a crowbar on the right shoulder. How the police had burst in and arrested him halfway through freeing his brother from the rope.

"Have you seen a doctor yet?"

"A doctor?"

"Paul, you must have found it hard to concentrate at school. Did you find schoolwork difficult?"

He waved his hand, shaking his head with a sneer. "It never made much sense to me, all those numbers, those letters. I didn't know what was going on most of the time. I didn't like school. The children teased me. They said I was thick. They said I was stupid. Maybe I am."

"That's no problem at all. The reason I ask is because we've arranged for a special doctor to come and see you soon. He talks to people who found schoolwork hard, like you did. He'll give you pictures and puzzles – things that are fun – for you to do, and the wonderful thing about them is that they have no wrong answers, so whatever you put is going to be right. That'll be good, yeah, mate?"

"I don't like puzzles. And I'm not your mate."

Kyle sucked a deep breath in, a convivial smile on his face. "Maybe some pictures then. Once the doctor has seen you I'll be able to prepare a defence for you, because I want you to be able to go back to your house and live there happily, doing what you want. Nobody wants to see you spend your life in prison."

"I don't. I always thought prison was for bad people. But I don't think I'm bad. I didn't do anything bad."

"I know."

'TIME'. The call came over the Tannoy and Paul was led away.

Although she found being away from her young child torturous, Sue wanted to spend the best part of the evening with Jeff, especially now she spent her days away from him. After a bite to eat at Brenda's insistence, she drove to the hospital in Greg's car, hoping the nurses would have good news about her husband's condition. Surprisingly they did – there had been a change in brain activity over the course of the day and more movement of his fingers and toes. The doctors were quietly optimistic that he was improving, but time would tell.

217

Ellen strolled into the room, the dark circles under her eyes more pronounced than before, and she was pleased to hear of Jeff's slight improvement, albeit wishing she had the same good news about her own husband. "How did things go with the new solicitor today?"

Sue took Jeff's hand, stroking it nonchalantly as she told Ellen about the debonair young bachelor she had met earlier. "He's very full of himself, but I bet he's good at what he does. The best part is that he's completely behind what we're doing, and you always need someone to believe in you. Dad took him to the prison earlier to meet Paul, but I'd left for the hospital before they got back, so I'll have to update you on that tomorrow."

"Thank god I've finally found you, I've been looking for you for days." Sue spun around and watched Alan Reeves breezing towards them. He nodded at Jeff's bed. "How is he today?"

"Pretty much the same, thanks for asking. What are you doing here?" Her answer was curt and Alan's shoulders sagged.

"Look, I know Dom's being heavy handed at the moment, but we can only report on what we saw, and it really looked to me like Paul was attacking the four men."

She rolled her eyes, shaking her head slowly. "I was there first, I saw Paul cutting the rope to free Jeff, well, all three men."

"I've read your statement. Tell me, you've mentioned a journal before, could you fill me in on that."

Sue sighed, wishing the police had listened to her and searched for it earlier, so the real attacker was in Hull Prison instead of Paul. "We haven't found it yet. I've no idea where Jeff put it."

Alan patted her shoulder briefly, a warm gesture to reassure her. "I know this is hard for you, Sue, but when you find it, let me know. As long as you promise not to mention anything to Dom. He's adamant Paul Mason's our man." He fished into his jacket pocket and pulled out a calling card. "That's got my mobile number on it. Try and find it. And don't visit Bert again." Sue smirked, which peeved him. "I mean it. He reported you."

He left and the two fatigued women glanced at each other, each reflecting surprised eyes. With a mixture of relief and astonishment, Sue gasped. "There is hope after all."

Chapter 18
Saturday 17th November

Kyle arrived at the Dawson household early in the morning after staying the night with his parents. Jack showed him to the kitchen table, where he laid out his notes in an order that made sense to him, covering the highly waxed pine. Jack pushed a notepad aside and set two steaming mugs down, one containing Yorkshire tea, the other green tea with a dash of lemon juice. He sat and regarded the young man. "So, you didn't tell me how it went at the prison last night."

Kyle was hesitant, choosing his words carefully. "I wanted to think about the things he told me before I filled you in. From what you and your daughter explained about Paul, he's pretty much what I imagined. I'm with you, though, I don't think he's guilty. That makes it easier to defend him."

Jack straightened, quizzical. "Defend?"

Kyle's sparkling eyes returned to the paperwork. "Yes."

"Kyle, we asked for your help to get him out, to find the truth, we never expected you to defend him. In all honesty, we can't afford you."

"I get that, Jack. The thing is, I told my superiors what I was doing this weekend, I told them what you told me. They were really interested because it's such a high profile case, and they said I could defend Paul, payment free, if I wanted. It was their suggestion."

Jack coughed, flabbergasted. "Kyle, we couldn't possibly expect…"

"Jack, old man. Trust me, the advertising and promotion my company will get from defending Paul Mason, from discovering the identity of the notorious Bonfire Night Killer – they won't be losing a penny from giving my time away for nothing."

Jack chuckled flippantly. "You have high expectations. That's good, because we feel as if we've been banging our heads against a brick wall. Before last Sunday's incident, the police were certain Paul was guilty of killing the two women, now they've tied the latest batch of killings to him. They're only seeing black and white, and I'm struggling to prove they should be looking at the greys in between."

As if an internal light had been switched on, Kyle's face brightened and a healthy glow settled on his cheeks. His smug arrogance also resurfaced. "Don't you worry about that, they've no chance against me. What about the lost journal? Have you found it yet?"

"No, but even so, that wouldn't prove that Paul was innocent. Apparently it just details the killings thirty years ago."

"It's my belief that if you organise the foundations properly, the building on top will be easy. If we can prove Bert Rock committed those murders, it'll shine a whole new light on Paul's situation."

"I know, but everybody involved in that era is dead now. Roland, Joan, Jeannie, Dorothy – need I go on? With only Bert left, he's hardly likely to confess after all this time, and that's what we'd need."

"I'll go and see him, I've got a way of twisting people around, getting them to spill." Jack could quite believe that. He so abhorred the man beside him who was doing him a colossal favour from the kindness of his heart. "You mentioned that you and your daughter went to see him last Wednesday and he wasn't saying much."

Jack shook his head solemnly. "Nothing. All we really learned was that he's a dirty piece of work and quite capable of killing in cold blood, in my opinion."

"No, that's not all he let you know. I think he also told you that something was in his bureau, because he wouldn't have shut it otherwise. I intend to take a look. Now, back to the journal. You say that Jeff was the last person to have it, that you know of, and that was before the incident on Sunday."

"That's what I think." Sue had entered the kitchen unnoticed, wrapped in a fluffy maroon dressing gown and matching slippers and carrying little Jacob snugly. "I stayed at Paul's on Saturday night and we found the journal on Sunday morning. Jeff showed me a couple of pages and it didn't make comfortable reading. At that stage everything seemed to fall into

221

place, because if Bert was the original killer, he probably also disposed of Dorothy and killed Fiona."

"So you know that he intended to read the entire journal on Sunday after you'd left? Let's just say he did. So, think, once he had finished it – you're his wife, you know him better than anyone – tell me what he would have done with it."

Sue took the baby bouncer from the worktop, pulled a chair out and sat, settling Jacob onto the fabric seat and tying the safety harness. She rocked him gently with her foot. "He would have hidden it safely, something of that importance. But if it was in Paul's house it's either still there, and access is banned due to it being a crime scene, or he took it to his car."

"You don't think the police have it?"

"Bert would have been arrested by now if they had."

"Right. So Jeff, would he not have kept it with him? If he had, maybe Bert took it. He's another option."

Jack switched the kettle on to prepare a mug of tea for his daughter. "Does Jacob want a bottle?"

Sue shook her head. "He had one an hour ago, thanks. Well, if Bert managed to get it, he won't have kept it, he would have burned the evidence, I imagine. Anyway, I don't think Jeff would have done that. If he'd finished the book, he would have put it somewhere very safe."

"His car then, like you said. Where's his car?"

"It's outside, I brought it back on Wednesday after we'd seen Bert. I haven't looked in it."

Kyle rested back on the chair for a while, his arms crossed as he contemplated the scenario. "So let's assume the diary is telling the truth, that Roland was the rapist and Bert the shooter. Why would that mean Paul couldn't have committed the latest killings? Think laterally."

Jack brought Sue's tea from the side and returned to his chair. He couldn't shake his dislike of the seemingly perfect man, but he couldn't deny that he was thorough. And concise. "The papers have reported that the gun used in Sunday's attack was the same one that was used to kill the women in the eighties. In the original killings Bert wasn't sexually motivated, the raping having been done by Roland, and Fiona Malik wasn't raped either. Nor was Dorothy, we assume."

"More importantly why would the killing start again now after a break of thirty years. A criminal usually has a trigger." Jack had to concede that Kyle was good, his mind working in the opposite way to his own and his daughter's. "In Paul's case they're using his father's sudden death as his reason for murder, but instead of proving Paul innocent, I want to prove Bert guilty. So what would have triggered him?"

"The journal? He might have heard about its existence." Sue sipped her tea, rocking the baby with her foot.

"Quite possible. If the two men were feuding before Roland's death, as I've been led to believe, Roland may have threatened to tell all from the grave."

Sue stood, finishing her tea, eager to get dressed now to search Jeff's car. Why she hadn't considered doing so before escaped her. "Don't you think that if that sort of threat had been made, Bert would have *sorted* Roland out a long time ago, rather than let it get to the stage where somebody else may be party to the secret. Like Paul."

A beaming grin spread across Kyle's face, his eyes twinkling, impish and glittering with life. "There you are, then. He somehow knows Paul has read it, so he recreates a killing from the eighties – bar the rape that he wouldn't, or couldn't commit – and implicates Paul in the murder by using his boots."

"But Paul said they weren't his boots."

Kyle sighed with a tinge of annoyance. "Okay." His tone dripped with sarcasm. "So he planted the boots he'd worn to murder Fiona outside Paul's house. Do you know why the four men were at Paul's house last Sunday?"

Sue nodded to her father to take over the conversation and left to get changed. "Jeff told Sue before she left on Sunday that he was going to tell Paul's solicitor about the journal. Benjamin Roberts must have gone over for that reason. Frank Butler is Jeff's superior at work, and as Paul was released from the cells that day, Frank must have been involved with that, which explains him being there. He might know about the diary too, but he's still in a coma as far as I know. The other man was

David Webber, Dorothy's estranged son. I don't know why he would be there."

Kyle raised his hand to his mouth, long fingers drumming on his lips as he soaked Jack's words in. "None of that gives Paul a reason to be violent. A high ranking detective who has just arranged his release and dropped all charges; his brother, also an officer bent on proving Paul's innocence. His solicitor: ditto, also working to prove Paul's innocence. He has no motive to tie them up and beat them, or worse. But, if he'd seen in the diary that Bert was guilty of the killings and found the man torturing the people who were trying to help him, he would have disabled him and tried to free the hostages."

Jack was impressed with this new way of thinking. "Hence cracking him across the shoulder; it puts his arm out of business and buys him time without severely maiming him. He would have picked up the gun and thrown it aside, an obvious move, and that would explain his fingerprints on it."

"Absolutely correct, Jack." Kyle beamed his superior winning smile and Jack squirmed.

The drugs had worn off and Jeff had a rare moment of clarity, and he thought back, clearly and concisely. Once more, he was submerged in his father's journal:

'Bert and I were excited all year, waiting for Bonfire Night. We knew what we were going to do, and for me — maybe for him too — it was the only thing that kept me going. I had the guilt of killing Jeannie, and for disposing of her body without a burial. I'd lost one child, not that he was my biggest concern, and I was struggling to bring you up on my own. Dot popped in every now and then, but she was busy with her family, and she wasn't interested in re-kindling our relationship, which I would have jumped at.

'Because I knew what we were going to do, I'd been watching the women of Colefield, picking somebody I really fancied shagging, and a couple of months before a young lass had moved into the village with her husband. She was really quiet, timid, and they kept themselves to themselves. They were pretty posh — I watched their furniture being moved in from my front room and thought how expensive it looked. I guess I fancied her but hated her for her money too. So to screw her would not only be great because she

was out of my league, but it would also put her in her place. Only thing was, I wasn't sure if they'd go to the fireworks display, they were so up themselves, so I picked another girl, just in case.

'I'd been watching the other girl a while when I noticed that Nessa, as I later found out she was called, had turned up at the event after all, and my heart flipped, it felt like Christmas had come early. She was with her husband but he didn't bother me, he was a nothing. Then she slipped into the bushes nearby. Bert and I ran swiftly through the trees and undergrowth and came up behind her. She was crouched down, pissing on the ground, her knickers round her ankles. As soon as she seemed to have stopped, I raced forward and grabbed her, silencing her with my hand over her mouth. I dragged her for ages – pants still round her ankles – with Bert walking beside me, keeping watch, and once we were back under the cover of the willow trees, I screwed her. It was so easy with her pants already down. I loved the scared look in her eyes; it turned me right on.

'I finished in seconds, I was so ready for it, and I wanted to go again.She was so tight, you could tell she hadn't had kids, I was so turned on – and so quickly – but before I could get back down onto her, Bert shot her in the head. I was devastated because he'd promised he wouldn't kill again, and I stormed off, adjusting my clothing. Instead of creeping through the trees and re-entering the village from the opposite direction, I just walked right into the crowd, eager to get home. Bert followed me.

'As soon as I got home I poured a large drink and seconds later Bert burst in wielding the gun. I shouted at him, asking him over and over: why? All he said was that he felt like it. That didn't seem a good enough reason to me, he'd taken somebody's life. I punched him, and that was when I realised how strong he was. He was a short man, stocky – he looked like a weasel – and I've always been tall and broad, so I had no reason to think he could beat me in a fight, but he did, and easily. He had me on the floor with the gun to my head and he swore that if I ever told anyone he would kill my son. He'd kill you.

'Our friendship wasn't the same after that. We acknowledged each other on the street, but I knew things had to change. I wanted to replace my wife, I needed a woman around to help bring you up, and I spent the next year searching. I went to every social occasion the village offered, and by the next summer I'd become friendly with a girl who had some mental problems and was slightly deformed. I didn't see her as attractive; she was just kind to me. She'd come round and play with you; you'd build blocks together, draw

225

pictures. But after a while, when I looked at her, well, I hadn't had sex in a long time, and she was probably capable. I tried to get her into bed a few times but it was like talking to a child, and I realised that if I was going to have her, I was going to have to force her.

'I suppose somewhere in my mind I began fantasising about the rapes, and my imagination built up this scenario where I forced her on Bonfire Night, and I resolved to do it, but this time without Bert because I couldn't trust him not to kill her. I swear I didn't know he was there when I lured her into the bushes. She was alive when I left. I only heard the next morning that she'd been shot dead, but I knew who had done it. I resolved there and then that I wouldn't rape anyone again, and I never did.'

Blackness crept from the edges of his mind and Jeff realised they had sedated him intravenously again. He was desperate to wake from the prison of his body, to warn the police about Bert, to see him behind bars, but he couldn't convey his wishes to anybody, and as long as the medical staff kept sedating him, he wouldn't be able to. He dragged his memory once more as he felt his muscles and mind relaxing towards sleep.

'The last time I spoke to Bert, aside from passing the time of day politely, was in nineteen eighty-two. We had a massive argument, and Bert made it clear that if I ever told anybody, not only would he kill you, but he'd go on a spree taking everybody around him down. I wasn't a good boy, but I didn't want that to happen, so I kept quiet. I've told you all this, Paul, because I wanted the truth to come out. I want you to find a way of paying Bert Rock back for what he did to those women. I know you can do this, Paul. You can read the final letter I've written for you once you've found a way of making Bert pay for his crimes. But be clever, because I don't want him to hurt you. If you can find a way of getting him caught without ruining our family name it would be the perfect retribution for me.'

In my room, Ellen screamed for help, pumping the alarm to summon the nursing staff. Two medics rushed in. "He's waking up. I think he's waking up. His eyes just opened. He looked at me."

Within seconds the room swarmed with nurses and doctors, all busy-busy, and a doctor leant close to my face, shining a torch in my eye. "Frank. Frank, can you hear me?" It was impossible to reply with the ventilating tube in my mouth. I choked on it, trying to push it out with my muscles, drag it out with my hands. "Frank, stay calm. We can remove the tube for you, but you must stay calm."

I forced myself to stop struggling – panicking – and as promised the doctor gently removed the tube, scraping the inside of my throat as it went. I gasped for breath, chest rising and falling heavily, causing me discomfort. I tried to speak but no words came, the inflammation in my throat so great.

I had no idea where I was and I couldn't remember anything except that Ellen was my wife. I groped for her hand and she clasped mine tightly, concerned, yet relieved. "Oh Frank, I'm so glad you're back with us, I've been so worried. You're in hospital, do you remember what happened?"

I wanted to respond, and I tried, but I was tired, so confused. I stared at her blankly, focused on her beautiful face and nothing else, although I sensed the doctors working around me. But they were irrelevant. After a while a doctor asked Ellen to one side and I watched her walk across the room, my eyes stinging, reddened and watery from the brightness.

"Mrs Butler, this is obviously good news, but we still need to be careful. With injuries such as these, he's liable to relapse. I'd like to keep him in intensive care for at least another night for observation. If his condition remains stable, we can move him to one of the wards."

She nodded, grinning, grateful, with tears in her eyes, and the doctor returned to my bedside, issuing orders to his colleagues in technical terms I couldn't understand. Ellen took her mobile from her handbag and dialled. "Sue, Frank's awake. Now maybe the truth can come out."

Sue, now clothed in jeans and a sweatshirt, explained my recovery to her father and Kyle Barrymore, who smiled. "Well, that's another visit to add to today's list."

"Frank? What can he possibly help you with in his condition?"

Kyle tapped his nose. "He was there. Let's get this clear, the things we need to do today. First, we can search Jeff's car for the elusive diary. That's number one. We need to go and see Bert…"

"We can't." Sue had removed a plastic bottle, teat and lid from the sterilizer and was waiting for the kettle to boil. "Bert knows me and Dad from last Wednesday, he's already reported us to the police and one of the inspectors in charge, Alan Reeves, has been to see me. We can't risk going there again."

Kyle's upbeat, conceited chuckle tinkled through the room, setting Jack's teeth on edge. "What can I be today then, a journalist? How about that? Everybody loves talking about themselves, and everybody wants their fifteen minutes of fame. Maybe if I tell him I'm from, say, the Daily Express, tell him I believe Roland Mason is guilty of the killings in the eighties and that Paul is for the recent murders, just like the cops are saying… maybe he'll fill the rest in himself."

"What! You can't do that. It would impede the investigation. It's corrupt." Sue dropped four measures of powder into the bottle of hot water, shook it, and stood it in a jug of cold water.

Kyle pointed to the bottle with a know-it-all expression. "It's much quicker and easier to make the bottle with cool, pre-boiled water and heat it up in the microwave."

Sue was speechless and her antipathy towards the smarmy know-it-all matched her father's. "Microwaves are not safe to heat baby bottles in, they have hot spots." She slammed the jug holding the bottle on the table and sat again, irritated.

He shrugged. "Not if you shake them well, but it's up to you if you want to go about things the long way. Anyway, I don't care if my way of getting the truth is unusual, if it gets some kind of admission, it's worth it." He sorted the paperwork on the table into an organised pile. "So we find the journal and I visit Bert, try and suck up to him a bit and get what I can out of him. Then we go and see Frank in hospital, see if he's got anything to add to the story. He's bound to remember the attack, so as soon as the police hear that it was Bert who attacked him, all of them, they won't have a solid reason to keep Paul in custody anymore. Then, we can work on getting him freed."

Aware Sue was sulking, Jack took over. "That's an ideal scenario, but somehow I think the police are dogged about incriminating Paul."

Again his dazzling, unconcerned smile brightened the room. "Not for long. I have ways with people that you just wouldn't believe." Jack's eyes met his daughter's and a wave of nausea swamped them both.

They decided to take Jack's Mercedes, as Bert would probably recognise Jeff's Vectra, and Sue's humble Micra was at the police station. The journal had been relatively easy to find; Jeff had tucked it under the carpet in the boot, beside the spare wheel. With Jack driving, Sue sat in the passenger seat reading aloud from the diary, which enabled her father to hear the details as well as Kyle, who was in the back, leaning forward with interest. They reached the quaint village and Jack parked on the roadside before reaching the houses. "If I drive any further, Bert might see me in the car. You'd better take over. Sue and I will take a walk around. Be careful though, this car's my pride and joy."

Kyle chuckled pretentiously. "Oh, no worries there, I'm a member of the Advanced Motorists, I'm an A-plus behind the wheel."

"Of course you are," Jack said under his breath. He and Sue, fists clenched, watched Kyle drive confidently around the corner before walking towards the heart of the village. They rounded the bend, grateful for the pavement that replaced the knobbly grass verge, and watched Kyle park outside the row of bungalows where Bert lived, stroll along the alleyway to his door and knock sharply.

They waited until he had gained access, and continued walking towards Paul's house. Sue breathed sharply, clutching her father's arm. "Dad, the crime scene tape's been removed and there are no coppers outside. We should be able to go in." She rooted for the keys in her handbag, bringing them out with a flourish.

Bert had been suspicious when he opened the door to the dapper man, his casual clothes clearly not costing casual money, but within seconds they were chatting away, both seated in the impeccable living room, as if they had been friends for years. Kyle hadn't found it easy to connect with the man, but getting people to open up was one of his many talents. He had introduced himself as Kyle Moore stating, after seeing the immaculate tidiness of the house, that he was from the Daily Mail; he was certain Bert Rock swung to the right politically.

Bert rested his arm, in a sling, on the side of the sofa to relieve the relentless aching from his right shoulder. "So, to what do I owe the honour of having such an esteemed journalist visit me?"

"I heard you used to be friendly with a man named Roland Mason, and my sources tell me he was the man who committed the notorious Bonfire Night murders in the nineteen-eighties. I just wondered what you could tell me about him."

"He was a bastard, a total bastard. You know he's dead, don't you? He was one of those people who use others for what they can get. He killed his wife, you know? It's common knowledge around here." Kyle kept quiet, listening intently. "They said that Jeannie left Roly and moved away with the young lad, and I don't know where the youngster ended up, but it definitely wasn't with his mother."

"Young lad?"

"Paul Mason had a brother, he…"

Kyle stopped him. "Yes, I know now, you're talking about Jeff Mason, the policeman who was hurt last weekend."

"Yes. I saw him you know, I knew he was the man who killed those women back in the eighties, but he swore he'd kill Dot Webber if I ever mentioned it to anyone. Well, he can't now because he's dead." His head sank, eyelids heavy. "And so is Dorothy."

Kyle discreetly scanned the room as Bert related his story and agreed with Jack's remark that the orderliness was faultless. He noticed the bureau and willed it to open so he could look inside. As an excuse for Bert to leave the room, he asked for a glass of water, but was directed to the tap in the kitchen himself.

Realising he would have to find another way of seeing inside the cabinet, he fetched a drink, then tugged a Dictaphone from his pocket. "Do you mind if I record this?"

"I take it you know about Roly's son, Paul? You know he's on remand for killing a woman on Bonfire Night just gone?"

"Yes, that's what brought our interest to Roland Mason in the first place."

"In that case, if it means that dumb idiot Roly dragged up – Paul, if you didn't already realise – gets put inside for good, I don't mind what you do." Kyle switched the tape recorder on and nodded. "I was always jealous of Roly, he had everything I wanted, a beautiful wife, a family. But he was nasty through and through and he was never satisfied with what he had, always wanting more. At first I believed his story that Jeannie had left him, and I felt a bit sorry for him, to tell the truth. I could tell he was broken by it even though, at the time, I suspected he might have something to do with her disappearance. Other than being a bad husband, that is. I rekindled our friendship and we began hanging out with each other, going on the pull together, looking for women.

"We went into Scunthorpe one night, and this was the first time I'd seen how dangerous he could be. He was fine at first, but the more he drank the louder he got, and eventually I persuaded him it would be a good idea if we went home for the night. He insisted on taking two women with us, but on the way to the bus stop he pulled his girl down an alleyway and I watched him rape her. Her friend just buried her face in my chest, crying. It wasn't only the rape that scared me though, it was the violent way he did it; she was terrified. He told me afterwards to keep my mouth shut and – I was quite a bad boy myself, stealing, stuff like that – I did what he told me. I never mentioned it to a soul. I reduced contact with him after that, I was concerned by what he was capable of.

"A couple of weeks later the first major fireworks display here in Colefield took place. I wasn't going to go. I wasn't interested and was going to have an early night, but the banging and crashing, all the flashing lights, they kept me awake. At about nine in the evening I got fed up. I got myself dressed and went for a wander around the field to see what the fuss was all about. I was hungry so I got a burger from a van, and while I was eating it I noticed movement in the bushes; I'm a keen game hunter so I notice things like that. I watched, and suddenly Roly darted out, grabbed Katherine James, a woman we both knew from the village, and dragged her underneath the willow trees. He clamped his hand over her mouth so she couldn't scream.

"I followed, curious, and also concerned for Katherine's well-being. I liked her, she was a good soul. I saw him push her to the ground, lifting her skirt, and I knew he was about to rape her, but I didn't do anything. Truth be told, I was scared of him. I waited for it to be over, which it was very quickly, and I expected him to leave her, but suddenly he pulled out a gun and shot her in the head. That's when he saw me. He dragged me through the undergrowth, for ages we ran with him pointing the gun at me, and finally he brought me into the village from the opposite direction and ordered me to his house. He told me that if I ever mentioned a word to anybody he would rape and kill Dot. I couldn't have that; you see I was in love with Dorothy and had been since I was a teenager. I probably still am, even though she's gone. Although she'd left me to marry Ernie my feelings never went away, and I would have protected her with my life.

"He knew he had me, my feelings for Dot were well-known. I promised that I would never say a word on condition he never killed again. He agreed. When the following two murders happened I knew it was him who did them but I never dared to say a word. As long as Dot was alive I wasn't taking any risks with her safety. But we were never friends again."

Kyle scratched his head, his beautifully tousled crop dislodged from perfection, yet even more appealing, and he drummed his fingers on his lips, debating. "That sounds pretty much what I suspected. I mean, it must have been very traumatic for you, wanting to do the right thing yet having such a terrible threat over your head. Is that why you ended up giving him an alibi? I mean, you did, didn't you?"

Bert cleared his throat, his cheeks reddening. "Yes, of course. He said he needed someone to say he had company, so I did. He terrified me. Will they do me for that?"

232

Kyle chortled affably. "I wouldn't worry too much about something like that. I think the police will probably be pleased that you're finally telling the real story at the crucial moment, which is now. You might get a rap on the fingers."

"So are you off back to London now?"

Kyle knew he had a chance and his mind began to whip up an excuse. "No, not until tomorrow, but…" He had it, it was perfect. "I'll tell you what, have you got an envelope?" Bert was puzzled as Kyle retrieved the memory card from the Dictaphone. "It's just if I send this by post, courier even, it'll get there before me. Then the girls can get started on the article right away. All I need is an envelope to send it in."

"Sure. Good idea."

Bert unfolded the lid of the bureau and Kyle's heart sped with relief. He spotted a pale green correspondence set, recalling that some distinctive mint coloured notepaper had been mentioned, so when Bert proffered a standard white envelope Kyle waved his hand to dismiss it. "No, give me one of the green ones. The girls at the office will love getting something a little different in the postbag." Bingo.

Bert followed him to the front door. "This article you're doing, when will it be coming out? I'll have to make sure I buy the paper that day."

"Well, it's Saturday today, so we'll probably have all the loose ends tied up by the end of the week. I'd like to think it could be headline news for next weekend."

Bert rubbed his hands together, his wide grin displaying the gap where the missing tooth had been. "And you think that my statement will finally have the identity of the Bonfire Night Killer revealed? The whole fiasco laid to bed?"

Kyle shook Bert's hand warmly, a dazzling smile beaming. "I think it will be the nail in that evil man's coffin, and also enough to convince the police for good that Paul was just following in his repulsive father's footsteps." Having issued the words Bert wanted to hear, Kyle left the property and headed back to the car. He started the engine and slowly drove around the corner, searching for Jack and Sue.

Whilst Kyle had been visiting Bert Rock, Sue phoned Alan Reeves to inform him they had found the journal. He was interested in the content but, aware he would be going against the instructions of Dom Townsend, his long-term colleague and supposed superior, he suggested they meet privately. In hushed tones he proposed a small café near her home in Hessle. He was surprised when she arrived without the baby. "I thought you'd have your son with you."

Sue shook her head as she sat opposite him at the table, waving a waitress across and ordering a white coffee. "No chit-chat, Alan, you're not my favourite person at the moment."

"Oh, I'm sorry. I, um, well, you told me you have the diary. Can I see it?"

"Alan, I'm not stupid enough to bring it with me. You might have told Dom about it and I know he's totally against what I'm doing. Look, the diary completely exonerates Roland Mason as the Bonfire Night Killer if what he's written is true." Sue tugged her gloves and scarf off, setting them on the table, her face reddening in the heat of the basic dining room.

Alan exaggerated a sigh, gazing at the ceiling with disbelief. "So this important document you told me about is simply a diary that an old man wrote prior to dying, stating he didn't commit a series of unsolved murders. And you are dumb enough to believe it." He rose from his chair, figuring enough time had been wasted.

Sue grabbed his sleeve, hissing through taut lips, "Sit down and bloody listen." Miffed, he followed her order, leaning back to allow the waitress to set the coffee on the table. "He admits to being there, he admits to raping the girls, but he has implicated, quite believably, somebody else for the killings. The relation of his account is thorough, Alan, and the man he's accused is certainly capable of the crime, in my opinion."

"Then let me see it."

"You don't get it, do you? First of all, if that man finds out about this as a free man, who knows what he could do. He's dangerous. He needs to be taken into custody for Paul and Jeff's safety, and that needs to happen before the damning information is released. Like I said, Dom's against this, who's to know that he…"

Alan leant forward, eyes flashing with understanding. "It's Bert Rock, isn't it? That's why you went to visit him the other day."

She focussed on stirring her unsweetened coffee. "I'm not saying who it is. What I want to know before I give you anything is that first, it'll be taken seriously, and secondly Jeff will have a police guard by his bed from now on. If the man Roland accused finds out he knows about this, it would be all too easy to sneak into the hospital and hurt him."

Alan finished the dregs of his own coffee, unsure what to say, and was relieved when his phone rang. He answered, listening for a few seconds, and his face paled as he ended the call. "I've got to go. I'll call you later."

"What's happened?" He ignored the question, slipping on his navy parka and swearing under his breath. Now Sue was pallid, her eyes wide. "Not Jeff?" She stood abruptly, the chair almost falling behind her, and grabbed at his arm as he left. "Alan." Her voice was shrill, laden with fear. "Tell me it's not Jeff. Tell me he's alright."

With his lower lip trembling, Alan gently wrapped his arm around her shoulders and guided her towards the door. "Come on, I'm taking you to the hospital."

Sue rushed into the room that had been a second home, but there were no beeping noises, no whoops of gushing air as the ventilator breathed for her husband. She wanted to scream, to rip the equipment from the walls, but instead her hands grasped at her own hair, tugging it, her heart overwrought and breaking. She could hear weeping and it dawned on her that the sobs came from her own throat. She turned to Alan, who stood tentatively at the doorway. "Then I have nothing left to protect. You can have the fucking diary, and you can add another murder to that bastard's rap sheet."

Unable to speak, bewildered, Alan bowed his head and strutted across the corridor, peering through the glass into my room, where I lay in semi-sleep with my wife by my side. Her

235

face was wet with the tears she had shed over the news of Jeff's death, encompassed in the knowledge that it could so easily have been her – the grieving widow – rather than Sue. Ellen spotted him and beckoned him inside. "I don't think Frank's had so many visitors in one day since he's been here. Pull up a chair."

He dragged a plastic seat next to Ellen and sat with his chin in his hands, elbows on knees. "Do you know what happened?"

"Only what Dom told me. Is Sue here?"

"I just gave her a lift, she's with him now."

"It seems his body just gave up. They re-started his heart, but when they tested his brain function there was nothing. They couldn't do anything." Ellen's eyes were fixed on my face, her words shallow, forlorn.

"What about Frank? I heard he woke this morning. Has he been able to say anything yet?"

She sighed deeply, stroking my hand tenderly, weaving her fingers through mine. "He's in and out of consciousness, but the doctor said he could possibly be out of intensive care tomorrow, so things are promising. Which makes me feel guiltier about poor Sue. On the same day I get my husband back, she loses hers."

Most of my colleagues knew Ellen and the respect they had for me reflected to her. My eyes flickered and I opened them a crack to see Alan's hand on my wife's shoulder. I struggled against the harsh grating in my throat and mouth and both visitors turned to me. "Frank, are you back with us?"

I tried to ask about my colleague, but the effort hurt the back of my throat, and neither Ellen, nor Alan appeared to understand me. I tried again, forcing a single word through the pain. "Jeff?"

In the absence of an answer from either adult, their eyes darting here and there to avoid mine, it was obvious he had lost his fight and my heart sank. I was aware I had been gravely ill for nearly a week – the nurse had explained after I'd regained consciousness – and Ellen had mentioned Jeff's similar condition. Bit by bit, horrific memory after horrific memory, I pieced together the final moments I'd had with Jeff. Praying that Bert was locked up securely, I tried to form the next word, but all I could manage was 'B...'

Ellen felt it pointless to keep the secret any longer. "Sue and her father have been digging into things and they're both certain it wasn't Paul who attacked Frank and Jeff. He's trying to tell you that it was Bert who did this to him."

"I've just been with Sue and she didn't say as much, but I guessed." Alan grasped for my hand before thinking better of it, and shoved his in his pocket. "Are you trying to say Bert, Frank? Bert Rock?" Ellen's eyes bored into the side of his face, her jaw tight, concerned. Alan stood and leaned close to my face. "Did Bert Rock do this to you?"

I was woozy with pain medication and struggled to remain awake for long. It took all the strength I had to manage a slight nod. His face disappeared from view and I felt a soft breeze as he dashed from the room.

As soon as Alan left intensive care, he called Dom. "I've just been to see Frank, are you still in the hospital?"

"I'm in the canteen. I needed to sit down after what happened to Jeff."

Alan scanned a map of the hospital on the wall, trying to make sense of the zones and blocks. "Gotcha. Get me a coffee, I'll be with you in a second." He jogged breathlessly down the stairs and along the corridor to the restaurant, and spotted his colleague as he came through the door.

He didn't make any sense at first, words tumbling out and tripping over each other, but Dom's stern glance halted him. He breathed deeply for a few seconds, controlling himself. "We've got the wrong man. Frank just indicated to me that it was Bert Rock who attacked him."

Dom leant back in the comfortable chair, arms crossed, a condescending tinge of amusement on his face. "Alan, you seem to have failed to notice that Frank's a very ill man. We have no intention of interviewing him until his condition is stable."

He was going to have to come clean and admit that he had discussed the situation with Sue Mason behind Dom's back. Dom was displeased, and hearing about the journal did little to impress him either. "Come on, Dom, you know as well as I do that the evidence we have on Paul is shoddy. What if Sue's right?

237

She swears that Paul was trying to help them when she went in the room, and remember that she was the first on the scene. She got there a good few seconds before us."

"When I walked into that room I clearly saw Paul Mason with a carving knife in his hand leaning over all four men. There was a gun with his bloodied fingerprints on it, a crowbar. What more do you want, Alan? What's shoddy about that?"

"Those seconds Sue spent before we arrived, she's told me she saw the scene completely differently to how you and I did. Why are you so adamant that Paul has to be guilty?"

Neither man had noticed Sue approaching. "Because Dominic Townsend is a self-righteous, pig-headed arse." They stared at the broken woman, the woman whose life would never be the same. She casually reached into her handbag, dragged out a beaten, leather-bound notepad and dropped it on the table. "You're right, Roland could have lied. You can either use the information that's in this book with a potential view that Bert Rock might have killed all those people, or you can ignore it. What the fuck would I care now, anyway? My Jeff's gone. Nothing matters to me anymore."

On hearing the dreadful news, Jack collected his numbed daughter from the hospital and brought her home. Brenda fussed over her for some time, while simultaneously tending to Jacob, whose sore gums had made him fractious. A rapping on the front door made the three adults jump, all lost in the agony of Jeff's death. On autopilot, Brenda answered the door and led Kyle into the lounge. "What's up, you lot? Did somebody die?"

Sue glared at him, a fresh crop of tears brewing, and she strode from the room, feet clattering on the stairs as she retreated to her temporary bedroom. However much Jack disliked the smarmy youngster, he knew he hadn't meant to be uncompassionate. He mooched to the drinks cabinet and poured two measures of Courvoisier, explaining the unhappy news.

"I am so sorry, I really had no idea. Do you think I should go and apologise to her?" Kyle took the proffered glass.

"No, I'll go and see to her." Brenda left and her softer footsteps climbed the stairs.

"I'm really sorry, Jack. Do you know how Frank's doing? He could be our final living witness."

"No, I've not heard anything and I haven't asked." He sat, cradling the glass in his palm. "To be honest, I can't think about this anymore, it's all come as such a shock. We thought he was on the mend."

Kyle leant forward. "Look, obviously your family has some grieving to do, so why don't I keep working the case on my own. I'm due back in London tomorrow because I'm in court Monday, but if I take the journal with me…"

"Sue gave it to the police."

"You have got to be fucking joking." Swearing somehow didn't seem appropriate with the suave man.

"She's washed her hands of it, for now, anyway. It's too much for her."

"From what you've all told me the police are desperate to put Paul away for this. Without that book we can't do anything more on either cluster of murders."

Jack's sad eyes, the black circles underneath deeper than they had ever been, caught Kyle's attention and he took a sip from his glass. "With all due respect, Kyle, and with the greatest thanks for giving us your time the past couple of days, but if the police choose to ignore the diary then so be it. It's not our problem anymore, now Jeff's gone. My priority is to ensure that both Sue and Jacob get through this and come out the other side with some semblance of a life."

Dom and Alan had cancelled their separate plans for the evening, settling at Dom's desk to pore through the journal. Eventually, eyes tired from reading the uneducated writing, Dom rested back on his chair and lifted his feet to the desk. He stretched. "Truth or a pack of lies?"

"I reckon if it was a pack of lies he wouldn't have admitted to the rapes."

Dom rubbed his fingers back and forth on his black moustache, thoughtful. "I guess there is that. Okay, let's assume that this is the truth for now, that Bert is the original killer. He's managed to get away with murder three times, and many years have passed since. Why would he suddenly start again now?"

Alan patted the diary. "He heard about this, that's my guess. So he kills Fiona and places the boots he was wearing at Paul's back door, having deliberately left a clear footprint in the mud at the scene."

"Have another look at the forensics report on the boots. If there was any evidence on them, check it against Bert's DNA and fingerprints – do we have fingerprints for him?" Dom checked his computer to answer his own question, tapping and clicking, waiting patiently. "Yes, we do, but they're old. As soon as we've picked him up, get a fresh set. Get forensics to test them against the gun as well as the boots, there may be some partials if he had held the gun."

Alan scratched his head, brow furrowed. "What doesn't make sense to me is that, in here," he tapped the journal again, "Roland states Dorothy was the love of Bert's life, so why would he not only murder her, but do so in such a vicious way?"

"I don't know. Look, we need to apply for a warrant to search his house when we've got him in. I'm sure any questions will be answered then. Just remember that we thought Paul was blackmailing Dorothy. Well, if he's not involved with the murders, maybe Bert was the blackmailer. Who knows? All I know for certain is that we need him in for questioning as soon as possible."

"Tonight?"

Dom shook his head. "No, let's wait and see how Frank is tomorrow.If he actually names Bert as his attacker, no judge will object to us keeping him in custody until his court appearance. That's something we can't guarantee yet, seeing as Paul's still locked away for the same crimes."

Chapter 19
Sunday 18th November

Bert had been tossing and turning in his bed for hours, his mind buzzing, and he was fed up. He had tried a swift shot of liquor twice to try and dumb his brain, but to no avail. He recalled the conversation with the journalist the previous day – his questions – and it dawned on him that the visit was dubious. Of course Bert had loved elaborating his hatred of Roland, and the idea that it might ensure Paul stay in prison for life, but would a national newspaper really be interested in little old him.

He cast his mind back to his youth, to the deep friendship he'd had with Roly and how it had been destroyed. And he thought back to the woman he had loved. He had admired Dorothy as he'd grown up. She had been a couple of years above him at school, a pretty, free spirit, and she'd always had a smile on her face. He had just turned thirteen when he saw her dressed as a bridesmaid, her dark locks curling over the shoulders of the pretty blue dress, dainty ankles in lacy socks enhancing the buckle shoes, and he had been struck with a powerful teenage lust, which had never ended. He'd been smitten, gradually worming himself into her life, and for a couple of summers they had spent the school holidays together, carelessly walking or running through the fields surrounding Colefield. They would dance in the sunshine, framed by the vivid green grass, the richly coloured flowers and the cloudless azure sky. When he turned sixteen, the third summer he had spent with Dot, he'd bravely kissed her. At the time he'd thought she would push him away, ridicule him for being two years younger and less mature, but the risk had paid off. She had succumbed willingly.

They'd spent as much time together as possible over the next blissful six months, around her cleaning job at the pub and his late night shifts poaching or stealing, which had taken precedence over his ailing schoolwork. He had been delirious with their clandestine lovemaking, ecstatic to be in the arms of the girl he felt destined to be with. The girl he loved. Until the day that bastard, Ernie Webber, had returned to the village from his stint in the army and turned Dorothy's eye.

Ernie was ten years older than Dot, a quirkily handsome man. Tall, with broad shoulders and a confident gait, he was a gentle giant, kind and loyal. Some would say weak. He had fallen for Dorothy as quickly as Bert had, but in contrast to the strong man of the world, Bert was nothing. At five-foot six and heavy-set, padded with a generous layer of fat, he had been no match to Ernie's looks, maturity or earning power.

Dorothy had always been the type of girl who would marry young, have her family at a tender age, and her parents had been thrilled, if not boastful, when Ernie became her beau. He'd asked for her hand in marriage within months, presenting her with a rock of a diamond that even Bert would have been too scared to steal on his frequent expeditions to thieve from surrounding villages. Bert knew he had lost the battle before it started, as Ernie had easily fired the fatal bullet into his heart as soon as he had stepped from the bus and caught Dorothy's eye.

Bert had meekly tucked his tail between his legs and bowed away from the love of his life, but inside he had been furious, and worked the anger out by increasing his night-time raids, now dragging Roland along with him. Roly had been an obvious choice of friend, they were similar in age and he had been a bad boy too, his unsociable antics frequently saturating the relentless village gossip. Bert had taken him under his wing and taught him everything he knew, training him to be sleek, stealthy and fast.

At first they had taken time to plan the robberies, spying on the houses, learning the routines and habits of the occupants, but the thrill had accelerated over the years and soon three houses a week wasn't enough anymore. They became more random, more opportunistic, picking likely houses within seconds and taking huge risks. Inevitably they had been caught, and as the severity of their crimes increased, the tap on the wrist from an angry policeman had elevated to court appearances and a few sessions behind bars. Having spent two months locked in dingy, cold cells their friendship had dissipated, neither wanting to repeat the dire existence of prison life, and they had recognised they were bad for each other.

Soon after their release, days apart from each other, Roland started dating Jeannie Merrick and they had soon become serious. The engagement came as no surprise, and nor did their marriage a few years later when she had been three months pregnant. Bert remembered how lonely the following solitary years had been, how dreadful it felt to see an old friend playing happy families and the love of his life bearing children with his rival. He had never met anybody special after Dorothy, satisfying his sexual urges with drunken housewives and wanton single girls on the rare nights he went to town.

Even though Bert had managed to persuade Dorothy to hook up with him on two blissful occasions, his disgust of Roland Mason intensified on hearing through the village grapevine that Dorothy had been having an affair with him. There had been no evidence, nobody had seen them together, but the subject arose too often to be coincidence. When Dorothy announced her first pregnancy, the tittle-tattlers had gone into overdrive as to the identity of the child's father. She had kept her dignity, never rising to the frequent tutting she received as she walked through the streets and eventually, when bonny David had been born, the villagers had found better, newer material to chat about.

Bert had watched from his window on many occasions, able to see Dorothy's house from his bungalow, and on a few instances had been sure he had seen a male figure covertly creeping towards her side door during the periods that Ernie was away on business. But if they had been having an affair, they'd been discreet. However, the seed of hatred had already been planted for Bert.

The years passed and Dorothy and Jeannie completed their families – nurturing babies, chasing toddlers, ironing school uniforms, breaking up bickering siblings – while Bert watched forlornly from the side-lines. His sensible, regular job at the steelworks had been the only thing to break the tedium of his lonely existence, except for the hunting season, when he could enjoy his only hobby.

Bert recalled when everything had changed: the night Jeannie died. Or should he say disappeared. He had seen her

243

sister, Joan, getting off the bus and watched as she brazenly strolled to Roly and Jeannie's house. The next thing he'd heard was that Roly was devastated because his wife had left him. But Bert remembered the strange thudding noises from the end of the garden the previous night that had prompted him to peep through the curtains in case an intruder was outside. He had heard a car start on the dirt track and leave, but he knew Jeannie couldn't drive. It had dawned on him then that there had been more to Jeannie's disappearance than a simple marital dispute.

A few days later, the events of that night still playing on his mind, he arrived at Roland's house with a bottle of whisky, a peace offering because he was sorry Jeannie had left. Truthfully, he had wanted Roly to confide in him after downing a few drinks, to reveal the darker side of the official story. They'd had half a bottle between them, sitting in the armchairs, when a noise had come from the kitchen. Roly had gone to investigate. Through the closed door, Bert heard Roly and Dorothy's muffled voices in a whispered argument, and realised that things were still very much on for the adulterous couple. The burning, jealous hatred had reappeared, and Bert knew that as soon as he had the opportunity, he intended to destroy everything that Roland was, wanted to be and ever would be.

Events happened, years passed, and Bert's revulsion cooled to a gentle simmer. When Roland took his secrets to his grave, it was without receiving retribution from his enemy. Until now, with Kyle Moore promising to unearth the dark secrets.

The thought of the journalist's name reminded Bert he was trying vainly to sleep. He swung his tired legs from the bed and poured a third shot of numbing alcohol, and, in afterthought, scribbled 'Kyle Moore' on the notepad he kept on his bedside cabinet. Something was odd about the man turning up out of the blue and he intended to find out what.

Now I had begun my slow climb up the recovery hill, I noticed the pain from my injuries becoming more apparent. I rang for a nurse and she fed some painkillers through my drip. Since the previous day when I had seen Alan Reeves, I'd been desperate to unburden my memory of the horrific events that had occurred the week before, and now my excellent friend – my most promising colleague – had died at the hands of the burgeoning psychopath. I wanted Bert Rock to be locked away for the rest of his life.

Lying pathetically on the hospital bed was tedious, regardless that the scenery had changed since I had been moved from intensive care to a regular ward. Every time the door of the four-bed section opened, the patients glanced across, hoping to see somebody other than medical staff to make the hours tick by faster. Seeing Dom and Alan made me want to skip and jump with relief. I indicated the water jug and Alan poured a small amount into a plastic cup, helping me to drink. "How are you feeling?" He placed the cup on the side and sat in one of the chairs Dom had pulled over.

I nodded, my throat still sore, and when the words came out they were rasping with the discomfort. "Okay."

Dom stood, a habit of his when he wanted to interrogate somebody. "Frank, do you remember what happened last week?"

I nodded again. "Clearly." Using as few words as possible I recalled the events of the fateful day, and enthused when Dom asked if Paul had been rescuing us when he and Alan had arrived at the scene. The two officers glanced at each other, then back at me. "Paul's innocent. Bert did this. You need to get him locked away. He's dangerous."

Dom shuffled his feet, the approaching sentence devastating to his masculinity. "We know that now and I'm sorry we didn't listen to what Sue was trying to tell us." I nodded my appreciation, regardless that I felt equally guilty. "We won't take a formal statement yet Frank, it sounds like you're struggling to speak, but we're going to arrest him now."

I was determined. Even if I only said a few words, a signed statement was prudent. I insisted they write my version down, no matter how long it took. I could cope now the painkillers were kicking in.

Bert replaced the handset and slammed his left fist against the occasional table, furious. He hated being lied to. He had felt uneasy since Kyle Moore's visit, and had eventually called the

Daily Mail offices to verify his identity. His suspicion had been spot on. The newspaper had never heard of the man, either employed by them or as a contractor. Bert had no idea who the impostor posing as a journalist could be, but something was going on behind his back and he didn't intend to take any chances. He sat back on the sofa, channelling his mind and utilising his anger to try and work out what to do.

Minutes passed and he remained clueless. He lumbered to his bedroom, tugging the curtain aside to take in the dramatic view over his rear garden. Flecks of sparkling white reflected from the branches of the trees and the grass, giving the scene an eerie grey hue. Only the muddy brown dirt track at the end of the garden broke the expanse of frost that blended with the heavy clouds on the horizon. In the distance, he could see the notorious copse of willow trees where four unfortunate women had met their demise. He hoped the peacefulness of the stunning view would help him think, but an unfamiliar ocean-blue car roof, almost completely hidden by the hedge that surrounded Paul's garden, and littered with frozen droplets of dew, was suspicious.

Bert threw an anorak over his jumper, without regard for his painful shoulder, and tugged his wellies on, pleased to be wearing his own comfortable boots after the difficulty he'd had walking in Ernie's oversized pair. He hurried through the door and trotted to the end of the garden for a better view of the car, and gasped. It was the same impressive Mercedes CLK that the bogus journalist had driven the previous day. So Kyle Moore was at Paul Mason's house. Aggravated, Bert began to retrace his steps, determined to confront the dubious fraudster, but a jaw-clenching creak stopped him and he nipped behind an apple tree at the edge of his garden, peering round to see what was happening.

An aging male came from Paul's house, and Bert immediately recognised him as one of the officers who had visited earlier that week, leading him to complain. Seconds later, the man he knew as Kyle Moore joined him, his bronzed skin and ash-blond hair brightening the bleakness. The two men shared a few words and laughed briefly. The sudden, confusing realisation that the charming infiltrator might be an undercover detective hit him and he scurried back to his home, desperately recalling everything he had said to the man, concerned he may have said something he wouldn't want the police to hear. He remembered the envelope. The pale green envelope that was part of a set he had used to tell Paul 'threats mean death'. Had the police found that one when they had searched his house? Had he even kept it?

He sat on the sofa, the winter jacket too hot in the warmth, and thought things through logically. If they had the letter, and they knew about him pointing a gun at Paul... If they tied the gun to the one he had used when he attacked the three men...

It was too dangerous. Bert ripped the sling from his arm, tossing it on the carpet as he raced to the bedroom to fill a suitcase, berating himself for his stupidity. "Why are you doing this to me, Roland fucking Mason? It's a cruel bloody trick." He emptied pants, socks, jumpers – anything that came to hand – into the suitcase, swearing foully in his flustered haste.

Within ten minutes he was ready and he checked the house swiftly to ensure nothing was out of place, snatching the discarded bandage and folding it neatly before dropping it on the arm of the sofa. He glanced through the bedroom window and saw the Mercedes was gone. Checking he had his wallet, he grabbed the keys from the hook and left the house, glancing around the quiet road surreptitiously.

Towing the case behind him, he walked the short distance to the edge of the village, surmising he was less likely to be seen if he waited for the number twenty-six at the stop on the outskirts of Colefield. He stood, shoulder aching, checking his watch every few seconds while he willed the bus to arrive early.

"Damn, I forgot to lock the back door." Jack took a set of keys from his jacket pocket and dropped them on his lap. He checked the mirrors and turned the car around in a lay-by. "Thank god I noticed before we got to the bridge. It's getting pricey, the amount of travelling I've been doing over it." He edged the car into a gap in the traffic, heading for Colefield.

"Thanks for your help back there, Kyle, you didn't have to come with me."

"I can see how distraught Sue is, and I know how much support you and Brenda are giving her, but nobody's been giving you support and I imagine you're pretty cut up about this yourself."

Jack felt the insane guilt he continued to experience every time he had a bad thought about his friend's overachieving son. "It is hard; I can't deny that. I liked Jeff a great deal. He was a perfect son-in-law and a damned fine husband and father. I shall miss him. I know I told Sue we would collect his belongings from Paul's for her, but to be honest I wanted to go anyway. I wanted to see the last place Jeff had been in before the attack."

"I can understand that. Wait a minute... Isn't that Bert Rock?" Jack slowed the car and the stocky man on the roadside bowed his head, pulling the hood of his anorak over his thinning, grey hair. "Stop the car. I reckon he's sussed out I was a fraud. I'll bet you he's doing a runner."

Bert had dumped the suitcase and was attempting to run along the muddy path leading away from the village, and although he was aging and unfit, he could move pretty quickly. His athletic skills, however, were nothing compared to Kyle's physical prowess. Within seconds he had caught up and rugby tackled the old man to the ground, shortly to be joined by bemused Jack. "What are you doing?"

"After all the work we've done to get him arrested I'm not bloody letting him get away now." Kyle sat astride Bert, clutching his hands together behind his back, and Bert wailed with the pain from his shoulder. "Have you got a tow-rope?"

"Yes." Jack returned to the car, baffled by Kyle's behaviour. He threw the rope on the grass and stood, hands on his hips. "He was probably just going shopping or something."

"With a suitcase?" Kyle deftly tied Bert's hands and used the rest of the cord to immobilise him beside a sapling. "You weren't going shopping were you, Bert? You've realised you haven't got away with the perfect set of murders after all. You wanted to get away, escape to a friend's house or something, and hope the police wouldn't find you. Well, you see, I'm not letting that happen. This case is the pinnacle of my career so far, it'll make me a million and more. My face will be on every newspaper and magazine in this country." With the knot fixed securely, Kyle stood back to admire his handiwork as Jack, amazed, watched. "Go on, Jack, don't just stand there. Find a camera and get a good shot for the papers. I'll be a hero. Oh, and call the cops or something."

Ellen prepared a small bag containing bananas, mint imperials, cup-soup sachets and other soothing foods to bring for her husband, an attempt to ease his sore throat. She had spent most of the week at the hospital, sleeping where she fell, tending only to her basic hygiene needs, watching over the man she loved with hopes and prayers, but now his condition was no longer critical she allowed herself some time away. She thought about Sue and her devastating loss, and although she was compassionate, she was emotionally detached because of the irrational guilt she felt about her husband surviving. She had avoided Sue since she'd heard the dreadful news.

Ellen collected the bag and her keys from the kitchen side and was about to leave when the phone rang. Tutting, she answered and her heart fell when Sue's distraught voice greeted her. "Sue, I've been meaning to call you. I'm so sorry."

"I know. So am I. I'll make this short, Ellen, I know how uncomfortable you must be with the situation. It's about the Bert thing. He's killed my Jeff. I don't give a shit about anything else, I just want justice for my husband."

Ellen wanted to slam the phone down and leave the house as planned, her priority her husband's recovery, not catching some killer. "I understand that."

Sue's voice cracked with distress. "Frank is the only survivor from that attack now, he's the only one who can tell the police what really happened. Please Ellen, I'm begging you, I know he's ill, but please get him to make a statement."

Ellen agreed and politely ended the call, shuddering with relief that the awkward, albeit brief, conversation was over. With less of a spring in her step, she called goodbye to her teenagers and began the familiar drive to Scunthorpe. I was sitting in my bed when she arrived and she beamed a smile as she trotted towards me. "I've brought you some goodies that shouldn't hurt your throat. How are you? Can you speak yet?"

I leant in for a kiss, and although my body ached, I felt hugely better for having had a decent sleep after giving my statement to Alan and Dom. "It still hurts to talk, but it's a lot better than earlier."

She sat on the chair beside my bed. "You look so good. Have the doctors said anything?"

"I'm improving well, out of danger apparently." The door opened, catching my eye, and I was surprised to see Alan again. "What are you doing back here? Haven't you got any work to do?"

He grinned as he approached the bed. "I came to give you the good news in person. We've picked Bert Rock up and he's in custody now."

Ellen gulped with relief. "Thank God. Have you already given a statement then?"

I nodded and returned my gaze to Alan. The sordid memories of the previous week jabbed at me, but I was determined not to let the experience bring me down. I clenched my jaw and willed the thoughts away. "Did he give you any trouble?"

Laughing, Alan explained how Sue's aging father and Paul's debonair new solicitor had captured Bert by the roadside and tied him up. How they had called for the police, who would have dismissed their claims as ridiculous had it not been for my statement that morning. I was relieved I had insisted on saying my piece, even though it had been physically and emotionally draining. "Have you questioned him yet?"

"Not really. I think Dom wants to wear him down a bit first, make him wait. On the evidence we have I don't think we'll have any problems getting extended custody if necessary. He's denying it all. Still blames Roland and Paul, and he's instructed a solicitor."

I leant against the pillow, amazed at how quickly I had tired. "I wish I could be there. This case has dragged and it would be so nice to be part of the clear up."

"You take your time, boss, treat it like an extended holiday." I snorted, giving him a cynical glare. "Okay, maybe not. Anyway, you know how cocksure Dom is, I'm sure he'll do the job justice."

Kyle and Jack had followed the police car to Hull and waited a while for news on Bert's arrest, but finally Jack decided to get home to his daughter. Kyle's train to London was due to leave early evening so he had a few hours to go, and he told Jack he would make his own way to the station. He would phone if he heard any news in the meantime.

As soon as Jack waved goodbye, Kyle phoned a fellow lawyer he had met at a black tie event in London. He explained the situation and made a proposal. Waiting for the return call was nerve-wracking, but he kept calm. Eventually his mobile rang and, relieved it was Quentin Forsythe, he took the call outside, breezing through the doors into the sharp, wintry sun. "Quentin, what have you got for me?"

"A couple of questions. First, did…" he hesitated and Kyle heard him leafing through paperwork, "did Paul Mason sign anything that instructed you to act on his behalf?"

Kyle chortled affably. "Of course not, I'm not stupid. I got him off, yes, and I have no intention of getting Bert Rock out of this, but I want the profile of the case."

"You're a tough cookie, Kyle."

"Have you thought about my suggestion?" Kyle was nervous, but it didn't show in his manner or voice.

Quentin sighed. "I'd rather do this face to face, but yes, I have. If Bert is willing to instruct you as his lawyer, then we want you to be part of our company. We're prepared to make you a partner. If you offer your services to him as a member of our firm and he accepts, I can have the paperwork drawn up immediately and you can sign on the dotted line tonight when you get back."

"Magic. You know my current contract with Gladstone and Peterson has a three-month competitor clause, don't you?"

"We can get around that, don't worry about it. I can't imagine a trial would happen before that anyway."

"Even in such a high profile case?"

"Look, there are problems to overcome, for sure, but Forsythe and Simmons want this case. It'll take our reputation through the roof. First things first though, we need to know if Bert will instruct you, because this deal isn't happening if he doesn't."

"I'm with you. I'll put on the charm when I see him, I'm sure he'll have no objections once I've finished with him."

"Somehow I don't doubt that, Kyle. Look, go in there as a representative of my company, tell him you're a partner, tell him he won't have to pay a penny towards the costs regardless of the outcome. If he says no, then you can carry on working for Gladstone and Peterson and we won't mention this again. If he agrees then, first of all, welcome to a lucrative partnership at Forsythe and Simmons, and secondly, call me and I'll get the ball rolling this end of the country."

Bert wasn't a stranger to police cells, although it had been a long time since he had last been inside one. He sat on the firm bed, head in hands, wondering relentlessly how things had become bad so quickly. His life wasn't wonderful, he had learned to live with loneliness, the tedium, but at least he'd had freedom. Now, with the dirt Roland Mason had spilled on him after his death, he realised he was unlikely to experience liberty again. He heard footsteps closing in and glanced at the door. Nothing prepared him for seeing Kyle's face. "What the fuck are you doing here, you psycho?"

A guard unlocked the metal-barred door and Kyle strode confidently across the tiny room, proffering his manicured hand. "Bert, we can meet properly now. My name is Kyle Barrymore, I'm a partner at top London legal firm, Forsythe and Simmons. I'm sure you've heard of them."

Bert crossed his arms tightly, rebuking the handshake. "No, of course I bloody haven't. Get out of here. You're a fucking two-faced liar."

Kyle strutted from one end of the room to the other and back, head raised arrogantly, hands in trouser pockets, apparently deep in thought. "Hmmm, I can see why, at this stage, you think that." He stopped. "The thing is, I heard about this case last weekend and it took my interest, so I came up north to see family and look into what was going on – I have many contacts up here. My sources told me they were about to release Paul Mason and arrest you instead, and it appalled me, setting a guilty man free and imprisoning the innocent."

Bert straightened, encouraged by the smooth patter, yet still confused. "But you were the bloody one who tied me up and called the bloody cops. My shoulder's still smarting from that."

"Ah, Bert, Bert," he waved his hands, a sorrowful expression settling on the handsome features, "they were going to arrest you anyway, don't you see that. I was on my way to see you to offer my services to you, when I saw you trying to run from the problem. I had to stop you. You see, if I hadn't they would have thrown the book at you. After all, an innocent man wouldn't run, that's the way they would see it. The good news is now you're in here, I can make sure that justice is done and you're set free. You just have to let me."

"What do you mean?"

"My fellow partners and I have been talking. We're willing to pay all the costs in your defence if you instruct me as your lawyer. This case will come to trial, there's no doubt of that, I'm afraid, and you need the best legal defence you can get. Forsythe and Simmons is a top company, we handle high profile cases all the time, and I'm excellent at my job. If anyone's going to get you released from this hell-hole, it's me."

Bert was perplexed. Whereas he appreciated the offer was first class, he had known the solicitor he intended to use for thirty years. "I don't know. I mean, that old guy you were with, he's a copper. How does that fit in?"

The affable, knowing chuckle rang through the room. "Related to Paul. I got him on my side to fish for dirt on him." Kyle paused for effect. He knew he was winning and smiled widely, ice-white teeth sparkling in the dull room. "Bert, you told me your story yesterday and I believe every word was the truth. I'm on your side. Agree to let me act on your behalf and I'll make damned sure that when you leave the trial, it will be as a free man."

"Is that a promise?" Bert's trusting eyes were pleading.
"You bet. You won't regret this."

Chapter 20
Crown Court – the Aftermath, 2015

Paul had finally spent some of his stashed savings and purchased a television set; a novelty, as it was capable of receiving a signal, unlike the one upstairs that he used with his ancient Atari games console. He'd had no choice; life was utterly lonely, a mere existence, and drowning in the mindless programs every night had become his world. His father's ashes were in an urn on the mantelpiece in the front room. Discovering Roland had killed his mother had caused much internal debate, and he had considered throwing them away with the rubbish where they probably belonged, but with Jeff and Dorothy no longer popping in all the time, the ashes were his only company.

He took a large bite of his hastily made cheese sandwich and flicked through the channels, searching for something, anything that would relieve his boredom until bedtime. After three years of court appearances and appeals strongly defended by Paul's old lawyer, the news that Bert Rock had been sentenced to life without parole had been a relief. Paul knew that, had it not been for his brother's tireless and subsequently fatal efforts to prove his innocence, it could well have been him in the dock.

Paul glanced at the clock, supping from the whisky bottle to wash down the bread in his mouth, and clicked on to the News at Ten to see the report he had watched a dozen times or more. Bert's committal was the headline news of the day and would litter the national newspapers, which he intended to buy, the next day. Leeds Crown Court appeared on the screen, an impressive building that turned the eye with its eclectic character, but today it was the crowd of onlookers held back by metal railings, the horde of reporters shouting and snapping their cameras, which drew the interest. Uniformed officers in fluorescent jackets lined the barriers and a secure van waited with its engine running, flanked by flashing police cars that were there to escort the truck for Bert's safety.

He leant forward, keen to study the familiar clips again. A huddle of smartly suited men emerging through the doors, the reporters bustling for the best shot, a short figure with hunched shoulders and an awkward gait, hands cuffed behind his back and a grey blanket covering his head. The devilish Kyle Barrymore with his twinkling eyes and chiselled cheekbones.

A series of photographs appeared on the screen showing the faces of the victims. Paul listened intently to the newsreader, her business-like voice detailing the murders: Katherine James, a dated image depicting a smiling, carefree woman; Vanessa Walton, a stunning, bashful girl with rich chocolate eyes and matching hair; Bernie Smith, with an impish, dimpled grin and twinkling green eyes. Fiona Malik wrapped in her husband's arms, with wild, curly hair, a fiery mass of orange that framed her dainty features, tumbling over her athletic shoulders. Four delightful women whose lives had been cut painfully short by a vicious madman. The madman who had just received a lifelong custodial sentence.

The screen reverted to the courthouse, now showing the blanket-draped man being assisted into the guarded van, whilst in the background, Kyle Barrymore, wearing a bespoke designer suit, took advantage of the media flurry with his shiny, blond fop of hair and his sparkling, winning smile.

Dorothy Webber's older face contrasted the young women's photos, her drooping jowls sagging over a once attractive face, the blue rinse adding ten years to her age. Paul felt tears burning. After all this time, he still missed her mothering and homemade meals. He dropped the crust of the tasteless sandwich onto the plate; it was cardboard compared to her delicious cottage pies and hefty fry-ups.

The images of Jeffery Mason, David Webber and Benjamin Roberts appeared on the screen and Paul couldn't take any more pain; it felt as if his heart was shifting physically in his chest. He switched the television to standby and threw the remote control on the coffee table. He drained the last dregs of whisky, hoping it would send him to sleep so he could tick off another meaningless day from his life.

Thirteen miles away, across the Humber River, Ellen and I sat in our easy chairs, each with a glass of bubbling champagne. We leaned towards each other and chinked glasses in celebration of the imprisonment of the elderly man. "Thank god that's over. It's been the longest few years of my life." The words couldn't possibly describe how I had faced the depths of hell since Bonfire Night three years before. Not only had I lost one of my best friends at the hands of the blanketed man on the screen, but I had also lost the use of my left leg. A routine operation to pin the shattered bone in place had resulted in nerve damage, and although I could manage on crutches on a good day, those days were coming less often.

Ellen touched my arm fleetingly, grateful love shining in her eyes for the fact I was alive. She finished her drink and set the glass on the table. "Come on, you, it's time for bed, don't you think?" My wonderful, caring wife pushed the wheelchair towards me and I eased myself to the edge of the cushion, awkwardly shifting from one seat to the other. "Don't forget you've got physio tomorrow." It was a common statement nowadays, the bane of my life...A pathetic and painful attempt to regain some mobility that realistically would never happen.

Still proud, albeit downtrodden, I wheeled myself into what had once been our decadent dining room, a place that had hosted so many wonderfully happy dinner parties with friends and family, including Jeff and Sue, now decorated neutrally to serve as a downstairs bedroom as I was unable to manage the stairs. With a single bed. Ellen's lips gently skimmed my forehead – a kiss for a dependent child – and bid me goodnight. I sighed; tomorrow I was going to try harder to walk again, no matter how painful it was.

Kyle had reached the level of popularity where he was welcome at any showbiz event, and he could guarantee column inches in broadsheets and tabloids, magazines. He was a frequent guest on celebrity quizzes and television chat shows. Being a partner in Forsythe and Simmons was, in itself, a lucrative career and money was never an issue in the top restaurants and five-star hotels, but the tens of thousands he earned from interviews and photo sessions sealed his luxury lifestyle and filled his bed with one beautiful woman after the next. He peeled back the Egyptian cotton sheet on his bed and ravenously pushed the buxom blonde whose name he had already forgotten against the pillows. She giggled and gasped, sighed and moaned, and seconds later he rolled to the side, spent and ready for sleep.

"Kyle, baby, don't you want to talk for a while?" This was the type of bimbo he detested: the ones who genuinely believed he wanted more from them than a quick roll under the covers. He groaned and pulled the deluxe pillow tighter to his shoulders, his head wallowing in the plush comfort. She sat up, sulking. "You know I can always do a kiss and tell on you? I'd make thousands."

"Fuck off." He turned his back to her in irritation.

Chantelle shifted her feet to the floor, the stilettoed heels she still wore digging into the thick pile of the cream carpet, and took her silk pants from the end of the bed where they had been discarded in haste, sliding them up her lusciously long legs, skimming her shapely thighs. She stood and tugged them over well-proportioned hips. "Fuck off yourself." She took a cigarette from the bedside cabinet and lit it, inhaling deeply as she planned her next move. "All I want is five minutes of your time, Kyle."

"Just shut up, will you, I'm trying to sleep."

With a flounce, Chantelle began to dress herself, jerking arms and body into the slinky, black Givenchy gown. "Right then, have it your way. I'll contact the press tomorrow."

Kyle was bored of the familiar conversation. He pushed himself up, a sneer on his botoxed features. "For fuck's sake. Do you really think I care?" She hunted dramatically for her Ralph Lauren diamante clutch bag, avoiding the stinging words. "I have fucking kiss and tells done on me almost every week. Do you really think one more will damage me? It's free publicity and I get laid too, a double whammy. Get your pathetic story out there and don't think for a second that I'll give a shit."

Chantelle strode angrily towards the door, stopping and leaning against the frame, her bleached tresses tousled and sexy. "You're a bigger bastard than I could ever have imagined, Kyle Barrymore."

"Yeah, yeah, get over yourself." He flung himself on the pillow, and by the time the front door of his stunningly styled, opulent apartment slammed, he was already asleep.

The chill in the air was uncomfortable and eerie, a gentle breeze that had no source. The smell that hung like a low cloud was terrible, a mixture of manly bodies, the metallic tang of iron, and dust. Bert lay on his side, the thin mattress beneath him hard and unforgiving. He tugged the starched cotton sheet up to his neck, followed by the woollen blanket, and wished he could scream from pure frustration. There would be no point, nobody would care. Every now and then, rhythmic footsteps would approach, soon disappearing into the distance as the guard did his nightly rounds.

This was the first night of his new life. The first night in the home that would be his for the rest of his years. His solitary cell at Full Sutton prison was roughly nine feet by six and, so far, had few comforts to personalise it. Over the three years he had spent on remand in Hull, he had studied theology, learning to believe in and eventually love God. The Bible was now his favourite book. But the one question that God wouldn't, or couldn't, answer was why Bert had been imprisoned for crimes he hadn't committed.

Bert reflected on his past, on the long-gone days when he'd had the freedom to eat what and when he wanted, to walk outside on a whim, to laugh with spontaneous joy. His had been an unplanned pregnancy and he had been born on his mother's forty-sixth birthday, the seventh of January, nineteen fifty-one. He had been a rascal of a child, always up to some form of mischief or another. His aging mother and father, parents for the first time as they approached their fifties, hadn't had the stamina to keep track of him and he had taken advantage of the situation, skipping school, getting into fights, and some petty pilfering from bakeries and newsagents. His early days of harmless crime had given him a clear choice in life: either find a job and behave, or continue the burgeoning career in theft and risk spending many of his years in jail. He chose the latter time and time again, until the police became fed up with seeing him so often and pursued through the courts for a custodial term. His third spell in prison, the longest at forty-three days, had been dreadful and he had chosen to clean up his act and find a responsible trade. He had never completely followed the law, the infrequent poaching provided him with luscious, rich game to dine on as a treat, or sell at the pub, but in general he had become a respectable man.

So how had he ended up in the place he'd rebuked by gaining employment at the steelworks? He couldn't comprehend how the lies of a dead man could make him pay such a high price. Roland had detested him for much of his life, but he hadn't, until now, realised how much. This act of revenge was cruel and Bert frequently imagined the ghost of Roland laughing with gusto in the spirit world.

Bert's shoulder had never recovered from the breakage, it was persistently stiff and achy, and he rolled onto his back, moving his arms as far from his body as the small bed would allow to ease the dull throbbing. His mind drifted to the young Dorothy, her beautiful, youthful scent and comely figure. The way she would dance in the fields, a bright ray of sunshine that glowed on the cloudy days, and sparkled when the sun shone. He had never come to terms with her death, even three years on. Someone else had killed her in revolting circumstances, yet he was serving time for her murder. Guilt possessed him as he recalled his dreadful treatment of her on the last night he had seen her alive, and despite his best efforts to block out the memory, it flooded back and was resolutely determined to keep him awake until the early hours.

He had been sure, with Roland having passed away, that the crude blackmail note was from Paul, and had scribbled a terse reply to frighten him from taking the attempt at extortion any further. When a second letter dropped through the door he realised that subtlety wasn't going to work with Paul, and he had devised a plan to scare him so much he would never try such a stupid trick again. It had quickly become apparent that Paul had no idea why Bert was brandishing a gun, and when Paul told him it was Dorothy who had been expecting a package that night, his heart had sunk, distraught.

But as the minutes ticked by, the sadness and betrayal had rapidly transformed into fury and he wanted not only a good explanation, but retribution too. He'd not done anything bad in the recent weeks, no arguments with neighbours, no slights, no lewd remarks to the young girls who played on the streets and fields. So what did she have on him? Anything? He couldn't think of a single reason for her actions. She also knew he had never been a wealthy man, so where she had thought he was going to find two grand from eluded him. He dismissed Dorothy with the same redundant sorrow he always had after remembering her.

The gun. He had kept the beautifully crafted Blackhawk 'Flattop', the fine detailing on the handle and the shining barrel a tribute to the years he had spent polishing and cleaning it, safely in a hidden compartment at the back of his wall-length wardrobe. Exquisite as the revolver was, a nineteen-sixties rarity, he now wished he had never found it. Years before he had been hunting in the woodlands that lay on the outskirts of Colefield, and investigated when hes aw a glint within some bushes. He knew he should have handed it to the police, but it was stunning, and he reasoned it wouldn't harm anyone to keep it himself, as long as he kept it secure. It never occurred to him that it may be the gun used by the Bonfire Night Killer. He wished he had handed it in all those years ago. Instead he had taken it home, cleaned and repaired it, hidden it away like a secret trophy. Until the night he had threatened Paul.

After Bert discovered that his beloved Dorothy had been blackmailing him, he had stomped uncomfortably to her house, wearing her late husband's Wellington boots, and threatened her. He had marched her at gunpoint on a mission that, looking back with the benefit of knowledge, was his ultimate mistake. At first he had considered killing her, his rage so insane, but a combination of opportunity and the eternal love he felt for the woman altered his plans dramatically. As they had been forging their path through the field, Bert holding the gun discreetly to her back as he forced her to lead the way, he had seen movement in the icy grass. Sitting on the cold ground and obviously drunken was a young, flame-haired woman. She had a lit cigarette in her bare hand and swigged from a clear-glass bottle that could have contained one of several spirits. He directed Dorothy towards her, whispering instructions as they approached. They stood close to the woman he now knew to be Fiona Malik. "Are you alright, love?" Bert had noticed the fear in Dorothy's voice, but only because he knew her so well. Fiona, her face wet from tears, had not found the unassuming, elderly couple a threat. "Why don't you come for a walk with us? You might feel better if you talk to somebody."

Fiona had sobbed an intoxicated, grateful acceptance and staggered to her feet clutching the large, half-empty bottle that Bert now saw was vodka. She dropped the butt of her cigarette onto the frost-flecked grass and the trio strolled into the copse of weeping willows. Dorothy, acutely aware of the weapon pressed into the excess flesh of her back, had pacified Fiona, whose woes were intensified by alcohol, with her gentle, motherly manner. When Fiona inevitably staggered and insisted on sitting beside a tree trunk, sheltered by the copious branches, it had seemed to Bert that Christmas had come early. The girl was almost comatose. In a shocking and unplanned move, he grabbed Dorothy's arm and forced the gun into her hand. He controlled her aim and ordered her to pull the trigger. She protested vehemently, weeping tears of apology. With shame he recalled the exact words he had barked at her: *'You knew I was still in love with you, and yet you're callous enough to believe I'm a murderer. Have you any idea how dreadful that makes me feel? Well, if you can believe that of me, then you can find out for yourself exactly how it feels to kill someone, because I can assure you it's a feeling I have never, and will never, experience.'* She had squeezed her eyes tightly shut, whimpering, as he forced her finger to close on the trigger, and the echoing gunshot merged into the popping and crashing of the fireworks that spewed from the neighbour's gardens a couple of hundred feet away.

The realisation that she had fired the shot that had fatally wounded the woman, who was now slumped, unmoving, on the cold, crackling ground in front of her, disturbed Dorothy deeply, and she found an inner strength. She had grasped the gun tight, shrugging unsuspecting Bert from her back, and aimed it at him.

They had struggled, her strength greater than he had expected, and suddenly the gun fired. Dorothy fell instantly with a low wail, petrified. Bert saw the blood pulsing from a wound in her hip, and the gun was in his hand. Instinct flooded him and he'd hurried away.

At home, he'd returned the gun to the secret compartment, deeply regretting having moved it. He had calmed his nerves with a stiff brandy, the glass shaking in his trembling hands, and when common sense had finally kicked in, he remembered the Wellington boots he had borrowed from Dorothy earlier that day. He tugged them off and replaced them with his own comfortable pair. Furtively, he took them the short distance along the dirt path into Paul's garden and left them by the back door. Now, if there were any footprints, the finger would point at Paul Mason. It wasn't revenge, but simple self-preservation.

He'd returned to his bungalow and drained another brandy, and gradually the enormity of what had happened dawned. He realised, with regret, that he must return to the scene and help the woman he still loved, regardless of her accusations.

But Dorothy hadn't been there, and he had never seen her again.

Bert had tossed and turned all night, certain the police would burst in and arrest him for shooting Dorothy and keeping an illegal weapon, but they hadn't. When he had awoken the next morning after a fitful sleep, he found the village swarming with police officers, and he had patiently waited for them to lock him away before throwing away the key. Bert stirred from the painful memories to smirk at the irony of his current, lifelong, predicament.

Uncomfortable again, Bert stiffly turned onto his left side, willing himself to sleep the shock of the sentence away. He tried to relax by counting sheep, but within moments his thoughts had returned to the day he'd heard Dorothy's body had been found in the landfill site, dumped amongst the rotting peelings and discarded rubbish. He recalled the consuming confusion as he wondered how on earth she had ended up there, half a mile from where he had left her.

Tiredness finally took hold and Bert drifted into a fitful sleep, lulled by the sound of the guard's footsteps approaching once more. He would never know – and God would never tell him – that the whole, disastrous incident had been witnessed by another man. A man who had hated his wounded mother enough to savagely beat her and leave her for dead in a wheelie bin, which would subsequently take her to the odorous resting place before she slipped from life on a hospital bed. A son who had incriminated Bert by slipping into his house when he'd left the door unlocked whilst taking the wellies to Paul's back door. A man who had stolen a distinctive green envelope and sheet of paper from Bert's house and scribbled a note explaining Dorothy's absence to Paul, whom he knew to be close to his mother.

Had Bert known the truth in the final three, tedious years of his life, caged in a secure prison alongside what he would call real killers and rapists, he would have known a semblance of peace – of exoneration – in knowing that he had unwittingly brutally beaten and shot the man who had destroyed the love of his life. David Webber, the son who had tortured and ultimately killed Dorothy.

As the aggressive bowel cancer took control of his body, his major organs shut down and the flesh covering his bones thinned to a paltry covering of parchment skin, Bert accepted his impending death with gratitude. He would never know that the man he had killed in his desperation to bury the past would never have been born had he not shared that last, passionate embrace with Dorothy forty-four years earlier.

Repenting his sins to the God he now believed in, he closed his eyes and slipped painlessly to his death, taking with him the shocking truth, now never to be told.

THE END

Biography

Ricki is also the author of Hope's Vengeance (2009), Unlikely Killer (2010), and Bloody Mary (2011), all published by Wild Wolf Publishing. She is a happy single mother of four, and now the elder two have left home she has more time to write and research. Her biggest interest is the study of true crime.

www.rickithomas.com